THE HARDER
THEY FALL

Also by Debbie McGowan

Champagne
(1st Edition: highblue, 2004;
2nd Edition: Beaten Track, 2012)

'Time to Go' in *Story Salon Big Book of Stories*
(Edited by Joseph Dougherty; iUniverse, 2006)

And The Walls Came Tumbling Down

No Dice

Hiding Behind The Couch Series

Hiding Behind The Couch (Book One)

No Time Like The Present (Book Two)

First Christmas (Short Story One)

THE HARDER THEY FALL

Hiding Behind The Couch Series
Book Three

by
Debbie McGowan

Beaten Track
www.beatentrackpublishing.com

Beaten Track

First published 2013 by Beaten Track Publishing
Copyright © 2013 Debbie McGowan

A CIP catalogue record for this book
is available from the British Library.

ISBN: 978 1 909192 21 8

Beaten Track Publishing,
Burscough. Lancashire.
www.beatentrackpublishing.com

For Paul and Mark.
You re-ignited my desire to learn.
Thank you: for your tutelage, for your trust; for everything.

Know that a little of you both will forever reside in 'Sean Tierney'.
Alas, he's a psychologist: sorry about that. IOU 1xPhD.

—◊◊◊—

This novel is a work of fiction and the characters
and events in it exist only in its pages and
in the author's imagination.

However, there are a number of events and characters
contained within that have been inspired by real people.

'Phil' is inspired by an exceptionally talented saxophonist, with whom
I have had the pleasure to work for a number of years.

'The Late Poets' is based on an awesome band from the North-West UK;
the song title mentioned is also the title of one of their songs.

'Andy' the bar owner is based on a bar owner of the same name.
(see also suave, debonair…)

'Zuza' and 'Michal' are based on two very real and very special people from
Poland, who set up a bakery project in the Nepali village of Syabru Bensi.
However, they did this independently, and the events I have narrated in
relation to this are entirely fictional.
Thank you Michal, for your help and advice.

Bakery Project Website: www.piekarniawnepalu.pl

"The weight of the world is love. Under the burden of solitude, under the burden of dissatisfaction the weight, the weight we carry is love."

'Song' - Allen Ginsberg

CHAPTER ONE

Descending through the heavy grey cloud towards Kathmandu, the liner jerked sharply to the left, the flicker of the cabin lights temporarily illuminating the sudden trajectory of in-flight magazines and near-empty plastic cups as they paused at the lip of a tray and then tumbled down into the aisle. Droplets of rain squashed flat and dispersed against the window, distorting the occasional too-close peak of mountain jutting high and proud, black and formidable. The passenger nearest reached out a hand without looking and pulled to a close the only blind that remained open. Even the crew were strapped to their seats, feigning a carefree conversation and convincing no-one, on account of the darting eye movements that accompanied it. The jet levelled out once more and the announcement came that landing would be underway imminently, with apologies for the turbulence of its undertaking, as if the pilots themselves were somehow to blame. Less experienced passengers sighed in relief; those with more flying hours under their belts closed their eyes in silent prayer to deities various and unknown. The danger was far from over, and with the sound of the rain amplifying the drone of the engines, it was a landing destined to remain secured in memory for the rest of their lives, however long these might be.

Dan touched his brother's arm, both envious and amazed at Andy's ability to sleep so soundly while travelling. He'd slumbered his way through the vast majority of the twelve hours they had spent in the air, not to mention most of the seven endured waiting for their onward flight from Istanbul, and now, with the noise of the engines once again rising to a scream, he barely stirred. Dan poked him in the side and he jumped.

"What you do that for?" he slurred with a stretch and a yawn.

"We're about to land." Dan lifted the blind with the intention of demonstrating how close to ground level they were, only to be met by an impenetrable haze of greyish-white. "Or not," he said dubiously. The engines continued to screech as the plane banked left and upwards.

"Whoa. Has it been like this the whole way?" Andy was now fully awake and rather in need of a pee, but it would have to wait. There was no way he'd be allowed out of his seat.

"Only for the last half hour or so." Dan closed his eyes. The turbulence was giving him nausea and he was desperate to get off the plane. He wasn't about to tell his brother this though, for it would be an admission of weakness; something else Andy was better at than he was. It hadn't gone unnoticed, but Andy did the decent thing and didn't say a word.

"Good, err, afternoon," the voice of the pilot again, not sounding quite so confident as it had a few minutes previously. "Unfortunately we have had to abort the landing, due to poor visibility. We have five minutes' worth of fuel, so we will not be diverting, but we will be taking a different approach within the next couple of minutes. Please remain in your seats. Thank you."

The flight was perhaps half-full, mostly hikers and others whose hobbies involved travelling, dotted with the odd businessman here and there, sporting not-so-casual casual attire, their gaze artificially focused on a laptop or tablet. Even so, the din produced by multiple voices repeatedly muttering "five minutes' worth of fuel" was quite remarkable. Andy glanced down the aisle towards the air stewards, one of whom sensed his eyes on her and turned and smiled weakly, but kept her poker face. Dan still had his eyes closed, so Andy picked up his two day old newspaper and flicked to a random page. The headline loomed large and significant: 'Families reeling after plane trip ends in tragedy'. He quickly closed the paper again and pushed it away, although he wasn't especially worried; he'd been on many flights far scarier than this, for instance, where one of the engines failed—he'd done that one twice—or indeed where the only engine failed. Fortunately it was a motor glider and the descent was all the more beautiful for the lack of noise, if not a little longer in duration than anticipated.

"How long till we land, d'you reckon?" Andy asked, his mind idling on that thought.

"Oh, I'd say less than five minutes," Dan retorted, without opening his eyes. It would probably have been less difficult if he did open them, for he was alert to every sound and motion. The entire craft shuddered from the vibration of the wings, dropping sharply before rising again just as quickly. All the while they were flying upwards and at a steep incline to the left, with bags sliding from under seats, their owners unable to reach out and rescue them. Then the noise stopped.

Cautiously Dan opened one eye and tilted his head so that he could see between the seats in front, and thereon diagonally across the plane. Everyone was still and mute, seemingly struck silent by terror. They were dropping rapidly, quietly out of the sky. They were all going to die. Dan screwed his eyes tightly shut again and swallowed hard in an attempt to alleviate the pressure in his ears, but it was useless. Gravity is an unbeatable enemy and there is no point fighting it. Instead, he, like everyone else aboard, allowed his mind to wander wherever it wanted to. He thought back to the last time he asked Adele to marry him, stopping long enough to regret not fighting harder, ignoring the pain in his chest as he fought to breathe. Why hadn't the oxygen masks dropped down? Or maybe they had, but he would need to open his eyes to find out and try as he might, he couldn't do it. He couldn't bear to witness his own death coming up to meet him. Back further still, to the birth of his daughter, bypassing the time he had nearly died and straight through the years to his early twenties, newly home from university, with his life ahead of him. Had he achieved everything he wanted? Of course not! Who has by the time they're thirty-eight? Such a ridiculous, nondescript age to die.

It had to be only seconds now until they hit the ground. Soon the screaming would start, of this he was certain, for he could feel the panic starting to well in his gut, the pressure rising in his head, his shoulders squeezing in on his blood vessels. No air. No breath. How much longer now? Would he know about it when it happened? To be one of the lone survivors, trapped along with the dead, waiting for the flames to engulf them; that, surely, must be worse than outright death?

At least he was with his brother and he was so thankful for this that the tears fell of their own accord, unchecked by pride or other false emotion. So often they had fought about nothing of any great consequence, not compared to this thing. Whatever had passed between them, however great their differences, all that mattered now was that Andy would be here with him at the end. He tried to reach out to his brother, but there was too much force against him and he couldn't move. The harder he struggled, the more difficult it became and then the screaming began. Not long now until it was all over, their lives to be consigned to some voyeuristic documentary. Dan found his god and relinquished his body.

CHAPTER TWO

A beautiful September evening: the setting sun cast a red glow over the garden; house martins chirruped and swooped above the rooftops; a faint smell of cut grass hung in the air, as gardeners undertook what they hoped would be the last mowing of the season. Adele fed the fish, checked on the baby, laid her hand against the wine bottle and decided it was chilled enough. She reached to the back of the cabinet and carefully extracted the two glass goblets, each more than capable of holding a whole bottle, and divided the wine equally between them. A minute or so later, the doorbell sounded, Shaunna's halo of auburn hair instantly recognisable through the frosted window. Adele picked up the two glasses on her way, handing one to her friend and hugging her at the same time.

"Thanks," Shaunna grinned. "How's your day been?"

"Blissful," Adele said, clanging their glasses together. "Quiet, unmessy, unmoody, unmenny."

"Unmenny?" Shaunna repeated in puzzlement.

"Yeah. Without men. In other words, absolutely perfect." Shaunna laughed. They adjourned to the garden and settled into a pair of large, wooden chairs.

"What have you been up to today?" Adele asked.

"Not much. Work, then went to see Dad."

"Oh right. Nothing exciting then?"

"Not really." Shaunna sipped at her wine. There wasn't much to say now they had cycled through the usual daily routine of pleasantries, which isn't to imply that they had nothing to talk about; just that after being friends for so long they didn't need to talk to fill a silence, but nonetheless would undoubtedly find much to fill it with as the wine loosened their tongues. This was, after all, the calm before the storm, so to speak: Eleanor and James were getting married in less than two weeks. Of course, Eleanor and her mother were so obsessively well organised that there was nothing whatsoever left to do, which was why all of her oldest friends, normally roped in to help with any and every social function they had put on between them over the years, were able to appreciate a glorious early autumn evening and share a bottle of wine, or two, most likely: Adele had planned in advance and the second was in the freezer, just in case they finished the first too quickly.

"Is your dress sorted now?" she asked. The order had been given that no-one was to wear blue, but only after Shaunna had been out and bought her outfit, which was bound to be the wrong colour; if she'd bought a red outfit, then that would have been Eleanor's choice too. These things always happened, maybe because they all knew each other so well.

"Yeah. I just swapped it for the green one," Shaunna explained. Adele nodded. What this line of conversation was actually about was that she wanted to be questioned on her own outfit. Shaunna was aware of this and was struggling to pretend otherwise, but Adele looked ready to burst, so she relented.

"And how about yours? What colour did you go for in the end?"

"I'm glad you asked," Adele breathed. She put her glass on the table and tottered back to the house, reappearing a few seconds later, clutching a burgundy faux-suede garment bag. Shaunna rolled her eyes and waited for 'the reveal'.

"Ta-da!" Adele declared, freeing the short flowery dress and jacket. The dress was predominantly orange, with large pink roses, and the cropped, single-breasted jacket was of the same shade of pink.

"Oh, it's very you," Shaunna gushed. Adele held the dress, still on hanger, against her front and twirled.

"My shoes are the same as these," she indicated to the black high-heeled wedges she was wearing, "only in pink, obviously."

"Obviously," Shaunna echoed. It was a lovely outfit, but it was one which only Adele could get away with, or maybe women under the age of nineteen who hadn't had children. Adele carefully replaced the cover and took the dress back inside, satisfied with her friend's response. On the way back, she switched on the garden lights and transferred the other bottle of wine to the fridge.

"So, are you all packed?"

"Nope," Shaunna replied in a flippant tone.

"Me neither." Adele was about to elaborate further when her mobile phone sounded. She squinted at the screen. "Message from Jess."

"Really?"

"She's coming round, it says."

"I bet you anything it's to do with her wedding outfit."

"Yeah, it is." She handed the phone to Shaunna to let her read the rest of the message herself.

"She bought a blue one too. How funny." She handed the phone back. Adele sent a response and swapped her phone for her glass.

"I told her to bring some more wine," she said. Shaunna nodded.

"Good idea."

George was straddled across three foot of loft space, a leg on either side of the water tank, unable to move backwards or forwards for fear of putting his foot through the ceiling below. Between them they had six suitcases; they knew this because they'd spent the past two hours wracking their brains, trying to remember where any of them were. So far, they'd located one: on top of the wardrobe in what was now George's room, but wasn't when it was put there, hence long enough for it to essentially be rendered invisible. As for the others: they could be anywhere at all, but, George suggested, the loft seemed the most likely place.

Needless to say, Josh claimed to know exactly where they were, but there was no way he was climbing up there. The bravest he could manage on that score was to get far enough up the ladder to reach through the hatch and deposit old case notes; if he ventured any further he'd need the fire brigade to come and help him down again. So, his contribution to finding the suitcases consisted of standing on the fifth rung up and shining a torch into the furthest recesses of the roof space, in the vain hope that it might somehow pick out the distinctive silhouette of a suitcase lurking in amidst the scratchy insulation material. Under the circumstances, he found the suggestion of buying a replacement wholly unacceptable, even if George went to buy it on his own. It was wasteful and unnecessary; they just needed to try harder, that's all. However, George had cramp in both calves and a bump forming from where he'd bashed his head on a rafter, and was beginning to feel very much not in the mood for trying harder. He took one final, long look around, declared mission unaccomplished and carefully tightrope-walked his way back along the beam to the hatch. Josh pointed the torch upwards, lighting up his companion's thunderous expression to dramatic effect. He clambered back down the ladder and waited.

"I don't care what you have to say about it. I'm going to buy another suitcase tomorrow," George stated. Josh waited to see if there would be any further justification for this assertion, but there wasn't. It didn't really matter that much, yet somehow, like most things of late, the mystery of the missing luggage had been blown out of all sensible proportion. The holiday, for want of a more appropriate name for it, was still two weeks away—plenty of time for further searching—but the decision had been made for him once again and if it had been anyone else (other than Ellie, perhaps, but even then) it would have annoyed him. George's bossiness was a revelation, in spite of knowing each other for thirty years, and he rather liked it, if he was completely honest. After so long living alone, making all of the decisions for himself, it was good to have someone with whom to share the responsibility.

By the time Josh folded away the loft ladder and made it back downstairs, George was sitting on the sofa, flicking through TV channels. Not another word was said about the suitcases.

All of the other stemmed glasses Adele owned were of a normal size, so Jess settled on a pint glass: a sensible move, considering she'd arrived with two boxes of wine. She'd also brought with her three different, brand new dresses, leaving the original choice of blue at home. Now they were laid out on the patio table, while Adele gave each a thorough analysis. The first of the three was very much like her own, in pattern but not design, for it was a swirling floor-length affair, with cupped sleeves and buttons all down the front. This was Jess's least favourite, although Shaunna liked it the most. The second was grey and lilac with a faint pin-stripe through it and was quickly dismissed as being too dull and a potential clash for whatever shade of blue Eleanor had in mind. The third was a very slinky number, in deep orange and red, with a slit right up the side. This was declared perfect for the reception, but not the ceremony, so it came down to a choice between number one or yet another shopping trip. Jess shoved the three dresses back in their bag and dumped them on the floor. She'd quite had enough of trying on clothes that she wouldn't normally wear and it made her realise just how far she'd come. Not so long ago she'd have been delighted to take any excuse to go shopping; nowadays she was happy to go with a best fit, so it was looking like the swirly, ankle-length frock. Decision made, she settled back with her friends to drink too much wine and discuss the wedding.

"Who're you texting now?" George asked without taking his eyes off the TV. The programme showing was a crime drama, filmed to look drab and grey, with a script to match.

"Ellie." Josh pressed the 'send' button and locked his screen. There was little point putting his phone away, seeing as the only delay in her responding would be the time it took her to type out an overly long reply.

"Let me guess. You asked if she had a spare suitcase? You know she'll freak if she thinks we're not organised."

"Actually, that's not what the message was at all. I was just checking on the stag party arrangements."

"An evening in a moody jazz bar? Some stag party." George's tone was terse, still bemoaning the hour spent crawling around the loft, no doubt.

"That's what James wanted, so what else could we do?"

"I still say we book a stripper."

Josh's mouth dropped open of its own accord, but then he spotted the telltale twinkle in George's eyes. Good. It looked like he was finally going to relent on his bad mood. "So what's up?" he asked in the most carefree tone he had to offer.

"Tired."

"Is that all?"

"Yep." George turned the TV off and stood up. "Sorry. Were you watching that?"

"No, no," Josh said lightly and moved out of the way so he could pass.

"Good night."

Josh watched as he disappeared up the stairs, a door slamming shut a few seconds later. It wasn't yet nine o'clock. "Good night, I guess."

Wine is an interesting beverage for many reasons, the main one being the sudden onset of its effects, something that the three women were now considering at length, through fits of giggles brought on by nothing of particular hilarity. Their helplessness was exacerbated further by the text message Jess received from Eleanor to ask if she had any spare suitcases knocking around. Quite why they found this so funny, none of them could say. Indeed, they were having problems saying anything at all. Alas, it was Monday and therefore a 'school night', as they still liked to call them, so once they'd all taken turns to visit the loo, Jess called a taxi for Shaunna and herself, and they bade each other a somewhat teary farewell. It had been fun to sit, just the three of them, in the warmth of the evening, chatting and appreciating the time away from their respective menfolk, who, they concurred, were all right most of the time, but every now and then it was nice to have some space, if only to get the house back in order. Interestingly, neither Jess nor Adele noticed how little Shaunna had to contribute to this discussion, and nor did they realise that there had been no call to confirm whether Dan and Andy had arrived safely at their destination, until the following morning, when the news of the accident was all over the TV channels.

CHAPTER THREE

Eleanor kissed Toby on the forehead and handed him back to his father, who promptly returned him to the baby sling dangling from his shoulders. Over the past month, as Toby gained control of his very wobbly head, the papoose had slowly replaced the suit and tie that was James's customary attire, although the shirt and trousers remained ever-present and perfectly pressed. It was difficult to say which of the three of them looked the most exhausted, and yet James was fully enjoying being a stay-at-home father. It was his privilege, as MD, to set in motion changes to what he now realised was a dreadfully outdated maternity leave policy, or 'new parent leave', as it was called in the comprehensive documentation he had drawn up, in between feeds and nappy changes, and emailed to his office. Eleanor repeated her earlier forehead kiss, this time with James as the target, and mouthed the word 'tea' on her way to the kitchen. James stifled a yawn and rested his aching back against the sofa cushion. What strength women had, he confirmed to himself once again.

Eleanor's pregnancy had progressed without a hitch, despite the doom and gloom of every health care professional they had encountered during that time. Was she aware of the risks of giving birth so late into her thirties? The question was incessant and unnecessary, and Eleanor had found it so difficult to stand up for herself, to explain that as a general practitioner of course she knew the risks, but these days so many women chose to start their family later in life that the odds of there being anything wrong were negligible, to her and James at any rate. They'd briefly discussed what they would do if the scans showed any abnormalities. The answer: absolutely nothing at all. Their child was special because it was *their* child, regardless of any challenges which might come their way. So that was that: Tobias Benjamin Brown was born on the sixth of August, three weeks before his due date, but of a perfectly healthy size—a little too healthy size-wise for Eleanor's liking, particularly as she was still a few pounds away from fitting into her beautiful wedding dress the way she wanted to. She wasn't so naïve as to assume she'd be back to her pre-pregnancy shape and had told her mum to allow a few extra inches; even so, her hips were so large and round now (Shaunna had warned her about this and James remarked frequently on how wonderful they were) and her boobs were a whole three cup sizes bigger (he liked those too), which was great; she'd never really had boobs before and hoped they'd stay long after she was done breastfeeding and expressing milk every night before she went to bed. The only downside, to be taken literally, was that by the evening, they were so heavy that she felt like she might topple over, but it was worth it to see James so happy caring for their son.

She returned with two cups of tea, to find both of them fast asleep, James resting his head on the palm of his hand and bound to wake with pins and needles, Toby with his cheek scrunched up against his father's chest. She set down the cups, carefully extracted the baby and took him to his cot. He didn't even stir. When she returned, James had slumped forward, his chin hidden inside the baby sling. He was in such a deep sleep that he didn't wake until she caught his ear with the strap while attempting to free him.

"Thank you," he murmured as she passed him his tea. It was an effort to lift the cup to his lips.

"How did the conference go?" Eleanor asked, smoothing her hand against his hair. He leaned into her and sighed contentedly.

"It did not, unfortunately. We waited for an hour, and even had a technician check to ensure that we were connected correctly, but they didn't sign in."

"Really? That's a bit strange."

"I thought so too, although as Jason says, we don't know what the technology is like over there. I assume they couldn't get a connection."

"I guess. Or their flight was delayed, perhaps?"

"Perhaps." James took Eleanor's hand and kissed it. "I should make supper," he suggested. She shook her head.

"You stay right there, James Brown. I will make us supper this evening. You have worked quite hard enough and it's very late."

James didn't protest at this and was once again fast asleep by the time she returned with a simple, pasta-based meal. Soon after, the 'young' parents went to bed, the missed video conference forgotten for the time being.

Josh was awoken by the noise of the vacuum cleaner banging against his bedroom door and turned wearily to check the time: 7:30? He'd clearly gone quite mad. He stumbled out of bed and threw open the door.

"George! What the hell?"

"Got a long day ahead and it's my turn. It says so on the rota."

Josh let out a small yell of outrage and grabbed his dressing gown. "That bloody rota," he muttered under his breath as he pushed past to the bathroom. "Who's stupid idea was it to have a rota?"

"Yours actually, Joshua," George called after him.

"You weren't supposed to hear that!" Josh shouted back angrily. He slammed the door and turned on the shower, which didn't quite drown out the sound of the vacuum cleaner, but it was halfway there. George was right; this was his fault, and all because he thought it would save any arguing over whether one was doing more than the other. He'd thought it was working too, until now: quite why it was necessary to vacuum at this time of the morning—well, it was entirely unnecessary, in fact, and about something far more significant than a spot of lint on the carpet.

Josh emerged from the bathroom half an hour later and just in time to hear the front door close. So that was it then. George was at university for the day and would hopefully return in a better mood this evening, although if he made it back before bedtime, then that would be just twice so far this month, which was September, and optional. George contended that it was quiet in the library and he found it easier to work there—just him and Sophie and a couple of postgrads on the desk. Josh had no grounds to criticise, for he'd spent many a summer break doing the exact same thing, but that was beside the point, and it was a point he had yet to fathom. Today was his first day off in months, which was what made George's antics all the more infuriating, although it wasn't as if he was without things to do. For example, there was still the shed to clear and a stash of wallpaper lurking behind the sofa, bought on the day before Eleanor went into labour. With James in Birmingham, Josh had just accompanied her to her last ante-natal appointment and only stopped off to take advantage of the DIY store's toilets, but decided to go for a quick peruse whilst she did what she needed to. When she finally located him in the wallpaper aisle, he had picked up the rolls for the lounge and was mulling over possibilities for his bedroom. Under any circumstance other than a heavily pregnant and unpredictably hormonal best friend threatening a tantrum in the middle of a vast, echoic superstore, he'd have probably thought up some clever comeback to her very public suggestion that he was acting on a sympathetic, primitive instinct to nest. Instead, he went for the safe option of giving her the car keys, paying for what he already had in his arms and getting her home as quickly as possible.

So, this wasn't exactly what he'd had in mind for his time off, but the walls needed doing and he was up now. He headed downstairs (George had filled the filter machine; apparently it wasn't quite so bad as he'd thought), tipped some cereal into a bowl and poured a very large mug of coffee: his essential fuel for the task ahead. He'd had plenty of opportunities to practise his wallpapering skills over the years; living on your own (and even before that being the only man about the house) does that for you, although his grandmother would fight him all the way, watching over his every move, questioning whether there was enough paste, was he sure the pattern was the right way up, had he left enough trim, or too much? It was no wonder he was such a perfectionist. Funny. He'd imagined he excelled above all others in this regard, until George moved in. And then he discovered precisely what true perfectionism looked like.

Josh scooped a heap of cornflakes into his mouth and shoved the bowl on top of the bookshelf so that he could move the sofa, pulling it into the middle of the room and retrieving the rolls of wallpaper. He still wasn't convinced this was a good idea, although with the sofa away from the wall, he remembered how much he disliked the colour of the paint and wondered why he'd chosen it in the first place. He turned on the TV, with the intention of tuning into a music station, but thought pop and dance music at this still relatively early hour might be a bit much, so he stuck on the news instead. It was a decision that immediately put an end to his interior design intentions. The remote control tumbled from his hand and cracked as it hit the corner of the table; Josh moved backwards to sit down on the sofa, forgetting completely that he had moved it, until it hit him in the back of the legs and felled him. He watched on, dazed, shocked, a futile hope forming in his head that he had heard wrong. Upstairs, his abandoned mobile phone tinkled away unanswered, vibrated across the bedside table and on the third missed call toppled off the edge and landed with a thud that was sufficiently loud to stir him out of his trance. He went upstairs and retrieved it, returning Eleanor's call on the way back down.

"Josh! Turn on your TV, quick!" she ordered him breathlessly.

"I've seen it."

"They didn't make the conference call last night."

"Oh God." Both of them went quiet and stayed that way for

several minutes, before Josh finally found his tongue again. "Have you heard from Jess at all?"

"Not yet. She's in court this morning."

"And Adele?"

"No, but then that's nothing unusual."

There was an undertone to the dialogue that consisted of each knowing they ought to try calling Jess and Adele, whilst hoping that the other would offer do it. Just as Josh was about to relent, his phone started to beep intermittently, indicating another call.

"Incoming from George. Hold on," he said, switching calls. "Hello?"

"Have you heard?"

"Yes. I'm just on the phone to Ellie."

"Does Jess know?"

And so the conversations continued in this manner for the better part of the morning, from Eleanor to Josh, to George, to Kris and finally to Shaunna. All the while Jess was in court, unable to be reached, and Adele wasn't answering. The staff on the advertised information line were either reluctant to share with non-relatives or simply didn't know any more than that which had been broadcast, but one thing was absolutely certain: Dan and Andy had made no contact in twenty-four hours and by now it was on every news channel, on the hour and in the ticker: a small passenger jet had crashed in Kathmandu; no-one was thought to have survived.

CHAPTER FOUR

Creatures of habit: they gathered first in the waiting room of Josh's surgery, then moved on to The Pizza Place, where the children could be entertained, or contained, depending on which adult was making the judgement. The children, thankfully, were completely oblivious to the dread surrounding them. Little Shaunna was clutching a fat, red crayon and happily colouring everywhere but within the outline of an elephant. Toby was slumped against one of James's palms, the other entirely covering the tiny tot's back. Josh refreshed the newsfeed on his tablet to see if anything different displayed, but the same words were etched across the screen and into his retinae. George glanced over Josh's shoulder and read them for himself. Again.

"How many planes land in Kathmandu on a daily basis? I mean, I realise it's not Heathrow, but surely the chances of it being their plane are pretty slight?"

No-one replied, because they were all silently following the same line of placation, desperate for the odds to be on their side. As well as this thought, Eleanor was ashamed to admit that she was worrying about the wedding. Andy had assured her that this was a quick round trip—no longer than a week, he'd said—and that they'd be back and all set for both the ceremony and the somewhat unconventional honeymoon to follow. If she'd doubted his word, it was not for reasons like this. Andy made and broke promises all the time, but they were inconsequential and within his control. She turned towards James and put her finger in Toby's hand. He gripped it tight and it made her feel better. James smiled and lifted his thumb to touch hers. She closed her eyes and held on to that feeling.

Kris's phone wasn't so loud really, but in the solemnity of the moment it broke through like a fanfare trumpet. He glanced at the screen and quickly headed outside to answer the call. It was his boss at the radio station.

"A quick interview, no more than two minutes," he coerced, eager to get a local twist on the news of the plane crash. Kris glanced back through the window at his friends. If he did this it might keep them safe from other prying journalists. On the other hand, it might bring even more to the door.

"I'm sorry, I can't. Not right now. We don't know anything and it might not even be their flight."

"I understand, but we know there were only two Britons on-board, so if you could just perhaps give us a quick line or two about how you're all feeling, you know, mention the humanitarian aspect…"

Kris hung up and threw his phone so hard it hit the pavement opposite, breaking apart and bouncing into the path of an oncoming bus. So there were two UK passengers. How was he going to tell the girls? He went back inside and headed straight for the toilets, locking himself in the cubicle. His heart was pounding and he could feel the tears pricking his eyes. He couldn't lose Dan, he just couldn't. Not now. It would be so unfair. He pressed his hands against the cool cistern, trying to steady his thoughts with deep breaths and distractions. He heard the door to the men's room spring to a close and waited for whoever had entered to finish using the urinal before he flushed the toilet. He rubbed his eyes and went outside.

"Hi," he smiled weakly.

"Alright?" The other man washed his hands and moved to use the dryer, but Kris was standing in the way, preparing himself to face the others.

"Sorry," he said and reluctantly returned to the restaurant. A short while later, the other man followed, acknowledging the group with a tip of the peak of his enormous hat, before disappearing through the kitchen door, leaving it to swing behind him.

"That's Wotto, I take it?" Kris asked no-one in particular. Four voices confirmed that it was. Krissi was in the kitchen too, where she'd been since they'd arrived and told her what was going on. He decided to go and check on his stepdaughter, because it was easier than telling his friends what his boss had disclosed. As he approached the kitchen door, he slowed right down. Through the circular window, he could see her leaning against Wotto's shoulder, a length of blue paper towel scrunched up and soggy around her red eyes and nose. Perhaps this wasn't the easy option after all, but she'd spotted him now, so it was too late. She feigned a bright, carefree smile and moved away from Wotto.

"How're you doing?" Kris asked.

"OK, I guess. You?"

"Yeah. OK."

"Good, good," she replied, collecting a clipboard hanging on a wall hook and busying herself with reading whatever was on it.

"What you up to?" Kris peered over the top of the clipboard.

"Ordering stock. My scanner's playing up."

"Right. What's that then?" He wasn't interested in knowing and she didn't especially want to explain, but she obliged anyway, understanding that her dad was probably feeling this a lot more than she was. Her dad. That's who he was.

"I'm going to err..." She dashed across the kitchen and disappeared inside the walk-in refrigerator. Kris watched on, rendered helpless by his own impending loss. Wotto came over and patted his arm.

"As I told her," he nodded in the direction Krissi had just taken, "you shouldn't think the worst. Don't grieve for them yet."

Kris lifted his eyes and looked straight into Wotto's face. He was young—no more than twenty-five, at a guess—with a bright, sincere expression. He'd seen pain; it was written all over him, yet it didn't drag him down. So much wisdom in those words.

"You're right," he nodded. "Thanks."

"She'll be OK, you watch," Wotto added, thumbing at Krissi as she emerged again, clipboard still in hand. "She always is."

"Yeah, she's tough," Kris agreed.

"You're not joking!" Wotto laughed and turned back to his preparations. The restaurant was due to open in twenty minutes and they were nowhere near ready. Krissi looked from Kris to Wotto, trying to ascertain what had passed between them. Kris gave her a wink and she came to him and kissed him lightly on the cheek.

"I love you."

"And I you," he said, returning the kiss on her forehead. "I've got a bit more information. It's not good news, I'm afraid."

Krissi stepped away and waited while he searched for the words to tell her what he had discovered, each one piercing right into her like a poisoned dart. Almost two years had passed since her selfishness had pushed a wedge between them and still she didn't regret what she had done. How could she now, when they were waiting, powerless and ignorant? Kris watched her carefully, taking in her reaction, for the first time truly understanding why she had needed to know the identity of her real father, and also finally realising that none of it mattered. She was his daughter: as good as blood, this love that filled his heart and kept it beating. However bad it was when they found out for sure, he knew that they would get through this together, the way they always had, and he would at last be ready to tell her the truth.

Opening time had merely shifted the friends to a table in the corner, where they dutifully sat, drinking purchased beverages and picking at a large pizza. None of them had an appetite, but they didn't know what else to do. Every so often, Jess's phone would beep and she'd glance at the screen, then return it to her bag. Shaunna was doing her best to entertain her young

21

namesake, who really could have done with having a nap, but was as obstinate as her parents when it came to doing the right thing. Adele was pressing a few escaped granules of sugar to powder with her fingernail and Eleanor was feeding Toby. James was standing by the door, watching George and Josh engaged in what seemed to be a very difficult exchange outside, each looking past the other. Kris noticed Jess begin to crumble and took her hand.

"I need some air," she said, getting up and pushing past him. She stumbled outside and walked a few yards down the road, in the opposite direction to George and Josh. A few seconds later, they came back towards the restaurant; Josh returned inside, while George stayed to talk to Jess.

"It's not their plane," Josh announced. "They landed a few hours before the crash."

"Are you sure?" Eleanor asked.

"Yes. I've just checked the flight numbers. Apparently there's been a big storm that's taken out the communications system in the city, which is why we haven't heard from them and also why the news channels couldn't confirm the flight details. Anyway, they're safe, as far as we can tell."

Adele began to sob and Shaunna rushed to her, hugging her tightly. Little Shaunna watched on in bemusement.

CHAPTER FIVE

The plane once again straightened out and slowed as it approached the airstrip from the opposite direction. Andy reached across his brother and opened the blind. The rain was torrential, the water that had accumulated on the tarmac creating a terrific spray, as the wheels bounced once, twice, then smoothed out, taking in the full length of the runway before they came to a halt. Some of the passengers cheered, although Andy wasn't able to share their sense of relief just yet; he turned to his brother, who was fast asleep, and decided, against regulations, to dash to the toilet while no-one was looking. By the time he returned, Dan was unbelted and out of his seat.

"Come on!" he commanded. Andy hesitated a moment, waiting for the telltale tension in Dan's neck muscles. After all these years he still loved to wind him up, although he was looking a little off-colour, so Andy took it no further. They shuffled forward and queued behind others awaiting their turn, some fussing with bags and belongings, unaware of the impatience building around them. Dan checked his watch and tapped his fingers on the back of a seat. They were going to miss the call at this rate.

It was the culmination of many months of planning and legal negotiations that could have been made all the more complex because of the emotive issues within which they were embedded, the final stage of setting in motion everything that had been ambitiously envisaged. Nine months had passed since Alistair Campion died, an unintended victim of a man crazed by loss and loneliness. There was still no credible explanation for why he targeted Campion in particular, but regardless, he was no more, and the fire had ensured his empire went with him. Almost.

Campion's wife died not long after and what was left of the business would have remained forever intestate, had it not been for the discovery of a singular son and heir. With the directors dispersed to other boardrooms across the UK, Alistair's estranged son Jason had finally and rightfully won his inheritance. If they made it to the hotel in time they might even find out what he intended to do with it.

Jason was no stranger. Dan and Andy had known him for years, in passing at least. Now in his early twenties, he still sported the moody, sullen attitude of his youth and insisted on wearing arty, dark attire even in the midst of summer, when the rest of the country was donning its shorts and vest, whatever the weather. He certainly hadn't inherited his dress sense from his father, nor, it would seem, his business sense, for it was apparent from all previous communications that he didn't want the money and was desperate to dispense with the responsibilities that came with it.

They at last made it inside the terminal and stopped at the first open area where they could get out of the flow of foot traffic. Dan was fidgety and felt sick.

"I'll stay and check in with the haulage people, if you like," Andy suggested.

"Yeah. Good idea. I'll get to the hotel and set everything up. See you there." Dan was already moving away, grateful that he could save face. The humidity wasn't helping much, although didn't normally bother him. Maybe it was something he'd eaten. The mere thought of food turned his stomach and he quickly stepped outside, gulping in a great lungful of mountain air. It was warm and moist, but wonderfully real compared to the plane, and it instantly eased the nausea.

Two groups of people congregated outside the terminal: passengers who had just exited and were now variously awaiting taxis or lifts, and then the taxi drivers, legitimate or otherwise, seeking to pick up a fare. Somewhere in amongst the latter group would be their connection and Dan started to scour the crowd, wondering how he might recognise this person. If he'd felt well, he'd have stayed with his brother, as their lift was someone Andy knew from his previous visit to Nepal. Dan rubbed his eyes and swallowed back the saliva, hoping it was the product of his mind rather than his stomach.

"Andrew!" a voice called from within the midst of waiting cars, a hand waving over the heads of the crowd, looming closer, until a smiling brown face came into view.

"Ah. Yeah," Dan said under his breath with a weary realisation of how useful it could sometimes be that he and Andy looked so alike, although it wasn't the easiest thing to explain to those who didn't know them well.

"Hello," the man said materialising in front of him, hand outstretched in friendship.

"Hi," Dan smiled and shook the hand.

"You are not Andrew, I see, but you must surely be his brother Daniel," the man smiled back.

"I am, though I prefer Dan."

"Of course. I am Bhagwan," he said, unhooking Dan's holdall from his shoulder without waiting for confirmation that this was acceptable. Dan was glad to be rid of the weight and followed him through the rapidly diminishing horde, to the rusty old pickup truck parked at an angle of almost forty-five degrees to the kerb. The man chucked the bag in the back and Dan winced, hoping the thud as it landed was his water bottle rather than his tablet, not that it would matter by the time they reached the hotel, judging by the inch or so of rainwater it was now swimming in. He climbed into the front and fastened his seatbelt, noting that his companion had not fastened his own.

"So," Bhagwan said, steering hard out onto the road. "You have not visited Nepal before?"

"No," Dan replied, grasping for the handle on the inside of the door in an attempt to stay absolutely upright, so sure he was going to throw up at any second.

"And what do you think of it so far? Wet, huh?"

"You could say that," Dan replied, although in all honesty it was no worse than September in England.

"Most people come when it is not monsoon season," Bhagwan explained, throwing the truck around a corner and accelerating sharply up a steep slope. Dan lurched forward and pressed his lips together. He was starting to sweat with the effort of keeping his stomach contents where they were.

For this reason, he didn't reply to the man's observation and felt terribly rude, but he really didn't want to risk opening his mouth, so he nodded and hummed, whilst Bhagwan narrated their journey through the current downpour, regaling him with tales of monsoon seasons past, where the roads were a foot deep in water, with graphic descriptions of floating excrement and other such unpleasantries, pinching his nose or adding sound effects for authenticity. None of this was helping at all.

By the time they pulled up outside the hotel, the urge to expel was so great that the best Dan could offer was a vague utterance of thanks and an apology before he bolted inside, on the lookout for anything that looked remotely like a toilet. To his delight, the symbols on the doors made for an easy mission. The man standing in the foyer watched on in bewilderment as his newest arrival sprinted straight for the restroom without a word.

Meanwhile, Bhagwan returned to the airport, where he parked almost identically to his prior visit and waited for Andy, who was in turn still waiting for the hold to be unloaded so that he could check their shipment had arrived in one piece. It wasn't an especially precious cargo—not to him or Dan—but when they had been charged with the task of coordinating the ordering and delivery, it was made apparent that the equipment was vital to the survival of an entire village. With this in mind, and the desire for a new adventure lurking just below the surface, Andy suggested they fly out and oversee the delivery in person. Dan had immediately agreed, although he hadn't seemed quite so enthusiastic since they left. He was very quiet, with none of his usual resistance to anything and everything Andy suggested.

After a wait of only half an hour, which seemed a lot longer in the absence of anything to do to pass it, a customs official confirmed that the equipment had been successfully unloaded and provided Andy with the number for the storage container, where it would remain until the following morning, ready to be transferred onto their transport to the village. Andy had readily entrusted Bhagwan with the task of arranging all of this, even though they had spoken just once during the past decade. He shoved the piece of paper with the storage container number deep into the zip pocket of his rucksack and headed out into the wet Kathmandu afternoon, genuinely thrilled to see his old friend and sharing a heartfelt embrace.

As they drove away from the airport, they caught up on the less complicated aspects of life in the years that had passed since they last saw each other, both much younger then and with fewer cares for the future. Andy had been hiking through the Himalayas at the time: the end of a three month treacherous journey across India. Unlike most of the other people he met on his travels, he wasn't driven by any convoluted need to 'find himself', or attain some sense of inner peace; he sought adventure and it's safe to say he found it the moment he accepted a lift on the back of Bhagwan's pickup—as far as he could tell the exact same vehicle he was sitting in now. Last time, it had been the depths of winter, when snow and ice had blocked the road down into Kathmandu, turning a ten hour drive into a two day trial interspersed with impromptu stops to work with others traversing the pass, to clear rocks and massive hunks of ice from the narrow carriageway carved into the side of the mountains. This time, nearing the end of monsoon season, he didn't expect it to be much safer and hoped his estimate of a one week round trip wasn't overly optimistic, afraid to let Eleanor down for many reasons, not least that she was the champion of holding grudges. She'd yet to forgive him for breaking his leg and 'shirking' in the weeks preceding Adele and

Tom's wedding two years previously.

Bhagwan was coming to the end of the bit where he talked about his family and his wife, with whom he had three children: two girls and a boy. The girls were twins, aged eight, and the boy was four. Since the birth of his son, they had been unable to conceive again, much to Bhagwan's sorrow. Andy thought it apt that ahead of them vast black clouds were forming, for he could sense where the conversation was going.

"And you, Andrew. Tell me of your beautiful wife and children."

"I, err, I'm not married." Andy began uneasily.

"Still enjoying the bachelor life, yes?"

"Something like that, yeah," Andy said, relieved to be off the hook. Just to make sure, he added, "My brother has a young daughter, called Shaunna. She's very precious."

"How so?" Bhagwan asked. Andy was only too glad to oblige him with the information. It was raining heavily again, the lightning flashes casting the mountains in ominous black relief, the back of the truck skidding occasionally, but mostly taking the terrain confidently in its stride. If Andy were the cautious type, then he might have been a little more concerned about the dangers of tomorrow's trip, but as with all these things, it was a challenge he'd accepted and therefore it had to be won.

They had arrived at the hotel, and he took money from his pocket, offering it to Bhagwan, who initially pushed it away, but eventually took it at Andy's insistence. He knew that what would seem a pittance back home was significant compensation in Nepal and he wasn't one to take advantage. Bhagwan thanked him for his generosity and stopped briefly to chat with the owner of the hotel (a distant cousin of some sort, like all the people in places like this), then left Andy to check in and find Dan. The owner of the hotel, who introduced himself as 'Alan', which Andy presumed to be a western name he had adopted to assist his guests, showed him to his room, indicating across the hallway to another door as they passed. Andy dumped his bag on the small bed, gave his face a quick freshen-up with a splash of cold water and went straight to Dan's room. By now he would have the connection up and ready for the video conference and would no doubt have some comment to make about his rather late arrival.

As it turned out, Dan had nothing to say. He opened the door and pointed to his tablet, abandoned on the bed. Andy squinted at the screen.

"No connection. Bugger."

"Yeah. Alan says the storm's taken out the phone lines, so there's not much we can do."

"An interesting choice of name, I thought." Dan didn't comment. "Oh well. Not to worry. It wasn't urgent, after all. We were only showing off really." Andy watched his brother carefully, noting how pale he was. "You OK?"

"Yeah. Tired, that's all. I hope they get it back up again soon. I could do with an early night. That 5 a.m. start is going to finish me off."

"Bhagwan is coming back this evening, to share some of his famous hooch. It's not bad stuff, actually."

"I'll take your word for it," Dan yawned and stretched, immediately wishing he hadn't. His chest felt tight and crampy and his balance was way off. He staggered slightly and steadied himself with a knee against the bed frame. Everything ached.

"You sure you're OK?" Andy asked again.

"I'll be fine," Dan frowned, "although no doubt you'd prefer it if I left tomorrow to you?"

"Not at all," Andy said defensively. The nine months they had been working together as Jeffries and Associates had gone even better than he'd expected, their perpetual sibling rivalry rarely rearing its head. On occasion, Dan could be offhand, his response underpinned by a misconception that Andy was somehow trying to stitch him up. The truth was that he had not once and nor would he ever try and get one over on his brother. If anything it was the other way around, a case of Dan assuming of others what was true of himself. Regardless, it was apparent that he wanted to be left alone to rest, so Andy headed back to his own room for a nap and a shower, with plenty of time before Bhagwan returned for an evening of drinking and singing. It was still early afternoon, with the hum of life and the pit-pat of rain floating through the open window. In spite of the humidity, there was a cool breeze, and Andy stripped to his boxers and lay on top of the sheets, quickly drifting off. He'd asked 'Alan' to wake him if he wasn't up and about by six o'clock, so could safely relax and enjoy the break from reality. Across the way, Dan was also sleeping, in fits and starts. He couldn't get comfortable and the waves of nausea had him dashing to the toilet so frequently he felt like he was undertaking a stamina run. Eventually he found a position where the sickness wasn't quite so severe and pulled a sheet around him.

In the event, Andy didn't need an alarm call and was up and in the shower by 5:30. He was already enjoying himself enough to waylay any guilt he might have about his motivations for returning to Nepal, for whilst they were honourable in most senses, he was still doing it by and large for the sense of adventure, and with Bhagwan for company, it would certainly be that.

The wet-room was quite something and typical of these kinds of places, he had come to realise on his travels. The locals could be living in relative destitution, barely enough to eat and only just keeping roofs over their heads, but the tourist hotels were kitted out to the highest possible standard. The shower, therefore, was the sort for which most British households would pay handsomely, with enough pressure to fell an elephant. Andy stepped out of the downpour to shampoo his hair, the lather disappearing immediately he put his head back under. When he emerged into the room a few minutes later, just as soon as he could tear himself away from the wondrous massaging effect of the water jets on his shoulders, he was breathless and refreshed. He unzipped his rucksack, pulled out a clean t-shirt and a pair of unnecessarily vibrant Bermuda shorts, gave his hair a quick shake and sat on the edge of the bed to put on his shoes. He managed to get the left one on before the commotion outside drew his attention and he limped to the window to see what the fuss was about.

Adults were looking down from windows and children shouted as they ran through the streets, their faces lit with the devilish delight of those who know they are delivering news that will fill grown-ups with terror, but are yet to comprehend why. Andy couldn't understand anything of what was being said and quickly put on his other shoe, nearly tripping over his untied laces on his way down to what could generously be described as the hotel's lobby. It was deserted, and Andy spied the owner outside, engaged in a hurried dialogue with a boy of about ten. He wandered out onto the street, the rain immediately soaking his clothes right through, and listened in on their conversation, hoping his show of interest might afford an interpretation.

"There is a plane crash," Alan explained, pointing over towards the airport. Andy followed the direction of the finger, but the sky was so dark and the rain so heavy that he could barely see past the end of the building and even the thickest black smoke could readily disguise itself in amongst the storm clouds. Seconds later, Bhagwan came tearing around the corner and skidded to a stop, the spray from the wheels of the pickup missing them by millimetres.

"A plane has crash-landed by the airport. It is very, very bad," he shouted excitedly, his expression much like that of the children running around delivering the news. In a country with such a low life expectancy, Andy wondered if this kind of tragedy had less of an impact than back home, where longevity was the quality by which most judged their health and wellbeing.

"There was a big explosion," Bhagwan continued, grabbing one of two large jars from the back of the truck and handing it to Andy. It was full and surprisingly heavy, considering the ease with which his small, wiry friend had hoisted it over the side, and Andy staggered slightly under the weight.

"Are there any survivors?" he asked. Bhagwan shook his head.

31

"A plane just like the one you came in. The airport is closed."

Andy ran his fingers through his hair, the thoughts toppling so fast around his head he was struggling to order them into anything he could act upon. He needed to tell Dan, and to try and get a message back to Jess and Adele, but the telephones were out. Would the news have made it to the UK yet? He hoped not and began to play through the scene of what would happen when it did. He was very close to the mark: wrong location, but the imagined reactions of his friends was spot on.

For several minutes more, the men remained standing in the street, the rain bouncing inches off the pavement, the children becoming less numerous and urgent in their proclamations. By now everyone knew about the crash, and they were treating it with a kind of boredom. Accidents were common here: trucks toppled off the mountain on an almost daily basis. Children and adults alike died of diseases long since eradicated in most of the developed world, or from malnutrition, particularly those who lived up in the mountains, and yet for all of this, the people of Nepal were so generous and welcoming. Andy recalled the kindness of those he had encountered on his last visit, offering a place to sleep and sharing their meals with no expectation that the favour would be returned. This was the real reason that they were here now, overseeing the delivery, because the young couple whose project this was were paying back. There was no profit in this venture, other than for those who believe in karma or an afterlife. Andy didn't care much for money, but Dan did, and it was a credit to Alistair Campion that he had been able to tap into some hidden benevolence within him in order to secure his help. Yes, his little brother was a very different person these days and the changes were definitely for the better.

They went back inside, and Andy went to tell Dan about the crash, but found him in a deep, unstirring sleep. He left him as he was and returned to the lobby, where there was a small room with old chairs and a broken TV. The two 'cousins' had already started on the hooch and offered up a china teacup. Andy thanked them and sniffed cautiously at the cloudy liquid, the fumes almost enough to intoxicate from this action alone. Bhagwan laughed and emptied his own cup in one go. Andy shrugged and followed suit. It didn't taste as bad as it smelled, although the last time he was here, Bhagwan had gone to the effort of decanting it into brown bottles and it was easy to avoid the sediment. The act of pouring it straight from the large earthenware jar had stirred up the sludge in the bottom, which was bitter and tangy to begin with, but became less so as the evening wore on. Bhagwan was staying over, not that the hooch would normally have stopped him driving, but it was important that they set off as early as possible, so as to make good time. The trip took upwards of six hours when the roads were clear and dry, and at this time of year, mudslides and river floods could easily double it.

The evening passed by so quickly, with Bhagwan narrating sagas of confiscated distilling equipment and arrests, each more elaborate than the last. Andy was enjoying himself so much (and was so drunk) that he almost forgot about the plane crash and the worry it would be causing back home. The phone lines were still out and looked set to remain that way for at least the next twenty-four hours, by which point they would be up in the mountains and far from technology. He tried waking Dan a couple of times, partially succeeding on the second, when he rolled over and swore. Andy decided it was safer to let him sleep; the news would keep. He went to bed himself just after eleven o'clock, leaving Bhagwan and 'Alan' to their songs and the remaining dregs of the first jug, saving the second for their planned return in a couple of days' time. And boy did he sleep; the next thing he was aware of was Bhagwan shaking him awake at fifteen minutes to five in the morning. He sat up carefully in anticipation of a thumping head and the dizziness that generally accompanied a night of heavy drinking, and was pleased to find that he felt perfectly well, other than some general stiffness from too much time sitting in budget airline seats. A quick shower and he went to check on Dan, to find he was already outside, policing Bhagwan's shuffling about of fuel and basic supplies to make room for the equipment they were to collect from the airport.

"Morning," Andy greeted his brother. Dan paused and glanced at him disdainfully.

"Why didn't you tell me about the crash?"

"I tried, but you were dead to the world. Feeling any better?"

"A bit." He attempted a smile, which only served to clarify that it was a lie.

"This isn't the place to come the hard man, you know," Andy warned. He'd watched a few people go down with altitude sickness and other illnesses that were relatively minor with the right medicine and plenty of bedrest, neither of which would be available to them once they were up in the mountains; thus, the best preventative measure was for Dan to be upfront about his symptoms, and about as likely as Bhagwan's truck suddenly transforming into a Lamborghini.

"I'm fine," Dan snapped, his neck muscles tensing.

"How's your head?"

He ignored this and went back into the hotel to collect their bags. He was feeling really rough, and just wanted to get on with the job without the constant enquiries about his health. He didn't travel well at the best of times, but the turbulence coming in to land hadn't helped, and he was trying his hardest to forget about the nightmare, or hallucination, or whatever it was, because it had been so real; his relief at finding they'd landed safely, however, was short-lived, replaced as it was by the return of the nausea and then the news of the actual crash. He even wondered momentarily if it was some kind of premonition, which wasn't the sort of thing he usually held any stock in.

Once everything was strapped down in the back of the truck, Andy climbed into the cab, shuffling across as far as he could without getting in the way of the gear shift, leaving Dan to take the seat closest to the door, for which he was glad, just in case the urge to vomit overpowered him again. Bhagwan checked everything was secure and started the engine; not the quietest or smoothest of runners, but reliable nonetheless and the local people took little notice of the noise. Dan took a deep breath and held on to the door, as the truck once again rattled its way along the main drag back to the airport, the complex in darkness apart from a few vehicles in the distance, working through the night to clear the debris and return to normal operations as quickly as possible.

It wasn't until they neared the warehouses that it became apparent that the place was shut down, which didn't make much business sense, as it was only really the runway that was out of action. Bhagwan pulled over and shouted to one of the drivers of the many trucks parked along the opposite side of the road, who confirmed that they weren't expecting any change for another eight hours at least, by which point it would be too late to start driving up the mountain. Bhagwan conveyed the news to his passengers, and Andy agreed that leaving it until tomorrow seemed like the most sensible strategy, so back they went to the hotel, where Dan went straight to bed, leaving Andy to see if he could find a way of getting a message home. After trying several local businesses, he gave up and decided to go and catch up on some sleep himself.

The airport was still closed the next morning, although the haulage warehouses were all lit up, now with twice as many articulated lorries lined up outside in varied states of loading, and men barking instructions at boys carrying sacks across the paths of ragged forklift trucks. Andy had memorised the number of the container and scanned the dark crates until he found the correct run of prefixes, pointing it out to Bhagwan at the last second. He slammed on the brakes and turned hard to the right, stopping a few feet from the container. Dan swallowed and opened the door. He was starting to worry about the logistics of the journey ahead. He'd seen the mountain roads on TV and it could only get worse, but there was no way he was going to be beaten by a bout of food poisoning, or whatever this was.

Andy was completely tuned into his brother's state of health, thus took more than his share of the weight of the enormous catering oven, walking backwards and balancing it on the dropped tail of the truck so he could climb up and pull it on-board, while Dan and Bhagwan pushed from the other side. It just about fitted widthways, but there was no way the tailgate would fasten, not without jettisoning the fuel and water, which would be somewhat counter-productive. Instead, Bhagwan took a rope from the cab and looped it around the back of the truck as best he could. Dan raised an eyebrow doubtfully.

"It's OK. I do this many times," Bhagwan assured him, with a tug on the tied end to remove any slack, before they all climbed back in the cab and started their journey up towards the mountain pass. By now it was light enough to take in the final remains of the crashed jet, not that it was recognisable as such. A few bent panels and some torn seats—a devastating reminder of the lives lost and a thought for the families left behind.

"Surely the phone lines must be working by now?" Dan asked distractedly, unable to look away from the crash site.

"We can stop and see, maybe?" Andy suggested. Bhagwan shrugged and pulled up next to a group of drivers congregated around their wagons, gabbling incomprehensibly and pausing only to smoke or spit. He shouted to them and they all stopped talking at once. One of them nodded. Bhagwan said something else and the man pointed to a window in a building a couple of hundred yards from their location.

"There's a phone in the office there," Bhagwan explained, putting his foot down and driving the entire distance without changing gear.

"Do you want to do it, bro?" Andy put his hand out to brace himself against the dashboard. It was already an instinctive response.

"No, you go," Dan muttered through gritted teeth. "You'll get more sense out of Jess than I will from Adele."

"I was going to ring Josh, actually," Andy said. "Safer all round." Dan gave him a swift nod in agreement and rotated on his seat to let him pass.

It took several attempts to get a connection, and several more before he received an answer; not surprising, as it was the middle of the night in England. The conversation was economical enough to have been a telegram. Andy reassured Josh they were both safe; Josh explained that the accident had been all over the news, but that they'd checked the flight numbers, so knew it wasn't theirs within a couple of hours of hearing about it. Everyone was fine; Eleanor had threats she would see through if they didn't get back for the wedding. Andy laughed, although was quite sure that it was no joke. They said their goodbyes and Andy returned to the truck, nodding to Dan to indicate that all was well back at home. Bhagwan gave him just long enough to get settled back into his seat and they were off again, heading for the pass and pleased that the rain had stopped, at least for the time being.

CHAPTER SIX

George tiptoed into the hallway and placed the brand new suitcase against the wall. In the time it took him to close the door, Josh had put the old suitcase next to the almost identical one George had just bought. He turned back and nearly tripped over it.

"Oh. You found it."

"Yes. It was in the shed, along with three others."

"What were you doing in the shed?"

"Looking for a paste brush. More to the point, what were *they* doing in the shed? Any idea?"

"I, err, well I guess I must've put them there."

"And you didn't happen to notice them, right in front of the lawn mower, you know, the last time you mowed the grass? Now when was that? Last weekend?"

George had nothing to say. Of course he'd known the suitcases were in the shed. He'd fully intended to dispose of them at the first opportunity, but with Josh taking a few days off work he hadn't got around to it. Now here was the evidence, right in the middle of the hallway, and he'd been caught out. On the plus side, the key was safely hidden away, so at least he knew the contents hadn't been discovered.

"I'll take it upstairs, shall I?" George said, reaching for the handle without waiting for an answer. Josh put out his foot and folded his arms.

"Not so fast, Morley. What's inside?"

"Nothing important. In fact, so unimportant I can't remember exactly what. Old documents. That sort of thing?"

Josh glared at him and he smiled nervously, fully aware of the colour rising in his cheeks. He really didn't want to share what was inside the suitcase. Josh moved his foot out of the way and stepped aside. George stayed where he was.

"Off you go then." Josh turned back towards the living room. "And when you're done you can come and give me a hand with this last wall."

George picked up the case and scurried away up the stairs, grateful to be let off for now, but knowing it couldn't last and hoping he could come up with something more convincing than 'old documents' before it was brought up again. He left the case behind his bedroom door and retrieved the key from the back of his underwear drawer, pushing it deep into his pocket before returning to the lounge, where Josh was pasting the last section of bare wall. The rest of the room was covered in pale cream paper with a singular red stripe running through it, and on the final wall hung one length of deep red, with a swirly, black, embossed pattern.

"What do you need me for?" George asked. "You've done perfectly well without me and I'm useless at wallpapering."

"I need you to check the pattern matches, because I can't tell close up." Josh said this in a tone that implied it was the most obvious thing in the world. He handed George a spirit level. "You know how to use this, I take it?"

"I can probably figure it out," he replied dryly. Josh grinned at him, picked up one of the pre-cut lengths and climbed halfway up the stepladder, from where he unfolded the paper and positioned it against the previous piece. George stood watching from across the room.

"You might need to come a bit closer," Josh suggested. George obliged and climbed the other side of the ladder, spirit level at the ready. Josh smoothed the top of the paper and moved his arm away so George could check the pattern: almost level, but not quite. They repeated this action a few more times, both becoming increasingly irritable the more their arms ached. Eventually George backed off and nodded.

"It's as good as it's going to get, I think."

"OK," Josh said, smoothing the paper down and trimming the ends. He stepped back and stopped alongside George. "What d'you think? Nice, isn't it?"

"It is, but didn't we only paint this about three months ago?"

"We did, but as I said at the time, I never really liked the colour."

"Can't say I remember you telling me that. I thought it looked all right."

"Well it's gone now, whatever. Do you think the pattern's a bit much?" Josh didn't, but he really wanted George to approve.

"No. I like it. Sean's got the same paper in his lounge. Sophie had me on the same routine in the Easter break, and I must say—surprising as it may seem—she's much harder to please than you are."

"*Exactly* the same?"

"Same pattern, but in green," George said, noting the usual agitation in Josh at the mention of Sean Tierney, his university housemate and long-time academic rival. "The red is definitely more tasteful," he added helpfully. Josh was satisfied.

"OK. Let's get the rest of it up and then we can order a Chinese takeaway, or something."

"I like your thinking." George re-armed himself with the spirit level, newly motivated by the offer of food. He hadn't eaten all day, because that was just how he was feeling and he wasn't alone. Everyone had been so fired up about the wedding, but the news of the plane crash, even with the knowledge that their friends in Kathmandu were safe, had been such a shock that it was proving difficult to get back on track. The other part of this was that Eleanor, who would usually have them running at her beck and call whenever there was a social function, had no requirement for them. She was far too calm for George's liking; he preferred it when she was her normal feisty self, over-reacting to all the small things and phoning Josh every five minutes to unload her burdens. OK, so the phone calls made him jealous, but this was how it should be. Perhaps the sense of foreboding was all in his mind, for he'd been waiting for her to explode for months and rationalised that pregnancy and motherhood were the reason for her change of personality, which was so complete that she almost wasn't the same person he had known for the past twenty-five years.

This train of thought had terminated at its natural conclusion just as the final corner of the last length of wallpaper was smoothed into place. Josh shifted the ladder away from the wall and moved to the other side of the room to admire the fruits of his day's work. He wasn't any good at plumbing and would struggle to do anything more electrical than change a fuse, but he was an excellent painter and decorator, even if he did say so himself. Perhaps not to a professional standard, although if he fancied a career change, then this wouldn't be entirely incongruent with his first choice of therapist. After all, didn't both jobs entail dressing things up to make them seem prettier? He looked to George to see what he thought, but whatever he thought it had nothing to do with the transformation of the lounge with a few rolls of embossed vinyl. Josh was about to ask the question of what was on his mind at the same time as George answered it.

"I was just thinking about Ellie."

"Why?"

"I don't know really. She seems different."

"In what way?"

"I'm not sure. Like the spark is gone."

"Hmm. I know what you mean, but I don't agree. The spark's still there. It just doesn't suddenly and without provocation erupt into a scorching wall of flame anymore."

George laughed. "Do you think she's happy?"

"Yes, I do," Josh nodded. "I think that for the first time in her life, she is actually, genuinely, completely happy. However, I am not." On these words, he picked up the bucket containing the remainder of the paste and walked out of the room. George stayed where he was, unsure how to respond. A moment later Josh returned and gathered up the scraps of wallpaper.

"What's wrong?" George asked.

"I mean I'm starving and want to get this cleared away so we can eat!" He'd been looking at the wall when he said it, so hadn't seen how George had taken his remark, but it was apparent that he'd misinterpreted his flippancy. Now he took the paper out to the bin and returned a second time, putting his hands on George's shoulders.

"I am very happy," he said sincerely, holding eye contact for a moment or so, then releasing him and leaving the room with the stepladder. It was several minutes more before he came back again, in a change of clothes and armed with a menu.

"Give me a hand with the sofa," he said, pushing one end back towards the wall. George managed to partially break free of the spell and did as instructed. He was so dumbstruck by what had passed that the most he could do was nod in agreement to Josh's suggestions on what they should order and spent much of the evening in the same dazed state. Something wasn't right. It had been this way for a while now, and he didn't know what to do to make it right. But Josh was happy. Once upon a time that would have counted for everything.

The next morning, George was first up and made a quick getaway, not wanting to face his housemate, in light of the previous night's engagement. Before he left, he moved the remaining suitcases from the shed up to his room, stuffed them in his wardrobe and locked the door, taking the keys to both this and the larger suitcase with him to the library. He didn't really have much work to do—that had been true of every day he'd spent there since the start of the summer break—but it beat staying at home with only his thoughts, or worse still, Josh for company. There was so much that needed to be said, issues he had with their living arrangements that were, it seemed, only an issue for him, and he was so angry with himself. Wasn't this what he'd always wanted? He and Josh were as good as living together. So what was he hoping to achieve? He set down his bag in an isolated carrel at the back of the library and sent a text message to Sophie to see if she was free to meet up. She'd been placed with a child psychologist, who had recommended she volunteer at an educational farm, taking children with phobias to meet the animals; the experience confirmed this was the area of counselling she wanted to specialise in.

They were about to embark on the second half of their two year diploma course and had decided to continue after this on the Masters degree programme that Sean and Josh were in the process of putting together—remarkable how they'd gone from being on only the most basic of speaking terms to working so amicably, if that was the word for it. The MA was drawn up and had been approved by the university, so now they were waiting on accreditation from The British Association for Counselling and Psychotherapy. To cap it all, they were also writing a paper together about ethics and confidentiality, which was causing some disagreement on a ridiculously childish point of contention about whose name should appear first on the article. Sean insisted he was lead researcher; Josh said it should be alphabetical, therefore his name should appear first. If they ever made it past this, it would undoubtedly be an excellent and provocative piece, because it was a topic on which they were both obsessively expert.

Sophie's reply confirmed that she was at the farm, but that George was welcome to join her later in the morning for coffee. He sent a message back to say that's what he'd do and settled down to some reading. His own specialised placement was working alongside a prison psychologist and mostly consisted of group anger management sessions with young offenders. It was both stressful and somewhat more tedious than he'd anticipated, as they were trialling a new programme, with two groups receiving the therapy and two groups 'on the waiting list'. So far, the anger management training was having little effect, but the psychologist had assured him this was usually the case. The real impact came at the end of the course, timed to coincide with release, when the intention was for him to shadow a probation officer as part of the follow-up.

The (marginally) more interesting part was working one-to-one with offenders declared sane by the criminal justice system, but who were clearly mentally unwell. Often this was down to depression as a consequence of their incarceration, although a few arrived in that state, including Eleanor's ex-husband. When George had informed the psychologist that he knew Kevin Callaghan, he was taken aback by her response, or lack of one, in that she didn't see any reason why he couldn't work with Kevin. It was only because George insisted that she agreed to take him off this case and gave him a different one instead—a fifty year old gay man who was on his sixth term for cottaging. The poor guy came from an age when intimacy was impossible by any public means and was still governed by that kind of non-sensibility. He was a lovely person and was once a successful businessman, but with a criminal record, he was relying on old friends to look after him in between prison sentences. Whilst the offence went by a different name these days, the problem remained the same and George didn't feel that his own sexuality was sufficient qualification for the task. The psychologist had set a programme of cognitive behavioural therapy in motion, so all that was needed really was to keep following the steps outlined in the case notes. However, he should only have been sitting in and observing, not delivering the treatment himself, and the only advice Sean Tierney had to offer was to tell the psychologist to stop off-loading the cases she didn't want to deal with. George hadn't asked Josh what he thought because he felt it would be inappropriate—truth be told, he was struggling to talk to him about anything at all—but imagined his advice would have been along the same lines.

A couple of hours spent reading previous research on anger management only served to make him more miserable, and he was glad when it was time to leave for the farm. Sophie was one of those people who was a perpetual ray of sunshine, able to quickly assess any given situation and draw out the positives from it. That's exactly what he needed right now, when he was feeling so dissatisfied with his life, albeit due to a set of situations of his own making. He dropped his stuff back at home (no-one was in) and caught the next bus out of town, passing through the village where Sean lived and onwards a couple of miles further to the end of the lane up to Farmer Jake's. It was a real pleasure to walk through the countryside on a warm, bright summer day, although not so much on a drizzly September day like today, so he kept his head down and marched on, only looking up whenever he heard a car coming towards him. On the third occasion of this, it was a 4x4 that was a little too wide for the road and he had to step up into shrubbery to get out of the way.

"Ouch!" He looked down at his knee to find a wasp hanging onto his jeans by its rear end and quickly brushed it off, rubbing at his leg and cursing under his breath, while it zigzagged its way across the field and out of view. He hobbled on up the lane, the next car slowing while its female driver stared hard at him. It was only when he met up with Sophie and she picked all the barbs off his jacket that he realised why the woman had given him such a funny look. He was covered in flowers and seeds and all sorts.

"I've finished for the day," Sophie informed him as she removed the last of the sticky seeds from his back. "Let's go get some lunch somewhere and you can tell me all about it." George gave her a grateful smile and climbed into the passenger seat of her tatty old car. Sean had bought it for her, although not out of kindness. It was so she could travel from home to the farm, rather than staying with him. He wasn't ready to share his space with anyone other than his cat, which suited Sophie just fine, but she didn't tell Sean that. She still lived at home with her parents, who were in their early sixties and very active with the local ramblers' association, so spent most of their weekends off on some trek or other through hills, along canal banks or across muddy fields—basically anywhere that was well served by public houses. At thirty-four, she could come and go as she pleased, and they had given over the top floor of the three-bedroomed house to her, in return for which she contributed a little towards the bills and looked after the place at weekends.

George couldn't come up with any useful suggestions for

where they should go for lunch, so Sophie decided on a little tea shop on the road between the town and the village. It was kitted out in the traditional style, for tourism purposes, with gingham table cloths set diagonally on the small, square tables and cakes under a netted dome on top of the counter. The two older women who owned it took turns to staff it from ten in the morning, closing at four in the afternoon, and served a very quaint range of traditional sandwiches. George shrugged indecisively at the menu, so again Sophie chose on his behalf and steered him to a table near the window, where he sat in silence, rolling the salt mill between his palms and staring out across the road. After a few minutes, Sophie extracted the salt and put it down firmly on the table.

"I assume this is still to do with the plane crash?" she speculated.

"Some of it, yeah, but it'll pass."

"OK. And the rest of it?"

He stopped staring out of the window and picked up the sugar dispenser. It was of the old glass type, with a chrome-valved lid, which was supposed to deliver a singular teaspoon of sugar when tipped, but usually managed about half that amount.

"Is it anything to do with Josh?"

The way he was gripping the sugar dispenser confirmed she had guessed correctly.

"What's he done this time?"

"Nothing. He's fine. Very happy, in fact. Or so he tells me."

"And you don't believe him?"

"Honestly? I can't tell whether he's happy or not. He's so…" George couldn't find a word for it.

"Emotionally distant?" Sophie offered. George shrugged. True: Josh could be very cold, but then he could also be overly emotional. Sean could fire him up like nobody else, and whenever Eleanor was down he would come out in sympathy, almost to extremes. But with George, he was exactly that: emotionally distant.

46

A tray appeared on the table between them, laid out with a pot of tea, cups and saucers, a small jug of milk and two plates of sandwiches. Sophie waited for the woman to unload all of these onto the table, thanked her and then poured the tea. George sat with his arms folded, staring into space.

"I know I've asked you this before," Sophie began cautiously, "and I've seen how tetchy the pair of you get whenever somebody brings it up." She paused to gauge his reaction before deciding it was safe to continue. He knew where this was going, but permitted her to ask. "Are you two actually together now? Romantically, I mean."

George sighed and shook his head. "I don't know. I don't think we are, but you'd have to ask him."

"If you don't think you are, then you're not," Sophie said bluntly. "Relationships are by consent and negotiation. Both partners have to feel they are benefitting equally and that's clearly not the case here."

George was beginning to feel very uncomfortable and Sophie sensed this.

"What did you get me?" He picked up half of his sandwich and peered in between the slices of bread.

"Egg and cress," she told him, even though he'd figured it out for himself. He glanced up at her and she smiled sympathetically. "I understand that you don't want to talk about it, so I'll just be here for you. If that changes, just say. The offer's open." She took his free hand and he nodded. Half of the filling fell out of his sandwich and landed on the table cloth with a plop. They both gasped and looked to the woman behind the counter, who was rearranging the cakes and didn't notice.

"Thanks," George said appreciatively. "I will tell you about the other thing that's bothering me though."

And so the conversation turned to his placement at the prison and how the psychologist was getting him to do all her work for her. Sophie didn't advise or comment; she just listened, which was precisely what he needed. By the time they had eaten their sandwiches and a butterfly cake apiece, he felt a lot better.

They paid the bill and went for a walk through the fields, sticking to the paths and avoiding any overgrowth. George stopped to stroke one of the horses that came over to investigate, amazed at how confident he was with large animals these days, so long as they weren't of the bovine variety. His time on the ranch evidently wasn't all a waste and Sophie asked him about it, from a professional perspective, keen to hear how he had overcome his fear of horses, although there was nothing methodical to it. He'd had no choice but to get on with it and the more time he spent with them with nothing awful happening, the less his fear that it might. It was classic desensitisation, coupled with a serendipitous incident involving a stallion (although he didn't see it that way at the time) that put paid to most of his phobias for good.

When they were ready to go, Sophie dropped him back home and gave him a hug in reiteration of her earlier offer. He kissed her on the cheek and waved her off, then went inside, where the house was still empty, leaving him time to consider his options and deal with the contents of the suitcases. It was Thursday, so Josh would be working late and George would make dinner. Afterwards, if he was still feeling the same, well, he didn't have a plan really, but one thing was for sure: he couldn't stand another evening of watching Josh flit up and down the stairs with bathroom cleaner, or washing, or whatever else he decided needed to be done right at that very second, acting as if everything was just the same as always. In fact, he was sorely tempted to take the shredder up to his room and get rid of everything once and for all, because there really was no point in keeping it anymore, not that Josh would appreciate the significance even if he did tell him what was in those suitcases. What he didn't realise, and never would have predicted, was that Josh had been snooping while he was out and already knew.

CHAPTER SEVEN

Dan was extremely uncomfortable, perched on the far edge of the pickup truck's bench seat, his head out of the window, partly to avert the nausea, but also because the windscreen wipers weren't coping well with the mix of heavy rain and mud splashing up from the road. Indeed, one of the wipers was completely dysfunctional and obstructing the view, although luckily not on the driver's side. All the while, Bhagwan pointed out various features of the landscape that they would have been able to see in clear conditions, but for now Dan had to take his word for it that it was beautiful. They'd been on the road for five hours, which would, again in clear conditions, have put them well past the halfway point, but they had at least another five hours ahead of them, so would soon need to stop for a rest and something to eat. There was a village more or less midway to their destination where they could normally buy local food; however, today there was a wedding and all the villagers were celebrating. It seemed a little ironic that they couldn't get any food when they were transporting catering equipment, although they were invited to share in the wedding feast. Andy refused; Bhagwan accepted. Dan hadn't eaten since his meal on the plane from Istanbul, but took up their offer of tea and was very pleased with himself for keeping it down.

Soon they were back on the road again, which was busier than before their rest stop, when they had only passed two other vehicles. It was also much narrower now, and manoeuvring around the other cars was a real and dangerous art. Bhagwan knew the route well and stopped in advance of particularly narrow passages, giving way to oncoming traffic, whilst feeling compelled to repeatedly point out that he wouldn't usually be this cautious. Andy still kept up the pretence of laughing at this justification, even though it was starting to grate on him. Dan napped on and off, drifting into a light sleep for a few minutes, then awakening if they swerved or hit a rock.

Further up the pass, a wagon was engaged in clearing a landslide, an operation that appeared to consist of scooping up a couple of tons of rocks and mud and throwing it over the side of the mountain. Bhagwan explained that the road was being improved by the Chinese authorities, whereas the wagon clearing the landslide was Nepali and 'unofficial'. Further on still, they came across a herdsman moving his very small herd of buffalo to new pasture. Bhagwan stopped the truck right in the middle of the road and waited until the lumbering beasts had passed before setting off again. After that there were a few other motorists, including two English motorcyclists, who had stopped to fix a puncture and were having a problem getting one of the bikes started again. While Bhagwan worked on the bike, Andy chatted with the men about where they'd been, sharing his own stories of locations they had in common. Dan stayed in the truck, rubbing his side, where there was a dull ache that coincided with the position of the handle on the inside of the door. He was feeling worse than ever and was desperate to get to the village. Fortunately, Bhagwan, who was a whizz with all things mechanical, had the bike up and running in fifteen minutes, and with less than an hour of travelling ahead of them.

Dan's head had slumped onto his chest and he had slid sideways so that he was leaning on his brother, the heat radiating through his jacket. He'd evidently been underplaying how unwell he felt, and it made Andy angry. They were now at an altitude of around two thousand metres, which was easy to cope with for most people of a good fitness level, but not a westerner used to living at sea level, and with a fever to boot. He knew that whatever he suggested, Dan would refuse to go along with his advice, and the sensible thing would be to return to

Kathmandu as soon as possible. They had planned to stay in the village until morning, to ensure that everything was correctly installed and in working order, before a final night at the hotel and then the flight back to Turkey. Whether Bhagwan would be up to driving a further six hours (at the very least) before tomorrow, was yet to be seen, but a glance at his companion gave him some indication. He was squinting through the mud-smeared windscreen and stifled his yawn when he realised he was being watched.

"Not far now," he smiled.

"Dan's sick," Andy told him. "He's got a fever."

"Not far now," Bhagwan repeated, nodding towards the road in front of them. Andy joined him in squinting and saw that the village was just up ahead. It disappeared from view as they rounded a bend, then reappeared again, the vibrantly painted houses standing out against the misty black of the mountains. Andy gently righted his brother, an action that awoke and startled him. He stretched and groaned and Andy pointed to the village.

"Thank God for that," he mumbled.

"Why didn't you say you were so sick?"

"I'm fine!"

"No. You're not bloody well fine at all. You've got a raging temperature and you're clearly in pain. Do you realise how dangerous it is for you to be in the mountains in your state?"

"Yes, Andy, I do. Or it would be if I was as sick as you think I am, which I'm not. I've got a touch of food poisoning or something, but apart from that I feel OK, so stop going on, will you?"

Andy could feel his temper rising and was trying to keep it contained, as they were now slowing down outside a little stone building with disproportionately large blue gates.

"Welcome to Syabru Bensi," a voice called from the other side of the gates, as a young, dark-haired woman came into view. Her face broke into a broad smile when she saw the oven on the back of the truck. "This is fantastic!" she said, and called back inside the building to her partner, who emerged a moment later to greet them.

"Hello, hello," he called cheerily, as Dan climbed out of the cab. "I am Michal and this is Zuza," he introduced in perfect English. "You are Andy and Dan, yes?"

"I'm Dan," Dan replied, shaking Michal's hand.

"And I'm Andy." He closed the door and walked round to greet the two people who had set up the bakery project. "It's great to meet you after all this time," he said, shaking first Zuza's, then Michal's hand. They had been communicating via email for many months now, so it was a bit strange to be meeting for the first time, when he felt like he already knew them.

"And also to meet you," Zuza smiled, wandering around the back of the pickup and inspecting the packing material, all of it impressively still intact. "The people here are so excited about this, but you must be tired and hungry. We should go inside." She said this, although it was apparent that all she wanted right at that moment was to tear off the plastic and cardboard and get at the oven. However, it was going to take several people to lift it from the back of the truck and take it to the building that was to be the bakery, producing the sort of bread and cakes that western tourists craved, hence destined to provide a significant income to this small, poor community. The Jeffries brothers didn't know much more than this about the project, other than that they'd had some problems transporting the equipment from overseas and up into the mountains. Andy had offered to take on the authorities, and with a few strings tugged in the right places, weeks of coordinating transport, three days of travelling through thunderstorms and monsoon rain, here they were. He was overwhelmed: such an incredible sense of achievement, and yet he knew it was nothing compared to how the young Polish couple who made all of this possible were feeling.

They followed Zuza and Michal inside the small guesthouse, with Bhagwan heading off across the village to pay a brief visit to another 'cousin'. Dan was glad to be inside of something that wasn't moving; it was colder up in the mountains than it had been in Kathmandu, and he was struggling because of this, combined with the thinner air. Andy pretended not to notice his brother's shivering, so as not to detract attention from their hosts, although he was going to have to say something soon. It was getting worse and, in spite of the spread laid out before them, Dan didn't touch a single thing, choosing instead to sip at the milky tea, occasionally showing some engagement with the conversation, but he was a bit out of it. When the opportunity presented itself, Andy pulled Michal to one side and asked him if he knew where he could find a doctor, hoping the answer wouldn't be in Dunche, or it would be as well to wait to get back to Kathmandu. Michal told him that there was a group of German tourists travelling through, one of whom was a doctor, and gave him the name of the family who were putting him up. Andy thanked him and returned to the table, where everyone, other than Dan, was eager to finish the meal so that they could unload the oven, and as soon as she felt sufficient rest time had passed, Zuza started dropping hints, asking how heavy it was, how many people they would need to move it, and so on. Michal was a little more tactful, and played along by ticking her off for her impatience. It made Andy laugh, but he could see how cruel it would be to stay and eat any longer, however delicious the food was, even if it was a bit on the spicy side. He signalled to Zuza that it was time, then held back a moment to get Dan on his own.

"I think there's a doctor staying in the village. I'll sort out for us to go and see him once the oven is off the truck."

He expected further protest, but all he got was a shaky sigh and a nod. Dan levered himself up from the stool with the aid of the table.

"No," Andy ordered. "You stay there. Let's be honest, you're not going to be much use in that state." Dan sat back down again and Andy patted his arm. "Just take it easy, all right? I'll be done as quickly as I can."

Outside, the Polish couple, along with several villagers, had already untied the oven and were doing an excellent job of coordinating their efforts, thanks to Bhagwan's bilingual instruction. Inside, Dan folded his arms and rested his head on top of them, slipping forward on account of his fever sweat, until his forehead came to rest against the table. He was in a deep, dreamlike state, but not quite asleep, and could hear the shouting outside, his brother's voice calling. So much for being able to cope without him. He lifted his head and grimaced, the throbbing in his temples like tiny pneumatic drills, the effort of moving his arms more than he could take, and he yelled out as pain raced up his torso and across his shoulders, tearing through every muscle. OK, admit it, he thought, you've got mountain sickness. It's nothing to be ashamed of. Even the fittest people find they can't cope with altitude. It doesn't mean you're weak.

Andy was calling again, but Dan could do nothing about it. He let his head slip forward once more and stopped fighting.

CHAPTER EIGHT

One of those unexpected September heatwaves, inasmuch as the weatherman on breakfast TV had been quite convincing when he declared "light rain across most of the country and unusually cool for the time of year". Jess hated the way weather presenters used language, missing key phrases with that strange, almost telegraphic speech they have developed over the years, and ultimately getting it totally wrong. So now she was sitting in her office, the windows as wide open as they would go, trying to tune out the car alarm across the road that had been intermittently disturbing the peace for the best part of the morning. She actually called the police this time, out of concern for her own sanity rather than the security of the car in question. Needless to say, they'd yet to materialise. She shrieked in frustration, shoved her too hot feet back into her shoes and stormed downstairs to her infuriatingly cool and composed receptionist, who was fully able to appreciate the through-draught from the wedged-open external door, unperturbed and oblivious in her earphone heaven.

"I'm gonna go out there and slash his damned tyres in a minute," Jess said to no-one at all, because Lois couldn't hear her and Eleanor had finished for the day. Lois did, however, pick up on the fact that she had said something and paused the playback on the voice recording she was transcribing.

"Is everything all right?" she asked in perfect RP.

"That alarm's been going off since half past nine. It's driving me nuts!"

Lois smiled. "On the plus side, the battery will be flat soon."

"It won't just be the battery that's flat if I find out who owns the blasted thing," Jess growled. Lois giggled and stuffed the loose earphone back in her ear, the sun reflecting off the silver chain dangling from her ear-lobe. Jess moved closer to get a better look at the tiny, sparkly gemstones, suspended like droplets of rain from the end of the chain.

"Sorry. Was there something else?" Lois removed the earphone again.

"Lovely ear-rings."

"Thanks. They were a twenty-first birthday present. Aquamarine is my birthstone—oh, that reminds me. I meant to give you this earlier." She lifted a stack of files and retrieved a small, white envelope from underneath, handing it across. Jess read the names on the front and frowned.

"Andrew and Jessica Jeffries?"

"It's from…"

"Your Uncle Rob. I know! It's a very old and not very funny joke. He's getting married again, is he?"

"Not that I'm aware of."

"Oh." Jess had been convinced it was a wedding invitation. "I guess I'd better open it and see what's inside, then."

Eleanor stopped off at the supermarket on the way home, for some nappies, washing-up liquid, sterilising fluid, cotton buds and several other items that had her questioning whether her days of shopping trolleys loaded with grown-up impulse buys were gone for good. As she queued at the one checkout that was open, she passed the time examining the contents of other shoppers' trolleys and baskets, amused by how easy it was to determine a person's lifestyle and living situation from their selected purchases. The man right in front of her, for instance, was clearly a student, with his instant noodles, cans of beans, strawberry laces and five-pack of doughnuts, whereas in front of him was a single career woman with bags of prepared salad and vegetables, pre-cooked chicken and a lone loose apple. Currently taking up the entire length of the conveyor belt was the weekly shop of a poor young mum with her two children, one in the trolley seat biting the handle and making a 'mam-mam-mam' sound as she did so. She was quite cute, with her rosy cheeks and blonde spiky hair, a small bunch of it partly secured in a little pink clip on top of her head. Not so cute was her older sister, who was harassing her exhausted mother almost to death with a teary, repeated request of "Please, Mummy?". Eleanor had all of this ahead of her and the prospect wasn't looking so grand from her current vantage point, particularly as by the time she'd made it through the checkout, there was a queue of six more people behind her and still no sign of any assistance for the poor bloke on the till. She took her change and bags and thanked him, giving him a sympathetic smile as she departed.

James had gone to Birmingham to collect Oliver, as per their haphazard, 'however it suited the previous Mrs. Brown best' custody arrangement: the summer holidays had been spent with his mother; now, with due disregard of newborn baby brothers, impending nuptials and honeymoons, Oliver was to stay with his father, to be returned a fortnight before he was due to start school, which coincided with their return from Wales. For all of this (not to mention working from home during the daytime sleeps, even though he was officially on paternity leave, and thus utterly exhausted), James was delighted. So, all things considered, it was fortunate Eleanor had decided to take the week before the wedding off work: the locum was coming in tomorrow to have a look through the patients' files, although it was the same doctor as had covered for her when the baby was born and nothing much had changed since then.

She arrived home to find an empty house, other than the white envelope addressed to 'Ms. Eleanor Davenport' propped against the coffee jar. She frowned and set down the shopping bags, too curious to leave it until everything was put away.

"Oh, good Lord," she said, as she pulled the card from the envelope and realised what it was.

Adele was vacuuming the hall when the post arrived and didn't notice until the pitch of the vacuum cleaner changed. She tugged the envelope away from the nozzle and squinted at the writing on the front.

"Mr. Daniel Jeffries and Miss Adele Reeves. Hmm." She placed it on the telephone table (she had always wanted one, even though the phone was in the lounge) and continued on her way, little Shaunna tottering along behind her with her own mini pink version of an upright Hoover, complete with the 'H' logo on the front, but with the batteries removed so it didn't play that dreadful music all the time.

Kris pushed the envelope across the table to Shaunna and raised an eyebrow.

"What's this?" she asked, reading the front. It was addressed to the pair of them.

"You'll never guess," was all he said. She eyed him suspiciously.

"It best not be money from Andy again."

"Can't be, with both our names on it," he pointed out.

Shaunna shrugged and put it down on the table, picking up her cup of tea instead. Kris tutted and continued folding the washing. Their sharing a house was still so entwined with having lived together as a couple that he saw nothing wrong with laundering Shaunna's underwear. However, she was starting to find it a little disconcerting, because some of it was new and he did insist on passing comment.

"This is lovely," he said, holding the silky camisole up against his chest and running his hand across the smooth surface.

"Thanks," Shaunna replied, bending her face towards her mug of tea so that she was peering at him through her hair.

"I don't remember seeing this before. I bet it's really comfortable to wear. It'd look fantastic with your red skirt. And those black pumps. Are you going to take it to Wales with you?"

"Why?" she asked dryly. "Did you want to borrow it or something?" He stuck out his tongue at her. The teasing was a way of covering up her discomfort and he quickly added the camisole to the top of her pile of clothes. He didn't do it on purpose.

"I'm a bit worried about the sleeping arrangements for this holiday," he said in a casual tone that he didn't quite carry off convincingly.

"Honeymoon," Shaunna corrected.

"How can it be a honeymoon when you're taking all of your friends with you? I can't even begin to imagine what James must think."

"I know what you mean, but we'll be fine, even if we do have to share a bed. It's not like we haven't done it before."

"True." Kris finished folding the last item and added it to his own pile. At some point they were going to have to brave telling everyone that their marriage was over. In an ideal world they would have said something months ago, when it first happened. Now he was desperate to avoid an inadvertent revelation, which would be inevitable if he asked for a change in sleeping arrangements. He knew he was making a big deal out of nothing; it was only for a week, after all.

Now that George had his very own laptop, he was able to sit and play online games for as long as he liked, although they'd somehow lost their charm since he'd stopped having to compete for screen-time. Instead, he was going through his emails and chatting with Sophie via instant messaging. He was, he claimed, supposed to be reading a report on token economies, but it was badly written and ill-informed, so he decided to give it a miss. Yesterday's lunch had really helped him get some perspective, although not with regards to Josh—that issue had yet to be addressed—but he'd decided to withdraw from his placement at the prison. It wasn't just that the psychologist was using him like a work experience kid: his time there had made him realise that this was absolutely the wrong type of counselling for him. In fact, he was starting to question whether counselling was for him at all, or if he'd merely pursued this career path to be close to

Josh. He was nowhere nearer finding the answer than he had been yesterday evening, when he'd also stalled on taking any action about the suitcases.

So, he and Sophie were idly 'chatting' away, when all of a sudden a message appeared from Joe, whom he hadn't spoken to since he signed over the ranch and was almost certain he'd removed from his 'friends'.

"Hey, G. How's it going?"

"Great, thanks. How're you?"

"I'm good. Just came on to say there's a fax come for you."

"Who from?"

"It's back in the office. I was going to send it on, but don't have a number."

George pondered for a moment. They didn't have a fax machine, so that wasn't an option.

"Can you scan it and email it?"

"Sure thing. It'll be a couple of hours. OK?"

"OK. Thanks."

And then Joe was gone again. George sat back and rubbed his chin. It was the first time he'd ever received a fax and a bit of a mystery all round.

Josh took the long route home, still trying to come up with a way of telling George that he'd looked in his suitcase. He sort of wished he hadn't—that he'd given him the chance to tell him of his own accord—but he was also relieved at what he'd found. In the hours between discovering the cases locked in the shed and when his curiosity prevailed, he had gone through all kinds of wicked possibilities, including the utterly absurd notion that George was hiding child pornography. It was entirely unfounded and driven by a client he'd been working with recently, who didn't have child pornography, but admitted to wanting to look at it. This wasn't the first time he'd heard this, although it didn't get any easier or less repulsive through repetition. The man was sick, in need of help way beyond Josh's capabilities, or at least that's how he felt about it when they were sitting in consultation with only floorspace between them.

No, George was nothing like that, and nor was he a drug smuggler (yes, he'd been through that one too), nor a transvestite (that one wouldn't have bothered him at all, apart from the hilarious image it created in his mind's eye), nor an armed bank robber (possible—he could have picked up some tricks at the prison) nor a serial killer (what kind of trophy would he take if he were? A snip of hair maybe, or a button off a shirt? That was much more like him). So anyway, the reality was still a bit of a shock, especially with the way he'd been acting lately, but nothing compared to what it could have been. The choice now was between owning up, or feigning ignorance, should George ever get around to sharing. It was a tough call. Josh parked up, turned off the engine and readied his door key in his hand, preparing himself for another evening of awkward pretence.

It was bound to be a bit of a challenge, sharing a house after living alone for so long, Josh reasoned, as he noted the sound of the running shower and observed the laptop strewn across the sofa, stupid little email icon blinking in the corner of the screen. He took a deep breath and continued through to the kitchen to make coffee, trying to reason away his annoyance. The thing is, George knew it irritated him, which made him wonder if he'd done it deliberately, but then he did it every time he was studying at home, so it was probably an innocent, but nonetheless infuriating, oversight. He filled the kettle and thumbed through the post, sifting out the obvious junk mail and restacking the rest for later perusal, stopping when he came to the white, handwritten envelope and examining it in an attempt to establish whether it was by a hand he recognised. He kept it in view as he spooned coffee into two cups (an assumption on his part), concluding that it was from someone male with a manual job (scrawled, angular, block capitals—it wasn't difficult), but otherwise he didn't have the faintest idea. The kettle came to the boil just as the bathroom door opened and closed, George bounding down the stairs a couple of seconds later, with a towel

61

around his waist.

"You want a coffee?" Josh called.

"Please," came the reply.

He poured the water into the cups and carried them, envelope dangling from his teeth, through to the lounge, catching a glimpse of his housemate slow-stepping up the stairs whilst he tried to read his computer screen, hold up the towel and coordinate his legs, all at the same time. Josh tutted and put down the coffees, carefully peeling the envelope away from where it had stuck to his lip. He opened it and pulled out the card inside.

"What on earth?" George stopped dead and almost dropped his towel.

"Oh no," Josh said, re-reading to confirm that his eyes weren't deceiving him.

"You're not going to believe this, but I've just received…"

"An invitation to a high school reunion?" Josh finished, walking out into the hall and waving the card so George could see it. "Me too."

CHAPTER NINE

The bread oven was wide and bulky, especially with so many people helping to carry it up the loose stone steps and into the bakery, with Andy left to do little more than supervise and cringe each time a corner snagged on a wall or someone slipped and lost their precarious grip on a sharp metal edge. If it had been up to him, he'd have left the packing materials where they were, although as Zuza had pointed out, they wouldn't have stood any chance whatsoever of getting the oven through the doorway with an extra six inches of polystyrene surrounding it. However, all his earlier assumptions waned to know-it-all complacency as soon as he stepped inside and discovered just how much had been achieved. The oven was the very last piece of equipment to be installed, and was set down in its final resting place, in amongst the racks and work stations, sacks of flour and stacks of baking tins. It was an incredible sight and he wasn't ashamed that watching the people of Syabru hugging each other and singing in celebration brought a tear to his eye, so overwhelmed by what he was witnessing that he temporarily forgot about Dan, fighting febrile hallucinations back in the guesthouse. Now his worries returned in full force, and he quietly attracted Bhagwan's attention to ask him if he knew of the family Michal had mentioned.

"Yes. I will take you when we are finished," he offered.

"Thanks," Andy said solemnly. He was so grateful for all that Bhagwan had done for them, but his priority was to get Dan help as quickly as possible and waiting for the revelry to reach a suitable pause wasn't really a luxury he could afford. Regardless, he told Bhagwan that he was going back to wait at the guesthouse, where a quick assessment of the situation saw him filling a bucket with cold water and using his last pair of clean socks to sponge Dan down, whilst his brother protested as wildly as he could in the state he was in. Bhagwan arrived about twenty minutes later and immediately went off on his own, the pickup truck skidding on the wet stone road as it pulled away. After a short while he returned with the doctor: a willowy, middle-aged man with a heavy accent, deep furrows in his forehead, and eyebrows like black fronds of fern fanning across his temples until they joined with his hair. He took out a stethoscope and placed it at various points on Dan's sweat-glistening torso.

"Heart is fast," he said, taking a thermometer from his pocket and poking it into Dan's ear. He frowned at the reading, swapped the thermometer for a penlight and shone it into Dan's eyes. He shrugged.

"Not mountain sickness, but what it is I can not say for sure. The Patan hospital will tell you. You take him there as soon as possible."

"How soon?" Andy asked. "Can it wait until tomorrow?" He was less concerned about missing the village celebrations than he was about being driven back down a wet mountain road that was deathly at the best of times, by someone who had already spent almost half a day behind the wheel. The doctor shrugged again. However, the fact that Dan wasn't involving himself in any of this discussion was sufficient cause for Andy to believe that it couldn't wait that long and Bhagwan had picked up on his friend's concern.

"We go now," he stated resolutely. "My cousin will make strong coffee and we'll be OK." He smiled and nodded reassuringly. The doctor was still waiting to be seen out and Bhagwan followed him towards the door. "It is OK. And when I am too tired we take turns."

Andy didn't much like this idea. It was one thing to race sports cars up and down deserted English country lanes; it was an entirely different matter steering an ancient pickup with lousy brakes and only one working windscreen wiper down a Himalayan dirt track in the pitch black, although one look at his brother told him that if that was what it took, then he would do it. Andy set about collecting their belongings, all the while watching out of the corner of his eye and stopping every so often to re-position the wet sock. Dan was drifting in and out of sleep and the sweat was pouring off him, but would he keep that sock on his head? Andy re-soaked it and put it back again.

"I swear to God, if I had a staple gun," he muttered. Dan made a sound somewhere between a chuckle and a groan and lifted his head.

"I feel like shit," he said.

"You don't say!"

Bhagwan came back with Zuza and Michal, who wanted to thank Andy and Dan properly and were disappointed they couldn't stay.

"No need for thanks," Andy smiled, shaking Michal's hand and embracing him. "We've done nothing, compared to what you have achieved here. It is truly fantastic."

"Ah, it is the people of this village that are fantastic, not us," Michal said modestly. Zuza came over and kissed Andy on the cheek.

"You take good care of your brother," she said. "Come see us some time perhaps, when we are back home."

"I'd really like that." Andy hugged her. "I'll email, soon," he promised.

Bhagwan picked up their bags, leaving him free to assist Dan, who by now could barely stand. Slowly, they stumbled their way across the room and outside to the truck, where the owner of the guesthouse was positioning pillows on the passenger side of the seat.

"I'll send money to pay for these," Andy said and Bhagwan translated. The owner waved him away, as if to suggest that it wasn't necessary, but it was. The people here had so little and yet they would readily share, indeed sacrifice what they did have to help a stranger. Once Dan was safely propped up with the pillows, Andy climbed in beside him.

It was so dark now that the previously poor visibility had effectively dropped to zero. A small group of locals had gathered with Zuza and Michal to give them a final farewell and then they were off, back the way they had come just a few short hours ago. As they settled into the motion of the road and their eyes became accustomed to the total lack of light, Andy moved across the seat so that he had a clear view of his side of the truck, and also to give Dan more space. He was curled up, his hands clasped as if in prayer, his cheek resting against them and his nose and mouth all squashed up. It wasn't an attractive sight; Andy looked past his brother to his friend, who was frowning hard and singing under his breath. This was going to be one of the toughest journeys they had ever undertaken.

There was little to do to pass the time more quickly, with so much effort required to navigate the treacherous road; sometimes they chatted about nothing in particular; other times both of them stayed silent so Bhagwan could focus on an especially difficult stretch, or negotiate with other road users the safest means of passing in the dark, always with a terrifying awareness of the steep drop only a matter of inches away. Occasionally they would maintain a good speed for many miles, where the roads had been re-surfaced with tarmac and were in reasonable condition, but then they would come across the site of a recent landslide, where any existing tarmac now joined the rest of the stones and rubble. Bhagwan was doing an incredible job of staying alert, even spotting a stray yak on the road ahead when Andy could barely see past the truck's bonnet. Dan was in a deep sleep and had fallen to the left, his head now resting on a pillow on Andy's lap.

"You are very close, yes?" Bhagwan observed.

"Yeah," Andy replied. The word was woefully inadequate and couldn't even begin to describe their relationship as it was now. True, they had always been close; they were part of the same friendship group and these days, for the most part, enjoyed each other's company. Underlying it all, though, were the remnants of hatred from too many years of secrets and it had taken its toll on them both. What Andy felt for Dan was beyond words. Dan was his little brother, and he could just about remember him learning to walk and talk; becoming a little human being instead of a baby. When Andy went to pee, Dan would go too, standing right next to him, watching and learning how to be a boy. When their mother came to collect Andy from his first day at school, Dan had leapt out of the car, his chubby little legs moving as fast as he could make them, to get to his big brother and give him the biggest hug ever. Soon they were both at school, and this need to be together was fulfilled through football and rugby. Their brief parting when Andy went to high school was almost intolerable: often mistaken as twins, the boys seemed to have internalised the closeness that this genetic association would have bestowed.

It was only as they reached the end of high school that their constant requirement to do everything together began to dissipate, and until recently, Andy had believed it was only natural: they had reached an age where they were individuals in their own right, with new friends and, more importantly, girlfriends. Dan and Adele's on-off relationship was a big part of this, for when they were together, Andy was left to find other friends to spend his time with, but none of them could ever replace that closeness.

With all that had happened over the past couple of years, they had been able to re-establish something more like how it used to be when they were younger. Their business was flourishing and they hadn't had so much as an argument in months, all this in contrast to the twenty-two years prior to that, when they had gone for long periods without even speaking and had given each other so many black eyes that they'd both lost count long ago. Now they were here: halfway down the Himalayas, with Dan in a potentially critical condition, and Andy felt completely responsible. He should have played the big brother card when Dan lied that he was OK, instead of trusting him to tell the truth. If the unthinkable happened, it would be his fault, for being such a coward.

These thoughts had taken them a further hour into their descent: another six to go, based on their outward journey, although the rain had stopped and they hadn't passed another vehicle for quite some time. Andy glanced across at Bhagwan and noticed him contorting his face into all manner of expressions that would have been comical in any other situation.

"D'you want me to drive for a bit?" he asked, his earlier fear subsiding the further down the mountain they travelled.

"Soon I would like a break," Bhagwan said, "when we reach the rest stop down here." He pointed to the road as it curved back on itself in a hairpin, before opening onto a wider stretch, where he pulled over. Once they were stopped, Andy observed that there were a couple of other vehicles in front of them, both also taking a break. The two men climbed out of the cab and spent a few moments stretching.

"Not long now," Bhagwan told him. "You finish the drive. Only three hours."

"Really? Wow!" Andy was surprised they had made such good time: four hours so far. At this rate they'd be back in Kathmandu by around five in the morning, which wasn't an ideal time to turn up at the hospital. He would have to make a judgement call on whether they could wait until daylight when they were a bit closer to their destination.

As was his way, Bhagwan had wandered off to relieve himself and talk to another man who was leaning against his lorry and lighting one cigarette off the end of another. Andy glanced back through the windscreen at Dan: his temperature seemed to have dropped a little, but even in the cab's dim light, it was clear to see his pale face still shining with fever.

Shortly, Bhagwan returned and took a pot and stove from the back of the truck, setting it down to brew some coffee.

"I had a brother too, but he died of blood cancer," he said, his attention artificially centred on stirring the pot. Andy already knew this and it wasn't the most helpful of stories to hear at this particular moment. It had happened just prior to his last visit to Nepal, and the grief remained almost as tangible now as it had been then, when it was fresh and raw. Andy watched and listened, as Bhagwan went on to explain how an American charity had paid for most of his brother's treatment and that this had made them hopeful. They prayed hard that he might live, but it was not to be. Now there was a son and daughter left of the five that there once had been. It was such a sad story, repeated time and again in countries like this, and standing there, in the middle of a dark Nepali night, Andy fully appreciated his wealth and his powerlessness in equal measure.

It was time to get back on the road: Bhagwan shuffled onto the far end of the seat and tried to close the passenger door, but without moving Dan across, there was no way it was going to happen. Carefully, Andy lifted his brother's upper body and held him up until all three of them were safely inside the cab. Dan stirred but didn't wake, and Andy slowly lowered him, his head coming to rest on Bhagwan's thigh.

"It's OK," he smiled, "you are my lost brothers." Andy turned away and swallowed back the tears. He was getting too soft in his old age. He fastened his seatbelt and hesitantly started the engine, checking that he could position the gears, before he set off, slowly, down the steep stony road. Three hours: that wasn't so long really. He chanced a glance to his left and saw that Bhagwan had tipped some water onto the almost dry sock and was tenderly wiping Dan's face with it. He quickly turned his attention back to the road ahead.

"We've not always been close," he explained. "I did something really stupid when I was young and Dan covered up for me. He's always done that, you know? Taken the blame when it was my fault. I got him into so much trouble at school sometimes. I'd go off on some mad thing or other and he'd just follow, idiot."

"Not idiot. He is the younger brother, yes? This is what we do."

Andy laughed. "Yes, that is what younger brothers do.

We've got another brother too—three years older than me—but we never felt the need to always be getting in the way of whatever he was up to. Still don't now, as a matter of fact."

"You two are the same. He is different to you perhaps, your other brother?"

"Very much so. Me and Dan—we like the same music, football team, girls. Other than Adele. She is stunning, of course, but she's always been off limits. And their little girl. Honestly, Bhagwan, you wouldn't believe how beautiful she is! She has the darkest brown eyes and she just sort of looks up at you, blinking those big eyes. She's going to be a heart-breaker when she grows up, for sure. And she's started to talk now too. She shouts 'Addy' whenever I go round to see them. She's just awesome. And she's growing up so fast. When she was born, she was so tiny you could fit her on your hand. Amazing!"

"You want children?"

The question took Andy by surprise. Luckily the darkness was hiding his face, because he hadn't intended to gush like that about little Shaunna, but Bhagwan was right. He did finally feel ready to be a parent, although he and Jess didn't have that sort of relationship, so it was unlikely they'd be experiencing the 'patter of tiny feet' any time soon, if ever.

"Maybe one day," he said cagily. "Tell me about your children. How old are they again?"

Bhagwan sensed that Andy was uncomfortable with having shared so much, so he duly obliged. With his work as a guide to western tourists, he could afford to pay for the older ones to go to school and he was very grateful for this. He dreamed of them going to university, like the students he often drove up into the mountains. How wonderful it would be if his children could travel the world and return with stories of all the places they'd been. For all of this wishful thinking, he said, he was thankful that they were healthy and had a good place to live, adding to this that when he went home he had to fix a leaking roof that had meant moving their beds to the other side of the house. Andy carried on driving, half-listening to this story, at the same time playing out the scenario of asking Jess if they could have a baby together. Once again, she'd remind him of how often he broke his promise not to do anything dangerous; his defence that danger kept finding him was no defence at all as far as she was concerned, and whichever way he looked at it, there would be no convincing her. Still, it had be worth a try, if only for that very small chance she might give him the answer he wanted.

They were coming down onto the city, the small dots of lights here and there shining up through the darkness of pre-dawn. Andy leaned left and right to stretch his shoulders and noticed that his companion, who had become quiet a little while ago, was sleeping. Less than an hour to go: the drive hadn't been so bad, all things considered. Even though it was still a very long way down, it felt safer now and Andy settled into the last leg of the journey, allowing his thoughts to return to their previous meanderings around the possibility of parenthood. Without warning, a pair of headlights were upon him and he slammed on the brakes, swerving to the left and skimming the wing along the wall of rock at the side of the road. With no room to move over, the truck driver kept coming, straight up the middle of the road towards them. Andy swore.

"He'll move," Bhagwan murmured sleepily. "They always do, right at the last minute."

Andy hoped he was right, because they were now only feet apart, the lorry horn filling the silence of the mountains and echoing back. Just as it seemed inevitable they were going to collide, the lorry veered off to the right, passing so closely that it ripped the remaining wing mirror clean off, before rattling noisily past and onwards up the road. Andy exhaled sharply. Bhagwan smiled and closed his eyes. That was far too close a call, but it had brought Andy's random thoughts to resolution. He would talk to Jess about their future, in particular his desire to be a father, before he was too old, or did something really, really stupid.

·

CHAPTER TEN

"Hi."

The voice was smooth and deep, like rich cream sherry, and instantly sent a familiar, yet long unfelt shiver down her spine. Her mouth bent itself into a smile without her conscious permission. She lifted her face, slowly following up from the casually crossed legs clad in clunky biker boots and almost too tight jeans, to the leather jacket, unzipped over the palest blue shirt.

"Hi," she said, her eyes finally meeting with his.

"My overly-efficient niece wanted to buzz and tell you I was on my way up, but I successfully persuaded her to let me surprise you."

"So it would seem," Jess replied carefully. She'd been here before and it was a dangerous, dangerous place. "To what do I owe this dubious pleasure?"

"Dubious?"

"Hmm." She motioned for him to come in and he did, sitting on the arm of the chair opposite hers. She sat back and tapped her pencil on her teeth, irritated that she couldn't get the corners of her mouth to budge. How, she thought, does he still do this to me?

"I felt I should come and explain," he said, as if this in itself were an explanation. She frowned, mouth still fixed in that stupid grin, and shook her head in confusion.

"About the reunion?"

"Ah. That. Eleanor's getting married next Saturday." As soon as she said it, she realised how ridiculously irrelevant it sounded, but he responded before she could elaborate.

"Ah!" he repeated teasingly, "but she's not getting married *this* Saturday."

"What I mean, Rob, is it's terribly short notice and we're all so busy with the arrangements." The second part was a lie, because it had all been taken care of, by Eleanor and her mother, weeks ago.

"Which is why you should allow me to explain." He slid down into the seat, leaving his leg draped over the arm of the chair, his jeans taut across his thighs. Jess looked away and he laughed, welcoming the compliment served up by her inability to hide her attraction. "I've been having tests for the last few weeks. You see, I was getting breathless going upstairs, or even just moving a bike." He paused to gauge whether he could just come out and say it. Having not seen her for around fifteen years, although they'd spoken on the phone every so often, he wasn't sure whether he should ease her in before he delivered the blow, if she felt it that way at all, but he saw he had her full attention, so opted for straight-talking. "I've been diagnosed with a potentially fatal congenital heart condition."

Jess nodded slowly, but was lost for a response. There was more he needed to say, thankfully, for it would give her time to come up with something appropriate to reply with.

"It could kill me tomorrow, or I could go on to live a perfectly healthy life and die of something else entirely," he explained. "But, the thing is, it *could* kill me tomorrow, though I'm optimistic that it'll wait until at least Sunday, so I can enjoy this little reunion I've thrown together at the last minute. I hope you're free to come."

"Under the circumstances, even if I wasn't I would be, if you know what I mean."

Rob laughed. "Yeah, I get you. And what about Andy? Is he going to come?"

"Andy's in Nepal," Jess told him and his eyes lit up. "I thought that'd please you. Nice invitation, by the way. And no, we didn't get married. Nor do we have six kids or a cabin in the

Swiss Alps."

Rob nodded, an almost imperceptible grin settling on his lips. This was the long-standing joke between them. Back in school, Jess and Rob had been an item on and off for a year or so, then finally called it quits when they went their separate ways after sixth form, she to university, he to his apprenticeship as a motor-cycle mechanic—the perfect job for him, because he was obsessed with the things. In the years that followed, they would meet up for dinner or a drink, or simply just chat online, and at some point in every conversation she would mention Andy, which eventually led him to predict that they would be married by the time they were thirty, with a brood of six little ones. She wasn't sure where the bit about the Alps came from. Yet, in spite of his acknowledgement of her relationship with Andy, and his own marriage that was no more, there was still an undeniable spark between them and it was bright enough for others to notice, including Andy. He liked Rob, but recognised him as his only real rival and it aroused an unhealthy and uncharacteristic jealousy.

"This heart condition of yours," Jess began, just as the door opened.

"Hey," Eleanor called, initially not noticing that there was someone sitting in the chair. Rob swivelled around to face her.

"Hello, Eleanor. I believe I've gazumped your wedding."

"Hello, you," she grinned and headed straight over to give him a hug. "How lovely to see you. And yes, you have gazumped my wedding. You're looking great, by the way."

"Thanks. You too. Who's the lucky man, then? Surely you haven't persuaded Josh Sandison to make an honest woman of you?"

"Are you kidding?" True enough, they were always together all through sixth form, as well as being each other's date for the sixth form ball, but the possibility of them ever having a relationship for real was never on the cards for lots of reasons. "You'll get to meet him shortly," she said, just as footsteps sounded on the stairs. "In fact, any second now!" James came into view.

"Toby is in his seat, ready when you are, and Oliver is playing a bubble popping game with Lois," he said, then looked past her and saw they had company. "My apologies," he added sincerely.

"This is my fiancé, James," Eleanor announced. "James, this is Rob Simpson-Stone, an old school friend." James smiled and moved forward as Rob stood and held out his hand.

"Congratulations," he said warmly.

"Thank you." James shook Rob's hand and stepped back so that he was next to Eleanor. Rob examined them both and nodded.

"A perfect match, hey, Jess?" he said, turning to her with a wink. She giggled.

"Anyway," Eleanor coughed, for effect. She'd seen this often enough before, but it was still embarrassing to watch. "I only came up to let you know I'm going home now. I'll pop in from time to time next week, but I'm hoping I won't be needed much."

"No. You just enjoy yourself. Go and have some beauty treatments, or something."

"Oh don't you worry, I fully intend to," Eleanor assured her. She gave Rob another quick hug. "See you tomorrow, I suppose." She wasn't impressed with the short notice, but she had nothing else planned and it would be great to see all her old schoolmates, now that she was at peace with herself.

"Yeah, about that," Rob said. "I'm glad you're here actually, as it's one less call for me to make. Don't forget the dress code."

Eleanor looked at Jess and they both looked back to Rob.

"Dress code?"

"Well, not dress code, as such."

James shook his head. He'd noticed the dress code. It was typed in bold print on the back of the invitation.

"Go on," Jess said, pushing Rob to elaborate.

"I think I might leave you to it," he said, moving towards the door. Eleanor sidestepped to block his way.

"Oh no you don't. What dress code?"

Rob grinned impishly. "You know how sassy we all looked at the sixth form ball? All you ladies in your fine frocks and high heels, us gents in our tuxes and bow ties?"

"Yes?" Jess and Eleanor asked slowly and together, realising exactly where he was headed with this.

"That dress code."

"You want us to wear formal ball gowns," Eleanor stated, not that there was any need to reiterate.

"Yes, but not any old formal ball gowns. Anyway, I really must be going now." He backtracked and gave Jess a quick hug, both of them holding a moment longer than was necessary. "See you there," he whispered close to her ear, drawing his lips across her cheek as he moved away. She felt her legs wobble and was glad she was still sitting down. Rob repeated the motion, though without the erotic undertones, with Eleanor, and shook James's hand once again.

"Good to meet you," he said. "You're a very lucky man indeed."

With that, he made his way, slowly and with a quick smile at Jess, back down the stairs. A couple of moments chatting with his niece Lois, and they heard his bike fire up outside, then speed off into the distance.

"I'll wait downstairs," James said observantly and did as indicated. Eleanor delayed until he was out of earshot.

"You are a very bad woman!"

"I didn't do anything!" Jess protested, which was the truth. If she had led Rob on, it hadn't been deliberately so.

"You didn't do anything to discourage him either," Eleanor pointed out. Jess had no defence to that one. "So did he tell you why he's suddenly organised a reunion?"

"He's been diagnosed with a heart condition of some sort."

"What sort, exactly?"

"He didn't say, but it's the kind that could kill him at any second."

"OK. Well, I guess that does explain things. What

medication's he on?"

"I don't bloody know! I haven't seen him for fifteen years. I'm hardly going to be asking him things like that now, am I?"

"I bet you'd ask him for his inside leg measurement."

"Know it already."

"Or the size of his…"

"And that too. James is waiting for you, he said. Hadn't you best be going?" Jess busied herself with tidying her already tidy desk.

"Fine, fine," Eleanor said, pretending to be offended, then as a serious aside: "If you need a bailout at any point, just give me a shout, OK?"

Jess looked up from her desk and smiled. "Thanks Ellie. I appreciate it, but hopefully I'll behave myself tomorrow."

Eleanor turned away before her expression betrayed what she really thought about the chances of that happening.

The dress code was the first thing Shaunna noticed—when she finally got around to opening the invitation, after much prompting and pestering from Kris—and she was utterly delighted, for in the farthest recesses of her wardrobe lurked a floor-length, red taffeta dress, with a swooping neckline studded with diamantes that continued in two parallel lines diagonally across the front of the bodice and down to the gently scalloped hem. It had been hanging there for twenty years, ever since her parents and Kris had plotted behind her back in a desperate bid to persuade her to attend the sixth form ball, and the design, with its flowing skirt, was such that it still fitted her perfectly, perhaps even better than it would have done when she was eighteen. She still had the shoes that went with it, although they were not really the sort of thing she would wear these days, but who would know? She unhooked the hanger and carefully freed the dress from its plastic cover, holding it up against herself and admiring her reflection, unaware that Kris was watching from the doorway, wearing his own sixth form ball outfit: not a tuxedo in the traditional sense, but a cropped silver jacket with rolled-up sleeves and matching fitted pants. The pointed shoes had been well worn on subsequent nights out and had seen better days, but it was nothing that a re-heeling and a spot of shoe polish wouldn't fix.

"Put it on," he said. He looked like Morten Harket, Shaunna thought, standing there, with his hands resting casually in his pockets, and she could feel the knot of sexual tension building within. She dismissed it with a shudder and shooed him away so she could do as he suggested. The fabric was so soft and sensuous against her skin, and she smoothed the dress down over her hips. It felt so good. She tossed her hair back over her shoulders and checked her reflection.

"You can come back now," she called out. Kris walked into her room—it had once been *their* room—and stopped in his tracks when he saw her.

"Wow."

He moved towards her to take in the full beauty of her cleavage, the silky fabric moulding perfectly around her breasts, before falling away until it collided with the outermost curves of her hips. He couldn't help himself and reached out and touched her bare shoulder. She tilted her head and trapped his hand with her cheek.

"Don't," she said. He held her gaze and she let his hand slide around to her back. He pulled her to him, until their lips were almost touching, and inhaled her scent.

"You don't want to. Is that what you're telling me?"

"Of course I want to, but…" It was so difficult to explain, to put into words the confusion she was feeling. He was the one who ended their marriage, not her. She still loved him, and yes, she still wanted him. The easiest thing in the world would be to give in to the temptation and satiate this hunger, brought on by months of famine and need. Then what would it be like afterwards? Could they continue to share their house, pretending to their friends that all was well with their marriage, when it was a farce? Or was it? After all, what was marriage, but an enduring partnership? And hadn't they endured!

Her momentary doubt was sufficient to allow the flames to die down to a tameable height; Kris released her and turned away.

"I'm sorry." His voice was so small, so distant, but she couldn't care for him, not the way that she had done, through those years of make-believe and then his breakdown. He was stronger now, ready to move on with his life, the way it was meant to be, which was absolutely not like this.

"Me too," she said, reaching out and taking his hand. He curled his fingers around hers, but remained turned away from her. Then he released her and walked out of the room. Shaunna sat on the edge of the bed and felt the fizz of tears forming in her throat, but she wasn't going to cry anymore.

Eleanor had been muttering to herself and throwing things out of the wardrobe ever since they'd arrived home, and James was happy to have the boys to entertain, for it was the perfect excuse to stay out of the way. Three times now she had come into the lounge and declared that she knew her dress was here somewhere; she'd seen it recently, when they were packing up in preparation for the move, all this with the intention of being well and truly settled in, first before Toby was born, and then before the wedding. Unfortunately, the builders said, it was beyond their control: the house wouldn't be finished until November. Something to do with the electricity supply, they said. She didn't care. She just needed to find that damned dress!

"Enna is cross?" Oliver asked. He still hadn't quite mastered the pronunciation of her name, but he was getting there. Sometimes he got the 'L' in it too, so it came out as 'Ellna', which was pretty close. He had no problem saying Toby, though, and took every opportunity to practise, with a constant stream of questions powered by the curiosity of childhood: 'Why is Toby crying?', 'Why can't Toby eat cornflakes?', 'Why hasn't Toby got any teeth?'.

"No, she's not cross. She's looking for something and she can't find it," James explained patiently.

"Why?" Oliver came back. Why, why, why.

"She can't remember where she put it," James replied, already planning the next response in his head, but Oliver was bored and had moved on to his toy car, zooming it up and down the table with 'nyerrrrrr nyerrrrrr' vocal effects, followed by 'crassssshhhh!' as he sent it flying like a miniature aluminium missile into the air and three or four feet across the room.

"That's it," Eleanor announced on her way into the lounge. She flapped her arms once to emphasise the permanence of this statement. "I give up. I must've thrown it out. I mean, who in their right mind would think they were going to need something like that again? And anyway, I doubt it'd go anywhere near me now, the size of my hips."

"What does it look like?" James asked. He swapped Toby onto his other arm and caught a whiff of recently filled nappy. He wrinkled his nose.

"I'll do it," Eleanor offered, laying out the changing mat, nappy and baby wipes. James handed his youngest son across, over the top of Oliver's head.

"What you doing, Enna?"

"Changing Toby's nappy, because he's had a poo," she said, hoping to avoid any 'why' by pre-empting it and only succeeding in demonstrating the foolishness of adults.

"Why do babies poo?"

"Because they don't need all of their milk."

"Why don't they drink less milk? Then they wouldn't poo."

"Oliver!" James raised his voice a little and his eldest son was immediately quiet. Eleanor didn't look up from the nappy-changing, because she sometimes felt James was too strict on the poor little fellow, who wasn't quite four and behaved impeccably for most of the time.

"I was thinking," James said, ignoring Oliver's brief detour, "if you have a good idea of what your dress is like, perhaps we could purchase something similar."

"Unlikely. My mum made it. No, I'll just have to wear something else. I don't suppose anyone's actually going to play along with Rob's silly game, so it probably doesn't even matter that much." Eleanor fastened Toby's nappy. "There ya go, stinky baby," she said, tickling his bare tummy.

"Why does Toby like tickles?" Oliver asked.

"I don't know, Oliver. Because it feels nice, I suppose." He leaned over his little brother and gently tickled his tummy. Toby looked up at him and smiled. Eleanor gasped.

"He smiled! James! Toby just smiled at Oliver!"

"He did?" James joined the rest of the family on the floor and Oliver tickled Toby again, with the same effect, though he was far less impressed than the adults and soon toddled off to play with his other toys, leaving them to wonder if the now dissipated smile had been a figment of their imagination.

"Why don't you have one last look for that dress of yours?" James suggested. Eleanor eyed him sideways.

"You're getting as bad as Oliver. No. It's fine. Really. I'll wear something else instead—maybe go to the mall tomorrow morning." Toby's crying brought an end to the discussion, and she picked him up from the changing mat, unbuttoning her shirt as she walked over to the sofa. Oliver paused to watch, his mouth open, question at the ready.

"Shush, Oliver," James commanded and his son frowned. "Come and help me with Toby's things." He passed him the baby wipes and indicated where he should put them. Oliver complied, then returned to playing with his car, leaving James to tidy away the changing mat and dispose of the dirty nappy. When he returned, Eleanor was almost done feeding Toby and hadn't even noticed he'd been gone so long. He took the baby from her and set him down in his cot for his afternoon sleep.

The trouble with moving four and a half thousand miles away, George was explaining to Sophie, was that it meant getting rid of all superfluous belongings, and therefore his tuxedo, and the ludicrous thirty inch, high-waist trousers that went with it, was long ago dispatched to a charity shop, with everything else he'd possessed prior to emigrating. Well, maybe not quite everything else, but that was a different story. He rabbitted on, while she listened, a smirk fighting its way onto her lips every so often, until George sighed loudly and thumped his elbows down on the table. They were back in the little tea shop, because it was a rather nice place to be.

Infuriatingly, George continued (again), Josh still had his suit *and* it fitted him perfectly, but of course why did he expect anything else from Josh 'just-so' Sandison? If ever things looked as if they might begin to change, he'd do everything in his power to ensure they stayed exactly the same, including his weight and his hairstyle. It was a shame the same rules didn't extend to his living quarters, because he was on about getting yet more wallpaper this morning: this time for the hall and stairway. Old-fashioned, Sophie suggested. Traditional, George argued, but she was right. Josh was old-fashioned and at some point would have to concede to the ineluctable changes in his life.

George was being contrite and he knew it, but this reunion was making him incredibly nervous. When they were at school, it was unheard of for people to be openly gay, and Kris had braved the verbal, and sometimes physical bullying that ensued from coming out. George wasn't so harsh on himself as to believe he'd been a coward back then, although he was feeling very cowardly about it now, because other than his closest friends, the people he went to school with were mostly unaware of his sexuality. He'd done his coming out in his twenties mostly, first at university and then over in the States, neither of them what he would class as positive, pain-free experiences, so he was hardly relishing the prospect of going through it all over again and quite frankly found it ridiculous that he should have to, at the grand old age of thirty-eight. To cap it all, speaking to Joe, albeit via online chat, had stirred up all sorts of uneasy feelings that he wasn't prepared to share with Sophie, as she didn't know about what had happened with the ranch, other than that he had sold up and returned to England.

So his options, she advised, were quite straightforward: either he was going to have to bottle out, make up some excuse and not go to the reunion at all, in which case he would regret it for years to come, or, and this was the option she favoured, he was going to let her take him shopping tomorrow morning and find an outfit bearing some resemblance to the original. She tilted her head to the side and blinked rapidly as a signal that she was awaiting his response.

"So what you actually mean is I don't have any choice whatsoever," George stated. She shrugged and said nothing. "OK," he sighed, "what time d'you want to meet?"

"That's my boy," she said, patting his hand encouragingly. "You'll have an amazing time, I know it."

Josh came home from work and went straight up to his room to search, not for his tux, which was already at the dry cleaner's, but for the item James had requested. He was bound to have one somewhere. Of course, he knew George had one (and then some) but he couldn't really ask without giving himself away. He stopped to listen for a moment, to make sure he was still home alone, took out his keys and unlocked the ottoman.

CHAPTER ELEVEN

Dan was almost unconscious by the time they reached the hospital, and they'd had to carry him in on a stretcher, but he was now safely ensconced in a side ward and hooked up to a drip, with various tests under way. Initial observations indicated that there was no swelling, so it definitely wasn't altitude sickness, thus the doctors instantly dismissed Dan's self-diagnosis; he hadn't been at a great enough elevation to cause it for one thing, and aside from the headaches and somewhat delusionary state, he had no other symptoms. What he did have was a dangerously high temperature and a blood test confirmed that his immune system was on the brink of shutting down. For the first few hours, Andy kept vigil, only leaving when asked to do so and taking these opportunities to try and reach Adele to tell her what was going on, knowing that each subsequent missed call would send her into further panic. Eventually he decided to give up on all counts, and returned to the hotel, where the owner was only too happy to have him back almost a day early, but was suitably sympathetic about the circumstances and took some food up shortly after he arrived. Andy was fast asleep, so 'Alan' left the food next to the bed and quietly closed the door.

Later in the evening, Bhagwan also arrived at the hotel, looking a little more refreshed and with the offer of a lift, but Andy had already left on foot, so he stayed and had a drink, before making his way to the hospital to wait for his friend, who was back sitting on the terribly wobbly and uncomfortable wooden chair at Dan's bedside. Nurses came and went, checking blood pressure or drip bags. Sometimes Dan would stir and mutter some thing or another that usually made little sense, then drift back into a state of semi-consciousness. By now, the test results were all back and indicated that he had picked up a particularly nasty virus at some point during the past few days. There was nothing more that could be done to help him; just a matter of time, they said. Andy rubbed his eyes and yawned. He was sick: of sitting watching over his brother in hospital beds, knowing that he was responsible. If he could have changed places right there and then, he'd have done so without hesitation. Telling Adele, when he finally got through, had been tougher than he'd anticipated: she started crying, and he took the full hit of her regret for rejecting Dan's marriage proposals. Regardless of Andy's assurances that she would have the chance to accept the next time, she wouldn't believe him, and why should she? He'd hardly proved himself trustworthy in the past.

Dan slept on fitfully, and incredibly Andy found himself nodding off, perched on that rickety chair. The first time it was the sensation of slipping off the edge that woke him; the second he nearly jumped out of his skin when Dan shouted out for him.

"Shh," Andy comforted. "You're OK. You're in hospital and on the mend."

"I wanted to…" Dan began. He couldn't keep his eyes open and his mouth was clogged at the corners with dried saliva.

"Do you need a drink?"

Dan shook his head. "Shaunna," he said. "You love Shaunna."

Andy considered this statement for a moment, then remembered his conversation with Bhagwan when they were driving back down the mountain. He'd thought Dan was asleep at the time, otherwise he may have been a little more stoic.

"Yes, I do," he admitted. "She's my niece. Of course I love her." Dan giggled and shook his head.

"Not that Shaunna, silly," he said. He sounded drunk. Andy put it down to the deliria and held a glass of water to his brother's lips.

"Here. Drink some of this," he said, gently tipping the glass with one hand, and holding Dan's head up with the other. "You're seriously dehydrated. That's why you're on a drip."

Dan lifted his heavy eyelids and glanced around the room, then closed them again. He spluttered against the flow of water.

"Where's Adele?" he slurred.

"At home. I've phoned her and everything's OK."

"When's she coming to visit?"

"She's not, bro. We're in Kathmandu, remember?"

"Ah yeah." Dan managed a weak laugh. "What about Kris? He'll be here later. Does he know?"

"That you're in hospital, or that he'll have to catch a plane to come and see you?" He ought not to mock him in his state, but he couldn't help it. It was probably a response to the stress, or shock, or whatever it was he was feeling now that was making him lightheaded and causing his to heart flutter, just so long as it wasn't the same virus Dan had, as he was now asleep again, the water gurgling against his oesophagus and making him sound like he was snoring. Andy rested his back against the chair and slowly exhaled. He was shattered.

Dan was out of immediate danger, so there was no reason for him to stay, and certainly no chance of him accidentally getting any sleep here. Quietly, he pulled himself to a standing position, stretched his aching legs, and made his way back outside, surprised and pleased to see Bhagwan, patiently waiting by his pickup truck and chatting to a man in a blue uniform. As he approached, the two men hurriedly finished their conversation, not that it would have made any difference if they'd been overheard.

"Another of your cousins?" Andy asked.

"Ah, no. Not this time," Bhagwan said, climbing into the truck and starting the engine. Andy got in the other side and glanced across, noting that his companion was cagey. He was too tired to even begin to contemplate what they might have been talking about before, but there was evidently something amiss.

"How is your brother?" Bhagwan asked, taking more care with his driving currently than he had given to it going up and down the mountain pass.

"Much better, now he's got some fluids in him. I'm not sure if he'll be up to flying home tomorrow, though."

"Do not worry, Andy. This is the best hospital in all of Kathmandu." He reached across and patted Andy's arm, then sped off towards the hotel, glad that soon he would be on his way back home for a good night's sleep with his wonderful family.

The next morning Dan was brighter and making more sense; however, the doctor explained that his condition had deteriorated, which made little sense and his English (he too was German and it was one of twelve languages he understood, to varying degrees) was not good enough to explain.

"One minute," he said, and left the room, returning soon after with another doctor who translated on his behalf. The gist was that although Dan was no longer dehydrated, his white cell count had declined further and they hadn't been able to identify the virus. He was now on intravenous antibiotics, to treat any underlying infection, but that was as much as they could do. Andy thanked them for explaining, then followed them out of the room.

"Excuse me, but when do you think my brother will be well enough to fly home?" he asked. The doctor who spoke English was about to translate, but the other doctor understood the question and answered for himself.

"Not for many days. Too dangerous for airline, not your brother."

Andy nodded an acknowledgement and returned to Dan.

"Looks like we're staying a bit longer than planned," he told him, expecting an outburst, but receiving only a half-hearted 'OK'. He probably didn't comprehend what he'd just been told, Andy thought. Regardless, it was time to call Jess and tell her what was going on. He always tried to avoid doing this when he was away, because she could be quite snappy on the phone, but with their return home an unknown he had to brave the storm.

"I'm just popping back to the hotel," he said. "Won't be long." Dan didn't respond and looked like he might be asleep again, so Andy left and told a member of staff, just in case.

Once again, it took several attempts to get a reply, on both the house and Jess's mobile phone, which made Andy wonder if it was still because of the phone system, seeing as he'd also struggled to get through to Adele. Alan assured him that the phones were working perfectly well, an argument sustained by the fact that he'd had far fewer problems when he'd called Josh a couple of days ago. When he finally got through to her, she sounded distracted and didn't have anything horrible to say, which turned out to be worse than if she'd laid into him the way she usually did, as this was a fairly good indication that he was going to get the full brunt of her wrath when he got back, whenever that might be. The way it was looking, they wouldn't make it home for Eleanor's wedding either, and she was equally formidable when roused. Andy started the walk back to the hospital, now so used to the rain that he didn't even notice it, although he was very aware of how hungry he was and decided to stop off for something to eat and drink on the way. The place he had in mind was one he'd frequented on his last stay, which these days was a modern-looking internet café, and if he'd known in advance, he'd have just sent Jess an email. Anyway, the deed was done, but he was pining for a bit of England, so he paid for half an hour's internet access and went straight to the BBC website, overjoyed at the site of that familiar logo at the top of the screen.

The default loading page was the international news section, and his cursor was hovering over the UK news button when he spotted the headline.

"Ah, crap," he said aloud. Now he knew why Bhagwan and the other man had stopped talking the previous night. Two dead, several more in a critical condition, all with an unidentified virus contracted in Middle East. OK, so this wasn't the Middle East, but it was too close and the description of symptoms too similar to be pure coincidence. Andy read the whole report, clicked through all the associated links, then searched for more articles on other sites, meeting the same information over and again. Suddenly his worries about Jess, and missing Eleanor's wedding, weren't quite so significant. He sat for five minutes or so, doing little more than sipping his coffee and staring at the same list of search results, before deciding to send Josh a message to explain in more detail what the situation was. He would know how best to tell Adele and the others, if the time came. As Andy typed, the emotion swelled within him, a mix of anger and grief, for he sensed that whatever the outcome of this journey, things were changing. His email to Josh was raw and honest, perhaps a little more so than he'd intended, but he needed to put this feeling into words, or else he would not have the strength to go back to Dan. At the end, he clicked 'send' without reading back over what he had written, for fear that he might regret any of it. He gulped down the rest of his now cold coffee and made his way back to the hospital, where Dan was awake and eating his first meal in almost a week; he instantly perked up at the sight of his brother.

"Wow, you must be feeling better," Andy said lightly, as if he hadn't just read all those terrifying news reports and sent a virtual confession to Josh. "What you eating?"

"Dunno," Dan replied through a mouthful of brown stuff. "Kind of tastes like spicy mud, but I don't care. I'm starving."

"No surprises there," Andy grinned, going to take a tiny morsel off the edge of the plate. Dan poked his hand with the fork.

"You'd steal food from a dying man, you would," he said jokily, so engrossed in his meal that thankfully he didn't see the reaction his remark had evoked. Andy pushed the thought from his mind and resumed his position on the rickety wooden chair.

"I phoned Jess earlier. Told her what was going on," he said.

"Have you told Adele?"

"Yeah. I'll have to call her again later and give her an

update." Andy checked the time on his phone, which he was carrying only for that purpose, as it didn't appear to work in Nepal. "Our plane leaves in twenty-four minutes, incidentally."

"I reckon I could've coped with flying home."

"Probably, but the doctors said the airline wouldn't let you on-board with an unknown virus."

"Especially one that's potentially fatal," Dan finished for him. Andy examined the floor. "It's all over the news, the nurse said, and I can tell by the way you're acting that you knew this already."

"Only just," Andy defended himself. "I read it on the BBC website on the way here. I wasn't going to tell you, because…" He couldn't go any further without giving away how he was feeling: that Dan was ill because of him and he was so dreadfully sorry. But they were brothers; if they were similar enough in looks to be mistaken for each other, then it stood to reason that they were similar in mind and soul too.

"Because you didn't want to worry me," Dan said, giving him the easy way out.

"That's right," Andy said, both knowing the truth.

"The doctor says the antibiotics are doing something. My temperature's back to normal," Dan added, finishing the last of his food and pushing the plate away. He picked up his empty water glass and peered inside it dolefully. Andy filled it for him and he raised it in thanks. "And I've stopped hallucinating, I'm glad to say. That's definitely not something I want to go through again."

"Bad, were they?" Andy asked, grateful to his brother for what he was doing.

"You could say that. The worst one was when we were coming in to land. I was convinced, one hundred percent, that we were crashing. No word of a lie. It was only when you came back from wherever you'd been that I snapped out of it."

"That must've been scary."

"Tell me about it. And on the way back down from Syabru, I thought we were about to have a head-on collision with a lorry.

90

Then I realised you were driving, so I knew it wasn't real and just kept my eyes closed until it went away. Actually, now I think on, that's far scarier: you driving a pickup truck down the Himalayas."

Andy laughed, for real this time. "D'you want to hear something even scarier? You weren't hallucinating!"

If there hadn't been rails on either side of the bed, Dan may well have fallen off in disbelief, not only that Bhagwan had allowed Andy to drive, but that he'd got them safely back to Kathmandu.

"Well, I guess thanks are in order then," he said, suddenly humbled by his true appreciation for what his brother had done. The rest of what they did was banter, but he could feel that there was a connection building between them that surpassed anything they'd had since childhood, in part down to the conversations he'd overheard on the journey back from the village. Before now, and Andy's revelation about the incident with the lorry, he'd assumed that what he'd heard had all been in his mind. Now he knew it wasn't, he also realised that there was something else he needed to do.

"What I said yesterday, about your feelings for Shaunna," he started.

"No need to explain," Andy stopped him. "You weren't making a whole lot of sense—probably the fever or the meds."

"That's where you're wrong. Yesterday I thought I was going to die. Today I'm sure I'll be just fine, but either way I want to say something I should've said long ago."

"We don't need to drag the Shaunna thing up again, do we? I thought we'd dealt with it, after the stabbing and...everything."

"I don't mean that bit of it. That bit was—unfortunate. Not the greatest description, I know, but if you can keep your mouth shut, you'll get why I'm saying that, if you haven't already figured it out."

Andy was entirely on Dan's wavelength and could have predicted word for word what he was about to say. What he needed to do was stop him from saying it, because it should not be put into words.

"I'm going for a walk," he said and quickly got up and left the room. Dan watched him leave and closed his eyes to rest.

CHAPTER TWELVE

Saturday morning: Eleanor got back home a little after ten o'clock, her plans to head out early and snag a dress for the reunion scuppered by a call from the husband of one of her patients, sent home to die and almost ready to face the inevitable. She wasn't complaining, because this woman had been one of the very first to transfer to her books, their initial consultation ending with a referral for a routine mammogram, which, if conducted earlier, may have detected the abnormality soon enough for the treatment to stop it from spreading. Now she was in the last few days, her family travelling back from their various corners of both country and globe to say their goodbyes. Eleanor's locum was on stand-by, but in this most emotional of times, it was she who could support them best and that is what she had promised to do.

Both of the boys were washed and dressed, and James was just adding the milk to a mug of tea he had prepared on hearing her car pull up outside. She accepted his offer of toast and went to change out of her nightdress (tucked into jeans and hidden under a hastily thrown-on sweater) and into something more suitable for a morning of traipsing in and out of changing rooms. She wasn't looking forward to it, with a baby and an almost four-year-old in tow, but she was getting very excited about the party and it was spurring her on. She quickly ran a brush through her hair and went to the kitchen.

"When you have eaten," James told her, "we will take the boys to your parents."

"They're probably out shopping themselves, I'm sure

we'll…"

"I have already phoned and arranged this with your mother," he assured her.

"Oh! Well, I guess that'll help me catch up a bit." Eleanor talked as she chewed her way through the toast. "I've got so much to do before tonight. My hair's a mess and I could do with a manicure, or some false nails, and I think my mascara's dried up. I was going to get some this week anyway, and then I need to wax my legs. Actually, why don't you drop me at the department store on the way? It'll save tons of time and I might find everything I need all in one go."

"I could do that, I suppose," James said thoughtfully, "although I think your mother will be expecting you to come along."

"I'll pop in once I'm done shopping. I'm sure she won't mind."

"Perhaps you are right," James hedged, thinking on his feet. "However, she did mention that she wanted to show you the, err, cake stand."

"She did that last Monday. We were both there, remember?"

"Ah, yes, of course," James confirmed with a nervous smile. Eleanor had finished eating now and was poking Toby's arms into his coat. James sent Oliver to put on his shoes and soon they were in the car, heading towards the department store. The traffic was on their side for once, and Eleanor reached down to unclip her seatbelt as they approached the main entrance. James drove right past, his hands firmly clenched around the steering wheel.

"What are you doing?" she asked. "You were supposed to stop and let me out first!"

"Oops," he said unconvincingly. "It must have slipped my mind."

"In ten minutes? I don't think so, James Brown. What are you up to?"

"Nothing at all," he said, feeling his cheeks burn. He was a dreadful liar.

"Right, well, you'd best put your foot down, because I intend to be home as close to midday as possible." Eleanor folded her arms and huffed.

"Are you cross, Enna?" Oliver piped up from the back seat.

"A little bit," Eleanor said, staring out of the passenger window.

"Why?"

"Enough!" James said this so sternly that Eleanor immediately turned and faced the front. He glanced sideways at her, fighting the urge to smile. They turned into the road where her parents lived and he stopped the car. "If you take Oliver inside, I will bring Toby." Eleanor glared at him, about to suggest that he should do it all himself, but by now she was intrigued to find out why it was so important that she came to see her mother, so she unfastened Oliver's seatbelt and took his hand, waiting by the car for James to remove Toby and his chair from the back seat.

"You go on in," James nodded to her. She looked down at Oliver and shrugged. He shrugged back and they went inside.

Her parents' house had been the family home, and with seven children, it had needed to be far bigger than it was, for it always felt like it was bursting with people, especially as, over a period of a decade or so, they reached their teenage years, each going off to university and returning bigger and surlier than ever. Nowadays, with just Peter left to 'fly the nest', the house was only ever full for birthdays or other family functions. Next weekend, for instance, her brothers and sisters and their respective partners and children would all be crammed in somehow or other, and Mum would be in her element, although the same wouldn't be true of her father. This morning, he was sitting at the kitchen table, reading the newspaper and trying to ignore the noise coming from the back room. (This was once their bedroom, but now housed an old three piece suite and all her mum's odds and ends associated with her pastimes as an avid knitter, seamstress, and cake maker, to name but a few.)

Eleanor leaned down and kissed her dad on the head.

"Hello, love," he greeted her, without looking up from the paper.

"Hi, Dad. What's she up to?" Eleanor asked, nodding towards the back room.

"Erm, think she's putting the final touches to your wedding dress."

"Really? I thought she'd already done that."

"Oh, well I don't know then," he said, shoving his chair back and going to fill the kettle, all without making eye contact, which was entirely in character. "You staying for a cuppa?"

"No, thanks. I'm in a bit of a rush, but maybe when we come back for the boys?"

"All right, love," he said. He'd filled the kettle right to the maximum line anyway (again, typical for him). The noise coming from the back room had diminished now to the hum of a local radio station, and Eleanor decided to go and find out what her mother was doing.

"She'll be out in a minute," her dad suggested, by way of a 'do not disturb' warning. Eleanor nodded her understanding and waited, although not patiently. James was taking his time too, and she was starting to feel quite irritated by the whole situation. The noise re-commenced and this time she recognised it as her mother's sewing machine, going at full throttle. The front door opened and James appeared, carrying Toby in his chair, and a large white and blue bag. He smiled innocently and Eleanor flared her nostrils.

"Is anybody going to let me in on the big secret, or am I expected to just stand here, stewing in my own juices?" No response, other than a nervous cough from her dad.

"Mr. Davenport," James greeted him, walking straight past her and into the kitchen. He set Toby's chair down on the table and shook his soon to be father-in-law's hand.

"James," her dad said with a courteous nod. They'd been introduced by their first names, which James refused to use, and it was a formality Eleanor found extended to her address of his father also. Right now, she wasn't feeling at all formal or polite, and let out a little shriek of frustration.

"Right. That's it. I'm going in," she declared, readying her hand around the door handle. Both James and her father gasped and she tutted. "Ridiculous men," she muttered. As she pushed down, her mother did the same thing from the other side of the door and Eleanor jumped.

"Hi, Mum," she smiled innocently.

"Good morning, sweetie."

"Hard at it, I hear?"

"Oh, I'm all done now," her mum replied in a matter-of-fact tone. "I'll show you, if you like, although it's not very exciting."

Eleanor raised an eyebrow in query and stepped past her mother into the room. Right in the centre of the floor stood the dressmaker's dummy that this time last week was draped in her wedding dress. And now...

"Oh my...Mum? How...?"

"You can thank James," her mother replied with a smile.

"And Josh," James clarified.

"And your mother's refusal to throw anything away," her father added dolefully. Eleanor reached out and brushed her fingers across the deep blue fabric.

"This is brilliant," was all she could find to say. She was having a problem taking it in. Here was an exact replica of her sixth form ball gown, right down to the intricately embroidered neckline. It could almost have been the original, apart from the somewhat curvier aspects of the cut. "This is truly brilliant," she repeated.

"When you couldn't find your dress yesterday," James explained, "I phoned your mother to see if you had left it here."

"No, I knew it was in the flat somewhere, I just couldn't..." She circled the dummy and shook her head in wonder. "Mum. How did you do it? It's the same fabric, the same design. It's..."

"Brilliant?" her mother laughed. "It was a bit of a challenge, but I've quite enjoyed it. Shame you inherited my ability to lose stuff, though. I can't find that lovely photo of you all at your ball anywhere, so James phoned Josh and he lent me his so I could copy the design. You remember how you wanted a full skirt, then changed your mind?"

"Did I?"

"Yes, sweetie, and it was a good thing you did, because I had so much fabric left over. I've given it a good wash, but you might need to spray it with perfume."

Eleanor leaned close and sniffed. "Ew. Mothballs. Nice!"

"So there you are," her dad said. The kettle had long since gone off the boil and he plodded back to the kitchen. "How about that cuppa?" he offered again.

"Go on then," Eleanor said, smiling and still shaking her head. She put her arms around her mother and hugged her. "I love you, Mum. Thank you so, so much. You're the best."

Unfortunately, George wasn't having quite so much luck finding a perfect replica of his tux, which he was really rather glad about. It wouldn't do for a reasonably well-built man (his own fault, for always cooking what Josh liked to eat) in his late thirties (nothing he could do about that part) to be wearing pants so tight, and he'd hated the jacket when he was eighteen, never mind now. What wasn't helping much was that he was still feeling anxious about going at all, although Kris had been very supportive when he'd emailed earlier to check they were still going together, and promised to steal all the limelight, not that he ever needed an excuse in this regard. George recalled how, at one point during their sixth form ball, Kris had taken to the dance floor, and he was an excellent dancer, but was really showing off, powered by too much vodka and a last chance to be himself, before he settled into life as Shaunna's partner and Krissi's stepdad. It was almost as if he were saying goodbye to his true identity, and in the intervening years, he had loved being both a father and a husband, not once regretting his decision to stand by Shaunna and her baby. But now he was back, he said, and ready to pick up where he left off, so George wasn't to worry. Nobody would care anyway, not these days, and who was he to say that half the lads hadn't turned out to be gay in the end?

"What about this one?" Sophie asked, waving a black jacket with red satin lining right in front of George's face and bringing him back to the present.

"Nah. Too…"

"Come on, George! It can't be that hard to choose, can it?"

"It really is, although I do like this one more than the last one. Maybe if the lining wasn't so—red?"

Sophie muttered something under her breath and returned the jacket to the rail, then scragged the others along, glancing at each and dismissing it with a 'no', or a 'definitely not'. George returned to staring into the mid-distance, pondering the viability of various excuses for not being able to make it to the party. A migraine maybe? He'd never had one in his life, so that wouldn't be particularly convincing. A stomach bug, complete with a good bout of diarrhoea? "Sorry guys, but my mum's not well and I need to go and stay over." No, that was tempting fate. Perhaps a suddenly remembered trip to see long-lost family down south? Now, that might work, if he put aside the fact that he didn't have any family, long-lost or otherwise, down south, up north, or anywhere else, for that matter. Well, there was Joe, but 'family' required more than DNA.

"A-ha!" Sophie said, finally, lifting the second to last jacket away from the others and inspecting it thoroughly before presenting it to her impossibly hard to please associate. "Is that 'less red' enough for you?"

George lifted the front flap and examined the grey lining. It was still very shiny, but not red, or blue, or, thankfully, pink.

"Well?" Sophie prompted. "And if you dare tell me it's too grey I swear to God I'll…"

"It's fine," George said quickly. "Let's just find some trousers to go with it and get out of here." He was usually a very enthusiastic shopper, but not today.

"Hallelujah!" she declared triumphantly. The trousers were the easy bit and five minutes later, they left the 'vintage' clothes shop with a full and authentic outfit. Now George just needed to find some shoes and get his hair trimmed, and they were done: all before lunchtime. Josh was working, so they decided to head back to the house for something to eat, seeing as they'd spent far too much time and money in the tea shop already this week. George made cheese sandwiches and took them through to the lounge, where Sophie was examining the décor.

"Sean's got that wallpaper," she said. "Best not tell Josh that though, I'm thinking."

"I already did. He didn't seem to care much, actually. Here." He indicated to her to sit on the sofa and handed her a plate.

"They do seem to be getting along better these days," she observed.

"Yeah. Just as well really."

After that neither of them spoke for a while, both busily munching their lunch and thinking back to how awkward things had been during the first term of their course, with Josh and Sean always at loggerheads. Their impromptu Christmas night out seemed to have brought an end to hostilities for the most part; there were still the occasional snipes at each other, although nothing compared to how it had been.

Sophie finished eating first and leaned forward to put her plate on the table, in the process spotting the game on top of the games console.

"*Crash Team Racing*. I haven't played that for years," she said, kneeling down to retrieve the case.

"It's one of our favourites," George explained. "Always good for a bit of friendly competition."

"Maybe we could get them to fight it out on this instead," Sophie suggested. George laughed.

"That's not a bad idea," he said. She still had the case in her hand, and he took it from her and turned on the console. "Come on then."

"Yay!" she said excitedly. He passed her a controller. "What are we playing for?"

"Err, how about lunch next Thursday?"

"Why Thursday?"

"I'm at the prison on Monday and Tuesday, and then it's James's stag do, so I'll be fit for nothing on Wednesday."

"I thought you were giving up the prison."

"I am, but I haven't got round to it yet."

"Just email them and tell them. I'm sure Sean and Josh will support your decision."

"Yeah, I suppose I could do that," George said thoughtfully. "All right then, lunch all next week. Except maybe not Wednesday. I'll see how I feel."

"Deal," she said and perched on the edge of the sofa cushion. "I'm so going to kick your ass."

"Ha! I don't think so."

George set up a new game and typed in their names, ready for the tournament to commence. The first two races went to Sophie, but soon they were level and stayed that way until it rested on the last race of the cup. Now things got really dirty, with them throwing everything they had at each other. As they came into the final straight, they were 'neck and neck' and crashing so often in their attempts to knock one another off the track that the rest of the characters had long since passed the finish line, but out of the pair of them it was Sophie who crossed first, by a fraction of a second. She leapt up from the sofa, punching the air in victory.

"Hardly a convincing win, was it?" George scoffed.

"Ooh! Someone's a sore loser!" Sophie said, making an 'L' against her forehead with her thumb and index finger.

"Definitely a fluke. I say we go for best of three."

"You're on!"

George restarted the game and they were off again, and he easily won the first race, but by the fourth he was wishing he'd bowed out gracefully after round one. At the end of the cup, Sophie threw down her controller and did a lap of the coffee table in celebration.

"Damn," George said defeatedly. "I guess lunch is on me!"

"Yup!" Sophie smiled. "I guess it is!" No time for a rematch, she helped George wash up, then left him to his afternoon of getting ready for the reunion party, but not without a quick restating of her superiority in the *Crash Team Racing* stakes on her way out.

"Told you I'd kick your ass," she said, giving him a hug and a peck on the cheek. "Now, you have a fab time tonight. Drink too much, dance embarrassingly and just enjoy yourself."

"I'll try."

"You better had. I want to hear all about it, over lunch next week." She grinned and George raised his eyes.

"Yeah, yeah. I'll beat you next time," he called after her as she bounced down the path, stopping at the gate to wave her fists in the air. George laughed and waved her off, then closed the door. "Time for a shower, I suppose," he said, glancing around the house to see if there were any other opportunities for further delaying getting ready. It was still only early afternoon, but when Josh returned he'd want the bathroom to be free so he could have a long, hot bath, and then he'd faff about with his hair for an hour or so, styling and restyling it, gelling it down, then washing out the gel and starting all over again. By the time he was done, it would look exactly the same as it always did, which was perfectly fine by George on any day of the week. With these thoughts in mind, he turned off the TV and trudged upstairs with the enthusiasm of a man going to the gallows.

Adele pulled another tissue from the glitzy cube-shaped box and dabbed at her eyes, sniffing loudly. Little Shaunna was playing with her doll, the only intermission in Adele's misery being the declaration of 'I-do-it' as the recently stripped toy was passed to her to be re-dressed once again. She didn't want to go to this rotten reunion in the first place. Of course, it'd be an entirely different matter if Dan were here, but he wasn't and he'd sounded so poorly on the phone that she'd struggled to find things to say to him that didn't involve asking if he was OK uncountable times. Even in his weakened state, he'd snapped at her in irritation and she couldn't take it. But that wasn't why she was crying. It was all Jess's fault. She sobbed again, dumped the sodden tissue ball with the others on the sofa and took another from the box. The baby toddled around the edge of the table and held out the doll.

"I-do-it?" she asked hopefully. Adele smiled at her daughter and took the doll and the little pile of clothes. And there was another thing.

As if she was still going to have her original ball gown! She didn't have the outfits she'd worn last summer, let alone those from twenty years ago. With her 'passion for fashion', there was no way she could possibly store all those clothes, and she was ruthless in getting rid of the ones she didn't want anymore, which was more or less all of them. The contents of her wardrobe were only ever as old as the latest trend; no room for sentimental holding on to 'this skirt' or 'that dress', simply because it prompted fond memories. If she'd wanted to go tonight, then she'd have immediately gone shopping for something new, but it was almost five o'clock on a Saturday afternoon. It just wasn't going to happen. Dan reassured her that he didn't mind at all, but then he would say that now, before the event. A few months on and he'd be throwing it right back in her face, with unfounded accusations of what she'd been up to in his absence. So she wasn't going and that was that. She'd sent Shaunna a text message to the same effect, which didn't lead to the anticipated relief she'd expected at getting herself out of it, given her reply of "u bloody well are! x". Why bother putting a kiss at the end? Shaunna just didn't understand, and now she'd fallen out with Jess too, so it was all so pointless. She stifled a further sob with a gulp and handed the newly dressed baby doll back to little Shaunna, then re-armed herself with yet another fresh tissue.

Whichever way she looked at it, she couldn't see what Jess's problem was. All right, so it made sense not to tell Dan and Andy about the reunion a couple of days ago, because they more than likely would've tried to get home for it, but now they couldn't, it really didn't matter that they knew, and she hadn't meant to tell him. That was the worst part. If she'd done it on purpose, then at least she'd have something to feel guilty about, but it just slipped out. Anyway, they knew now and there was nothing she could do to change that, so Jess was going to have to get on with it. Adele sniffed resolutely, dumped the discarded tissues in the bin and went to make a cup of tea. Just as the kettle boiled, the doorbell chimed and she knew instantly who it would be. She had to have some kind of tea detector. It was the only possible explanation.

"Hi," Shaunna smiled breathlessly, having marched round immediately after responding to the text message.

"Hi," Adele replied and turned her back. Shaunna followed her into the kitchen and eyed the recently made tea.

"Perfect timing," she grinned, getting herself a tea bag and a cup and placing it next to Adele's.

"Yes. How do you do that, by the way? Can you smell it or something?"

"That's probably it," Shaunna laughed. Adele shook her head and filled the second cup, handing it to her friend. They took their tea through to the lounge, where little Shaunna held out her naked doll to adult Shaunna.

"I-do-it?" she asked, blinking her big brown eyes. Shaunna took the doll from her and waited while the toddler retrieved the pile of clothes from the floor, passing over one item at a time, which she duly replaced on the doll, talking to Adele as she did so.

"Tell me again why you're not coming tonight."

"I'm not in the mood."

"A couple of Martinis and you'll be fine."

"And with Dan being sick I...I just don't want to go."

"That's rubbish. It's not because he's sick at all. It's because he's not here, but don't you worry about that. I'll make sure he knows how much you missed him and what a horrible night you had without him, and how you didn't drink, or dance, or talk to anyone because you were so miserable."

"And Jess called me a stupid bint," Adele added.

"She calls you that all the time. It doesn't normally bother you." She handed the doll back to her tiny namesake. "Ta," she said.

"Ta," Little Shaunna repeated, immediately re-commencing the clothes removal procedure.

"Anyway, why did she call you a stupid bint?"

"Because I told Dan about tonight."

"Right," Shaunna frowned. "And that's a problem because?"

"She said they'd try and find a way to get back for the reunion."

"Surely it would take too long? Isn't the flight, like, eight hours?"

"Even longer than that, I think. Which is exactly what I mean. What does it matter? I didn't tell him on purpose. I wasn't trying to spite her, or anything."

"Well, as you say, it doesn't matter, hun, which is why you are still coming tonight." Adele opened her mouth to protest, but Shaunna put her hand up. "I don't care what Dan has to say about it. I want you to come. I missed the first one, remember? This is *my* sixth form ball and I want to spend it with *my* best friend."

Adele couldn't argue with that. However, there was still the matter of having nothing to wear, but yet again Shaunna pre-empted the protest with a show of her palm. "You asked Alice to babysit tonight, yes?" Adele nodded to confirm she had. "Phone her and see if she can come now. We're going emergency shopping."

CHAPTER THIRTEEN

Andy was furious to begin with, but by the time he'd got through to Jess again, his anger had expanded into something so massive that he could hardly speak; she wasn't saying much either. He knew exactly why she hadn't mentioned the reunion, and it had nothing to do with stopping him trying to fly home, not that it would have been an option at any point, let alone with only hours to go before it was due to start. The boredom was bad enough, without this to contend with and he couldn't stand to be in the hotel a moment longer. He put on his trainers and went running.

A couple of hours on and he was still none the calmer for it. This wasn't the first time she'd kept something from him. In fact it was starting to become something of a habit. First the shopping addiction, then the dates with Kevin Callaghan last year, which was, quite frankly, idiotic, because she'd put herself in great danger by being secretive, not that any of them knew it at the time, but the way he was feeling that was by-the-by. Running at this altitude was hard-going, which was all the better, because if he didn't drain this rage from his system he'd end up killing someone. As it was, anybody who happened to inadvertently get in his way became the unwitting victim of a muttered string of expletives that fortunately they could neither hear nor understand. Friendship with benefits? What fucking benefits? The adrenaline kicked in again and Andy increased his pace as he turned a corner, right on time to run straight into a man carrying two large bins filled almost to the brim with tiny, brightly coloured, round beads, which predictably flew out of his hands, their contents exploding into the air and rolling off in all directions.

"Oh shit," he said, slowing to a stop. "Sorry. Sorry, I'm so sorry."

The market stall owner glared at him, a look of pure fury on his face. There was little else Andy could do, other than stay and help retrieve the beads, all the while repeating his apology, whilst other traders packed up for the night and shouted questions about what had happened. Needless to say, the anger he had been feeling prior to the collision was now matched by that of the stall owner, but even in his current state, Andy could appreciate the humour in what had happened, with passers-by slipping and sliding as if on ice, apparently in too much of a hurry to stop and wait for safe passage. It took nearly half an hour to gather all of the beads that hadn't rolled out of view or been scooped up by local children eager for a freebie, by which point he was almost his usual self, and made his way back to the hotel, taking a little more care this time. A good, long shower, something to eat and drink and he was feeling much calmer, until, that is, he arrived back at the hospital.

"Alright, bro?" Andy called on his way into the room. Dan stirred and turned to face him.

"Yeah. I'm OK." It was a statement derived from social nicety rather than truth. "Did you see the doctor?"

"I didn't. I can go and get him for you, if you like."

"No, he wanted to speak to you, that's all."

"Oh right. What about?"

"Something to do with quarantine. Not sure, to be honest."

"Hmm. OK. Well, he knows where to find me," Andy said, already wondering how long he needed to stay before it would be acceptable to leave again, not that he had anywhere better to be. He wanted to go home, to sort out this situation with Jess. He wanted to be at the reunion, to make sure nothing happened, and there was not a damned thing he could do about any of it. He felt the anger attempting to resurface and pushed it back down inside.

"What time is it?" Dan asked. Andy checked the clock on his phone.

"Quarter past nine."

Dan nodded to indicate his understanding and his eyes drooped shut again. This was how it had been for the past two days: short periods where he seemed almost back to normal, followed by relapses into drowsiness and sleep as his immune system attempted to rebuild its defences. Yet again, Andy gave thanks for Dan being such a fitness fanatic. This was the virus that had already killed lesser mortals, although he could also sense his anger turning towards his brother and was trying to rationalise it. Too much time to think: that was the problem, and he'd forgotten to bring his tablet with him again. He still had his phone in his hand and wondered whether the cost was worth it for a few minutes of trying to open a web page only to give up because the connection was so flaky. Before he reached a decision, the doctor came into the room, wearing what could only be described as a biohazard suit.

"Ah. Good. You're here. I'll get a bed for you," he said, picking up Dan's chart and flicking through the various sheets of paper.

"Sorry?" Andy had no idea what the doctor was talking about.

"I told your brother earlier. He has not told you?"

"Told me what?"

"The World Health Organisation have put out a quarantine directive."

"Dan mentioned quarantine, but that's all he said. What does that mean?"

"I'm afraid you have to stay here, until we run tests to see if you have been infected or not."

"Are you kidding me?" Andy could feel his hands balling into fists, the pulse in his temple quickening, the hairs all over his body prickling.

"We'll take samples right away, and if they are clear you can leave, but you won't be able to come back to visit. This room is now closed to anyone other than staff, and we must take all steps…"

"For fuck's sake," Andy hissed. "This is utterly fucking ridiculous."

"I understand you are worried, Mr. Jeffries."

"Worried? I'm not fucking worried, I'm livid. I'm stuck in Kathman-bloody-du, whilst my girlfriend is getting ready to go to a party and, much as I'd love to trust her, I know she's going to cheat on me. And you think I'm worried? That's what I'd be if I didn't know exactly what she's going to get up to tonight with Rob fucking Simpson-Stone. Worried. Ha!" Andy shook his head and turned away, both outraged and embarrassed that he'd mouthed off, at a doctor who didn't even know him.

"I'll go and get the blood tests," the doctor mumbled apologetically and hastily left the room. Andy stayed facing the wall, fighting the urge to punch it hard enough that they wouldn't need to stick needles in him to get blood.

Dan had listened to this outburst and was pretending to be asleep. He was shocked by what he had heard—not that Jess would probably end up doing a bit more than flirting with Rob, but that Andy felt the way he did about it. He knew, like all of their friends did, that Jess and Rob had always had a thing for each other, and he'd seen his brother's jealousy surface a couple of times before, but not like this. He was actually rather proud of him and knew he'd feel the same if they were to exchange places. But what surprised him most was Andy displaying how he felt so publically. It wasn't like him—yet another trait they had in common—and he would be appalled by his behaviour now. Dan opened one eye a fraction of an inch and peered through his lashes at his brother, who was still facing the wall and pressing his palms against it. He was trying to contain his temper; Dan recognised the stance and hoped the doctor would return soon, or they'd be paying for a new hospital room.

A few moments later, the doctor came back with various tubes in a kidney dish, took Andy's blood samples and left again, all without a word spoken by either of them. Dan continued to watch through slitted eyes, closing them as soon as it appeared as if Andy might look his way. He'd decided that it was the virus making him come over all sentimental, because for the past couple of days he'd been so glad to see his brother and could feel the respect he had for him increasing to an almost exponential extent. It was Andy who had made the decision to set up the business; it was Andy who had set in motion the arrangements for this trip; and it was Andy who had safely brought him back down the mountains to the hospital. He wanted to reach out and reassure him that everything would be all right, but he couldn't, in part because it wouldn't, but also because saying anything would mean revealing he had heard every word and Andy wouldn't be very happy about that. At some point though, when he'd calmed down, Dan was going to have to say something, as this wasn't really about whether Jess and Rob did or didn't get it on at the reunion, or at least, that wasn't the whole story.

The door opened and the doctor, along with another member of staff, also garbed in a full body suit, came into view, the latter backing into the room, pulling the end of a bed, one of the wheels squeaking as it turned against the resistance of a stuck brake. Andy took a deep breath and slowly let it go before he turned around, side-stepping so that they could position the bed against the wall that had helped him to keep his anger in check. The second man left the room and the doctor was at the door before Andy called out.

"Listen, mate, I'm really sorry about before."

"No need, no need. It's not a good situation and totally understandable." The tone of his voice indicated that a nervous smile was probably lurking unseen behind the mask. Andy nodded his appreciation, waited until the door closed and threw himself on the bed. It was surprisingly comfortable, certainly more so than the one at the hotel, but this was the pits. The rage had turned him morose and as he stared up at the grey ceiling, he felt tears trickle from the outer corners of his eyes. He'd seen this coming two years ago, when everything came to a head with the Shaunna situation, and Jess had pushed him away. She'd promised to stand by him, and to be fair, she'd seen through on that promise, but her resistance back then, and the deceit since: not telling him about the reunion was merely the confirmation of what he'd been trying to ignore. It was over between them and he was going to have to find a way to come to terms with it.

It was strange that only a couple of days ago, he had been thinking up ways of putting it to her that they try and start a family. In the time that lapsed between the realisation that this was something he wanted and Dan's revelation about Rob's last minute party, he had run through so many possibilities in his mind, trying to decide how he felt about fostering or adoption, so sure that Jess wouldn't want them to have a baby of their own. She loved her career. It had always been the most important thing in her life; even when she was in jobs she hated, or had got herself in hot water with an over-amorous senior partner, it remained her priority. She'd never taken him seriously, he could see that now, and that was precisely the demise of their relationship. He promised to tame his wild ways, took the job in Dubai, set up the business with Dan, all actions designed to show how sensible and responsible he could be, but now he knew that this wasn't what she wanted at all. She used to scream and shout at him for being reckless, upset at how he'd put himself at risk and how much he worried her, but in reality, this was what attracted her to him in the first place. Now he was a boring thirty-nine year old, with a wonderful, grown-up daughter for whom he could take none of the credit, and what for him was the equivalent of a steady job, and Jess was no longer interested. Everything she'd asked of him he had given and she'd thrown it right back. Andy sniffed, turned towards the wall and curled up.

Dan rolled onto his side and watched his brother's shuddering back. If they'd been at home, he'd have taken him off somewhere to drown his sorrows, but here all he could do was watch on, so close and so far away. It was quite some time ago, maybe as much as fifteen years, when Adele had really hurt him for the first time. They'd been sharing a house near to where Shaunna and Kris lived now; rented, because he was only a couple of years out of university and still trying to find his way in the job market. So, he was in his first real job and she was working as an assistant to an exceedingly talented yet demanding old seamstress who had escaped Nazi Germany, hidden by her mother inside a roll of silk, or so the story went. Adele hated that job, but made good tips, and they saved every bit of spare cash they had for that holiday. She wanted to go on a cruise, and that's what they did: only a week, because they couldn't afford more than that, picking them up from New York, then a round trip via the Bahamas, before returning to New York to fly home again. They were so excited to be going on a proper holiday together, and Dan had been all set to propose to her during their time on-board.

That first ring had long since landed at the bottom of the ocean, flung from the top deck when he saw her with the singer from the ship's band. For three nights he watched her flirt, ignoring it as best he could, because harmless flirting was something he could take, if he constantly reminded himself that that was all it was. The fourth night: he went to the bar to buy drinks during the break in the performance, taking his place in the horde of other passengers waiting to be served. What Adele and the singer didn't realise, or perhaps didn't even care about, was that whilst they could no longer see him, he could see them, and what followed went so far beyond harmless flirting that just as soon as Dan returned with the drinks, he ended their relationship there and then, knocked the singer unconscious with one punch and stormed out of the bar, straight up to the top deck, from which he launched the engagement ring, along with the wristwatch Adele had bought him for his twenty-first birthday, over the side and down into the formidable, black fathoms far below.

When they returned to England, Andy came to pick them up from the airport and knew without recourse to words that they had broken up. He dropped Adele off to stay with her parents, at her request, left the car outside Dan and Adele's house, and took him straight to the nearest pub, where they drank until they threw up. Even now, he could remember sitting on the edge of the pavement outside that pub, sobbing his heart out, with Andy's arms around him, shushing and soothing him the way their mother used to, on occasion, when they'd grazed a knee. The next day it was back to business as usual: he dismissed Andy's kindness with a snide remark about how he had fallen for and played his pre-designated role in the whole act he was putting on to get back at Adele, although it was an 'act' he went on to repeat with Kris a couple of years later, before he found a way to toughen up his heart, along with his body.

It pained him now, to think of how cruel he had been to Andy back then; yet, when he needed him, he was there at his side, as always, and right at this moment, the thing he wanted most in the world was to do the same for his brother. Slowly, he pushed his legs to the edge of the bed, where they slumped with a thud, the aches of being bed-bound for two days sending shooting pains down through the soles of his feet. It was a mammoth effort to sit up, and his head was spinning. He took a moment to steady himself and carefully dropped down onto the floor, then silently padded across the small distance to Andy's bed and sat, his arm resting on his brother's shoulder, the crying no longer silent. Andy reached up and laid his hand on Dan's, so glad that he was here.

The next morning, bright and early and after a very poor night's sleep on both counts, Dan and Andy tucked into some cornflakes, which the doctor had requested on Andy's behalf. In spite of his appalling language and attitude, the doctor felt sorry for him, and went on to explain, in a very awkward fashion, that he'd received a letter from his girlfriend a few months ago, telling him that she was with someone else. He too had felt completely powerless and so angry that he'd have flattened the other man if he'd been anywhere near him at the time. Andy repeated his previous apologies and thanked him for his understanding. He was still hurting, but perhaps less so for having people around who empathised with his predicament. Dan was quite chirpy this morning too, and they chatted about small, inconsequential things, to fill the time and the emotional void that was making Andy feel so sick that he was extremely surprised when his blood tests all came back clear. Even better news was that the hospital had sent samples off to be tested by the experts, and these had confirmed an isolated case of good, old-fashioned, seasonal influenza virus, albeit a little early in the season. Dan's immune system was kicking back and he was definitely out of danger, although he still wasn't allowed out of quarantine for at least the next twenty-four hours, nor to fly for another twenty-four after that, while further tests and analyses were undertaken, just to be on the safe side. Meanwhile, Andy had been given a whole array of anti-viral treatments, along with a flu jab.

"I'm going back to the hotel," he said.

"No worries," Dan responded. He'd hoped he would decide to keep him company for the duration of the rest of his stay, but could totally understand why he'd chosen not to.

"Hang on, I wasn't finished," Andy said, a little annoyed at the presumption. "I'm going back to the hotel to shower and get some of my stuff, then I'm coming back. You'll go mental if you have to stay here on your own."

"I'll go even more mental if I have to stay here with you!"

"Thanks!" Andy patted his brother's arm, no need for words, and headed back to the hotel. He was going to ask Alan to investigate the flights situation on his behalf, or at the very least, get in touch with Bhagwan, as he had more contacts and would probably be able to sort something out for them. By now it was almost 9 a.m. local time, so around 3:15 a.m. back home, and the party, along with anything else that came of it, would be over.

CHAPTER FOURTEEN

"I don't think I've ever before been so glad that this place was open till seven on a Saturday," Adele said—to herself, it turned out. She giggled and stepped out of the revolving door onto the street, waiting for Shaunna to do likewise. They were carrying a bag each: in Adele's was a dress for the reunion, not a million miles away from the one she'd worn when she was eighteen, and in Shaunna's a pair of shoes, two sets of matching bra and knickers, mascara, false eyelashes and a large, expensive bottle of perfume, courtesy of Adele's old colleague on the Chanel counter. It had been a very successful trip all round, and they'd had quite a lot of fun, a bit like last minute Christmas shopping, where almost anything will do. Not even the store manager, Adele's ex-husband, Tom, suddenly appearing by the lingerie section when they were mid-way through choosing which sets to buy had ruined their hour of frantic dashing up and down the escalator between the Ladies' Fashion department on the first floor, and Lingerie and Footwear on third.

"Don't you think it's a bit freaky that the men's shoes are right next to all these knickers," Shaunna whispered, watching Tom out of the corner of her eye. He was trying to look busy, shifting pairs of brogues around the racks.

"Now you come to mention it, yeah," Adele agreed. She stood on tiptoes and peeped over the rail. Tom glanced her way and smiled the quickest smile she'd ever seen flash across someone's face. She giggled. "He's quite pathetic really, bless him."

Afterwards, they'd even had time for a quick coffee and slice of carrot cake in the coffee shop on the top floor, before making their way back down in the juddery old lift, and through the hot, breezy, perfumed air of the ground floor, emerging red-cheeked and stuffy-nosed onto the street, where they were now waiting for a taxi. Given that they were going to the reunion together, Shaunna suggested stopping off to collect her things, before they both went back to Adele's to get ready. Apparently Kris had booked the taxi to pick them up from there at seven-twenty, which gave them almost an hour.

When they arrived home, Alice had just finished washing up after little Shaunna's dinner, and the teapot was ready for pouring. She staggered slightly as the two women bounced into the kitchen, well and truly in the pre-party spirit.

"Phew!" she said, waving her hand in front of her face. She closed her eyes and opened them again. "I can barely see you through the clouds of perfume."

Adele giggled. "And she really means clouds," she explained to Shaunna, although after nine months, she and Adele's quirky childminder were well enough acquainted for her to know all about Alice's synaesthesia. Nonetheless, it was a phenomenon that still fascinated Adele.

"What colour is this cloud?" she asked.

"Hold on, dear," Alice replied, pouring the tea into the cups. Once she was done, she turned back to face the two women and watched the air for a moment. "Gosh, it's a terrible jumble! Pinks, lilacs, yellows—have you been trying on all of the fragrances at once?"

"Not far off," Shaunna laughed, taking one of the cups and sipping carefully. "Ooh. Wonderful cuppa, Alice, thank you." Alice smiled happily; she did pride herself on her tea-making.

It was time to get ready and they took their drinks with them to the bedroom, tuned the TV to a classic hits music channel and cranked up the volume. Back in the lounge, little Shaunna startled at the sudden noise and put her finger to her lips.

"Sh-sh-shhh," she said.

"Yes indeed," Alice agreed, for she was quite startled herself.

Eleanor had been ready for more than an hour, or at least, her hair, make-up and nails were done, and she was sitting in her dressing gown, eating a fish curry and sweet potatoes. Oliver didn't like fish curry, he said, many times, poking at it with his fork. James was trying his best to ignore what he saw as blatant insolence, at Eleanor's suggestion, but even she was starting to get a little impatient with Oliver's stubbornness. It was a phase; one she'd experienced firsthand with her younger brothers and sisters, and their offspring also. Regardless, the fish curry was all he was getting, and his equally obstinate father insisted he could eat it or go hungry. Eleanor left them to fight it out and went to put on her dress, which fitted perfectly and made her feel beautiful. The only problem was, as it had been the first time, that she couldn't reach the zip to fasten it, and she returned to the kitchen to ask James for help. He stopped clearing the table and wiped his hands.

"They are cold, I am sorry," he said, carefully gripping the tiny silver tab of the very fine zip resting in her lower back.

"I finished now," Oliver said adamantly. James glanced over at the uneaten curry.

"A little bit more, Oliver, please," he said. Oliver located the smallest piece of fish he could find and jabbed at it with his fork with such force that it shot off the plate in Eleanor's direction. She closed her eyes, terrified to look and see if it had hit her dress.

"Go to your room!" James commanded his son.

Oliver started to cry, but that wasn't going to work.

"Now!"

He climbed down from the chair and stomped off to the little bedroom that was his whenever he was staying, where he screamed and cried and stamped his feet.

Eleanor cautiously glanced down at her skirt and sighed in relief. "It missed!"

"There you go," James said, the zip now closed all the way to the top, and the two fiddly little hooks secured so that it wouldn't come down again. Eleanor turned to face him and smiled. He put his arms around her waist, pulling her close.

"Are you sure you wouldn't like to stay home instead?" he murmured, kissing her neck and inhaling her perfume.

"Mmm. Whilst that's a very tempting proposition," she breathed, "I think the flouncing four year old might put a bit of a dampener on things."

"Alas, you are too beautiful, and so right, as always." James released her, looking genuinely disappointed. "What time do you need to leave? Only I will need an extra ten minutes to put the boys in the car. Fifteen, if Oliver is still playing up."

"Oh, I forgot to tell you," she said. "George has ordered a taxi. It's coming at ten past seven."

As predicted, Josh had washed his hair three times since he came home from work. The first was superseded by 'an accident with a bottle of styling spray', the second made him look like 'a chip pan after it's been on fire' and the third put him right back to where he'd started. All of this was a shouted dialogue, with him tearing around upstairs, and George offering food, making cups of coffee, checking if he was anywhere near ready, and so on, from downstairs. After no response for a good ten minutes or so, George went through to the kitchen, catching a glimpse of his reflection in the kettle's chrome surface. He hated bow ties, thought they made him look like a clown, especially when he was younger and his hair was that bit longer, or more accurately, wider, because it was very curly and grew outwards, not downwards. As he made his way back to the lounge to wait out the last five minutes before Kris was due, Josh came tearing down the stairs and dashed past him in a blur. Bewildered, George followed him, fully inhaling the scent of aftershave in his wake.

"Have you seen a…ah!" Josh pulled the pink silk scarf free of the sofa cushion. He draped it around his neck and turned to George. "OK. I'm ready, and with five minutes to spare. How impressive is that? *And* the dry cleaner got rid of that blackcurrant stain—not bad after twenty years, huh?" He pointed at his pristine trousers to emphasise the point and smiled. George didn't respond. He just stood there, staring, and with a very odd expression on his face. "What's the matter?" Josh frowned, examining the front of his shirt. "Don't tell me I've spilt something down me already."

"No, you haven't," George uttered. "You look..." What could he say? Hot? So damned hot that I could push you onto that sofa right here and now and hang the party? Could he ever have said anything like this to Josh? "You look kind of like Don Johnson, only..." This wasn't going well at all. He tried again, settling on: "You look very dapper."

"Thanks." Josh still seemed somewhat puzzled by George's reaction. "So do you, although how is it that you've reached our age without being able to fasten a tie properly?"

"Well, on the ranch we found they kind of got in the way of herding and clearing out stables and stuff," he said nervously, as Josh approached him. "And they don't go well with t-shirts," he added, fighting two completely incompatible urges: to back away, or grab him and kiss him. His heart was beating so hard and so fast that Josh felt it against the side of his hand and placed his palm on George's chest, which only served to make the situation a hundred times worse.

"Are you feeling OK?" he asked.

"Yeah. Why?"

"You heart's racing. Excited about tonight? It's going to be great fun."

"I hope so," George mumbled, willing his tie to be done already.

"There you go," Josh smiled and gave it a final tug to straighten it, just as Kris knocked on the door. George was unbelievably relieved to have a reason to move away.

"Hey," Kris greeted him. "Everything OK?"

"Yeah, sort of."

"I'm really looking forward to this party. Are you ready?"

"As I'll ever be."

"Good, good. More to the point, is Josh ready?"

"Cheeky!" Josh called from the lounge. "I've been ready for ages."

George shook his head and held up his hand, mouthing the words 'five minutes'. Josh appeared in the hall a couple of seconds later and looked out, past George and Kris.

"Is that...Oh my God, it is, isn't it?" He walked straight past them, examining the black limo parked outside.

"Yep. The exact same one," Kris beamed. It was a long shot, but he figured that limousine companies kept their cars for as long as they worked and looked up to the job, so he'd phoned the company who had provided them with their car for the sixth form ball and asked what the chances were of getting the same one. Twenty years on, they managed to find it, and all because Kris remembered a drunken remark from Dan about the number plate matching his initials, delivered as part of an elaborate tale of how he was going to be rich enough to have his own chauffeur-driven limo when he finished uni. He hadn't quite reached that point, but he wasn't doing too badly, and some of the cars he'd owned probably hadn't cost that much less anyway.

"Right, let's get going then!" Kris urged them on. It was seven o'clock and they were picking up Eleanor at ten past, Jess at quarter past and Shaunna and Adele at twenty past. It was going be tight, but traffic allowing, they would be there on time, unlike the original deal, where Adele's fussing with her hair was matched by more of the same from Josh; add to this a last-ditch attempt to persuade Shaunna to go and they'd arrived almost an hour late.

When they reached Eleanor's apartment, Josh went to the door, as she had been his date last time and this was, as far as possible, what they were intending again. With Dan and Andy stuck in Kathmandu, Jess was going to 'play gooseberry' to Josh and Eleanor, Shaunna and Adele gladly paired up, leaving Kris and George together—a far more comfortable arrangement the second time around, but for George's nervousness about seeing all his old classmates.

"Wow," Josh said as Eleanor's front door slowly opened and revealed his friend in her floor-length, deep blue dress. "Ellie, that's stunning."

"You're looking pretty fine yourself, Mr. Sandison," she smiled, and carefully stepped down next to him. "These shoes are a bloody nuisance, though."

Josh held out the crook of his arm for her to take and they strolled along the path, towards the waiting limo. In the back, Kris was pouring Champagne into glasses and handed one to each of them as they settled into their seats.

"I can't believe this is happening. A limo and everything! It's...I can't believe this is happening!" Eleanor beamed at the other three, her eyes wide and glittery with eye shadow and wonder. To them she looked the same as she always had, even though they were not privy to the lament that went with trying to hide the bags of six weeks of new baby with foundation and clever eye liner. She looked back at James, who was standing in the doorway, holding Toby; Oliver was standing next to him, sulking. Eleanor waved briefly and turned her attention to her friends and her Champagne.

Next stop: Jess. She wasn't wearing her dress from the sixth form ball, nor anything remotely similar. They all knew this, because it had been the most revealing gown of the night, not that she'd cared. Back then, she was only too happy to have her full cleavage on display, although that dress revealed a fair bit more than mere cleavage. Instead, she'd opted for the one she'd bought as a potential choice for Eleanor's wedding—the red and orange slinky number with the slit up the side—and it was perfect for this occasion, other than if common sense had prevailed, in which case she'd have been wearing a polo neck and trousers.

"Excellent! Who organised this?" she asked, lifting a long, shapely leg over the door sill.

"Kris," George and Josh exclaimed in unison.

"Nice work!" she said and gave him a peck on the cheek,

once she'd carefully slid along the seat until she was opposite George. Kris handed her a glass of Champagne.

"Glad you appreciate it," he smiled. Just the two 'girls' to go now. Shaunna had sent him text updates throughout the saga of persuading Adele to come to the reunion, so he was aware of what had caused the problem in the first place and somehow had to broach the subject with Jess. "You upset Adele earlier," he said quietly.

"Did I? Good. She's so ditzy sometimes. How did I upset her?"

"By calling her whatever it was you called her."

"I can't remember what I called her, but she deserved it. She told Dan about tonight, when we'd agreed we weren't going to tell them until they got back."

"Actually, that was your idea," Eleanor said in the least accusatory tone she could muster.

"Sort of," Josh said, trying to defuse the situation before it got out of hand. "We all agreed that we shouldn't tell them until it was too late for them to do anything about it."

"Whatever, there was no need for her to mention it at all," Jess said defiantly.

"It wouldn't do any harm to apologise for calling her names, though," George suggested. It was, he thought, an entirely reasonable thing to suggest, but Jess didn't agree.

"Apologise? To Adele? Are you being serious, George? I'm not bloody apologising to her, when she'll have done it to stir things up, and she damn-well succeeded too. Andy went absolutely nuts on the phone. He's probably gone and got himself into all kinds of trouble and it's all down to her."

George looked down at his lap. He wanted to challenge what Jess was claiming, but he didn't think he could find the correct combination of diplomacy and assertiveness, so he stayed quiet, as did everyone else for a couple of minutes. They were almost with Adele and Shaunna now and there was no way they could get in the limo with things the way they were. Josh looked to George, who was sitting to his right and playing with the stem of his Champagne flute, then to Jess, sitting opposite, running her finger around the rim of her own glass. He took George's hand in his own and gave it a squeeze, an action that wasn't going to calm or reassure him, not the way Josh was making him feel tonight. Unaware of this, Josh kept hold and started to speak to Jess, but not as a friend; as a therapist.

"It is possible to say you're sorry for one specific aspect and not compromise on anything else. You could perhaps apologise for the name calling, but at the same time make it clear that you don't agree with what she's done. What do you think?"

"Oh no!" Jess said loudly. "No, no, NO! I'm not playing this game, Joshua. I'll tell you what. I'll say sorry to her, but not because I am sorry. I'll do it to keep the peace. She's so bloody thick she won't even realise. How about that? Does that suit your requirements, dear counsellor?" She tried to stare him down. He maintained eye contact and didn't say a word, until it was she who looked away. She threw back the rest of her Champagne, slamming the empty glass down on the black felted mini-bar, with no effect whatsoever. They had pulled up outside Dan and Adele's flat by this time, and the two remaining friends were already on their way out to the car, giggling and squealing like they were teenagers once more.

"For fuck's sake," Jess hissed, then turned on her best fake smile as they clambered in, Shaunna first, followed by Adele.

"Hi!" Adele said brightly, looking around the group in the back. "Ooh! Champagne. This is great, you guys."

Kris passed the last two glasses to the newest passengers and they both slurped giddily at the contents. It was apparent that it wouldn't make a jot of difference whether Jess apologised or not, because Adele didn't seem remotely bothered by what had passed between them. This was all down to Shaunna's good work, knowing precisely how to talk her friend around, so that she was aware that what she'd done, whether deliberate or not, would have been quite hurtful to Jess. Unfortunately, she'd stopped short of advising against bringing this up in conversation.

"I just wanted to say," Adele began, swivelling in her seat to face Jess. Shaunna was sat between them and shrank back as far as she could. "I'm really, really sorry for telling Dan about tonight."

"Thanks," Jess grunted begrudgingly. "And I'm sorry I called you...whatever it was I called you."

"Oh, that's OK," Adele smiled. This time it was Josh who stared into his lap. He'd seen that smile before and it wasn't a good sign. Adele wasn't quite as dense as she liked to make out and had a malicious streak that was usually reserved for Dan. Now it was directed right at Jess and the close proximity of the warring factions didn't give any room for manoeuvre, physically or psychologically. "I totally understand," she continued, unperturbed by the presence of the other six people—seven, including the driver, who was safely concealed by a relatively soundproof black screen. "I mean, while the cat's away. And of course you don't want Andy worrying about all that, not when he has Dan to think about. So you're right. It was a stupid, selfish thing to do."

Eleanor couldn't believe Adele had just said it. They'd all thought it, but no-one would ever have said it. And now it was Jess's turn.

"Don't you dare come the moral high ground with me, you cheap little slut! Who was it that was pregnant with one man's baby and marrying another, in your big, tacky meringue of a dress, pretending to be the innocent little bride? And as for Andy worrying about Dan. After the shit he's put him through over the years? But then it's no bloody wonder is it? Not when he's got to put up with you!"

Shaunna cleared her throat and Josh glared at her, his eyes imploring her not to say a word. They were going to have see this one through, because however well-meant or carefully chosen the intervention, it would be taken, distorted, and used to beat them by whichever got a good hold of it first. Their driver chose this moment to pull back his screen and inform them they had arrived.

"Thank merciful God," Josh muttered. He, Eleanor, George and Kris waited, until Adele, then Shaunna, then Jess, got out, the latter storming straight across the car park after Adele, leaving Shaunna shell-shocked and standing on her own. Through force of habit, and because he cared, Kris shuffled past the others and went to her. In the distance, they could still hear Jess and Adele screaming at each other.

"I'll go see if I can talk them down," Eleanor said, although she didn't envisage success. She glugged the rest of her Champagne and edged along the seat, hoisting her dress up to her knees in order to step down onto the tarmac. "Bloody skirt. Now I remember what a damned nuisance it was last time. See you in a mo." She paused to readjust her outfit, then disappeared from view, leaving Josh and George alone in the back of the limousine.

"Well, I suppose this might mean they get it out of their system before they ruin everyone's night," Josh remarked.

"Um, yeah, I suppose," George said quietly.

"You don't think you started it, do you? Because it was going to happen, whatever any of us said."

"No, it's not that. It's, err…what I mean is…I dunno, maybe I should keep my mouth shut and leave the talking to you."

"Hey, remember what happened with Ellie? Imagine how that would've ended if you'd left it to me. No, what you said was right, but Jess didn't want to neutralise the situation. She was spoiling for a fight and we all know why. Anyway, time we went inside and joined the party, don't you think?"

Josh gave George's hand one final squeeze and released it, then shuffled along the seat and out into the evening air, seemingly oblivious to the effect that his uncharacteristic behaviour was having. George stayed where he was: he needed a moment to try and get his head together, a confused mass of arousal and reluctance pooling like a pit of tar in his stomach. He remembered now, when it all started; that mind-numbing crush that rose up around him, drawing in on him until he could think of nothing else. Time had quelled it to a constant ache, like an untreated abscess, and more recently still, it had mutated into a wish only partly fulfilled. Had his compromise of accepting a house-share with Josh destroyed his chances of ever having a relationship with anyone else? He'd begun to think this was so and had been well on the way to convincing himself that it was enough. But now the crush was back, with a vengeance, only this time he wasn't sure he could beat it into submission.

"Are you coming?" Josh poked his head back through the open door.

George climbed out and smoothed down his trousers, his eyes averted.

"What's up?"

"Nothing."

"Another one of those 'it's too complicated' things, is it?"

"Something like that, yeah. I'm dreading this." There. He'd said it.

"Why?"

"Because coming out was tough."

"You once told me that you never stop coming out."

"Did I? That was quite profound, and also total bollocks."

"I disagree. However, do you really think no-one at school figured out you were gay? Anyone who matters will either have realised long ago, or decided they don't care one way or the other. Just be yourself and have fun. All right?"

George shrugged. "That's easy for you to say."

"Maybe, but look." Josh pointed to Kris, who had just paid their chauffeur and was now chatting to a couple of new arrivals and playing up his 'gayness' to full effect. George frowned sulkily.

"There's no way I'm doing that," he said.

"You don't need to. Just be yourself," Josh repeated. "Now come on, let's go!" He walked away towards Eleanor, who was waiting impatiently outside the entrance, leaving George to trail behind. Kris fell in step with him and gave him a nudge.

"Have you seen?" he asked, nodding towards Jess and Adele, who were still bickering, but looked as if they might have reached enough of a truce to enjoy the evening ahead; they hugged awkwardly as they made their way back to their other friends.

"That's something," George grumbled. He shoved his hands in his trouser pockets and huffed.

"Come on, grumpy-pants." Kris looped his arm through George's and pulled him inside.

CHAPTER FIFTEEN

The party was certainly not in full swing, and didn't really start swinging until the majority of the guests had consumed a couple of drinks or more, most initially experiencing that same mix of nervousness and excitement at seeing their fellow sixth formers twenty years on. The slenderness of youth had long since departed for most of them, as had the hair of around half of the men, but they were still of an age where mid-life vanity had yet to lead them into embarrassing attempts to comb over shiny pates or don ill-fitting pants. In passing conversations, some confessed that the outfit they were wearing was not the original article, which was 'thrown out ages ago', they'd say quickly, thoughts flitting to their attempts to shoe-horn themselves into said garment during the past couple of days. Kris was proud to declare to everyone he stopped to talk to that his suit *was* the one he wore when he was eighteen, even if it had been a year of mental illness and sustained lack of appetite that had determined his ability to fit into it. Likewise, Shaunna's mingling was made easier by the option to lead questions about her teenage pregnancy into responses incorporating the dress she was wearing, bought by her parents two decades ago.

"Of course, I was too busy looking after a toddler to come to the last one, but at least this didn't go to waste in the end," she'd say, sweeping her hands down her sides and giving them a little spin, revelling in the resulting compliments about how beautiful she looked and repeated suggestions that perhaps having children earlier was the way to go.

Josh leaned on the bar and watched the whole affair from a

distance, fascinated by the continuities and the ease with which people were falling right back into the relative orderliness of their old friendship groups, when often they hadn't been in touch since high school. The only notable exception, for it was clear he was still a very long way off relaxing into the flow of the evening, was George, always a couple of steps behind Kris, glad to be downstage and cutting off conversations with quick, blunt responses. Eleanor was on her way back across the room, having visited the Ladies' yet again (her fourth trip in the hour and a half they'd been here) and it was a relief to be certain that this time around it wasn't to induce vomiting, but to stick another plaster on the back of each heel. Give it another half an hour, Josh thought, and I'll be carrying those shoes.

"Enjoying yourself?" Adele interrupted his observations and waved a ten pound note in front of her so as to make clear to the bartenders that she, along with about fifteen others, was waiting to be served.

"I am, actually. You?"

"Yeah. It's lovely to see everyone again, although I can't believe I used to be such good mates with that lot." She subtly tilted her head in the direction of a group of women in short dresses and platform heels, skin aglow with the unmistakable orange of spray tan and sunbeds. "They're so shallow. I mean, when I was sixteen I probably bitched like that too." She affected a squeaky, mimicking tone: "Oh. My. God! What *does* she look like in that dress?"

Josh laughed. "That sounded just like—what's her name again? That one in the cerise pink nightdress."

"Cherise, funnily enough." Adele told him and they both giggled.

"You were always better than them," Josh said. "You know that, don't you?"

Adele lowered her eyes modestly. "I don't think so."

"I do."

He was doing that mind-probing thing again and she hastily eased herself into a gap that opened between two of the people waiting at the bar, although it wasn't far enough away to escape.

"Shall I just shut up?" Josh suggested.

"Oh, it's OK. I don't mind really," Adele smiled, too brightly.

"No, I'll just shut up." Josh sipped at his glass by way of confirming that he really was done, even though he was seriously tempted to tell her how much he admired her for challenging Jess earlier. Adele was served soon after and gave him a kiss on the cheek as she passed by.

"Thanks," she said.

"What for?"

"What you said, and what you didn't say." He nodded his understanding. Yes, much more astute than they gave her credit for. "Anyway," she continued, "I'd best go find Shaunna. Last time I saw her, she'd been cornered by Zak 'freaky-stalker' Benson. He's not bad-looking these days, but, ugh!"

"Good luck!" Josh called after her, as she tottered on her absurdly high heels around the perimeter of the empty dance floor. It would probably take a few drinks more before she or anyone else felt brave enough to strut their stuff in front of their once overly judgemental peers, although some were starting to look almost ready now. Cherise and her friends, for instance, were starting to move in time to the music, their usual fixation on self-image temporarily shelved in favour of criticising others. The conversation they were having was ludicrous, and Josh followed it by listening where he could and filling in the gaps with non-verbal cues. They were talking about Kris.

"Didn't I tell you?" Cherise was saying to the broad-shouldered, peroxide blonde to her left. "I said, that Kris Johansson isn't gay. He just needs showing what to do with it, I said."

Josh took a slurp of his pint in order to stop himself from laughing. Peroxide Blonde was watching Kris and nodding meaningfully. What was her name again? Sharon? Chantelle? Something like that.

"So you offering, Cherise?" she said and the two of them

tittered loudly.

"You must be joking, Shelle." Ah yes, that was it, of course. Shelley Harrison: captain of the girls' hockey team and looking like she could still do the business.

"I heard him on the radio the other week," Brunette Bob piped up. Josh remembered her all right, but he'd never known her name. She was one of those girls who trail along behind the in-crowd, not quite brash or common enough, but trying their hardest to gain an invite.

"You never did," Cherise remarked cuttingly. Brunette Bob looked indignant, but she said no more on the matter. Josh felt sorry for her, because she was probably telling the truth. What a shame she still felt the need to fit in with these dreadful people.

All the while he had been listening to this conversation, he had been aware of the fourth individual who made up their group: someone for whom, alas, a hair-based nickname was not required. She'd been watching him for quite some time, which was why he'd continued to focus on the other three, as looking away would be as dangerous as making eye contact. He really didn't want to talk to Suzie Tyler, his constant companion through the boy-girl seating years. She was an exceedingly nasty piece of work, and he caught that sneer as it morphed artificially into a wide, teeth-bared smile. She was coming over.

"Hi, Josh," she called on her approach, waving at him. He nodded.

"Hey, Suzie. How are you?"

"Oh, I'm great, thanks for asking. On your own?"

"I was," he said coolly. She affected a giggle.

"You haven't changed much, have you?"

"Nor have you."

Back in school she had instigated so much trouble, not just for Josh and the others; she didn't discriminate. Hence, he was overjoyed to find at the start of the fourth year, that firstly she was no longer in most of his classes, and secondly, the boy-girl seating arrangements had by and large been abandoned. Even so, she was the one who took it upon herself to tell the rest of their year about Shaunna's pregnancy, and she was supposed to be one of her friends. The rumours were horrific, cruel lies of how she had been 'gang-banged' by all of the lads at the party, which was why she didn't know who the father was. At the time, Shaunna was off school with morning sickness, so they were able to shield her from this; not so from the nickname of 'Shaunna Whore-nessy' that they'd come up with in her absence. What clever girls, Josh thought sardonically: well done them.

Suzie had been standing next to him for a couple of minutes, swaying to the music and casting her vicious eye around the room for her next victim, and much as he didn't think any of them deserved it, he was hoping she'd find someone else soon. A few seconds later his prayers were answered, although Kris probably wouldn't be quite so grateful.

"See you," she said, slithering away. Kris's face dropped as he saw her heading in his direction, but he quickly switched to performance mode and turned on his best smile.

"Hi, Suzie. How fabulous to see you," he said loudly, kissing the air next to each of her cheeks in turn. George glanced over at Josh and rolled his eyes.

The dance floor was still empty, but a few people had moved closer, including a group of men, one or two of whom he instantly recognised, standing right on the corner, trying to look like they were engaged in some kind of macho discussion about football when it was nothing of the sort; this much he could tell from some of their gestures. Tagging on at the very outskirts of the group was Martin O'Brierly, no taller or less round than he had been in sixth form, although his red hair wasn't quite so much of a 'shock' these days, more of a smattering of red dots, shaved close and showing off the skin roll against his shirt collar to optimum effect. He really was a funny-looking little man, but then so were the others in his selective grouping. They were the geeky, average achievers, who, by reason of acne, ginger hair, obesity or other irrelevant physical property, had struggled to make friends with either sex. It was apparent from the way they were standing that they certainly weren't friends with each other, and their conversations consisted of bland explanations of the various boring jobs they did. Peter Parsons, it would seem, was a network manager with responsibility for 'a very powerful, robust system', which he'd set up singlehandedly. The rest of what he said used terms such as 'giga-hertz' and 'terabytes' and Josh lost interest. In response, Jonathan Shipley was boasting about his 'unbelievably successful' web design company, with 'literally hundreds' of clients who were too stupid to question how much he was charging them for something they could have done themselves.

Meanwhile, a few feet away, was the group that Andy and Dan would have been part of if they'd been here tonight. In the US, they'd have been The Jocks, with their height and athletic build. Dan's friend 'Aitch' was holding court, using his pint as a prop to illustrate some kind of fancy manoeuvre. This group had honed their social skills to such perfection that every smile, laugh, nudge, utterance of 'Yeah?' was almost choreographed. Josh stifled a yawn just in time, for Aitch had spotted his attentiveness, excused himself from the group and was coming his way.

"Josh. Good to see you," he smiled as he approached, vast, firm hand outstretched. Josh allowed his smaller, rather feminine hand (by comparison) to be shaken.

"You too. It's great to see so many people here, isn't it?"

"It is. No Dan though?"

"He's in Nepal. He's not very well either—picked up some virus or other."

"I saw something about that on the news. It's killed a good few people, they were saying. So, what're you drinking?"

"Oh." Josh was a little taken aback by the sudden switch mid-sentence, but Aitch wasn't to know how worried they'd all been. "I'll get these," he suggested.

"No, I insist. I was buying one anyway."

"OK. Lager, thanks."

"Righteo." Aitch queue-jumped about six other people and handed Josh his pint. "I take it you've had no more trouble from that Callaghan bloke?"

"No, thankfully. He's in prison now. They decided he was sane after all."

"Figures," Aitch said, picking up his own pint. "See you later." And off he went, back to his fellow meat-heads. It was at this point that Josh realised Eleanor hadn't made it back to him, even though she'd only been just across the room, but that was a good twenty minutes ago. He scanned the crowd and eventually found her; she was talking to Shaunna and Adele and switching her weight between her feet. Their conversation was animated and serious and he could tell it was about Jess. He followed the direction of their occasional furtive glances, to a dark corner behind the DJ, where Rob and Jess were standing, their faces very close together, Jess flirting so obviously that it would be impossible to miss. She and Rob had always been this way; in fact, she was like this with any charming male company, and it didn't necessarily need to be of the heterosexual variety, from what he'd seen over the years, with both George and Kris coming in for the occasional brush with those long legs. However, that kind of flirting was safe, or safer, and Andy certainly didn't consider either of them a threat. Rob was a different matter and Adele was right. This was a case of Jess taking the opportunity of Andy's absence to engage in one of her favourite pastimes, and who wouldn't, if they were blessed with that figure and those looks? But it was a dangerous game she was playing and it could only end badly.

"She's going to get herself in serious trouble one of these days," Eleanor said, stumbling towards Josh and leaning on him to steady herself so that she could remove her shoes, then looking around for a stool to put them on, but there weren't any free. Josh tutted and held out his hand. She smiled and draped the ankle straps over his index finger.

"I think that day might arrive sooner than we think, too," he added.

"Well, so long as it's not before next Saturday," Eleanor remarked. Her glass was empty and she looked at his almost full pint in disdain.

"Aitch bought it."

"Did he? That was nice of him."

"Not really. He wanted to know where Dan was. I think the pint was just recompense for being a reliable informant. I take it you want a drink then?"

"How thoughtful of you to offer," Eleanor grinned. She was sticking to orange juice and lemonade, on account of breastfeeding, but she was going to have a couple of 'proper' drinks later on, if she was in the mood. At the moment, she was enjoying watching everyone else become intoxicated, and had already witnessed a couple of interchanges that probably wouldn't have taken place in alcohol-free conditions. These kinds of occasions tapped into long-buried sentiments of wars waged and won (or lost); on her way across to Josh, for instance, she'd overhead one of the 'lads' apologising to one of the 'girls' for being so mean to her at school. For her part, she acted out a convincing acceptance, but Eleanor remembered the many times that she and this other girl had both been hiding out in the school toilets, while she engaged in her ritual oesophageal abuse and the girl stood, arms folded and angry tears streaming down her face, insisting she was never coming to school again. An apology twenty years too late was never going to cut it.

"Shall we go and find somewhere to sit?" Eleanor suggested. "Only my feet are killing me."

"Me too!" Josh remarked, holding up her shoes and wrinkling his nose.

"They don't smell, do they?" She looked mortified.

"Nah. No worse than usual, anyway," he grinned and she poked him in the ribs. There weren't many tables in the room, and most were already taken, so they squeezed up in a corner with a bunch of other people, all with that same look of 'being too old for this kind of nonsense'. Meanwhile, the DJ was ready to start cranking out some tunes, and Adele and Shaunna were first on the dance floor, with others quickly following their lead.

"Have you seen Kris and George recently?" Eleanor asked.

She had obviously followed the same train of thought, as Josh had also been wondering why Kris wasn't already up there giving it his all.

"They were over there somewhere just before," Josh shouted, pointing over towards where most of the guests were still standing in their various groups. The DJ had turned up the music. "Jesus! I know we're all getting on a bit, but we're not bloody deaf—yet!"

"Pardon?" Eleanor shouted back. Josh looked at her, trying to decide whether she was joking or not. She sipped her drink and turned her attention to the dancers and he followed suit. Adele and Shaunna were having a great time, completely regressed to their teenaged days, when this was all they ever did, not a care in the world, giving themselves over completely to the music and the joy of being together, in their own little bubble of oblivion. Far behind them, mostly obscured by the brightness of the lights, Jess had her back turned and was standing in front of Rob, who was leaning against the wall. It was impossible to see more than this, and Eleanor was glad, because what she didn't know couldn't incriminate her. She hadn't forgotten her offer of bailing Jess out if the need arose, but as things were it seemed that this was the last thing she wanted. For all of what had been said in the limo, she and Andy weren't officially together. All of the friends knew of their closeness, which had grown over the past few years, but they weren't an item, so Jess was free to flirt, or even have a fling with Rob, if that was what she wanted. With any other man, it probably wouldn't have mattered near half as much, and she had to know that her actions could not pass without consequence.

A mixture of boredom and woe was starting to take over, so when the next track was a Wham! number, Eleanor grabbed Josh by the arm and pulled him to his feet. He left her shoes on the seat and followed her, feigning reluctance as they nudged their way into Adele and Shaunna's circle of two. They hardly seemed to notice. The next song came on and Josh contemplated sneaking off and leaving Eleanor with the other two women, but then realised he was really enjoying dancing. It had been so long since he'd done it that he'd forgotten how much fun it was, not that he was particularly good at it, but it was liberating to just let the music take over, and so he danced through the next track, and the one after that, and so on, until it was Eleanor who wanted to stop.

"I'm just going to the loo," she explained edgily.

"OK," he replied. This wasn't the same as the previous visits, he could feel it, and as he watched her meander bare-footed through the crowd and off down the hallway outside the ballroom, he cursed himself for not paying attention to her mood. He'd let the moment take over and in the time that had lapsed, something had happened. He started to worry, that worry rising to panic when he felt his phone vibrate and saw she had sent him a text message, which read:

Please can you come to the ladies ASAP? x

He downed the rest of his now-warm lager in one go, went straight to the Ladies' toilets, which were directly opposite the Gents', and waited outside the door. Women smiled quizzically or sympathetically at him as they emerged, having already passed him once on the way in. Another text:

I'm in the second cubicle from the door. x

Well, he thought, isn't that just great? All these women wandering in and out and she wanted him to go in there too. He took a deep breath and pushed against the door.

"This is the Gents', mate," a surly voice called from behind. He glanced back and identified the owner—one of Dan's friends who was there at the time of 'the unfortunate incident in the showers'. Terrific.

"Err, yeah, I know. Thanks anyway," he said, blushing. There was nothing for it, but to put his head down and push on through. "Sorry, ladies," he announced, as he speed-walked past the women lined up in front of the mirrors, all engaged in make-up re-application and a snide conversation about some poor soul who had been foolish enough to wear red shoes with a black dress. Cherise Williams et al again; and there he was thinking it couldn't get any worse. He tuned out and lightly tapped on the second door along.

"Ellie. It's me!"

The bolt clicked and the door opened a couple of inches.

"I'm so sorry, Josh. I've got a bit of a problem," she said, ushering him inside and locking the door again. He heard the conversation on the other side switch to hissed whispers.

"Right?" he asked hesitantly. At least she hadn't been vomiting, which was a good sign.

"I knew I should've expressed before I came out, but I didn't have time. It was stupid of me, and now I…"

"I'm sorry, Ellie, but I haven't got a clue what you're on about."

"Right. See, there's this thing called a let-down, which is basically triggered when a feed is overdue, or you think about the baby, or something."

"OK. Still not following."

"I'm leaking milk, Joshua! And if it goes through to my dress it's going to leave two big fat round nasty stains on my boobs!"

"Ah," he said. "Now I understand. So what am I supposed to do about it, exactly?"

"I've phoned James and asked him to bring me some more breast pads, but these ones are soaked." She nodded down the front of her dress, which she was holding away from her body. Josh glanced around the cubicle and spotted the absence of toilet paper.

"Do you want me to go and get some loo roll for the time being?"

"Please," she nodded frantically. He unlocked the door and emerged into the crowded communal area, where Cherise and her pals instantly stopped whispering and glared at him. He flashed them a quick smile and checked the other doors. They were all locked.

"Balls," he said and turned straight back. "They're all engaged. Here: have this." He unwrapped the pink silk scarf from his neck and held it out to her.

"Oh, Josh, thank you, but it'll stain the fabric and you'll never get it out. Apart from which, where would you put it for the rest of the night?" She started to make a creaking noise and jiggled uncomfortably.

"What's the matter?"

"More sodding milk. I might as well give up now and just go home."

"Oh no you don't. It'll be fine," Josh assured her and pushed the scarf down the top of her dress. "Now you have no choice. I'll go and wait outside for James."

"OK." She shoved the scarf down inside her bra. "I love you."

"Love you too," he replied, as he once again exited the tiny cubicle, bashfully making his way back through the women and out to the corridor, receiving some very odd looks along the way. He stepped out into the fresh air and was grateful for it, because his face was burning, from alcohol consumption and embarrassment. Soon after, James pulled up and wound down his window to pass through a bag of small round pads; they looked like wound dressings.

"I hope no-one's watching," Josh mumbled. "It might be a bit tricky to explain. Thanks for this."

"No problem," James replied. "Is she enjoying herself?"

"She was until she had a—can't remember what she called it now."

"Let-down," James confirmed. "She usually feeds Toby in the evening and expresses for the next day."

"Ah, I see. So, essentially she's made enough milk to feed him for the next twenty-four hours. No wonder her pads were soaked through. Anyway, best go deliver these. Thanks again. See you later."

James nodded his goodbye and drove off. Josh headed back

inside and straight for the Ladies', but then something caught his attention, just on the outskirts of his peripheral vision. It was George and Kris, and they were…

He pushed the door to the toilets open with so much force that he almost hit someone in the face.

"Oh God. I'm sorry. I wasn't looking where I was going," he said, running now to get away. He hammered on the cubicle door and edged through the gap, handing the pads to Eleanor. She pulled his scarf free of her bra and bent to pick up her bag.

"What do you want me to do with this? I suppose I could put it in here and—what's wrong?" She'd turned back to face him mid-sentence and he looked terrible.

"I just saw, well, I think I saw, err…"

"What did you see?"

"Err, I…it doesn't matter. I probably imagined it."

"All right then, what do you think you imagined you saw?"

"George and Kris," he said. She shrugged, failing to see the significance. "Together."

"What? You mean 'together' together?"

"I think they were kissing."

"Seriously? Are you sure?"

"Oh, I don't know. Maybe I was mistaken?" Josh suggested, willing it to be true. "I mean, the way George was feeling, I can't see…and Kris wouldn't do that, would he? No, I must've imagined it. Forget I said anything."

Eleanor bit the inside of her cheek thoughtfully. "This'll kill Shaunna—if you're right, of course, about what you think you imagined you saw, or whatever it was."

Josh wanted to shout "It's killing me too!", but how could he? Aside from the fact that he was standing in a cubicle in a women's public toilet, he hadn't told anyone—not even Eleanor—how jealous he felt when George showed an interest in someone else, and he was convinced it was pure egotism on his own part. For everything he'd said about the attention being unwanted, he, just like any other normal person, was flattered to know that he was loved and desired. But Eleanor was right.

Shaunna was the one being cheated on here, or at least this is how it seemed to them right now, for George had kept his promise to Kris and said nothing about the affair with the guy at the radio station. On top of this, Kris and Shaunna were still trying to come up with a way of telling their friends that they had effectively been separated for nine months, and had reached a perfectly workable means of sharing their house. But sooner or later it was bound to come out, and it looked like that time had arrived.

CHAPTER SIXTEEN

The flight schedule between Kathmandu and Istanbul was poor at the best of times, but Andy and Dan had everything stacked against them. First off, two airlines had cancelled all flights due to the current weather conditions. Of the remaining two, one refused to take Dan because of his 'virus' and the other was booked right through to next weekend. The only suggestion the agent had was that they provide contact details and hope for a cancellation. And then, once they'd got to Turkey, they'd have to hope there were seats available for the flight back to the UK. Andy hung up despondently and shook his head.

"The first available flight is on Saturday," he explained to Dan, who had earphones in and was half-asleep. It was so good to have music to listen to. Andy turned the tablet and hit 'pause'. Dan opened his eyes and removed an earphone.

"What?"

"I said, there are no flights until Saturday."

"Crap. What we gonna do?"

"Go on Saturday, by the looks of it. I can book the tickets now and then sort out a flight back from Istanbul, or we can leave it and hope for a cancellation. What d'you think?"

"Book the flights. If a cancellation comes up we can make a decision then, but I'm done with adventure on this trip." Dan put his earphone back in and hit the 'play' button.

"Guess it's up to me then," Andy said and started over with the phone calls to people, whose English, whilst being far better than his Nepalese, was still rather limited when it came to understanding their flight requirements. Ellie was going to have them hung out to dry for missing the wedding—well, she probably wouldn't, because it was beyond their control, but even so, he really didn't want to miss it. So far he'd only made it to Shaunna and Kris's, which was, in retrospect, the only one that counted for anything. He'd missed Adele and Tom's; he'd missed Ellie's first wedding, and he'd deliberately stayed away from Jess's partnership ceremony for obvious reasons. This, he was starting to accept, was the problem. For Jess, the so-called benefits of their friendship were in the sex, not the emotional support he gave her, pepping her up through failed relationships, lousy jobs and then setting up her own practice. It sounded like a bit of a gender switch, because although the sex was important, to him it was more about having someone to go home to. In spite of the constant ear-bashings about his lack of sense, only once had she shunned him, and it was entirely understandable, but it had hurt, because it was about trust, not desire.

Yet again, Andy's thoughts had trespassed into thinking about her and it really was too painful to keep revisiting. The only consolation was that there was a slim chance he had misinterpreted her intent in not telling him about the reunion, and her subsequent reaction to his knowing; that is, she jumped straight on the defensive, which he took as a sure sign that she was guilty of something. Still, so long as they got home for the crazy group honeymoon in Wales, there would be plenty of time for autopsies, or rather, he could but hope, relationship-saving surgery.

Eventually, with much confusion surrounding booking the flights on the one hand, and asking for notification of cancellations on the other, everything was set so that at the very least, they were going to be back home by Sunday night. It was far from ideal, with Dan almost ready to leave hospital and another five days to fill, but he was getting better by the hour, so perhaps they could go out and enjoy themselves in the mean time. To be honest, Andy didn't feel very sociable, so it was going to be quite a drag getting through the rest of the week, even if Dan suddenly made a full recovery overnight, which was highly unlikely. Andy had caught flu when he was younger, and it was bloody awful, even in comparison to smashing up his legs in the car crash, which was the most severe injury he'd had in all his years of travelling, diving, surfing, hiking, climbing, racing, parachuting, gliding…in other words, if it suited the word 'extreme', then he was up for giving it a go. And that was the only other potential positive which might come out of breaking his pact with Jess.

Now that Dan had set up his tablet for him, Andy decided to suffer the expense of using the internet, if only to relieve the boredom and the requirement he'd developed to repeatedly dissect his feelings, and search for mountain climbing in Wales. It might not be a patch on the Himalayas, but it sure as hell beat sitting in a room for another week, watching on as the world did its thing, while he stayed stock-still, being something he wasn't because that was what had been asked of him. Ellie was right when she told him that he shouldn't change who he was for Jess, and now he was starting to appreciate precisely what she had been getting at. It wasn't that he couldn't see it through. If that was what it needed, he'd have done it. So, a little adventure in Wales was a win-win situation: if he got Jess back, then great; and if he didn't, well at least he'd be doing something he enjoyed.

Dan was snoring loudly in the bed across the way, his earphones tinkling unheard by their wearer, irritatingly tinny and loud to Andy. He got up and stretched, pressed 'pause' again, and returned to his web search. There was lots of stuff to do in the Brecon Beacons, which was where the cabins were located. He could go paragliding, if the mood took him, or abseiling. There was even a bungee jump over a fast-flowing river. He'd not done bungee jumping yet, so a new challenge.

He was so engrossed in his planning and scheming that he didn't hear Dan stop snoring, or notice him make his way across to spy on what he was up to.

"That's your porn, isn't it?" he said, glancing over Andy's

shoulder. He immediately closed the browser window.

"Err, yeah. I was looking for stuff to do in Wales next week. We'll arrive home on Sunday night, by the way."

"We're going to be in big bother."

"Tell me about it. You know, I was just thinking about something Ellie said to me a while back, just before I gave all this up." Andy indicated to the blank screen of his tablet, but Dan knew what he meant. "She said that Jess didn't need me to do it for her, give up my lifestyle and everything. She was right."

"In what way?"

"Jess needs me to be myself, not the miserable bastard I've become recently."

"Right," Dan remarked dryly. "You know the real problem here? You're trying to understand what she wants. She's a woman. You've got no hope, bro."

"That's disgustingly sexist."

"Yep. And it's all based on experience. How long have I known Adele? More than thirty years and I still haven't a clue what she wants."

"That's because it's Adele."

"It's because she's a woman," Dan said knowingly. With that pearl of wisdom, he went to the adjoining bathroom and stayed there for a good half an hour. He'd grown quite a beard while he'd been ill, and Andy assumed he was shaving it off. He reloaded the page he'd been reading earlier, and adjusted his pillows; it certainly beat sitting on that awful wooden chair. When Dan finally emerged, he was showered and smelled of toothpaste, but his beard was still intact.

"Are you planning on keeping that?" Andy asked, pointing at his brother's chin. It would've taken anyone else several weeks to grow something so long and dense.

"Maybe. I quite like it."

"And will Adele like it, do you think?"

"There you go again," Dan smirked. Andy ignored him and returned to his browsing, giving him the low-down on all the different activities he intended to try in Wales, but Dan was only half-listening, his mind drifting back homewards to Adele and little Shaunna. Even if it did prove impossible to give his two girls what they wanted, he'd never stop trying. This much he had come to realise in his time in Nepal.

CHAPTER SEVENTEEN

Mid-September and Autumn was beginning to show its face, the first fall of leaves fluttering around their feet as they made their way along the winding path through the graveyard. Eleanor was going to church with her mother, because she'd agreed, sort of in payment for her ball gown, and because her father was going to the train station to pick up his twin brother, who had flown over from Ireland for the wedding. Ben, Luke and Teddy would be arriving between now and Tuesday, in time for the stag night, so there was much to do on this so-called day of rest, and her mother continued to fidget throughout mass, eager to get home and get on with the vacuuming, bathroom cleaning, mopping, wiping down of walls, making up of beds, and so on, in the midst of which she would still cook a perfect roast dinner. She really was quite an incredible woman and it was apparent from which parent Eleanor had inherited her organisational talents.

Meanwhile, on this quiet Sunday morning, Kris and Shaunna decided to take Casper to the beach, for last night they had each individually realised just how big a task they had set for themselves in pretending, for the entire week's holiday in Wales, that they were still together. Over breakfast, Kris had tentatively proposed that they discuss how best to tell their friends that they were separated, and Shaunna's initial response wasn't promising, but she was a little more receptive once she had a cup of tea inside her. So they set off on foot, Casper with his Frisbee firmly clenched between his teeth, and walked 'cross country' to the nearest stretch of coast, which wasn't the prettiest, but a perfect place to take a dog on a day like today. It was a view shared by many others, with Casper temporarily forgetting about Frisbee fetching in favour of giving a traditional canine greeting to each and every one of his kind that he came across. A woman with two Dalmatians was a little taken aback when she saw the daft yellow Labrador lolloping eagerly towards her, and dropped both leads on the sand, where they trailed along behind her two dogs as they darted here and there, chasing each other through big puddles of sea water. When they eventually wore themselves out, she caught hold of their leads and unclipped them.

"I always worry about letting them off," she explained, "because they're so boisterous and incapable of doing anything I tell them to. They're brothers, you see, and I've had them since they were pups. Both deaf as doorposts." She held up her hand and signalled to one of the dogs, who immediately came to her, and she gave him a treat. "The trouble is getting them to look at me," she said, and signalled again. The dog ran off after his brother and down towards the wake, with Casper bouncing behind in a close third.

"Whereas I have the same problem because he's too dopey," Shaunna said, whistling loudly with her fingers. Kris rubbed his ears. "Sorry," she grinned. Casper continued on his mission to catch up with his spotty new friends. "Ah well, he won't go too far. He's too much of a wuss."

"He's very handsome. Is he a gun dog?"

"No, although we did try him with search and rescue training, because The Dogs' Trust said he came from a specialist breeder. It cost a fortune and the only thing we learned was why he wasn't kept on. He's useless."

"He's very loving though," Kris justified. "He's a loyal pet— a dog of leisure."

"Yeah, it's the same for my two," the woman agreed. "Some of these breeders haven't a clue. Anyway, I'll see you."

"Bye," Shaunna and Kris responded, watching as the woman moved away from them, walking backwards and waiting for the optimum moment when her dogs were looking the right way. It came and she signalled for them to come, the pair of them tearing up the beach at speed and skidding to a halt, throwing a trail of sand in the air. She gave them both a treat and continued on her walk. Half a minute later Casper arrived and ran in circles around Kris's legs. Kris threw the Frisbee along the beach and off they went, repeating this action as necessary, while they talked about the best way to approach their problem.

In general it wasn't really a problem to them at all, as they'd had plenty of time to come to terms with it. Apart from the small glitch when Shaunna was trying on her dress, they'd lived entirely separate lives in most respects. They still shared meals together, and bought household shopping, because it made more sense than doubling up on items that were more expensive in individual sizes. But the social and sexual aspects of their day-to-day activities were no longer of concern to each other. For instance, Shaunna had also seen Kris with George the night before, and found it a little odd, but it didn't bother her in the slightest. When she used to joke that she'd turned Kris straight, it was out of a need for reassurance that he was all that he claimed to be, but she never truly believed it. So, once the shock of his affair had passed, she found she was strangely at peace, and because Kris could finally be himself, his mental health improved by leaps and bounds, with immediate results. He was back at work within a couple of weeks, was eating properly again and starting to enjoy the little things in life, like walking the dog, reading a book—in other words, everything he'd always done when they were together; he also went out at weekends with some of the guys he worked with, and she didn't care to know what he was up to when he didn't come home.

Kris's only worry was that they hadn't told Krissi. She'd hinted at the question once, when she'd been visiting and noticed that her old room was filled with his stuff, but she seemed to accept their explanation that they were clearing out the wardrobes to fit new ones, and let it go. The longer they left

149

telling her, the harder it became and they agreed that she needed to be the first to know. Shaunna sent her a text message, inviting her round for lunch, and nodded to indicate that she had replied in acceptance. So that was the first step complete. Also easy, by comparison, was the decision of what to say to their parents, and they decided against telling Shaunna's dad, who was a little forgetful in his old age and wouldn't cope with the news very well. Kris's parents were accepting of his sexuality when he was younger, so although they might be a little saddened by the marriage break-up, they wouldn't judge him badly for it. Still, there was no urgent need to tell them, as they lived too far away to find out by accident. Alas, the same was not true of their seven closest friends, or at least, the six who didn't yet know.

So, should they tell them all at the same time? This was Kris's first suggestion, and on the surface it seemed a good one. It would mean not having to repeat themselves over and again, and no awkward questions about their living arrangements. The big downfall to this approach, aside from Dan and Andy's absence, was that there were some who needed to know before others; Adele was Shaunna's best friend, and would feel dreadfully betrayed if she didn't hear the news first. And then there was Eleanor, who would instantly go into a panic about the wedding and the cabin bookings for next week. In conclusion, telling everyone at once was a bad idea.

By this point in the conversation, Casper was exhausted, but would happily have continued fetching the Frisbee for as long as someone threw it for him to fetch. However, they'd been walking for almost two hours, thus had a return leg of the same duration still ahead of them, and by the time they arrived home, everything was sorted out. They were going to give the dog a quick shower to get rid of the sand, have lunch with Krissi and tell her, go and see Adele, and then Eleanor, and leave everyone else until tomorrow. By Tuesday, they would all know, giving them a full three days to let it sink in before Eleanor's wedding.

As with all plans, it didn't go quite as they'd hoped.

Casper happily complied while Kris washed the sand out of his coat, and even shook before he was out of the bathroom. At the sound of Krissi arriving, he tore down the stairs and leapt at her, nearly knocking her right back out of the door, and into Jason, who was standing just behind her.

"Yuck. Couldn't you have warned me in your text?" she said, wiping the mix of water and dog saliva off her face. She took off her coat and kissed her mum's cheek.

"Sorry, hun." Shaunna was just finishing up with the salad and had already laid out the chicken and potato wedges.

"And he stinks," Krissi added, patting Casper's very wet head. "Doesn't he?" She addressed this question to Jason, who wouldn't have answered it even if he hadn't been preoccupied with trying to pick short, yellow hairs off his very black jacket and jeans.

"Err," he said and smiled weakly.

"Don't say things like that," Kris warned jokily as he came into the kitchen, his clothes completely soaked. "You know what your mum's like." Unfortunately, the warning came too late, because Shaunna had already abandoned the salad, the uncapped bottle of dressing discarded in favour of a handful of lit incense sticks, which she positioned in the holders placed here and there around the downstairs rooms. She returned, unceremoniously tipped the dressing over the salad, gave the bowl a shake and dumped it on the table.

"He doesn't smell that bad really, Mum," Krissi said apologetically, then coughed, largely for effect, although the incense was sending out quite a lot of smoke.

"It's too late. You've said it now," Shaunna snapped and sat down opposite her daughter. Krissi looked to Kris, who gave her a wink to indicate that the curtness was not directed at her.

"This looks yummy," she tried.

"Help yourself," Shaunna said. "You too, Jason. Dig in. You still look like you need feeding up. Don't you eat?"

"Yeah, I do…" he began.

"Like, chips and crisps and the odd apple, if you can be

151

bothered," Krissi interrupted.

"That's so not true," he protested.

"It so is," she argued.

"Anyway," Kris interjected. It was all done in fun, but there were more serious matters to attend to. "Clearly we didn't just decide to invite you to lunch for the sake of it."

"Oh, thanks!"

"Like you've ever needed a formal invitation before!"

"So why did you invite us? I assumed it was us? Not just me?" She looked worried.

"Jason, you are more than welcome," Shaunna assured them. She was glad that Kris had taken the lead and was feeling a bit less stressed about the whole situation.

"Thanks, Mrs. Johansson," he mumbled. He took the smallest piece of chicken and a tiny scoop of potato wedges and positioned them carefully on his plate.

"That's why you never eat. You spend so long trying to make it look like a work of art," Krissi said, watching him push the wedges into an arc with his fork. He ignored her and picked up the outermost wedge, chewing on it and repositioning the others at the same time. Krissi tutted and turned her attention to her own food. "Anyway, you were saying?"

"Err, yeah," Kris said, suddenly nervous, now he was being put on the spot. "The thing is..." He picked up some salad and carefully carried it to his plate. "Me and your mum..." He made a big fuss out of selecting a piece of chicken. "What I'm trying to say is..." He did the same with the wedges, almost replicating Jason's earlier behaviour.

"We're not together anymore," Shaunna finished for him. She waited, watching her daughter's face for a reaction. None was forthcoming.

"Right?" Krissi said, expecting more.

"That's it, really. We thought we should tell you."

"Oh. OK. I thought it was going to be something serious, like Grandad was sick, or something."

"It is serious!" Shaunna said crossly.

"I didn't mean it wasn't serious, did I?"

"What did you mean?" Kris asked. This was not the response either of them had predicted when they were talking about it on the beach.

"I mean, I knew. We knew, didn't we, Jason?" She nudged him. He nodded and busied himself with cutting a tiny morsel of chicken from the portion on his plate. The knife slipped and the smaller piece flew off the table, right into the mouth of the waiting Labrador.

"Nice catch, Casper!" Krissi said. "So yeah. All that nonsense about clearing out your wardrobes. Pfft!"

"And you're all right about it?" Kris asked.

"Don't be soppy. Of course I am. I'm a big girl now and it's not like I have to put up with the pair of you trying to keep out of each other's way, is it? You got a boyfriend yet, then?"

Kris was in the process of swallowing a slice of tomato and had to gulp it down before he'd chewed it, almost choking himself by doing so.

"Krissi!' Shaunna shouted. She couldn't think of anything else to say, but it was enough for her daughter to realise that she had overstepped the mark. She played with her food, feeling very foolish in the long silence that followed, eventually broken by Kris as soon as it looked like they were all finished with their meal.

"Anyone for dessert? We have chocolate fudge cake…"

"No, we don't. We ate it last week," Shaunna reminded him.

"We don't have chocolate fudge cake, but we do have apple pie and ice-cream."

"Sounds good to me," Jason said, momentarily forgetting his usual sullen disposition, but reverting just as quickly. Krissi tutted again.

"Me too," she said. Kris looked to Shaunna, who confirmed with a nod that she'd have some and started to clear the table. So that was the first revelation over and done with. Next: to tell Adele.

It hadn't really been that late when they'd left the reunion party the night before, but it was too late for Alice to go home, so she'd stayed over, gone home to feed Albert, and then come back again to watch an old black and white movie. It was something they had taken to doing whenever Dan was working away—a bit of light relief from looking after a very active toddler who refused to nap until early evening, and something Adele was surprised to find she enjoyed immensely. When Shaunna rang the doorbell, it was just coming to the big finale, and Adele scowled at her without saying a word. Shaunna glanced at Kris, and they stepped inside, observing the scene before them and hanging back to attend to the koi pool, in the absence of any other occupation.

"She didn't say she had company," Shaunna whispered.

"What do we do? Leave it until tomorrow?"

"No. Let's go and see Ellie and try again this evening." She tiptoed over to Adele. "We'll come back later," she whispered.

"What?" Adele said, without taking her eyes from the TV.

"We'll come back later," Shaunna repeated more loudly.

"OK," Adele replied absently, leaving them to let themselves out.

"I could murder a double vodka right now," Kris said, as they walked back down the road to catch the bus to Eleanor's apartment.

"Ugh. Not sure I could," Shaunna grimaced. "I'm absolutely knackered. I reckon we've walked about ten miles today."

"Yeah. Pretty close to it."

Fortunately they timed their arrival at the bus stop perfectly, and flopped into the nearest seats, physically and emotionally drained. They all lived relatively close to each other, so they were at Eleanor's front door within fifteen minutes, and could hear from outside that somebody was screaming. It turned out to be Oliver, having his second tantrum of the day, and all because James asked him to get a nappy from the bedroom.

"Ignore the shrieking child," Eleanor said, sending them through to the lounge, right past Oliver. Shaunna and Kris did as they were told, and perched uneasily on the edge of the sofa. James finished putting a clean nappy on Toby, picked him up and looked around.

"Here. I'd love to hold him," Shaunna offered. James passed the baby to her and she settled back into the sofa, taking the bottle of milk Eleanor brought a moment later: she had considerably more experience than the pair of them, and Toby settled happily into his feed.

"You should visit more often," Eleanor remarked, for Oliver had also quietened down, and was standing in the doorway, waiting to be allowed to return. This was the rule that James had imposed: if he was upset, he was to go and be on his own until he was no longer upset. It wasn't working.

"Come back now, Enna?" he asked, sniffling.

"Yes, Oliver. Get a tissue and wipe your nose." He did as she told him and stood next to Kris, examining his hair. It was light brown with blonde highlights, which probably seemed quite strange to Oliver, with his black curly hair. Eleanor's hair was also dark in colour, and Oliver couldn't help but stare. Kris smiled at him and he smiled back.

"Yep. You should definitely visit more often," Eleanor repeated.

"You might change your mind when we tell you why we've come," Shaunna said. Feeding the baby was making her feel relaxed and in control, and she was ready to do the talking this time around.

"Sounds ominous. Should I sit down for this?"

"Probably."

She shrugged and sat in the armchair. James finished clearing the baby changing equipment away and left the room.

"You don't have to leave on our account," Kris called after him.

"I am quite sure you would rather I did," he said and continued on his way. Eleanor examined both of her friends, trying to second-guess what they were about to tell her.

"Please don't say you can't come to the wedding. Not when

Dan and Andy won't be there either."

"God, no. We wouldn't miss it for the world!" Shaunna reassured her. "And before I go any further, it won't make any difference to the arrangements for the holiday, so don't worry about a thing. That's why we wanted to tell you now."

"OK," Eleanor said, relieved, her curiosity taking over.

"Kris and I decided to separate last Christmas," Shaunna told her.

"I'm sorry." It was an automatic response.

"Don't be. It's all OK between us, but it wasn't working out. We're still sharing the house. The only thing that's really changed is that we don't share the same bed."

"Lots of couples do that these days, don't they? Have their own bedrooms, I mean?" Eleanor was a little out of her depth with this. If it had been a patient telling her the same news, she'd have coped perfectly.

"They probably do, but we're not actually a couple anymore. We might even get divorced some day, but there's no rush. We're quite content with things the way they are for now." Shaunna shifted forward so that she could wind Toby. "As I said. It makes no difference to any of your wedding or honeymoon plans, but we thought we should tell you before you found out another way."

"Last night," Eleanor looked at Kris as she spoke, "Josh said he saw you and George together."

"Yeah. That's what we were worried about. Or at least, I didn't know Josh saw us, but thought someone probably did and might say something, although that was just a spur of the moment thing. Me and George aren't 'together'. He does know about this, though."

"But he hasn't told Josh?"

"No. I asked him not to."

"Ah. That makes sense. You know the way he stresses out when he thinks any of us is going to get hurt. He'll probably be relieved to know the truth."

"Are you OK with it, Ellie?" Shaunna asked. Toby had

sicked up on her hand, but she just took a tissue from her friend and cleaned it up without any fuss.

"You're a real professional, do you know that?" Eleanor laughed. "Yeah, I'm fine. I was a bit shocked at first, but you've never really had a conventional relationship, so I guess you're not about to start having one now. And a good thing it is too. I'd hate to be the only one acting inappropriately for my age."

"I wonder if we'll ever grow up?" Kris mused.

"I hope not," Eleanor said sincerely. "Although it suddenly hit me the other day that Andy's going to be forty next year."

"Don't remind me," Shaunna groaned. "I'm already feeling old. And at least there's no chance of you suddenly becoming a grandmother any time soon."

"Krissi's not..."

"She's not pregnant, no, but you never know. She and Jason have been living together for ages now, and they've been friends since high school."

"That doesn't mean they're about to start a family," Kris reasoned.

"As I say, you never know."

"It sounds like us lot," Eleanor observed, "friends since high school, which is no excuse for rudeness. I'm sorry; I forgot to ask if you'd like a cup of tea, or coffee."

"No, thanks. We've got to go and see Adele. We went there first, but she was watching an old film with Alice, so we thought we'd come and tell you." Shaunna shuffled forward and passed Toby to his mother.

"I got to be first. Yay! I do feel important, but I won't mention it to Adele. Good luck!"

"Thanks. We'll need it." Shaunna hugged her around the baby. "And if you need a hand with anything, just give me a shout."

"We should be all good to go, but thank you." She gave Kris a hug and waved them off. "So..."

She closed the door and turned to James.

"What do you think of that, Mr. Eavesdropper?"

157

She knew he'd been standing in the hallway the whole time and had heard every word. Interestingly, he had nothing to say, and nor, for once, did Oliver.

By the time they arrived back at Adele's, she was alone and reading a magazine, looking quite comfortable in her pyjamas and very much not in the mood for company. Nevertheless, she let them in and offered them a cup of tea. They both refused, having agreed on the way there that actually a double vodka (or equivalent) was definitely on the cards, just as soon as they'd done the deed. They'd also agreed that Kris was going to start off this time, because Shaunna was terrified of how her friend was going to react, knowing her the way she did.

"Shaunna asked me to explain what's going on, because she's a bit upset about it," he began. This was part of their planned strategy.

"Oh dear. What's the matter, sweetie?" Adele simpered and knelt on the floor in front of her friend, blinking up meaningfully. Shaunna closed her eyes and covered her face, hoping that her desperate attempt not to laugh would be misinterpreted as crying. It appeared to be working, as Adele was now smoothing her arm.

"Last year, I did a really stupid, selfish thing," Kris continued. This was the part he wasn't too happy to admit, and they hadn't intended to tell anyone, never mind Adele, whose propensity for gossip would see it spreading around their friends in record time. But he was doing it for Shaunna, he reminded himself, and took a deep breath. "I had an affair."

Adele gasped in horror.

"With a married man."

Adele gasped again.

"And Shaunna found out and threatened to tell everyone what I'd done."

"You'd deserve it too. That's despicable."

"But I'm so ashamed," Shaunna mumbled incoherently through her hands.

"Why are you ashamed? You didn't have the affair. *He* did. I can't believe you could be so..."

"Selfish and stupid. I know. But I was. I am. I hurt Shaunna and I love her so much."

"How can I trust you anymore?" Shaunna wailed from behind her hands. Adele pulled her close and Kris turned away, struggling to contain himself. He was somewhere between laughing and crying, for what he was saying was true, but they'd been through it all and rebuilt their friendship. Everything was how it would have been if he'd been honest with Shaunna from the very start.

"It's OK. There, there," Adele comforted.

"We're going to stay together for now. In the house," he explained sorrowfully, "and maybe one day, if Shaunna ever learns to trust me again, we might try and make it work like it used to."

Adele scowled at him, then lifted Shaunna's chin with her finger. "Is that what you want, sweetie?" she asked. Shaunna nodded. "Then I'll be here for you."

"I'm sorry. I can't take this anymore," Kris said, and ran from the room. The front door slammed a second later.

"I've got to go after him," Shaunna cried, still through her hands.

"You can stay here if you want. Dan won't be home until next weekend, and I'm sure we can fix up something, just as soon as we get back from Wales."

"Thank you, Adele. You're such an amazing friend." Shaunna hoped she could carry this off long enough to hug her and leave. She accomplished the hug, and slowly walked to the door, her face turned downwards, occasionally affecting a sob. "I'll phone you in the week," she offered as her parting words.

"OK, sweetie. You know where I am," Adele replied, giving her friend a final hug, and watching her trudge down the path and onto the pavement.

"For God's sake, shut the door already," Shaunna muttered through gritted teeth. The door closed and she picked up her pace, meeting Kris at the corner of the road.

"And the award for Best Actress in a Leading Role goes to…" he said. They high-fived each other and burst into fits of laughter.

"Right. Which way to the nearest pub?"

CHAPTER EIGHTEEN

Kris had phoned George to give him permission to tell Josh, and after carrying the secret for nine months, he was eager to share. Indeed, he would have done so immediately, but for one not so minor problem: Josh wasn't talking to him, which is to say, he wasn't ignoring him entirely, but since Saturday night, their conversations had consisted of George saying something and Josh responding with, at best, a singular word, more often a shrug and sometimes a nod. For instance, to the question "Would you like a cup of coffee?", he generally found it in himself to nod in agreement, whereas "What's the matter?" resulted in a shrug, and "Are you OK?" usually deserved an utterance in the affirmative, even though he clearly wasn't. George had no idea what he had done to upset him, or even if that was what was wrong, but one thing was for sure: it was the first time ever he was glad to be going to the prison for the day, in spite of Sophie's suggestion that he just email to tell them that he wasn't going back. So off he went, on a train journey with three changes, followed by a bus that stopped half a mile up the road, relieved that it was the very last time he'd be doing it, whilst appreciating the opportunity to try and figure out why Josh was being the way he was. He couldn't help thinking that, if anything, it should be the other way around. For now, though, there was the more pressing matter of getting himself out of jail.

Thus, George's tactic with the prison psychologist was to tell her that he'd had a change of heart and didn't want to work with offenders after all, which was true, although it was her attitude towards him that had led to this realisation and he was well aware of the possibility that with a different placement he might find he'd made the right choice to begin with. Her response only cemented his certainty that it was the correct decision; she knew he didn't have it in him, she said, and he'd had it fairly easy. Well, he thought, if being dumped with your friend's psychotic ex-husband, a man with an addiction to cottaging and a group of eighteen year olds, each with a list of GBH convictions too long to fit on one A4 printout, was 'having it fairly easy', then she was right. She granted him permission to finish off his paperwork and leave straight away, making him feel like one of the offenders they treated when she took him to hand in his ID badge and other paraphernalia.

Back on the bus, three trains, and home again, unsure how he was going to pass the rest of the day, his thoughts constantly switching between the obnoxious cow at the prison and Josh's current mood. What he didn't expect to find was that Josh hadn't gone to work at all. Instead, he was sitting on the sofa, reading an old hardback book and sipping at a very large cup of coffee. George stood in the doorway and watched him. He was trying hard not to pay attention, but it was utterly pointless trying to fool George, of all people.

"Are you ever going to tell me what's wrong?"

Josh shrugged but said nothing.

"Agh! What's the fucking point?" George stormed upstairs, slamming his door, and not for effect. Josh lifted his head and stared at where he'd been, then closed his eyes. A few more crashes and bangs, George came back downstairs and went straight out again. Josh threw his book across the room, followed by his coffee cup.

Several hours later, when George returned from his sitting alone in the library until they told him to leave, he couldn't believe his eyes.

"Why are you doing that?"

"I don't like it," Josh replied.

"My God! Four words. In one sentence!" He took his bag upstairs, pausing in his room as he tried to decide whether he should just stay where he was and forego food, or risk yet another rebuttal. He was too hungry.

"You eaten?"

"No."

"D'you want something to eat?"

"Do you normally ask?"

"No, but the way you're acting, I just don't know what to do for the best."

Josh grunted.

"So. Shall I make something for both of us?"

"If it wouldn't be too much trouble," Josh responded indifferently and waited until George was out of sight before continuing up the wall with the scraper. He didn't really hate the paper that much, although having the same as Sean Tierney didn't sit too well, but that wasn't why he was taking it down. The coffee came out of the carpet fairly easily, but the lighter parts of the wallpaper pattern were completely ruined. It was an outrageous act, which surprised him; he didn't lose his temper, ever, and it was just as well, because making a habit of it could turn out to be very expensive. Luckily, the coffee had only hit the one wall, and he'd been thinking about replacing the paper anyway, so the other three, which weren't the same as Tierney's, as far as he knew, could stay just as they were for now. In the kitchen, the sound of pans colliding heavily with the hob signified that he wasn't the only one who was feeling it, and that helped tremendously. It was George who had done this to him, so why shouldn't he suffer too?

They sat in silence for the rest of the evening, both picking at their meal, and Josh taking the plates to the sink, although not trusting himself to wash them, for fear that a fork might accidentally fall out of the cutlery drainer, or some other such irritation that in the general scheme of things would remain just that, but right now had the potential to wreak considerable damage. He hated feeling like this: he was used to being in control of his emotions, but he was so wound up that even if he did want to tell George why, he wouldn't have been able to do so. He collected his book from the lounge and went upstairs; a minute or so later he came back down with a box, took it out to the car, and repeated this action once more before he stayed upstairs for good. All the while, George had pretended to be watching TV, waiting until it was safe to go to bed himself.

The next morning there was more of the same, both recognising that they had just hours to reach some sort of truce, before James's stag night. Neither of them was especially looking forward to an evening in a jazz bar with all of Eleanor's male relatives and James. With this breakdown in communication, it was going from bad to worse. However, as George predicted, seeing as Eleanor was Josh's best friend (he was sick of hearing this phrase), he finally took it upon himself to break the silence.

"I will tell you what's pissed me off at some point," he started, "but for now we just have to make the best of it."

"Well that's not going to work, is it?"

"Why shouldn't it? You only need to know that I'm angry, and it's because of something you did. I'm sure it will come to you if you think about it hard enough, and if it doesn't, then that merely serves to illustrate that I'm right to be angry."

"Come again?"

"No. Figure it out for yourself," Josh said tersely. He was dressed for work and left soon after. George washed up from the previous night's meal, even though that wasn't how it was supposed to be, and threw himself into the vacuuming (for the sake of something to do) and deep contemplation. A few hours on and all he had to show for it were the most spotlessly clean carpets in the western hemisphere and a headache. There was, he thought, one person who would know, if anyone did, what was the matter with Josh, and much as he didn't want to bother her with anything so 'trivial' at the present time, he didn't see as he had any choice. He gave Eleanor a quick call to ensure she was in, and headed straight round, using the walk there to formulate a means of working the problem into a rundown of the arrangements for the rest of the week. This turned out to be a very useful approach, as she didn't seem to pick up on how terrible things really were, for he presented Josh's bad mood as part of a more general narrative of how he was avoiding him by tidying his room, or decorating, or drawing up cleaning rotas, speculating that it was because he was worrying about the wedding. She listened to everything he had to say, whilst folding tiny clothes and adding them to a precarious pile that toppled several times during his oration. She just picked them up, folded them again and continued to listen. At the end, she filled the kettle, led him to the lounge and sat him down.

"You need to stay out of the way for a while," she said. "Have a coffee with me, go home, get your stuff for tonight and come back."

"Oh, it's not that serious. Is it?"

"Probably not. As you say, he's most likely just stressing about the wedding, and he hasn't said anything to me about you upsetting him." She left the room to make the coffee and called back from the kitchen: "There's nothing I can really think of that you've done wrong." She came back with the cups. "I mean, he did see you with Kris on Saturday night, but we were more worried for Shaunna than anything else. We didn't know about them not being together anymore, of course."

"And Josh still doesn't know. Kris said I could tell him, but the opportunity hasn't actually presented itself, seeing as he's not talking to me. Worse than that, I've known since it first happened."

"Yeah, Kris told me that."

"So what did he say, Josh, I mean? About Kris and me?"

"Nothing much. Well, nothing at all really."

"Maybe not that then. Ah, man! Why can't he just tell me what's up?"

"Because that's the way he is."

They sat and drank their coffee in silence; James had taken Oliver to the park and Toby was fast asleep. It was wonderfully peaceful and quite possibly the best thing about being friends for so long; being able to sit and share each other's company without needing to talk just for the sake of it.

165

"This is all wrong," George said after ten minutes or more of listening to only the sound of the baby monitor's occasional click, or Toby squeaking in his sleep. "Why aren't you in your usual pre-function frenzy? You'd normally be racing about like a headless chicken and fretting that nothing was getting done. Shouldn't we all have tasks assigned and be telling you to chill out every five seconds?"

"Well, the thing is, that description you just gave? Let's just say I'm my mother's daughter and if you were to go round there right now, my dad and brothers would be tearing their hair out, while she barks orders at them, like a crazed sergeant major."

"Right, so everything's in hand then?"

"If my mother's in charge it's more than in hand, I guarantee it."

George nodded his understanding and finished the remainder of his coffee.

"Are you coming back?" Eleanor asked.

"Yeah. Not sure why you think it's necessary, but I would rather keep out of his way."

"All I'm saying is the way he storms off when he and Dan fall out is only a teeny, tiny taster—ask that lecturer of yours. He's been here, done this, got the t-shirt and the leather elbow patches."

"Sean?"

Eleanor raised an eyebrow.

"Oh really? Tell me more."

"I don't really know anything more than that. Josh turned up in Newcastle once, totally unannounced and in an unbelievably foul mood. He wasn't exactly up for sharing, either. In fact, he hardly said a word to me the whole time. Sean arrived a couple of days later and they had one hell of a fight—not fisticuffs, obviously, although I did have to intervene on behalf of my flatmates—but they went home together afterwards, so I guess they must've sorted things out."

George frowned thoughtfully. This sounded like it might have been the start of the on-going dispute between Josh and

Sean, and probably wasn't relevant to *his* current predicament, other than to demonstrate the lengths to which Josh would go in order to avoid confronting a problem. Nonetheless, he was still curious.

"And you've no idea what it was over?" he asked.

"None at all. I wasn't allowed to mention it, but I think Josh just needed some space." George looked worried and Eleanor patted his arm. "Look, I'm sure it'll pass, eventually. A bit like really bad constipation." She grinned.

"And on that beautiful analogy, I'm going. See you in a bit."

Josh was still at work, so the coast was clear for George to grab his things and go straight back out, but he needed to know more about what Eleanor had told him. In fact, by the time he reached the house, the need was so great that he did something he'd never done before: he went into Josh's bedroom.

It was an alien place to him and he looked around, trying to decide where he would be most likely to hide any keepsakes. The room was light and airy, with plain walls, curtains and carpet, all in the same shade of pale cream, with very little in the way of furniture: a double bed, a small bedside cabinet with a lamp, clock and a book, a bedding chest, a wall mirror and a shelf lined with bottles of aftershave and deodorant. Fitted wardrobes extended along one wall, with lift-up flaps above them; George opened each in turn, standing on tiptoes to peer inside. Most contained jumpers, folded neatly and piled one on top of the other. He pushed a hand in amongst them to see if there was anything concealed behind or within, but came up with nothing every time. Likewise, the wardrobes underneath contained only what one would expect, although the end cupboard was stacked with ancient psychology journals, and he lifted a couple from the top of the pile: they were copies of the *International Journal of Psycho-Analysis* dating back to the 1920s and probably worth a fortune. He carefully put them back, closed the door and pivoted to face the other way, biting his lip thoughtfully. The only other storage space in the room was the ottoman, which seemed too obvious a place to look, but he decided to do so anyway. It was locked and there was no key.

Now, at this stage, the right thing to do would be to leave well alone. He'd already trespassed into Josh's personal space, whilst fully aware of what a privilege had been bestowed on him to be invited to share the house. Josh was very private and did everything he could to stay that way, sometimes to an almost extreme level. He wasn't, for instance, the sort of person one might catch making a towel-clad dash back from the bathroom, not even when home alone; nor, as George had often found to his cost, did he appreciate personal belongings being left lying around shared spaces. So the right and most respectful thing to do was to leave the room exactly as he'd found it and never set foot in there again.

What George did instead was take out his keys and try them in the lock. None of them came close, so he searched the room again. He knew his friend well enough to also know that he was bound to have a spare key somewhere, but discerning precisely where that might be would take precious time he didn't have. By now he was so obsessed that common sense was little more than a distant voice calling out to him to stop what he was doing. He needed to know what was inside that chest. He returned to his own room, took a hanger from the wardrobe and unbent the hook on his way back. He didn't really have a clue what he was doing, but had been led to believe that a straightened length of wire could break most locks. Unbelievably, it yielded straight away, and he soon found out why. It wasn't a proper lock, but a catch, which lifted when pressed, presumably because most bedding chests contain just that. This one was, on the surface, no different, with a few duvet sets and a pair of cushions at the top. George lifted the cushions free and peered into the space below.

This was what he'd been looking for: the letters, photographs, diaries—all the personal effects that might finally tell him what he needed to know. For it was no longer just about understanding how he had upset Josh. They'd been working and living together for the best part of a year, in almost every sense a couple. He had always worshipped him and always would, but he kept himself closed off—from everyone. OK, so he would freely tell them all that he loved them, and could positively gush with gratitude if he felt it appropriate, but the real, underlying emotions were carefully managed and contained, like the contents of the ottoman, and his current bad temper was only the second time ever that George had seen him on the brink of losing that control, the other being due to extreme sleep deprivation and stress. The mere existence of these photos and letters indicated he did care far more deeply than he was prepared to admit to his friends, but at this moment, what George wanted to know above all else, was what had happened between Josh and Sean. For now, though, the chance was lost, as Josh was due home any second, and a car had just pulled up outside. George quickly replaced the bedding and lowered the lid, quietly slipping out of the room and back into his own as the front door opened and closed again. He could feel his heart pounding and tried to steady his breathing, listening to the sound of keys being set down, the click of the kettle being turned on, all amplified above their usual volume by the excitement of almost being caught in the act. Josh came upstairs, and stopped on the landing.

"George?"

He panicked. He was supposed to have returned to Eleanor to avoid this happening. What was he afraid of exactly? This was Josh, after all. George cleared his throat and opened his door, feigning a stretch.

"Hi."

"We need to be ready by seven," Josh informed him. "OK?"

"Yeah. Cool."

Josh nodded and went back downstairs. George quickly grabbed his bag of clothes and made a dash for it.

"I've got to go and see Ellie. I'll meet you there," he said and disappeared out of the front door. Josh carried on making his coffee. He'd expected George to have gone somewhere else to get ready and was surprised to find him home, but he wasn't going to think about it. During the course of the day, he'd been able to gradually suppress his anger, and whether George was there or not, he was bloody well going to enjoy James's stag night.

George was halfway between home and Eleanor's apartment when she phoned to warn him that James's mother and father had arrived unannounced, his father apparently having decided that he would like to go out with his son before his impending matrimony. He got the impression that what she was really saying was that he would be best not to come at all, if that were possible, so now he was really stuck. He couldn't go back to the house when he'd fled so hastily, and a quick return call to Eleanor confirmed his interpretation, so he headed for the only other place he could think to go: Kris and Shaunna's.

"You know what I was telling you on Saturday night?" George said by way of a greeting when Kris answered the door. "Well, it may have come to a head already. Can I get changed here?"

"Sure," Kris stepped aside to let him pass. "You can use my room. You know where the bathroom is. Use whatever you need."

"Thanks." George dashed up the stairs. He had less than an hour to get ready and make his way to the jazz club.

Back at home, Josh was taking his time, and not because he was enjoying the chance to get ready in peace. His usual trick of redirecting wasn't working and as a consequence he was so wound up that anything even remotely energetic was sending him into such an agitated state that he daren't risk it. He sat and drank his coffee, checking the time every so often and trying to ignore the blank wall. Half an hour left; he needed to shower and change. Surely even he could do it in that amount of time? He plodded to the kitchen and rinsed his cup, then up to the bathroom to turn on the shower, and to the bedroom. On the floor, to the right of the ottoman, was a cushion. The vision turned him statuesque, as there only two possible explanations for it being there. The first was that he'd left it out the previous night; the second, and this was not his favourite by a long shot, was that George had been through his things.

The possibility made him cold inside, but not angry. Perhaps it was simply that he couldn't get any more angry than he already was, or that he had no grounds to complain, given he had done the same thing himself a few days ago. So now they were even. Josh knew George's secrets and he knew his. That might make it easier to resolve the matter once and for all. He picked up the cushion and put it on top of the ottoman, too little time to go and get his keys, when the shower was running and he only had twenty minutes left.

There again, he mused as he left the house precisely twenty minutes later, a little adrenaline can go an awful long way. He climbed into the pre-booked taxi and arrived at the jazz club with ten minutes to spare. None of the others were there, so he bought a bottle of beer and perched on a bar stool, allowing the music to wash over him, like cool rain on a hot summer's day. He was feeling much calmer, and only experienced a minor surge of annoyance when George came over.

"You were quick," he said, taking the next stool along.

"Yes. I should get angry more often."

"Hmm. Perhaps not."

George ordered a beer and they sat, intermittently sipping at their bottles while listening to the female vocalist and pianist creating the low-key jazz backdrop. It was faked, the listening, a convenient excuse not to speak to each other. The singing was soulful, the singer a small, dark-haired woman whose voice rose from her abdomen in waves, each note urging on the previous, as it flowed out across the room. There was nothing wrong with the music; it was beautiful, but that sustained sense of control in the singer's voice, as if she were holding back an almighty yell, mirrored George and Josh's situation so closely that it was almost painful. James and his father made a timely arrival, closely followed by Eleanor's father, uncle and brothers, but it was the two Browns who initially drew their attention and they were pleased for the distraction. Mr. Brown senior was a glimpse into James's future; greying hair in an identical cut, the same squared chin and deep brown-black eye colour. They were both dressed in what they considered to be casual attire, and here again the choices they made were strikingly similar. As the Davenport men ordered drinks, Josh and George switched to watching them, noting the tiniest, most subtle hints of their friend seeping through the interactions of her male kin. Josh had met them all and knew Mr. Davenport senior very well, so had no problem identifying which of the twin brothers was Eleanor's father, although George was struggling.

"Until you spot the more obvious differences, I'll give you a clue. Ellie's dad's wearing the black sweater," Josh told him.

"And their clothes are not a more obvious difference?"

"At the moment, maybe. You'll see what I mean."

James passed a tumbler to his father and indicated to an area in the corner of the room where there was enough space for their group to sit or stand. His father held back, waiting for James to make his way around the rest of the men, greeting each and pointing to the free tables, and so they all assumed their various positions for the evening, George and Josh taking the two chairs opposite one sofa, Eleanor's brothers Ben and Luke taking the next two along, while her dad and her uncle shared a sofa with second youngest brother, Ed (or Teddy, as his family insisted on calling him). Peter, the youngest Davenport, sat next to James, whereas Mr. Brown chose to stand for the time being. George thought it might be to avoid sitting too close to other people and immediately offered his chair; Mr. Brown brushed the offer aside, although not in an ungrateful way.

"Too many hours sitting in the car," he explained briefly, "but thank you." He almost smiled.

A muted round of applause signalled a changeover of musicians, with this particular ensemble having been at James's request, and consisting of a drummer, sax player, bass guitarist and the same pianist as before. With the exception of the saxophonist, the band were all older men, which somewhat depleted George's optimism that things might pep up. If he'd been feeling a little out of place at the reunion, then he was positively irreconcilable now. He barely knew any of these people, and as the band started to play their first number, Josh moved over to the sofa to chat to James.

"Well isn't this the best fun I've had in ages," George muttered under his breath. Even Mr. Brown senior was absorbed in the music, leaving him feeling very alone. So much for having a hangover on Wednesday, he thought. He downed his beer and went off to the bar to buy another, choosing to stay there for the time being. He took out his phone and sent a text message to Kris: "Wish you were here."

A few seconds later, the reply came: "Is it awful?"

He sent back: "Feel like a fish out of water - again!"

Kris had been invited too, but had declined the invitation, and his next message simply reiterated why. "I think James only invited me out of politeness. I don't really know him that well. Drink more beer!"

"Ha ha! I intend to. Speak later."

George put his phone away and watched Josh and James from afar. They were engaged in quite a heavy conversation, as far as he could tell, leaning in to each other to talk or listen, whilst keeping their eyes focused on the band. Brief applause, followed by the drummer clicking his sticks together, and into a slightly more up-tempo number. Mr. Brown senior came over and took the stool next to George.

"This is not your sort of music, I take it?"

"Not really. It's very good though."

"I agree, though I prefer classical music myself."

"I'm more a dance music man."

"By this, you mean modern dance music?"

"Yeah, but not that dreadful racket they play on the radio these days."

"That is an appalling noise, I quite agree." Mr. Brown held up his empty glass by way of indicating his requirement for a refill; it was a request that was immediately met. He ordered a bottle of beer and passed it to George. "We should return with our drinks and imagine that we are enjoying the evening," he said. His tone was stern, yet conveyed his sympathy.

"Thank you," George replied, taking the beer and following Mr. Brown back to their tables. He was right; this was James's night and he was being inconsiderate. To redress the situation, he honed in on the only other person who looked like they were hating every minute.

"Hi, Peter. How's it going?"

"Not too bad."

"Finished uni?"

"Yeah, last year. Just trying to find a decent job now. At the moment I'm working for the council, at the recycling centre."

"What's your degree in?"

"Environmental science."

"Oh well. At least it's relevant!" George joked. Peter laughed.

"That's what people keep telling me. It's a job, I suppose."

That brought the conversation to a close, for George could think of nothing else to say, or nothing he could actually say, as he knew Peter was also gay and with a couple of drinks inside him, the urge to tell him to stop living a lie was on the brink of getting the better of him. Seeing the damage it had done to Kris, not to mention the trauma he'd put himself through at the reunion, gave him a sense of being qualified to pass comment, but then he could also, even at this level of moderate inebriation, appreciate that Mrs. Davenport would not cope well with the revelation of her youngest son's sexuality.

More applause and the band began another number; James stood up, ready to go and replenish his drink, only to be greeted by a chorus of offers. He looked most disconcerted.

"You're the groom. You're not supposed to buy your own drinks on your stag night," Josh reprimanded him. He opened his mouth to protest, but Ben had been very quick off the mark and was already back at the table with a large glass of red wine. He passed it to his future brother-in-law.

"Sit," he said. James did as he was told. "And don't make me have to tell you again," Ben added with a wink.

"Just like Ellie," George laughed.

"Yes," Josh agreed. Eleanor and Ben were very different to look at, but their personalities, mannerisms and the way they spoke were almost identical.

"So, how's the talking job these days?" Ben asked Josh.

"Same as always," he responded, and off they went. George swigged at his beer and nodded to James across the table.

"Are you enjoying yourself?"

"Yes, thank you. I was very worried when you and Josh suggested a stag party. I have seen many men subjected to dreadful humiliation on these nights."

"Well, I promise you nothing like that is going to happen tonight," George said sincerely, then added: "Ellie would kill us."

"That is very true," James laughed. "I was just telling Josh about our young sax player over there." George turned to watch him for a moment. "He's just started studying music at university; a very talented young man with a natural ear."

"Yeah. He sounds pretty awesome, not that I know much about jazz."

"He was one of Alistair Campion's protégés. He started to get into trouble at school, although nothing too sinister: a couple of skirmishes with the police. They did the decent thing and sent him to Alistair, who loved the music more than I do. I daresay that is where my own passion for jazz originated."

"I never met Alistair Campion," George said thoughtfully, "but it sounds like his death was a loss to us all."

"Indeed," James agreed, momentarily absorbed by the grief of losing the man who had influenced him most in his life. He would have been here this evening; he was to have been his best man. "However, his few remaining assets are in good hands," he added with a hopeful smile.

"How so?"

"Jason Meyer, his son. He is quite exceptional and has many of his father's traits, including a keen eye for a business opportunity and a knack for persuading people to invest in his ideas."

"So Campion Holdings isn't defunct then?"

"It lives on as Campion Community Trust. Jason asked Dan and me to become trustees, and we, of course, accepted."

"Congratulations."

"Thank you. And now I must communicate with my father, or else he will wonder why he allowed my mother to talk him into driving up for this evening. Excuse me."

With that, James arose and carefully stepped around the low table, making his way over to his father, who actually looked quite content to be left alone. Josh and Ben were still engaged in a witty dialogue about various shared experiences over the years, while the other Davenports were ready to commence a not very well thought through drinking marathon. The Irish influence was strongest in Eleanor's uncle, who still lived in Dublin and had a fantastic, melodic accent; the more they drank and talked, the stronger Eleanor's dad's accent became too. They were on the stout by this point, although this bar served an American one, much to their vocalised dismay. Still, they were dauntless in their endeavour, and Eleanor's uncle now had Luke and Ed ready with pints in hands.

"Three, two, one, go!" The two lads tipped their drinks and glugged, black liquid trickling down their faces and necks. Luke finished first and slammed his empty glass on the table. Raucous cheers all round; now it was Ed versus his dad, apparently the rule being that the loser went through to the next heat. Poor Ed looked like he was about to throw up, but was putting a very brave face on things. The men stopped to applaud the band and Eleanor's dad signalled to George, inviting him to join them in their drinking game. He shook his head, happy to be only an observer. The band were taking a break, and the bartender put on some background music, turning it up a notch, evidently in an attempt to drown out the 'Stout Wars' taking place in their corner of the club.

"Is that alright for you?" A young male voice spoke and

George turned to find the sax player standing right behind him, a pint of lager in his hand. Condensation dripped off the glass onto George's shoulder and startled him. "Sorry about that, mate," the sax player said hurriedly. He looked as if he was expecting George to start a fight over it.

"Don't worry about it," he smiled. "You're doing a fantastic job, by the way."

"Yes, it's excellent, Phil," James said, shaking the sax player's hand. "Thank you for agreeing to play tonight."

"Thanks for asking me."

"This is George," James introduced him and he nodded an acknowledgement. "This is Phil, the young man I was telling you about."

"So, you're enjoying the music?" Phil asked.

"Yeah. It's great. I think you might want to crank it up a bit when you restart, though." George could only just hear himself above the current round in the drinking contest. Phil laughed.

"I'll have a chat with the lads and see what we can do," he said, and headed back across the club, stopping at the bar so James could buy him a drink, before returning to the stage. It would seem he was true to his word, for when the band started up again a few minutes later, they were much louder than previously and the best thing of all was that no-one seemed to mind. In fact, a few people were dancing, which was rare for this establishment on a Tuesday night. The party atmosphere was also bringing in extra customers, and the lone bartender was doing an excellent job, helped by most people drinking bottled beers and shorts that were quick to serve. It was only the Davenport louts making his job more difficult, with a dozen empty glasses cluttering the table next to them. George collected as many as he could carry and took them to the bar with him on his next trip. While he waited, he passed the time watching Eleanor's dad and uncle throw back what must have been something like their tenth pint. Now he could see what Josh meant: in spite of similar hair cuts and sharing the same build, height and facial features, they no longer looked identical to him. Having relied on the initial distinction of the black sweater to clearly identify who was who, he was now absolutely certain that he would never mistake one for the other again.

"See? I told you," Josh said, joining him at the bar.

"Yes, you did," George replied. It was the first time they'd spoken all evening and by now he'd had enough to drink to brave saying something. "Hey, I'm really, really sorry about Saturday."

"What about Saturday?"

"Me and Kris. I mean, if what we did hurt you, it wasn't..."

"That's not what this is about! And before you go any further, I know he and Shaunna have broken up, and that you knew from the outset but kept it to yourself, and it's nothing to do with that either."

"It isn't? Ellie told me you saw us together, and I thought..."

"Whatever you thought, or she thought, you're both wrong. Admittedly, I wasn't impressed that I only officially got to hear about the break-up courtesy of Adele, and I was even less impressed at the sight of the two of you slobbering all over each other, when, as far as everyone else was concerned, they were still having full marital relations. But you and Kris, well, you've always been like that."

"Not since we were at school, which was the only reason we ended up...doing that on Saturday."

"That's just it. The only difference between Saturday and any other time is that you and he kissed." George really didn't want Josh to publically broadcast his sexuality to the entire crowd of patrons standing at the bar, but he seemed ignorant to this, or didn't actually care. "What I'm talking about," he continued, "is the underlying desire to take it further."

George shook his head in disbelief. "So..." he lowered his voice to an angry hiss, "it's because you think we want to screw each other? What the hell difference does it make to you if we do?"

"None, really." Josh's reply was cool and dismissive.

"Well that's just great, isn't it?" George snapped angrily, but it was more to hide how hurt he was. "D'you know, I think I might just go and stay with my mum for a few days, until after the wedding, because we're getting nowhere and it isn't fair on Ellie and James."

"As you like. If you'd rather sleep on a couch than sort this out, then that's up to you."

"No. I wouldn't, but if you won't talk to me, then I don't see I have much choice really. And for the record, I do not want to have sex with Kris. Not then, not now, not ever."

"Whatever, George. Believe me, the pair of you are terrible when you're together. It's that 'first love' thing. You'll always have some hold over each other, but it doesn't necessarily mean anything. Anyway, thank you for apologising and coming clean. I guess I'll see you on Thursday."

Josh said no more and returned to the table, picking up the conversation with Ben right where they'd left off. George watched him until he could no longer bear to, and turned his attention back to the Davenports, the younger men in a far worse state than the last time he looked. There was only one thing for it, he realised, as he watched Luke throw back a pint of stout and stagger. The prospect of further snooping around Josh's bedroom was not one he relished, but somehow he had to get to the bottom of what was going on, find a way to get through to him before it was too late, and it seemed like the other option was probably the lesser of the two evils: he was going to have to talk to Sean Tierney.

CHAPTER NINETEEN

In a restaurant not so many streets away, Jess and Rob were having dinner. Their table, against the back wall and secluded by a well placed pillar, bore a candle, a single rose in a vase and two half-empty wine glasses. Jess had been telling him about a recent case, where the wife was having an affair and wanted out, but her husband refused to leave the jointly owned marital home. It was a dull and only vaguely pertinent story, but she was finding it so very difficult to converse tonight. In contrast, Rob was laid back yet receptive, listening attentively to all that she said.

"I'm sorry. I'm so boring," Jess laughed to hide her embarrassment.

"Not at all," he assured her and took her hand. "I've always found you…fascinating."

She blushed, but brashly held his gaze. "In what way?"

"Only in a good way."

"And yet you play so hard to get?" she remarked lightly. This followed from their parting in the early hours of Sunday morning, when she had invited him to stay the night. His refusal was all the more frustrating when they had remained physically close throughout the party and he was so very clearly aroused by her. She licked her lips—an unconscious gesture, which only registered a split second later—and quickly picked up her wine glass.

"There's no rush, is there?" He didn't want to put any pressure on her. She needed to be genuinely receptive to his advances.

"Well, you tell me. After all, you're the one with the potentially fatal heart condition. Was that why you went home on Saturday?"

"No," he laughed, "although I didn't think of that. It's not much of a turn-on, having a great hulk of a man collapse on you mid-climax."

"I'd be prepared to take that chance," Jess responded, surprised at her own boldness.

"All in good time." He lifted her hand and kissed it, his lips lingering against her skin and sending a thrill chasing around her entire body. "You need to decide what you want most."

"I know what I want most," she smiled; he returned it.

"You know what I'm talking about. If we are going to do anything about this, then it's only right to end your relationship with Andy first."

"We're just friends," she assured him again. This had been the recurring theme of the last fifteen years, but its importance was magnified by their renewed romantic involvement over the past few days. "Anything else we had is over."

"Are you sure about that?"

"I'm certain."

The waiter arrived with their main course, providing brief respite. When he left, Rob took her hand again and gazed into her eyes.

"You need time to work things through. I'm not prepared to share you, Jess."

"And why should you?" She withdrew her hand. He was driving her wild with this constant checking that he wasn't pushing her into something she'd regret later.

"Why don't we wait until after Eleanor's wedding?" he suggested.

"Because I don't think I can wait. I want you, Rob. I've wanted you since Saturday night. The only thing stopping this from happening is you." She picked up her fork and speared a floret of broccoli. "I'm ready for this," she continued, biting the top off the vegetable. "If you're not interested, just say so."

He watched her for a while, her expression purposeful and serious. Then he started to laugh.

"A woman who's prepared to proposition you with greenery stuck in her teeth isn't to be doubted, I suppose," he said. Jess immediately put down her fork and probed her teeth with her tongue. "And even pulling those ridiculous faces you are still sexy." He shook his head and began eating his own meal. They continued in silence, other than occasional requests to pass the salt or queries about filling glasses with wine. Afterwards, they chose two desserts that they both wanted to try so that they could share. Rob carefully positioned a morsel of cherry sorbet on his spoon and held it up towards her. She steadied his arm with a hand around the wrist, and closed her mouth around the entire bowl of the spoon, slowly withdrawing. He watched her closely, his knee finding hers beneath the table. She extended her leg and rubbed it up the inside of his thigh.

"So," she said, "are we still going to wait until after Ellie's wedding?"

"Like hell we are!" He threw down his spoon, the waiter's attention attracted by the clattering. It was unintentional, but served a useful purpose nonetheless. "Can I have the bill please?"

Two minutes later, Jess climbed onto the back of Rob's powerful bike and they roared off towards home. It was light again before they parted company.

George's mum was a very odd little Mancunian woman who wore rollers, all day every day, whether she was going out or not. Sometimes, if she had to pop to the supermarket, she'd just stick a hat over them, which made her look even more ridiculous and people would stare, but she wasn't bothered. She didn't believe in heat treatment and insisted it was the only way to control the frizziness that she had passed on to her only son. For all of this, she didn't stand out from any of the other women in the block of council flats, many of whom could, on occasion, be spotted chatting across iron-railed balconies, heads draped in hair nets, cigarettes drooping from corners of mouths, as they hung out their washing for the world to see, should it ever look their way. This was the last remaining tower block in the town and it seemed like the council had given up trying to re-house these retired housewives, instead choosing to wait for them to leave of their own accord, by hearse or otherwise.

She didn't have to live like this; it was her choice: yes, she was that stubborn. When George inherited the ranch from his father, his first thought was to sell it and buy them a house somewhere better, but his mum was having none of it. She didn't want "that filthy bastard's stinking fuckin' money", she said, uncaring that it was George's father she was talking about. And then she went out to 'fetch some cigs', scarf draped over rollers and off to 'the Paki shop'. He cringed with embarrassment every time she uttered those words, as she had just ten minutes before, when she bustled past and awoke him. George lifted his head and glanced at the old carriage clock on the cluttered mantelpiece.

"Why doesn't she buy a bloody new one?" he thought aloud. He tried to turn over so he could get his phone out of his jacket, which was just out of reach on the coffee table, next to an ashtray full of cigarette ends, but he couldn't move his legs.

"Come on, Monty." He nudged the small yet surprisingly heavy Westie with his leg. The dog grumbled, circled a couple of times and lay down again. George pulled his legs free and sat up. "Ooh. Headache."

Now, much as he'd had what could reasonably be described as 'a skinful' the night before, he was quite certain that the banging in his head was due to oxygen deprivation, in the smoky, nicotine-tinged living room of his mother's pokey, ninth floor flat. She didn't believe in opening windows, "too fuckin' chilly and a total waste of leccy". Even the poor dog was yellow. George sniffed the arm of his t-shirt, but he couldn't tell if it smelled of cigarettes or not. He went to put the kettle on, using the time it took to boil to visit the bathroom.

The bathroom: pristine, but so full of stuff you could hardly move without knocking a shampoo bottle or a loofah into the toilet bowl, so he stood with his legs together and his elbows in, carefully aiming his shot ("Fuckin' men, are you all fuckin' blind, or what?") and wondering what he was going to do about the lack of toothbrush. He spotted a bottle of mouthwash, flushed the toilet and gave himself a quick spruce with cold water ("Don't you touch that fuckin' immersion switch, or else."), swooshed his mouth with the absurdly strong, green liquid, and arrived back in the kitchen just as the kettle clicked off. His mum's best china mug was the only one devoid of stains. It was the one he'd bought her for Mother's Day when he was nearly eight—just before his father left. He filled both this and the next cleanest one he could find with tea and returned to the living room. The flat wasn't dirty, but presumably the nicotine had also tainted her eyes and she couldn't see the orangey-yellow hue hanging in the air and clinging to all of her belongings. The dog started barking to indicate she was on her way back along the draughty, urine-scented corridor from the lift, and she duly arrived, half-burned away cigarette hanging from her lip.

"Ta, love." She took the mug of tea from him, shoved the duvet to the end of the couch and sat down, pulling the dog onto her lap. "I'll take you out for a piss in a bit, Monty love," she said, ragging the little dog's ears. He didn't seem to care at all.

"I'll take him now, if you want?" George offered. His mother released the dog. "Come on then," George cajoled, picking up the red lead from the coffee table. It brushed across the full ashtray, sending a grey plume into the air.

"Fuckin'ell George. Be more careful!" She brushed the light dusting of ash off the surrounding table. George didn't respond. He clipped Monty's lead to his collar and made a hasty exit, coughing his guts up as soon as he was out in the corridor, whereupon he discovered the source of the smell of urine, when Monty cocked his leg on the bins and turned on his heel, ready to go back inside.

"Let's go for a little walk," George said, pulling the reluctant mutt away from the bins and in the opposite direction. He needed fresh air and still had some way to go before he'd find any, down eighteen flights of stairs (how many times had he climbed these?), past discarded polystyrene trays of chips and curry sauce, empty beer cans and cider bottles, then out onto the expanse of muddy, threadbare grass at the bottom. He could, of course, have taken the lift, but he thought he'd save that delight for the return journey. Monty didn't appear to mind which he did, and gladly trotted down the stairs a couple in front, stopping off to mark his home turf several more times, and then to bravely challenge a Rottweiler, before they emerged into the world outside. George wandered around the perimeter of the grass, watching the little dog as he darted about on the end of his running lead, sniffing at patches to determine if they were worthy of a leg-cocking, then squatting down to do his other business. George hadn't thought to bring a bag to clean up (not that his mum would possess such a thing), so picked up an empty crisp packet and used that instead. The 'poo bin' was bolted to a post that was in turn bolted to a low wall, and this is where he decided to stop after he'd deposited the crisp packet.

When he lived here, he didn't really think about the sort of place it was. It was just home: not the nicest of neighbourhoods, admittedly, but people did still stop to pass the time of day, and would take in parcels for the flat next door. Alcohol and drug abuse were no more of an issue here than in any working class community, where unemployment had already hit hard, long before the double whammy of prolonged recession. The council's promise to tidy up and renovate the block had dropped off the agenda before he left, but for his mum and all the others who had resided here for the best part of their adult lives, it would always be home. So, regardless of whether he was the first in his family to get a degree, and these days was privileged with middle class luxuries and lifestyle, he would always be this: a working class boy.

And he was ashamed, not of his social background as such,

but the fact that he'd kept it from his friends all these years, lying about it whenever it came up in conversation. The most they knew was that his mother lived in a flat that was too small for her to have him stay when he came home from the States to visit. He may even have implied that she was quite well off, and it was an easy deception to uphold, for she had made sure he was never without. She might be a chain-smoking bingo addict these days, but she had been an elegant, beautiful woman in her younger years, and this was his dad's doing. He loved her and was proud that she was his mum, grateful for her sacrifices so that he could stay on at school and go to university. For all of this though, there was no way he could stay in that flat another night. Today he was going to talk to Sean, not that he believed for one minute he would give the information freely, but from what Ellie had said, he'd been as close to Josh as any of them, maybe even closer.

Monty was done with sniffing and running and was currently busy cleaning himself, not a care for who might be watching, with his back end on full view.

"Come on, Mont," George said and the little dog followed him back along the path and into the lift, which reeked like vomit, although there was none, back up to the ninth floor, where his mother was on her tenth cigarette of the day.

"I'm off, Mum. Thanks for letting me stay." He leaned over and kissed the cheek she offered without turning her attention away from the TV. It was one of those shows where people fought their private battles in front of a studio audience, with shrieking women and couldn't-give-a-shit men. If she'd been paying any attention at all, she might have recalled that his request last night was to stay until the weekend, but he held no sway here these days and she was too busy shouting at the people on TV ("Fuckin' right an' all, you tell 'im, love!"), so George just gathered his change and phone and made a quiet exit. Yes, he was still a working class boy at heart, but he'd seen the greener grass up-close and couldn't go back to where he once had been.

It was probably an abuse of their friendship, but the easiest way to make contact with Sean was through Sophie. She was working at the farm, so he sent her a text message to ask for Sean's number, under the guise of needing to chat with him about arranging a new placement. It wasn't really being deceitful, and he would tell her eventually, but right at this moment he didn't feel up to explaining. Her unquestioning acceptance of his cover story made him feel even more guilty about using her, but he now had Sean's mobile phone number and knew he was working at home today. A quick call was all it took to see him heading out of town on the bus to Sean's house, and he was relieved to find that the archaeological pit in front of it had been filled in since the last time he was here—with Josh. The memory of the pair of them laughing uncontrollably, as they tried to clamber out of the muddy, three foot deep hole, stung like vinegar in an open wound, and it was this that drove him towards Sean's front door, in spite of his metaphorical, rather than actual, cold feet.

Given that it was only a little after ten in the morning, he probably shouldn't have been surprised to find Sean still in his pyjamas and dressing gown, unshaven and hair sticking up on one side of his head, looking so distantly removed from the clinical psychologist who delivered their lectures that it was almost possible to forget they were one and the same person.

"I'm sorry. I can see I've caught you at a bad time," George said.

"Not at all, George, not at all. I was about to go for a shower when you called, but thought I'd wait. Come in, come in." George accepted his invitation and stepped into the hallway, waiting while he closed the door. The house was filled with the aroma of tea and porridge, and Sean wandered onwards to the kitchen, scratching his head, which made his hair stick out even more. He took a spoonful of porridge directly from the pan and put it in his mouth, waving his hand to indicate that it was hot.

"Still not mastered that microwave sorcery," he explained. George laughed lightly. "Will you have a cup of tea?"

"I'd love one, thanks."

Sean proceeded to get a cup, holding milk over it (George nodded) and then a spoonful of sugar (George shook his head), before filling the cup from a canteen-style teapot.

"There y'are," he said, pushing the cup towards his guest. "Shall we sit down?"

George followed him into his lounge and waited to see where he should sit. He'd already spotted the wallpaper—the one that was the same as Josh's, until he ripped it all down again.

"So what is it you need, George? Soph mentioned you'd been having a tough time at the prison."

"Err, yeah. It was OK really, but not for me," he said nervously. He hadn't expected Sophie to say anything at all, not after he'd told her last week that he'd sort it out himself. He really didn't want to get the prison psychologist in trouble. These things had a habit of coming back to get you later.

"Ah right, well. Maybe we need to arrange a couple of mentoring sessions and chat about where you want to be heading. How does that sound?"

"That'd be really helpful, thanks."

"I'll check my diary later and drop you an email."

So that was the easy part done, and without stirring things up. All good so far, but how to broach the other bit? He sipped at his tea, feeling very ill at ease, with Sean's eyes constantly burning into him, interpreting his every action.

"That porridge might be a bit cooler now. Think I'll give it another try," he said, the words loaded with subtext. As he passed by, he patted George on the shoulder. "Give you time to gather your thoughts. Then you can tell me what's really on your mind."

George was relieved and horrified at the same time. Was he really so transparent? Of course, Sean was a professional; he'd seen Josh do the same thing many times before, reading the subtle changes in people's body language, the words waiting behind pursed lips. He was starting to get a bit of a knack for it himself, although he was a long way from reaching their level of almost telepathic ability. In the kitchen he could hear the clanging of the spoon against the side of the pan, and a one-sided dialogue between Sean and his cat, to whom he was explaining that they had company and he was to behave. Soon both the clanging and the talking stopped, and George braced himself. Sphinx the cat came in first, jumped lightly onto his lap and curled up in a purring, fluffy ball. He was a truly welcome distraction.

Sean came back and took his seat on the sofa, legs crossed and tea resting on his stomach. He didn't say a word, instead waiting for George to begin to speak. This was the humanistic approach in full effect and he wondered how many times he was going to be asked what made him think 'this', or why he felt 'that'. But this wasn't a therapy session; it was an information gathering exercise. Like doing research—yes, that was a much easier way to approach it.

"I'm not sure how to—" he started. Should he just ask outright? Or perhaps gradually build up to it, set some context first?

"You want to talk to me about Josh," Sean stated.

"Is it that obvious?"

"To anyone else, maybe not. To me, and to your man Josh, yes. Sometimes I think he wishes as much as I do that it wasn't so. It can be a terrible burden. It would be nice to be able to turn it off, but there you go. I don't suppose we can have it all the way we want."

"You and Josh lived together."

"Shared a house as undergraduates, and for a while afterwards, yes. Until I royally screwed things up. I suppose he told you."

"Not really. He told me that you left to complete your PhD and he didn't like how you went about things, but that's pretty much it."

"He said that, did he? That's interesting. Interesting, and fifty percent the truth. I made some bad choices with my research, he's right about that. But it wasn't me who left. It was

189

him."

So Josh had lied about that then. George chewed his lip whilst he pondered the appropriateness of his next question. He ought not to ask it and probably knew the answer already, but it was the only chance he was going to get. "I know this is a bit too personal, and that you're with Sophie, but were you and Josh ever…"

"Lovers? Not at all, no. As you say, I'm with Soph and I'm very much a ladies' man. As for Joshy—after all this time I couldn't tell you for sure. He's always been too tied up working or looking after his friends to have a relationship." Sean paused. "It's the only thing he's been able to keep from me."

George rubbed his temples. The headache hadn't diminished any and was possibly getting worse. He concentrated on stroking the cat and tried to centre his thoughts. So far, what Sean had told him hadn't been particularly informative, although the fact that he couldn't see into Josh's emotional side either was some consolation. After all, if he couldn't, then what hope was there for anyone else?

"He's a good little partner, aren't you, Sphinxy? If they'd let me, I'd take him to the hospital with me. He'd do so much good."

"Yeah," George agreed. Without the cat on his knee, he'd have probably decided to wimp out by now, but Sphinx was making sure he wasn't going anywhere, so he decided to grasp the opportunity. "I don't know if you remember Eleanor. She's a friend of Josh's and mine. We were all at school together."

"Sure, I know Eleanor. What an incredible young woman she is, or was. You know, before Josh left, and you'll think I'm making this up, but he destroyed the house. He didn't do it all in one go, like when someone loses their temper and smashes up the furniture. This was much more controlled. The first thing was his bed. It took a couple of weeks for me to discover he was sleeping on the sofa, and his bed was in pieces all over his room. We had a big table and dining chairs, it was daft really, but that's what the landlord gave us, so we kept it. We spent many a night there, studying and drinking into the early hours. Well, that was the next casualty, and more in keeping with your smash it up with an axe kind of thing. He'd decided it was taking up too much space and we were going to get a new one, but of course, we never did. After he moved out I had to replace it or lose the deposit on the house. There were a few other things: the TV, most of the pans—my God he must've scrubbed the hell out of them, the state they were in—and then one day he left, without a word. I found out he'd gone up to Newcastle to stay with Eleanor, and I followed him, because I felt responsible."

"Because of your PhD?"

"Because he gave me unconditional love and I threw it back in his face. I didn't realise at the time that this is what I'd done. See, all through our time as undergrads, we were so close, because we were so alike. Getting our degrees mattered more than anything else and we worked so damned hard for them. Or he did. It was only in our third year we started to have some disagreements, well, huge arguments they were, in reality. Our professor was pushing us towards postgraduate study, and made it clear he expected us to toe the line, but Josh—he's not so good at doing as he's told, whereas I didn't care, as long as it got me the first I needed. Even then, he beat me by a long shot, but he was never one to brag about it.

"So, we carried on sharing the house for a while after, both working on our Masters, but it wasn't the same as it used to be and it was an unimaginable strain on our friendship. We were both looking for a way out, to get away from that professor, who was still trying to dictate where we went with our research, and to get away from each other. I got an offer to transfer to Bristol, straight onto the PhD programme, and I wanted to talk to him about it, get his opinion, but I didn't get a chance. Never the right time, you know?"

Sean had been staring into the mid-distance throughout, but now he made eye contact with George: the same kind of look he gave them during lectures when seeking affirmation that they had understood. Apparently, on this occasion it was not forthcoming. Sean returned his gaze to its previous fixation point and continued.

"When I followed him to Newcastle, Eleanor left us alone in her little tiny room up at the university there, and told us to sort it out. I was all for it, but Josh, he wouldn't say a word. Sure, we screamed and shouted till we were blue in the face, but he wasn't really saying anything. I kept pushing, trying to get past the shield he'd put around himself, but I couldn't do it anymore. He shut me out. Completely. He came home with me, but not long after, he left for good—sent me a letter to say he'd found somewhere else to live. Last Christmas, when we got drunk together, was the first time we'd spoken about it, and I missed him so much. We were like soul mates. I hurt him and he couldn't tell me how, so I couldn't make amends."

The two men sat in silence for quite some time after Sean had finished speaking, pondering over the same problem. This all made a lot of sense to George, for it was to the letter the way Josh was acting now. Whether it helped to know this was difficult to tell, as he still had no idea what he'd done to hurt him and hitting him with a barrage of questions could only make matters infinitely worse. He needed a means of further narrowing down the possibilities.

"When Josh left, was there anything else going on? Were you seeing anyone, for instance?"

"No. I was too busy with the groundwork for my doctorate. Why? Where are you going with this?"

"Honestly, I have no idea. We're missing something here."

"Yes, we are. We're missing Josh's perspective. If you find a way of wheedling it out of him, let me know what it is," Sean laughed, although there was much sorrow behind it.

"Thanks for being so open about this. I won't mention a word of what you've told me," George said, lifting the cat off his lap and placing him on the chair. Sphinx carried on purring and pulled in his tail.

"Ah, I don't mind you sharing, if it will help my old friend. I don't like to think of him being this way, which I assume is why you came." George's shrug was non-committal. Sean understood. "I love him like he is my own brother. Actually, that's a terrible comparison. I hate my brother, but you get the idea."

"Yeah," George smiled. "Thanks again." Sean saw him out and he walked to the bus stop, his mind working overtime, so much so that he would have missed the bus, were it not for the woman who came running up the road with her hand out so that it stopped anyway. He sat near the back and stared, unseeing, out of the window. He was determined to get to the bottom of this, for his own and Josh's sake, because they couldn't carry on indefinitely, living in the same house like a pair of overgrown 'roomies', an invisible, unbearable weight hanging over them that could drop at any second.

It wasn't yet midday, so, safe in the knowledge that Josh would be at his surgery, George went back to the house (he was finding it very difficult to call it 'home') to shower and pick up some clothes. Much as he didn't want to impose on anyone else, he was going to have to ask Kris and Shaunna if he could stay with them for a couple of nights, if possible until after the wedding, the plan being to confront Josh on neutral territory: the cabin they were sharing in Wales. As he made his way up the road towards the house, he sent Kris a text message asking him to give him a call in his lunchbreak, pausing to click 'send' before he fished out his keys.

"Oh Jesus!"

George pushed the door a little harder, the resistance against it increasing with every inch that it crept open. He let go and it sprung back.

"Right," he said, using his body this time, until the gap was wide enough to squeeze through. Just the other side of the door, folded into a clumsy heap, were all of the carpets and he clambered over them, pausing at the summit to inspect the living room; no further damage to report there. Likewise, the kitchen looked to have survived this latest bout of what he could only describe as 'uber' spring-cleaning. George shook his head in despair and returned to the hallway, trying not to damage the foam underlay on the way up to his room, where he sat on the end of the bed, head in hands, trying to come to terms with what was happening. This was a side of Josh that he had never seen; he had watched him so intensely for so long that it was almost impossible to comprehend. It was the antithesis of hoarding, like he was purging his life of whatever it was that he saw as the root cause of his troubles, a material manifestation of the extreme emotional control. George wanted to help, but felt utterly powerless; not even Eleanor had any knowledge of this facet of Josh's personality; Sean still didn't understand what was wrong, so what chance was there for a trainee counsellor who couldn't even see through his first major placement? Just as he was beginning to slide into a state of hopelessness, his phone rang and he answered it in relief.

Kris didn't ask any questions about why he needed to stay; it was bound to be far too complex and personal for George to want to share, so he just said yes and reassured him that it was no problem at all. Shaunna wouldn't mind either, he said, and they could sort out the sleeping arrangements when he got there. Kris would be home a little after six, a good hour before Josh finished on a Wednesday, so he would be able to avoid him completely. With that sorted, George gathered a few bits and pieces of laundry to make up a load and took them downstairs, tripped over the pile of carpets and sent the bundle of socks and underpants flying in all directions. He didn't swear at this stage, and instead just scooped them up and took them through to the utility room, dropping them in front of the washing machine so he could remove his jacket. He wasn't sure that a few stray cat hairs would be sufficient to set off Kris's allergy, but it wasn't worth the risk, so he shoved that in the machine, along with the rest of his clothes, added detergent and turned the dial, with no effect. A quick examination of the connections behind the machine revealed why: both hoses and the power cable were disconnected. Now he swore.

"Why, Joshua, why? Why the fuck can't you just fucking sit

down and talk about it, like normal fucking people do?" He reconnected the machine, pressed the 'on' switch and waited for the sound of water filling. All was well; back over the carpets and up the stairs, straight to the ottoman in Josh's bedroom; only that and the bed had survived. Enough was enough.

Now he knew how the lock worked, he had the trunk busted open in seconds, and this time there was a new addition to the selection of trinkets inside: a large, blue photo album, with loose photos threatening to slip out of the sides. He carefully lifted it free and knelt back. The spine of the album was cracked and ready to break apart, and he shifted his position in order to both allay pins and needles (underlay is not a particularly soft surface for prolonged kneeling) and also so he could lie the fragile folder flat on the floor. This was it: the point of no return. Carefully, using both hands, he opened the front cover and began.

The first photo was a little strange, but didn't surprise him, given the circumstances. Josh's parents died when he was young, not that he'd shared this information with George, of course, but his grandma did the first time he went round for tea. She was Josh's maternal grandmother, and her daughter had married a man twenty years her senior, then died from complications after surgery to remove an ovarian cyst. Josh was only a toddler at the time, and could only vaguely remember his mother; his father died a few years later, from a heart attack, so it was all very tragic but not particularly extraordinary. Thus, the 10x8 portrait photograph of two urns was a bit morbid, but George could fully appreciate why he had it.

The next few spreads were of Josh and his grandma celebrating Christmases and birthdays, some of the snapshots having come away from the little cardboard corners that secured them to the pages, and George was tempted to set them back in place, but it would give him away. Josh was a very cute little boy, with a flash of blonde hair and a pale, round face, his eyes so blue and bright and troublefree. His prevailing passion for sweaters was already apparent, as in most of the Christmas photos he was donning a Fairisle knit, in red or green and patterned with reindeer or snowflakes.

On to the next set: these were school photos, starting at primary school, with individual and class shots, and on the former, poor Josh had really suffered for the school photographer's hair comb. Some of the photos, especially what George assumed was his first high school photo, made him look like the stereotypical trainspotter, and he'd forgotten that Josh used to wear glasses. He wondered why he didn't wear them anymore, but it was another question he couldn't ask without revealing his snooping. Now he was into the annual class photos, and started to recognise some of the faces, a few of whom they'd seen at the reunion. It was fascinating to compare the assortment of scruffy teenagers, some lanky, some not, at the midpoint in their high school years, to the best-frock, keeping up of appearances in their early middle-age. Evidently they all recalled themselves as being far more attractive and glamorous when they were young, but the reality was they looked like a bunch of unwashed renegades. George had arrived at the sixth form photos, and yet he was only halfway through the album, curious to look ahead, but prepared to wait it out.

The first two photos were of the year group for their lower and upper sixth years. He scanned across the lines of tiny likenesses, easily naming some, struggling to even remember knowing others. There were over a hundred students in their year, and they'd all stuck to their own little cliques, nowhere more evident than in these photos. He could remember as if it were yesterday the whole saga of Andy, Zak and Aitch hanging back when the upper sixth photo was taken, because they were not officially part of their year group and were made to feel like total failures when they had to restart their A Levels. Still, they were doing better for themselves now than some of the so-called successes: the swotty girl on the front row, for instance, who wasn't at the reunion, although he'd recently seen her working on the checkout at the convenience store, her job since leaving sixth form with straight 'A's. There was no doubt a perfectly good explanation for her apparent lack of ambition, but she'd been too arrogant and full of her own self-importance for George to care to know.

On to the sixth form ball photos: as well as the unofficial photos they'd taken during the night, the blurriness increasing along with their blood-alcohol content, there were those taken by the official photographer, and Josh had every single one depicting the elements of their current friendship group. There were the generic 'lads' and 'girls' ones, which included between them everyone but Shaunna; then there were several more of pairs and trios in various combinations: Andy and Jess; Andy, Dan and Adele; Dan and Kris; Kris and him; Josh and Eleanor, and so on. Seeing them all now, it was easy to spot the problems they were facing then. Eleanor appeared drawn and in pain, and had probably spent most of the evening vomiting up the three course meal. Kris looked exhausted, perhaps from trying to support Shaunna and Krissi. Andy and Dan were tense and standing as far apart as they could, generally with someone else in between them. Adele was the same as ever, although her nose was bigger and her boobs were smaller.

Looking at himself, he would have believed he didn't have a care in the world, but this was the night his infatuation started for real. From being mates, going on bike rides and hanging out together at Josh's house, to doing what they had to do to get Ellie through her bulimia, it had been nothing more than friendship, albeit on a deeper level than most of those endured in childhood and adolescence. Any sexual attraction he felt was either suppressed, or directed at Kris, in private and far away from school. Then all of a sudden, right in the middle of the sixth form ball, whilst everyone drank and danced the night away, it hit him. He was totally and absolutely, head over heels, interminably, in love; with Josh.

And then they all went off to uni, and he had a good time. He joined the LGB society, met other guys, no requirement to keep his sexuality hidden. The longer he stayed away, the easier it became to push Josh from his mind, but he never succeeded completely, and each time they returned for the summer break, the whole thing would start up again. The worst time of all was when he came back for good. Eleanor and Jess were still studying; Dan had stayed in London; Adele was working full time. Andy had attended their local university, and stayed around just long enough to save up for his adventures, before he was off around the world. Meanwhile, Kris took all the work he could get and spent all the time in between with Shaunna and Krissi.

And then there was Josh: still at university, but not so far away really. At first he seemed quite receptive to George's weekly phone calls, and didn't dismiss outright his suggestion of going to visit, but he kept putting him off. Then he stopped answering the phone, or got his housemate, whom George now knew was Sean, to field the calls on his behalf, because he was 'at the library', or 'in the loo', or anywhere else but on the other end of that phone. George knew these were excuses, but there was no way he could confront Josh and demand the truth.

It would be another four years before he told anyone how he felt, and it was the worst decision he ever made. First he mentioned it 'in passing' to Kris, who didn't pick up on how he had contrived to bring it up in conversation, thus didn't pass comment at all. Next, he tried to tell Eleanor, but she was too caught up in her new romance with Kevin to think about anyone else. So he just went for broke, called Josh, arranged a movie date, and blurted it out in the popcorn queue. The real indication of how horrific the evening was from there on was that he had no recollection whatsoever of what the film was, nor what happened afterwards. However, he had no problem remembering the weeks of ignored phone calls, and the return of the lying about 'being too busy' whenever he tried to talk to him about it. Eventually they re-established contact, in a protracted form and always in the presence of other friends, but it was never spoken about again.

Then George's father died and left him the ranch, and in a naïve, last-ditch attempt, he wrote Josh a letter, pleading with him to come to America, as friends, and see how things went, because in all of the time that had lapsed since he first confessed his love, Josh hadn't said 'no'.

These reminiscences had occurred in tandem with the documenting of the same period in photos: the holiday they all went on to a tacky tourist resort in Spain on their first summer break; the somewhat more authentic trip they took to the Lake District the following year; the twenty-first birthday parties, Eleanor's first wedding (which was just after he told Josh how he felt and thus had permission to miss), and lastly Kris and Shaunna's house-warming, which doubled as his leaving party. These photos revealed nothing new: George examined himself in them, impressed at what an excellent job he'd done of carrying on as if all was well, when he felt like he was dying inside. But now he'd reached an era that was unfamiliar: the years he was away in the States.

Up until this point, he'd not felt particularly guilty about looking through the album, for the photos were mementos of shared experiences, but now he was crossing a threshold, about to trespass into Josh's personal, private recollections of the ten years he had been away. For the first time, he was aware of just how appalling it was to be doing this. If the tables were turned, he'd find it very difficult to forgive Josh for prying, and still he kept on flipping those pages. The first few photos were nothing special: a trip to France with Eleanor, with the anticipated set of shots of them both atop the Eiffel Tower and standing outside the Louvre. A full two-page spread was dedicated to an excursion to the Freud Museum, with some seemingly random shots of people on the London Underground. George examined the first two or three of these in an attempt to fathom what they were about, but it was far from obvious, and he gave up and moved on. Next up was the visit they all made during his first year in America. He was terribly homesick, and so excited to see everyone that he took them on a tour of the full extent of the ranch, boasting about how many acres there were, and the number of horses and cattle he owned. Since then, he'd come to realise that compared to some of the other ranches nearby, his father's was about as impressive as an allotment would be to a farmer, but even so, his friends shared his early enthusiasm for the place. Or so he'd thought.

Three page turns later, George was wishing he'd left well alone, because now he was more confused than ever. At first, the photos of their visit were precisely what he would have expected: Andy and Dan clowning about in the airport; unattractive shots of Kris and Shaunna on the plane, fast asleep and with their mouths hanging open; group portraits of them all sitting together outside the house, which looked a lot worse in the photos than he remembered it being, and it had been pretty awful. He could even recall these photos being taken, with Josh setting the timer on his camera and then racing to get into position before the shutter went off. But it was all the other photos after this that were really freaking him out. George flicked backwards and forwards through the pages to check that he wasn't seeing things. No, it wasn't just his imagination. All of the photos were of him.

"OK," he said, trying to control his breathing and on the brink of hyperventilating. There were still a few more pages to go, and he reluctantly turned to the next one, with a very clear idea of what he thought he'd find, and yet hoping he'd be proved wrong. It was like a technicolour diary of his visits home, sometimes appearing with other people, but mostly caught on his own, and almost always staring wistfully into space. The very last page was of Adele and Tom's wedding, finally with a few photos that didn't include him, because he'd only arrived later in the day, a moment marked by a sneaky shot of him leaning down to kiss Eleanor whilst glancing around the room. To see his obsession documented so graphically was beyond embarrassing. He felt as if he'd been stripped naked. He dropped the album back into the ottoman, no longer curious about the rest of its contents, replaced the cushions and bedding, and stumbled from Josh's room along to the bathroom, absently turning on the shower and catching a glimpse of his reflection in the mirror. He looked as ghastly as he felt and had the urge to escape, to get out of there as quickly as possible. He turned off the shower again, grabbed an old jacket from the back of his door, threw a few changes of clothes into his rucksack, and left.

CHAPTER TWENTY

George tried to walk slowly, his racing pulse and soaring adrenaline levels pushing him to break into a run, but he needed time. He couldn't possibly share his discovery with anyone else, not even Kris, and wasn't yet up to faking being his usual self. If it had been at any other time and relating to anything other than Josh, he'd have gone to see Eleanor. Without this option, he had to find a way to push it from his mind, if only for long enough to ensure that the others wouldn't ask what was wrong. As it turned out, he didn't have too much to worry about, as when he arrived at Kris and Shaunna's, she was trying to persuade him that the most sensible arrangement was for George to sleep in the lounge, on the sofa, or they could get a camp bed out of the loft. They'd obviously been discussing it for some time.

"Are you OK with the sofa?" she asked, bringing George a cup of tea before he'd even taken his bag from his shoulder.

"Or he could have my bed and I'll share with you," Kris repeated. He hated having people stay on the sofa. It was one of those funny little irrational things and he knew it, but that's how he felt. Casper dropped a tea towel at George's feet and he picked it up, bewildered.

"I don't really mind. I'm just grateful to you for letting me stay, so put me wherever suits you. I'll even share with Shaunna, if that's easier all round."

"Yes!" Shaunna said. "That's a brilliant idea!"

"Are you kidding me?" Kris scoffed. "You're not sharing with Shaunna," he told George.

"It was only a suggestion," he muttered. Casper prodded him with his nose. "Maybe Casper will share his bed with me, what d'you think?" He tickled him behind the ears, and the dog turned away to have his rump scratched.

"He'd probably let you!" Shaunna remarked, then to Kris: "So your choice is he either sleeps on the sofa, or comes in with me."

"You won't want to," Kris said to George. "Her feet stink."

"Bugger off!" Shaunna took the tea towel and flicked it at Kris.

"Just be glad she didn't suggest top and tailing," he added and pulled in his behind just in time to dodge a second hit.

All of this row was conducted in jest, and so, unconventional as it was, George and Shaunna were going to share the double bed, with Kris in his single bed in the room next door. Now that they had told people the truth about their relationship, it was apparent that they were happier than they'd ever been, sharing their house and doing things together as best friends. George was just a tiny bit jealous, although not so much as to get in the way of being pleased for them and as the evening wore on, he felt himself relax in their presence, enjoying the chance to sit and watch TV without worrying about saying the right thing, or constantly waiting on a signal from Josh as to how he was really feeling. Kris was reading a script and Shaunna was browsing through a magazine, which she passed to George once she was done. Later, when she went up for a bath, Kris turned to him and waited until he looked up.

"I'm not going to ask how you're feeling, because I could tell when you arrived that things are really bad."

"I'm OK," George said lightly.

"Really?"

"I'm OK now," he clarified.

"Well, that's all I'm going to say. I'm here if you need me. We both are."

"Thanks. You've done more than enough already."

"It's the least I can do after you helped me out so much last

203

year."

"Well, I hear that's what friends are for."

"Yeah," Kris said, rolling his eyes at the cliché. "But you've been warned, so don't come crying to me tomorrow. Her feet really do smell."

"Even after she's had a bath?"

"Especially then," Kris winked. George laughed and they each returned to their respective reading material.

The problem with knowing you've got a problem is that it doesn't always follow that you know how to resolve it. The grout between the bathroom tiles was as white as it had ever been, and still he was fighting the desperate, almost uncontrollable requirement to take a hammer and chisel to it. The tiles were fine. They didn't need replacing. Neither did the carpets, but it was a bit too late for regret when they were at the rubbish tip already. So *he* had been back to the house, and left wet clothes in the washing machine. Fair enough, he'd have had trouble drying them, when the tumble dryer was in the back garden, but that was beside the point. And he'd been in the ottoman again.

"MY ottoman, George," Josh said aloud. His voice echoed around the bathroom and out into the empty, carpetless house. "In MY room. How could you?"

The fact that he'd been through George's suitcase without his permission didn't make it any less of an intrusion. He was in half a mind to go straight round to George's mother's and have it out with him. He'd lied about that too, and Josh had never revealed that he knew where they lived, to protect him from the cruel judgements of others. He'd have fought harder last night, when he declared that was where he was going, if he'd believed George would last more than one night away. He'd got that wrong then.

Josh looked at the tiles again, commanding himself to leave them alone, and felt his way out of the room, with eyes closed; the less he saw, the less likely he was to want to destroy it. He edged blindly along the wall and opened the door to George's room, the only one left untouched, for it was the only place immune to this compulsion. He sat on the bed and stared at the wall. There had to be a way to make this go away again. All that was required was willpower and a little thought adjustment. If they could just get through Ellie's wedding. He lay down, resting his head on the pillows, inhaling George's scent and trying to resurrect his crumbling resolve. His phone vibrated underneath him and he ignored it, clutching at the pillows and letting that scent take him over. Just a little bit longer, and he'd leave it behind him. Forever.

"Sorry it's so late," was how Sophie started her phone call to George. "Are you at home?"

"No," he said suspiciously. "Why? What do you need this time?"

"Hey! I've only ever done that to you once."

"Twice. Both times involving a cat."

"All right. Twice, but anyway, I was just ringing to warn you that Sean's on his way round to your place."

"At eleven o'clock at night?"

"Yeah. He's been drinking. By the state of him I'd say he's been at it all day. He was drunk when I got here about three hours ago."

"Oh hell. I'm actually staying over at a friend's. Thanks for letting me know, Soph. You OK?"

"Yeah—a bit confused and stuck with this sodding cat again, but I'm all right. Are you?"

"Not really, but I need to go and find out what's going on. I'll catch up with you tomorrow, yeah?"

"You mean you're going to turn up for lunch this time?"

"Ah. Sorry. I totally forgot. I'll see you at one tomorrow. Promise."

Sophie hung up and George carefully pushed back the duvet. Shaunna was fast asleep and facing the other way. It was a very odd sensation to be sharing a bed with a woman, or indeed, with anyone at all. He threw on his clothes and picked up his shoes, creeping out of the room and along the landing as quietly as he could. A floorboard creaked underfoot, and he paused, listening out in the hope that he hadn't disturbed anyone. Casper gave a small woof from downstairs, but otherwise the house was in silence. He left a note on the pad on the kitchen table, took his jacket from the back of the chair, and stepped out into the blustery night.

Sean tripped up the step into Josh's porch, fell against the front door and laughed at himself.

"Saves knocking," he said, standing back in the full expectation that the door would open at any second. When it didn't, he looked around for a doorbell and couldn't find one, so hit the door with the flat of his hand a couple of times. The noise made Josh jump awake and he sat up, startled and disoriented. He'd fallen asleep on George's bed. Another bang on the door was necessary before he realised what had woken him, and he made his way down the stairs, lightheaded and unaware of how late it was.

"Sandison. Open the feckin' door!"

Josh took a deep breath and counted to ten in his head. "Just bloody perfect." He opened the door and glared. "What are you doing here? And how much have you had this time?"

"Enough to tell me that you and I need to have a little chat."

"It's..." he took his phone from his pocket, ignoring the seventeen missed calls, "...gone eleven. Are you insane?"

"I don't think so. Am I?" Sean glanced past Josh and lost his balance. "I mean, is it me who's ripped up all the carpets? And what else, Joshy? Have yer taken yer bed to pieces again, or no?"

"Oh please just go away. This is neither the time nor place to have this conversation."

"There is no time or place for it. Did yer think I'd forget?"

"I hoped you might." The dog next door was barking and a couple of lights had gone on across the street. "Come on. Five minutes. That's all you've got."

Sean staggered past him and fell against the wall.

"So, what is it you want to say?" Josh closed the door and absently flicked the snip.

"Well, that's just the thing, isn't it? I still don't feckin' know what I'm supposed to say," Sean smiled, his eyes bloodshot and wandering on account of all the whisky he'd consumed.

Josh pointed to the lounge: "In there. Sit, before you fall down and do yourself an injury."

Sean nodded in thanks and pushed off the wall, sending himself headfirst through the door opposite and half-falling onto the nearest chair. Josh sat on the sofa and rubbed his eyes. He hadn't seen Sean this drunk for a very long time, thankfully, because he did have a tendency to ramble on about things that in the heat of a drunken moment undoubtedly seemed important, but meant little the following day. This felt a bit different, and, he supposed, if he did have to put up with unannounced visits with the house in this state, then at least it was only Sean who was seeing it. He examined his carpetless floor and folded his arms.

"A bit of regret there, Joshy? When did yer take 'em up?"

"This morning. They needed replacing."

"Ah right, so. You got some new ones ordered already, have yer?"

"Not as such." Josh turned away.

"I'll have that cup of coffee now," Sean said.

"I didn't offer you one, but seeing as you're in no fit state to get home again, I suppose I don't have a lot of choice."

"I could get home, no trouble at all. But I'm not going anywhere, not until you talk to me."

Josh didn't reply and instead pushed past him and went to the kitchen, where he filled the kettle to the top so that it took longer to boil, and stayed with it, taking as much time as he could to make the coffee. He didn't want to do this now. He didn't want to do this ever. As if things weren't bad enough already. Perhaps it was some sort of conspiracy: let's see how long it takes for Josh to crack. The anger crackled under his skin; he took a few slow, deep, steadying breaths, picked up the two cups and made his way back to the lounge. Another bang on the door and half the coffee landed in a brown puddle on top of the underlay. He took the cups to the lounge, dumped them on the table, and went back to the door, stepping outside and closing it behind him.

"George. Now's not a good…"

"I know. Soph phoned to tell me Sean was coming round."

"Yeah. He's drunk, but I can handle him."

"Are you sure?"

"I'm sure."

George moved to leave, but then hesitated.

"It's all fine, I swear," Josh assured him. "Can we talk about it tomorrow? Try and clear the air a bit?"

George nodded and turned his back. Of course he would want to sort it out tomorrow. It was Ellie's hen party tomorrow. Best not let anything as inconsequential as this ruin her fun.

Josh watched him walk away. "Oh, and George?"

He paused, with his hand on the gate.

"Could you let me back in?"

George huffed, came back up the path and took out his keys.

"What would you do without me?" he asked. For once he wasn't fishing for more, because he'd already found all the confirmation he needed. Josh loved the attention, but he didn't love him. The only thing left now was a hope that they could resurrect some sort of friendship out of this mess.

"I'd fall to pieces," Josh replied earnestly. George was a little taken aback by this, but didn't react. "And get really cold," he added. George smiled and unlocked the door.

"See you tomorrow. Good night."

This time he went for real, the sky maybe a little clearer than before, and Josh returned to the lounge to dispose of his unwelcome guest.

"Right, you. Drink that coffee and tell me what this is about."

Two dates in as many nights: Rob insisted he had to go, as he had an early start in the morning. He would see her tomorrow night, anyway. Jess held on to him a little too long and he reluctantly dragged himself away. She stood shivering in the doorway, until the roar of the bike was no more than a distant hum, then went to bed, alone.

Mrs. Davenport's fridge was, and had always been, an immaculate contraption, not to be adorned with magnetic letters, toddlers' attempts at abstract or surreal watercolours, or shopping memos, which was, of course, why it now bore a twelve page list of 'things to do'. With only two days until the wedding, she was as frantic as predicted, but it was the same kind of controlled panic in which Eleanor was expert, and she could maintain this state for several weeks in succession. She thumbed through her mother's list, noting the names copied at the top of each columned page. Charlotte came up behind her and looked over her shoulder.

"See that?" She pointed at all the ticks in the column headed with her name. "How awesome am I, please?"

Eleanor laughed at her sister's boast. "How frightened are you, don't you mean?"

"Ha! She doesn't scare me." Their mother descended the stairs in time to catch this last declaration.

"Who doesn't scare you?" she asked menacingly.

"Err…" Both of the sisters made themselves look busy.

"Is anyone putting the kettle on?"

"I will," Eleanor offered, "since I'm not allowed to do anything else."

Their younger sister, Tilly, had yet to arrive, and wasn't going to be impressed by the number of tasks she had to complete before this evening; yes, the pages were also organised, not only by day, but by time. This afternoon, for instance, Tilly had to contact the reception venue and check that they knew how many tables were required. Eleanor took the milk from the fridge and glanced at Charlotte's section of the list again.

"How have you done everything?"

"I just have."

"No. Look. It says here 'Friday, a.m.: contact florist to confirm drop-off time for bouquets'. Presumably you swapped the Beetle for a time machine?"

"Nope," Charlotte said smugly and took out her mobile phone. She pressed the screen a few times and handed it to Eleanor. On display was the florist's automated confirmation service, with live tracking of deliveries.

"Clever."

"Told you I was awesome."

Their mother had bustled off on yet another mission and could be heard shouting at some poor soul at the top of the stairs.

"All right, Mother. I'll do it now, even though it's only seven-thirty in the morning. The neighbours must think you're bonkers."

Charlotte scanned down the list of tasks under Teddy's name. "He's dead right," she said, pointing to the relevant item. Eleanor leaned in to read it.

"He can't do that now. It's raining. Aside from which, the grass looks perfectly fine to me, and even if it didn't I'm not getting married here, am I?"

"Ah, but you forget! The car is picking you up from here, which means the photographer will be snagging a few cheeky shots of the bride leaving the family home, which means..."

"The lawn needs mowing," Eleanor finished. "He'll electrocute himself."

"I think I saw that on page twelve," Charlotte grinned. "So, why are *you* here this early?"

"I just popped in on my way back from visiting a terminally ill patient. She's holding out for her son to arrive back from Australia. Guess when his flight's scheduled to land!"

"So, all this careful planning and you're going to do a bunk in your wedding dress to attend someone's death bed?"

"It won't come to that, I'm sure," Eleanor said optimistically, although she hadn't thought about what she would do if it did. "I'm going now, anyway. Good luck. And if you need to escape for a while, there's a perfectly good pub on the high street."

"Thanks," Charlotte retorted sarcastically. "See you tonight."

Josh stepped out of the shower and yawned. It was a bit of a struggle to keep his eyes open—not surprising really, considering it had taken a full three hours to convince Sean that a) there was no whisky, and b) he ought to go home. In the end, he'd had to phone a taxi on his behalf and physically push him out of the house, closing the door in his face. Even then he continued babbling, as he meandered towards the road and presumably into the taxi, although for all Josh knew, he could have passed out on the pavement and not moved since. But at two o'clock in the morning, he didn't care one way or the other, just so long as he was gone. The emotional interlude had wiped him out, and still his mind persisted in tearing around in circles, relentlessly seeking out aspects of his surroundings that needed changing. The curtains at the top of the stairs, the lampshade hanging from his bedroom ceiling—every object he passed brought with it a ceaseless surge of anguish and as he lay on the bed, staring at the suddenly offensive lamp above him, he gave up on the notion of sleep.

The options, then, were to get either the stepladder or his laptop, both with the ultimate objective of replacing the curtains and the ceiling lights, for now he came to think on, they could all do with an update. He got out of bed again, thoroughly disappointed with himself for failing to fight the urge, but at least Sean's visit hadn't been all in vain, for he was planning to order the replacements in advance, if only to stave off further admonishment from that bloody know-it-all. As if he was going to book an appointment with Tierney. As if! He didn't need him or anyone else telling him that what he was doing was mad. He knew it was mad. He was mad.

Self control, of sorts, came an hour or so later when, with a virtual shopping cart crammed with interior furnishings and the cursor hovering over the 'checkout' button, Josh had a mischievous thought. He typed into the address bar and watched, as the login box automatically filled itself with the email account details. They had been stored on his laptop ever since George first returned from the States, when he had needed internet access to oversee the delivery of the house, then later, to contact his lawyer and make arrangements for the transfer of ownership. In the time that had lapsed since, not once had it occurred to Josh that he could access George's email, but it did now.

It had to be said that he kept a very tidy mailbox; down the left of the screen were folders labelled by the types of messages they held, whilst his generic inbox contained only his latest unread mail: a message from Eleanor entitled "Re: BOGOF cravats anyone?", which made Josh chuckle in spite of himself, another from 'RaymoJack', with no subject, and three mailshots from online book shops. The one from RaymoJack (AKA Ray Jackson: one of the ranchers) intrigued him especially, as to his knowledge, George had cut all ties with the ranch when he sold it, and although it would give him away, he was sorely tempted to click on the unread message. However, it was the folder labelled "TTWDTA" that held the greatest allure, thus this was his first port of call. The list of messages took what seemed like forever to load, dimmed out and enticingly unclickable until they did, and he spent the time trying to discern the acronym. When the screen finally brightened, he knew he was in the right place, for these were messages not from, but to Eleanor, with a few to Kris: around two thousand in total. He started at the top and began to work his way down.

LOL Kris - see you later. x

Hey Ellie,
Your mum is fabulous. I bet you look stunning!
G x

His suit still fits him - surprise, surprise - so am going with Soph from college. Thanks anyway. x

How about this - you come to the stag do and then I'll talk to him. Deal or no deal? x

So far, so very uninformative. 3:30 in the morning and another 1,996 to go: he needed a more efficient strategy and paused for a moment to think.

The problem was that most of the messages had no subject specified; however, they were sorted into chunks by date, and some were also bigger than others. He scrolled down the list, on the lookout for sudden gluts of several larger messages, stopping when he reached a number sent in quick succession, over the space of four days last Christmas. One was to Kris, the rest to Eleanor. Clicking on the topmost of these, he came up trumps, for an entire dialogue appeared below. For ease of reading, he started with the very first message sent and worked his way up to the most recent interchange.

Hi George,

I just wanted to say thank you - again! I still can't believe what you did, you were amazing. We're on the way to Ben's now, and guess what? I'm going to have a baby!!! Wow, it feels really weird typing that! You're the first person I've told (best Josh doesn't know that, I'm thinking), other than James anyway. I don't think it's properly hit me yet, and I'm dreading telling my mum and dad. They think we only got together a couple of months ago. Eek!!!

Well, that's all I wanted to say really. Thank you, thank you, thank you. I love you! Hope you both have a brilliant Xmas.

Ellie x

====================

Hey Ellie,

I only saw your message after you phoned Josh, so technically he is the first person you told, but OMG! I'm going to be an uncle again! You have no idea how excited I am!!!

We're having a *quiet* Christmas, apparently. Josh says he's got to go and see his grandma tomorrow, so I'll go to my mum's. As for the day itself, I don't know? Make us dinner and sit around watching the Queen's Speech, I guess. Moan, moan, moan.

Have a fab Christmas - your first one with James - how amazing! And what does Ollie think about the baby, or haven't you told him yet?

Hope the present is still all right. I bought it before I knew, obviously!

G x

p.s. give the little man a big hug from *Dorge*

====================

Hi George,

The Queen's Speech? Tell him to stop being such a miserable git. Seriously, he'll have the pair of you turning into that old couple from *The Muppet Show*, you know - the two old men in the box? Can't remember what they're called, but you know who I mean.

Got to fess up, I opened your present already and it's lovely! I didn't know they made alcoholic hot chocolate and in all those different flavours! I can't wait to try the Cocoa Cachaca, and they've got long dates on them, but I might have to chance just the one. I'm sure that'll be OK.

By the way, Charlotte asked if she can hire you as a bodyguard to sort out her ex. He's been phoning her non-stop since we got here and let's put it this way, she's made it **VERY F***ING CLEAR** she doesn't want to see him ever again!

Ellie x

p.s. Ollie thinks it's awesome that he's going to have a little brother/sister, but he's more interested in knowing when Dorge is going to take him to play on the slide again.

=====================

Hey Ellie,

Aww, Ollie's too cute. And how funny is your Charlotte? Tell her hi from me, but I definitely won't be doing anything like that again…not for a while anyway!

Statler and Waldorf you mean?

LOL - more like Hinge and Bracket!

So yeah, it's Christmas night and I'm stuffed. I made us a really intimate dinner, with the full works - found the best herby roasties recipe ever! Josh seemed to enjoy them, but you know what it's like when you cook it yourself. Kind of loses its magic.

Anyway, he's in the bath (so wish I hadn't bought him what I did, I'm never gonna get him out of there!) and it's been a nice day I suppose. I'm loving being here of course, but…well you know the rest.

G x

====================

Hi George,

Happy Boxing Day! Not! It's a bit mental here. Oliver had a massive tantrum this morning, and Ben (the younger, not my brother, who is being an arse, incidentally) watched him, then said "Don't be so silly Oliver!" You should've seen his face! Whatever, it did the trick and now they're playing with Ben's train set, although they had to wait for my dad and James to get off it first!

You'll have to give me that recipe - sounds amazing! Better still, you can come and make them for me! Only kidding, but you should definitely BOTH come round for dinner soon TOGETHER!!! And yeah, you're right - it tastes so much better when someone else cooks it. In fact, I reckon everyone should have someone to cook for them - it kind of makes you feel special, if you know what I mean. Like my mum and her unbelievable Christmas dinners. If I can be even half as brilliant as she is…agh! Think my hormones are going to my head.

Our Charlotte's about to kick off (again), so I'll leave it at that and give you a call when we get back to arrange something. Just one more day, thank God!

Ellie x

The darkest hour before dawn was when Josh's failing eyesight finally gave him the willpower to stop trawling George's email and get some sleep. Unfortunately, it meant he was still as exhausted descending the stairs now as he had been six hours earlier going up them, and he really didn't want to get into the habit of surviving on caffeine again. Nonetheless, it was definitely time for coffee. He filled the filter machine and eased himself onto the kitchen cupboard, selecting a recipe book at random and flicking through the pages in reverse.

Since George moved in, they had built up a mini-library of cookbooks, and there were now all manner of herbs and spices in cupboards, on racks, and anywhere else they would fit. He did seem to really enjoy cooking too, but Josh's tastes were traditional and fairly basic. Thus, he could just about withstand a bit of garlic in his pasta, or some sage and onion stuffing, but he'd be happier with a plate of shepherd's pie any day. He was aware that this train of thought was a means of concocting a reason to ask George to leave, because last night he'd concluded it was the only way, and almost succeeded in convincing himself that this was what he wanted. Deep down, he knew it wasn't; that, in truth, he was terrified his efforts to make things right would only serve to send him away again.

What was adding to this fear currently was George's absence. Sure, it was still early in the day, but he'd made the offer and fully expected him to arrive at the 'crack of dawn'. He was starting to question whether he was playing some kind of game, making him wait, seeing how long he could suffer in silence. If that were the case, then it was entirely unnecessary. He was ready. There would be no more games. He jumped down from the cupboard and went to get his phone, typing the text message on his way down the stairs:

"When are you coming home? I miss you."

He sent it and put his phone in his pocket, then took it out again, typed a second message, read it back and pressed 'send' before he lost his nerve.

George heard his phone beeping in the distance, although he knew it wasn't actually in the distance, because he was in that half-asleep, half-awake state where dreams merge in and out of reality. He rolled over and stretched, the sensation of another person in the bed proving to be the most effective alarm clock in the world.

"Morning," Shaunna yawned, flicking her hair out of her face and straight into his.

"Good morning," he replied. Now it all came back to him. Shaunna spun her legs off the bed and sat up.

"Cup of tea in bed, or is that a step too far into weird?"

"No. That'd be lovely, thanks," he said, reaching over for his phone. He read the message and was about to lock the screen, just as another one came through. He scrolled down, read the second message and threw his phone down on top of the duvet. Then he sat up and read it again.

"Bad news?" Shaunna asked.

"I am definitely awake, aren't I?" She nodded. "This isn't a dream?" She shook her head. "Read this." He passed her the phone. She shook her head again and passed it back to him. He reactivated the dimmed screen and gave it to her once more.

"You still want that tea?"

"No. I'm good for tea, thanks."

Shaunna smiled and headed downstairs to put the kettle on for herself. Kris had already left for work. Meanwhile, George had the quickest shower he'd ever had, scrubbed manically at his teeth, decided to forego the shave and cleared the stairs in three bounds.

"I'll see you later," he called on his way out. Casper cocked his head at Shaunna as if awaiting an explanation.

"Humans, huh?" she said. She finished making her tea and took it back to bed, Casper beating her to it and making the most of the still-warm spot on what had become his side. A day off to herself, followed by Ellie's hen party. It didn't get better than that.

George cut diagonally across the road, slowing his pace as he neared the house. He hesitated. This was entirely new ground and he wasn't sure how to act. Was he to pretend that everything was the same as it had always been? Should he knock, or just let himself in? He paused at the gate to give himself thinking time, and to prepare for the possibility that the message was some kind of hoax or misunderstanding.

"Are you going to stand there all day?"

He glanced up to find Josh leaning against the doorpost, looking the way he always had, yet somehow very different. And then it came to him in a flurry of realisation; he had dropped his guard.

Walking up that path was the strangest experience, and he imagined it to be how a moth would feel if it developed a level of self-awareness which allowed it to reason that irrespective of how attractive that bright, shiny object appeared to be, it probably wasn't the moon; but it *might* be, and it was worth risking everything for that small, impossible chance. Josh watched him, a gleam of impatience (or was it eagerness?) in his eyes, willing him inside, into the trap.

"I'm scared," George said.

"Me too." Josh moved to allow him to pass in close proximity, but then blocked him with his arm. "I'm so scared, George. I don't know if I can do this, but I've got to try. I can't lose you."

"You're not going to lose me. Don't you understand that yet?"

"I don't understand anything anymore. I've spent so long being 'Josh Sandison, therapist', I'm beginning to think that's all there is of me."

"Whoa. Way too existential. I haven't had my breakfast yet."

"I've made you breakfast."

"You have?"

"It's a bit fancy. Poached eggs with rosemary and black pepper."

"You cooked for me."

"I did. Everyone should have someone to cook for them. It makes them feel special."

"OK. Now I really am scared," George joked. It was a decoy, for he knew that this singular statement was a deliberate confession; he hadn't been the only one snooping. Josh slowly lifted his arm away to let him pass, and followed at a distance, noting his acknowledgement of the pile of documents in the lounge, and then the breakfast he had prepared.

George perched on the furthest end of the sofa and glanced at the papers on the cushion next to him, having initially concluded that this was more of the same mass clear-out operation, but now he recognised the blue photo album.

"Are you going to eat your breakfast? I won't be offended if you don't."

"No. I am going to eat it. I'm starving and it looks delicious. You hate cooking."

"Yes, I do, but I sort of enjoyed it this morning. I didn't even know if you were going to come, but I had to take the chance."

"You think I'm going to ignore a text like that?"

"I hoped you wouldn't, which was why I sent it. I'm sorry."

"There's no need to be sorry, unless you only said it to get me to come back."

"I didn't."

George picked up his fork and knife and sliced through one of the yolks, the yellow liquid cascading onto the slab of toasted wholemeal below. He cut a chunk off the bread and put it in his mouth, feeling terribly self-conscious, even though Josh had left the room, knowing that his presence while George ate would have this effect. The food could have been warmer, but otherwise it tasted wonderful. He loaded another large hunk of toast with egg, the yolk dripping onto his chin on the way to his mouth.

Josh waited in the kitchen, listening for the clatter of cutlery that would signal George had finished. He was on his second jug of coffee and felt jittery. The caffeine wasn't helping that feeling, but it was keeping his mind focused. All those years of complete self control were taking their toll and the desire to crawl back inside his shell was almost irrepressible. Even this momentary lapse in concentration meant he missed his cutlery cue, and George had brought the empty plate. It was a welcome sight, because to ask if he had enjoyed his breakfast would have made it about the cook's performance, not George's pleasure.

"Thank you," he said, putting the plate in the sink and turning on the hot tap.

"I'll do that."

"That's not how it works," George protested. Josh leaned over and turned off the tap.

"You've got egg on your chin."

George reached past him to grab a paper towel. They were standing so close that it was unbearable and he could feel his legs wobbling. "Has it gone?" he asked, his breath catching in his throat.

"Almost."

Josh took the towel from him and dabbed at the offending spot, but he was no longer paying attention to what he was doing. Their eyes were deadlocked and neither wanted to break away. Eventually it was George who did, and Josh took the opportunity to pour two cups of coffee. He had never felt so nervous, his hands shaking so much that he was struggling to hold the jug. George watched and waited, then picked up both mugs and carried them through to the lounge, the trail of splashes a good indication that he was fairing just as poorly. Now they were seated either end of the sofa, with Josh's personal treasures an insurmountable obstacle separating them, both sipping at their coffee, so painfully aware of their own and each other's every movement. George had found a tiny scrap of lining paper still attached to the wall and was using this to distract himself from the pressure of the photo album against his thigh; it was like waiting to be shot with your own gun. Josh was employing a similar strategy with the power button on the games console, and when the silence broke, they both spoke at once.

"You played *Crash Team Racing* with Sophie."

"And you had the nerve to call Zak a freaky stalker."

George was first to respond, just as soon as he recovered from the shock. So that's what he'd meant. Who'd have guessed that a quick game to pass the time could do so much damage?

"I'm sorry. I'm not sure why it upset you, but it wasn't intentional." They still weren't prepared to look at each other.

"It's OK. I knocked the button with my knee and your scores came up on-screen. She gave you a bit of a thrashing, didn't she?"

"Yeah, you could say that. But why does it bother you?"

"I don't know, really. I think it's because it's always been something we do together, just the two of us, and you did it with someone else."

"I cheated on you, in other words?"

"I guess that's it, yes. It was like it wasn't exclusive anymore."

"That's crazy. I mean, I kind of understand why you feel that way, but it's still crazy."

"But not quite so crazy as what I've done to the house, or you going to talk to Sean."

"Ah. He told you. I thought he might."

"Which was why you came back last night."

"No. I came back because I was worried what might happen, with him being drunk, and you being..."

"Crazy? Well nothing much did happen. We talked, or should I say he did; he left—eventually—and I spent the night on my laptop."

"Reading my email."

"Yes."

By now, each knew that the other had been through their personal things, and were both working on the assumption that the intrusion was absolute, but that was not the case. George had got no further than the photo album, and Josh had likewise seen little more than the pictorial biography of their life apart, from George's point of view, and thirty or so email messages. It was only now, with Josh's next words that this became apparent.

"I didn't read all of your emails, but the ones that I did—you never say how you really feel about us, do you? And that's what bothered me, you know? I thought you were just keeping it from me, but all those messages to Ellie and not once do you say outright how you feel. The photos you've kept tell the same story as mine, but the words…"

"Hold it right there, Joshua." George put down his coffee and went upstairs, returning a short while later with the big suitcase and using it to push the table out of the way. Josh watched on in puzzlement, as he left the room again, this time bringing back with him the rug from his bedroom floor.

"See all of this?" he said, nodding at the suitcase and Josh's pile of documents, whilst spreading the rug on top of the underlay. "This has come between us for long enough." He smoothed the rug and sat on it, his back resting against the sofa, then patted the space beside him. Josh raised an eyebrow, a smile creeping onto his face as he slid to the floor.

"No more lies, OK?" he said.

"OK," George agreed reluctantly, because this felt a lot like entrapment.

"Do you remember when we cycled along the canal bank and you swerved to avoid those ducklings and fell off your bike?"

"How could I possibly forget?"

"And we were going to camp out in my back garden."

"Ha ha. We were, weren't we?"

"And you were going to tell me a secret."

"Yeah. But I had to go to hospital."

"What was it?"

"I, err, I can't remember."

Josh twisted around, carefully extracting from the pile an aged and fragile piece of purple sugar paper, on which was stuck the most dreadfully out of perspective drawing of a tower block, and below it a short, handwritten poem:

This is where my friend lives,
High up there, on the ninth floor.
I'd like to go and play, but he
Won't open his front door.

He says he doesn't live here,
But I followed him one day.
He counted out two hundred stairs
And gave the game away.

When people ask him where he lives
He's frightened as a mouse.
He even tells the teachers
That he lives in a big house.

But I know where my friend lives:
It's a big house in the sky.
I'd like to go and play some day
Then he won't have to lie.

CHAPTER TWENTY-ONE

She wasn't sure how she didn't hear it ring, but there was the missed call to prove it. Adele dialled her voicemail and held the phone to her ear with one hand whilst using the other to organise cleansers and moisturisers for her next client: one Ms. Eleanor Davenport. She hung up and clapped her hands in delight.

Not so delighted was the recipient of a similar message, sitting at a desk loaded with a week's worth of unfiled paperwork due to life's other far from little distractions, not to mention a PA on sick leave with flu. No voicemail, though; just a terse text message stating that Andy and Dan had secured a cancellation and would be back by late Saturday afternoon.

When George finally pulled himself together, having fled the room in tears some twenty minutes previously, he and Josh agreed that however painful, shocking or embarrassing their confessions, they would stay where they were until they'd worked through everything. Even now, as he unlocked the case, he was again overwhelmed by the poem. All right, it wasn't going to see Josh being named Poet Laureate any time soon, but it wasn't bad for a second year high school English assignment. To think he'd known all this time and kept it to himself. George sniffed and blinked away the tears.

"I don't know where to start," he said emotionally. "And there was I, thinking I'd be mortified if anyone ever set eyes on these…things. Yet, you shared that with me. I…I…" He was off again. Josh rolled his eyes.

"Man up, Morley. It's going to get far worse than that, believe me."

"I'm going to get a toilet roll," George suggested and waited for approval before he left the room. His phone was on the table and it started to vibrate across the surface. Josh peered at the screen.

"Sophie's ringing you," he called. George returned with the roll of tissue.

"Ah, hell. That'll be to remind me about lunch." He reached his phone just as it stopped and called her back straight away. "Sorry, Soph. I can't make it today."

"Now why did I have a feeling you were going to say that?"

"I'm a big disappointment, I know."

"Have you been crying?"

"Err, yeah. But I'm OK."

"Are you sure?"

"Yeah, thanks. I've got to sort something out. Are you free tomorrow?"

"Ohh. I suppose so. It best be important."

"It's more important than you'd ever imagine."

"All right. Same time tomorrow?"

"I'll be there, I promise."

"Hmm. I'll believe it when I see it. Bye."

"Bye." George hung up. "Right. Where was I? Ah yes." He lifted the photos out of the way and pulled out a dog-eared sketchbook, the first two-thirds of which was filled with his A Level art project. He passed it across to Josh, who ran his hand over the cover.

"Equinenergy?" he read.

"I thought it was really clever at the time."

Josh slowly turned the pages, stopping to examine each one in turn. "It wasn't just clever at the time. These are incredible." The sketches portrayed horses in motion, with their profiles blurring into the background to indicate direction, and even though they were in chalk and charcoal, they were so vivid, so lifelike. "I think the only drawing I've seen of yours is that doodle you did when you psycho-analysed me. Now I know why you were forever hiding in the art classroom."

"Yeah, it didn't really go with the macho image."

"Like I ever cared. I honestly didn't know you were this good." Josh's admiration was evident.

"They're not that great."

"They're tons better than my poem." He'd passed the centre of the book now and could feel George getting fidgety. "Here." He reached into his pocket and pulled out a tiny, black velvet bag. "This might distract you for a while." George took it and cautiously pulled apart the draw-string top, tipping the contents onto his hand.

"No way! You kept this?" He turned the Lovehearts sweet over and ran his finger across the worn and faded letters.

"Well it does say 'FOR KEEPS'. Oh, and I also kept this." Again, Josh delved into his pocket, extracted the small object and dropped it into George's hand. It was a bulb from a set of fairy lights.

"What's this?"

"You don't remember." Josh had continued through the sketchbook and had now reached a page that stunned him to silence.

"Don't remember what?" George asked, trying to hide his shame.

"When we...err..." Josh tailed off, so taken aback that he'd lost track of what he'd been about to say, because this sketch was of him and it was such a true likeness that he immediately started searching his memory for the time it related to.

"I did that when I was in Aberdeen," George explained. "It was how I imagined you to be at the time."

"You weren't wrong," Josh laughed. The drawing saw him sitting at a desk with his chin resting on his hand, deep in thought and staring into space above the piles of books that surrounded him, although it wasn't a space really, as it contained a very smudged, rough self portrait of the artist. He turned over a couple more pages to confirm that he had reached the end. "So, anyway," he said. He could sense George's continued discomfort and closed the sketchbook without further comment. "That first Christmas after we started uni?"

"Hmm?" George said vaguely.

"You helped me decorate the tree."

"I did?"

"At my grandma's?"

"Oh. Yeah. That was when we couldn't get the lights to work."

"And we went and bought some spare bulbs," Josh prompted. George nodded and smiled. He remembered now, but he wanted to hear the rest of the story. "And all the way home you kept singing 'You Light Up My Life', until I threatened to plug you into the mains instead. Well that, my dear friend," Josh pointed at the tiny glass lamp, "is the only bulb left over."

"'You Light Up My Life'. Man, that was so cheesy," George laughed.

"No." Josh's expression remained sincere. "Because maybe I'm finally going to get my chance." George's heartbeat quickened, although he couldn't help himself and started to laugh again. Josh tried to look affronted, but failed.

"Yes, you're right," he agreed. "It is cheesy." He took the bulb and the sweet and put them back in his pocket. "What's next?"

George returned the sketchbook and picked up a handful of letters. "A whole lot more cheese, I'm afraid. I wrote these when I first moved to America, with no intention of you ever reading them. I nicked the idea off you, actually. I think it was Dan, or someone—whoever it was, you told them to write letters to the person who was making them feel bad, to get it out of their system."

"Mmm, and I nicked the idea off my grandma, although you're also supposed to destroy the letters once you've written them." He reached into his pile and pulled out a sheaf of cream writing paper. "I have some too," he said, deadpan.

"Should we really be doing this? Only I might have forgotten about singing you tacky love songs, but I haven't forgotten how lonely…"

"Yes, we must," Josh interrupted. "As you said, these things have come between us for too long. I have matched you point for point on every painful, lonely or just downright embarrassing memory you've shared. I think we just have to treat this like one big and slightly bizarre game of Happy Families."

"But without the 'happy' part?"

"We'll get there one day," Josh said, the words serving to reassure himself as much as George. They exchanged the letters and began to read, instantly so absorbed that they temporarily forgot they were in the company of the author.

Dear Josh,

So, here I am, sitting on the porch, on a wooden rocking chair and
I feel like one of those old-style ranchers. It's sunset, and the
mountains - I wish you could see them. Even though I know in my
heart that it will never be this way, I still can't help myself, and
imagine us sitting out here, having a beer and watching the sun go
down together. And I wonder if it would have been different if I'd
told you when I first fell for you, instead of pretending that I was
happy being friends.

I must admit I hoped that once I got here, it wouldn't hurt so
much, but it does. Don't get me wrong, some days I only think
about you occasionally, you know the kind of thing - I'll be making
coffee and I'll remind myself of the way you drink it. Or like the
other day, when I was in the store, and suddenly remembered the
time you knocked down that big stack of Pot Noodles. At least that
one still makes me laugh, even now.

Today though, I just couldn't get you off my mind. Everything I
did reminded me of you and it made me feel so miserable and
homesick, but I know I can't come back. Right now I don't think
I'll ever be able to face seeing you again, especially if you've found
someone you like, or maybe even love, but I can't think about it. It
might seem selfish, but I hope you never do fall in love, because it
can tear you apart. I should know.

The sun's nearly gone now, so I'll have to stop writing. Maybe I'll
go post this letter tomorrow, but then again I'm still a coward. And
I still love you.

Forever,
George

Dear George,

Six weeks ago today.

We were all standing there at the departure gate, watching you board that plane and leave for the very last time.

Six weeks.

It seems like a lifetime. Ellie cried all the way home. Well we all did.

Except me.

I couldn't cry, and not because I didn't feel like it. Because I was afraid the tears would never stop. How do I live with knowing that I am the reason you left? If I'd said yes when you asked me to go with you, would it have made you stay? Oh George, I really wanted you to stay. I needed you to, and now you're gone.

The others won't talk to me about it, which is probably because they think I don't care, but the truth is I care so much. You're the only one I've ever trusted. Much as I love Ellie, she has let me down so many times. She doesn't realise how much it hurts me, and I can forgive her, of course I can. But you have always been here for me and I miss you. You might find that hard to believe, when I don't tell you honestly how I feel. Well, I'll tell you now. I love you, George. I always will.

Be happy.

Josh

Dear Josh,

You've no idea how wonderful it was to have you all come over to visit. It's a shame you couldn't stay longer. I hope you'll be able to do it again soon, or part of me does. The problem is that seeing you has only made me miss you more. I was kind of getting to grips with it before (as in I only thought about you ten times a day instead of a hundred!), now it's back again to the way it was. It actually makes me feel physically sick and I can't eat or sleep, which is definitely not like me. One of the guys who works in the stables even said I looked a bit scrawny the other day, so yes, I've got it bad again.

I asked Ellie if you get my letters (not the ones like this) and she said you do. I'm kinda glad about that. I worry you'll forget all about me, and I'm sorry if you hate getting them. It does hurt that you never reply, even though I totally understand why. You don't want to give me the wrong idea. I promise you, Josh, I get the idea perfectly well. I don't like it, but I know I make you uncomfortable. You don't want a relationship. It's OK.

Actually, it's not OK. I don't know why I wrote that. It's not OK at all. I've never even looked at anyone else since I told you I was in love with you. It doesn't matter to me these days. Even if it did it would make no difference, with all these dusty old STRAIGHT cowboys. I say this as if I know you're gay, and I honestly have no idea if you are or you're not. The only thing I know for sure is that I'm still in love with you and it sucks.

Forever,
George

Dear George,

Since we got back, I've been thinking about you all the time, and how happy you looked out on the ranch, riding the horses. My mind keeps returning to when Maggy was put to sleep and how devastated you were. I wanted to hug you and make the pain go away, but I just didn't know how. When I saw you out there, you looked like a real pro, so proud and so confident. I realised you didn't need me anymore, and that's been pretty hard to come to terms with. I don't think I ever will, if I'm honest.

I got two letters from you at once last week. Are you ever going to rebuild that stupid house? I do read your letters. I keep every single one of them, even though you don't put anything in them that I want to read. And I pretend to the others and to myself that I find them annoying.

Don't stop writing to me, George.

And don't you ever rebuild that house.

I'm ready for you to come home now.

Love as always,
Josh

Dear Josh,

I've taken to torturing myself lately. Not in a physical way, although I was reading a report in the paper the other day about some study they've done - you've probably read it already and know exactly what I'm on about - I can hear you now, going 'Ah yes. That was conducted by so-and-so, in such-and-such-a-year'. Anyway, it was a study into S&M where they said people who are into that sort of thing only do it to cope with mental pain, so maybe it's not such a bad idea after all. I'm kidding, of course! About the S&M at any rate.

What it is, is this: when I can't get you out of my mind, I tell myself that you've forgotten all about me. You see, I used to convince myself that even though we were thousands of miles apart, I was in your thoughts, like you are in mine. Yes, I knew it was make-believe, but it made me feel better to know that I wasn't suffering alone.

These days it's more like toothache. You get a real bad one and you press on it. The pain gets worse, but then the endorphins kick in and it stops hurting so much. Believing you don't care - it's just like pushing on a toothache. For a while anyway, but I'll take any relief I can get.

I got internet now, so I guess you'll soon be getting your letters by e-mail, not that it will make any difference. You don't read them anyway, but you know I have to keep on sending them. At least you'd know if I died! That's my other torture device by the way. Would you come to my funeral? Would you even grieve for me? I don't suppose I'll ever know.

Forever,
George

Dear George,

I left my favourite pen at your house. I can't believe I did that. It's the one you bought me for my twenty-first birthday, you know the one. It's blue and gold, with my initials engraved into the clip. I treasure that pen, even though it ruined a brand new shirt a while back, but I still kept it in my pocket.

It's silly, but it made me feel like you were closer somehow.

Your last letter was a bit abrupt. I wondered if you'd found the pen and thought I'd left it deliberately, but I swear I didn't. I keep thinking maybe I should drop you a line, ask you to keep hold of it for me if you find it, but I never know what to say. These letters I write help a little, knowing as I do that I can't tell you how I really feel.

The absolute honest truth, George, and it's going to sound so corny, but there must have been some kind of spark that ignited between us at the sixth form ball. I've loved you ever since, so why haven't I told you? That's probably what you're asking yourself, or you would be if you were reading this letter. I can never give you what you want. That's the bottom line.

I don't know if you remember, but when we were in third year, Dan caught me staring at you in the showers after PE and called me queer. We weren't friends with him then, and I didn't have a clue what it meant, although obviously I found out eventually. I still can't forgive him, especially as his idiot mates found it so hilarious. They didn't let it go for weeks. To his credit, Dan never called me it again, and I'm pretty sure he won't have any recollection of it ever happening.

Anyway, my point is this: I *was* staring at you, but not for the reason Dan thought. This whole sexual intimacy thing is lost on me even now, at the ripe old age of twenty-eight. But I saw it in you, that look of longing in your eyes, surrounded by naked bodies. I kind of envy you for that.

So there it is. You are the first (and only) person I've loved, and the first person I psycho-analysed, albeit accidentally. When you told me you were going, you accused me of not caring about your feelings. That's all I've ever cared about. I only wish you knew.

Always yours,
Josh

Dear Josh,

I'm glad to say that my depression has lifted now. Seeing you guys again was great, especially because you all had to stay for another two weeks. I don't imagine your patients would agree, but 'this patient' was glad of the therapy.

Thank you for being here and listening, even if you did it with your therapist's hat on. Is that how you cope? I guess it's a lot like Kris's job really, pretending to be someone you're not and delivering scripted lines. That's a really cynical view, I know, but that's how it seems to me.

We had a 'horse whisperer' come to the ranch last week. She was totally awesome to watch and I learnt so much from her. Some of the guys didn't take too well to having a woman tell them how to handle the horses, but we're used to Ellie bossing us about, so I had no problem at all! So this horse whisperer (her name was Mary-Ellen, believe it or not) tells me I'm a natural and it's not that I'm afraid of them, but that I'm responding to their fear. She talked me through some relaxation exercises that help to keep you calm.

It's awesome stuff, man!

See, we got this new stallion (he's enormous in every sense of the word!) and no-one can get near him. He kicked Ray (one of the guys) in the ribs when they were getting him off the truck and then he bolted. And guess who reined him in. Yep! I can't believe I did it. Ray says that makes me a proper cowboy. Yeeha!

I'm glad the stallion's not staying though. Once he's done the business he's going back to the stud farm, and the doc said Ray's ribs are nearly fixed too. I think you probably met him in passing - he's a great guy and totally up-front about everything. He's the only one here who knows I'm gay, or the only one I've mentioned it to. I told him all about you too (not the bit about my unrequited love - it's one thing admitting to bat for the other side, another entirely to act like a girl, or that's how they see it here).

Anyways, it's almost dark again, so I'm signing off.

Forever,
George

George had finished reading a couple of minutes earlier and was going through his photograph collection while he waited for Josh to finish also. There were hundreds of snapshots, bent and tattered from being tossed about in the back of trucks, or dumped uncaringly in cargo holds, so much so that they were jumbled and no longer in any discernible order, but the one that had wriggled its way to the top of the pile was the one that was the most telling of all, now he'd read the letters. It was taken right after Josh graduated with his Masters and it was of the two of them, standing back to back, Josh wearing his cloak, George wearing the mortar board that went with it. They had their heads tilted back against each other and they were laughing. He smiled at the memory of those innocent times, before he'd told Josh he was in love with him. Today, for the first time, he knew he had done the right thing.

Josh had come to the end of the letters, but had returned to the first one and was re-reading it.

"I'm going to make more coffee," George said.

"I'll come with you."

"Are you serious?"

"Yes George, I am completely serious. I think we've wasted enough time and right now I want to spend every minute with you."

"OK. If you say so."

Well this was new: Josh being clingy and affectionate? It would take some major getting used to, George mused, as he carried the cups to the kitchen, with Josh following closely behind, still engrossed in the letters.

"I want to do this," he said, pointing at a paragraph. George considered pretending he didn't know what 'this' was, but it would have been a lie.

"Then we should."

"Not necessarily in Colorado."

"Will South Wales do?"

"Nicely. Hmm, sunset, mountains, cabins with balconies— great, so long as it doesn't rain the entire week." Josh continued to thumb through the rest of the letters, his brow squeezed pensively. "This bit with the horse whisperer? It's the only time you actually sounded like you were enjoying yourself."

"Yeah. It was amazing. I didn't realise how easy it was to tune into animals, or get them to tune into you. Horses are really responsive like that. You just kind of get into this zone where suddenly you know exactly how they feel and what they're going to do next. The first time I did it was so weird, like magic, although it's really only about correctly interpreting their posture and movement."

"Body language—same as with people," Josh said. He had been watching George closely and his eyes had lit up with a joy that wasn't there when he talked about any of the other work he'd ever done, including counselling. But now George was aware that it was he who was being read instead of his letters, and he turned the tables.

"Tell me about that spark."

"You already know. You just read it."

"Tell me anyway." George leaned against the cupboard and looked at him expectantly.

Josh closed his eyes and concentrated, trying to visualise, smell, hear everything about that moment. He had repressed it so long ago and so thoroughly that it took time to recapture, reforming itself gradually and with an entirely imagined grainy film effect.

"OK," he said, "this is how I remember it. You were buying a round of drinks and I was sitting at a table with Ellie. She was stressing out about us losing our chairs, even though we all had allocated seats from the sit-down meal. You brought the drinks on a tray and nearly tripped with it. I got up to try and help, but it was too late. My drink slid right off the tray and all over me. You blushed and screwed your eyes tight shut. When you opened them again you realised I was staring at you and you smiled, and I couldn't look away. It was like you'd changed into someone new, right there before me, and I couldn't take my eyes off you. It made me feel dizzy, sick—I'm getting the same butterflies now, just thinking about it."

"No way!"

"You don't believe me?"

"Yes, I believe you. Just...wow, man. That's..." George shook his head in amazement.

"What about you?" Josh asked, feeling very vulnerable now he'd finally told him the truth, or at least the start of it. "And don't just say 'from the moment we met' again, because we were only in junior school! When did it happen for real?"

"Well," George began, his face breaking into a smile, "it was also at the sixth form ball. I was buying us a round of drinks and you were sitting at a table with Ellie. I think she might have been stressing about us losing our chairs and I'd been to the bar...need I go on?"

They both laughed and continued to gaze at each other in wonder that after twenty years they'd finally discovered they fell for one another at the very same moment. What to do about it: that was the question.

"Kettle's boiled," Josh said.

"Yep."

"Best make the coffee."

"Yep." George snapped out of it and poured water into the empty mugs. Josh tutted and pushed the coffee jar towards him, their hands touching briefly in transit and making George gasp. It was electric. Josh turned away.

"Is that why you didn't tell me?" George tried to make light of the question, as if it mattered less than the granules of coffee tumbling from the spoon in his shaking hand. "In your letters—the sex thing?" The lack of reply was confirmation in itself. "Josh. Please don't push me away, not now."

"I'm not. It's just..."

"I know. I read your letter. You still feel the same?"

"Which is why we could never make it work. I watched you on Saturday, battling to be yourself in front of all those people. And I was so proud of you, for knowing who and what you are and having the guts to show them."

241

"You don't know what you are. Is that what you're saying?"

"That's the problem. I don't think I'm anything. Oh, I'm not saying I don't get aroused, but obtaining sexual release isn't the same as having a sexual relationship."

"So you've never wanted to...act on it?"

"Once or twice, but not in general, no."

George had been stirring the mugs the whole time and was still stirring them now. He stopped immediately and handed one to Josh.

"So what's changed? Why tell me all of this now, if you're so certain it won't work?"

Josh couldn't answer him, not because he didn't know, but because it was still too painful to explain. He tried to unravel a couple of threads from the full version. The thing was that he'd always loved George, but he'd convinced himself that he couldn't possibly be *in love* with him, because he didn't want to have sex with him, or anyone else. That was why he'd denied the way he felt; however, since they'd been living together, it had been a constant struggle to keep those feelings locked away and his defences had finally reached breaking point.

"You've been so distant," he said, still grasping around in the rest of it for something more meaningful to add.

"I've been distant?" George asked incredulously.

"Yes, I know I have too, but I thought you were leaving me, and I think it must've flipped a switch in my head. Remember that client I had with Asperger's Syndrome?"

"Sort of."

"When I told him I'd never been in love, I honestly believed that."

"Hang on." George wanted to check he was getting it right. "So, you think being in love with someone means you should also want to have sex with them?"

Again, the absence of a response gave Josh away.

"Do you realise how ridiculous that is?"

"Is it?"

"The other day, when you accused Kris and me..."

"I didn't accuse you."

"Let me finish, please?"

Josh sipped his coffee by way of assent. George rephrased and continued.

"You said there was always something between Kris and me, that we wanted each other, but it didn't necessarily mean anything."

"It's true. Just because you desire him..."

"I don't."

Josh looked at him in confusion.

"Kris and I have never had sex. He was my first boyfriend and I was his, so yes, maybe we do have some kind of hold over each other, but that wasn't why he kissed me at the reunion party. He was trying to prove a point, that no-one would care, and he was wrong. Suzie Tyler is still a vile bitch."

"Don't get me started on her," Josh warned. "She was looking for someone to victimise all night and I know it's not much of a consolation, but the majority of people don't share her very warped view of the world, so try not to take it personally."

"Hmm. That's what Kris said too. Even so; being called names hurts, however old you are, and it could've been avoided."

"Did you love him?"

"Yes. I still do, as a friend, although sometimes he really pisses me off, especially when he pulls stunts like that. Growing up where I did, you don't go around advertising it, and I know he thinks he's doing it for all the right reasons, but it's a different world."

Josh stayed quiet for a moment, to take in this response. It didn't make him jealous to hear that George still loved Kris and no doubt the feeling was mutual. However, the question he had asked was not quite the right one.

"Were you ever in love with him?"

"Do you mean that, or are you asking if I ever wanted to have sex with him?"

Josh was still struggling to distinguish one from the other.

"No," George replied, for the answer was the same either way. "I've never been in love with anyone but you."

"And what about sex?"

"Well," he said coyly, "I wouldn't say no. We've known each other for thirty years and I've been in love with you for twenty of those. I'd be lying if I told you it had never crossed my mind."

Josh was flattered, but far from reassured. In his anxiety, he absentmindedly picked up the dishcloth and started brushing the spilled coffee granules into his hand.

"But it's not that important," George said. "The way you start cleaning when you're stressing out, or hide behind your hair when you don't want me to know how you're feeling? That's the stuff that matters."

"I don't understand."

"Today is the first time we've ever talked about sex. Doesn't that tell you something?" Josh shrugged and moved towards the sink. George intercepted and disarmed him of the dishcloth. "Are you listening?" He waited for eye contact. "Good. I'll try and keep this short and simple. You see, there are lots of things I love about you. Your smile, your eyes, the way you snort when you laugh, and how you spend hours messing with your hair for it to end up looking the same as ever. I love that you're intelligent and quick-witted, and that little know-it-all thing you do when someone says something that you think is stupid. I love your obsession with having everything in the right place, and the look of contentment you get when it's all 'just so'. I love how you try not to offend me when you hate what I've cooked, and how you always put the knives back in the right place when you wash up. I even love…"

"OK! I get the message!" Josh put his finger on George's lips. It was an action that both silenced him and momentarily stopped him breathing. Josh smiled and released him. "Although I still don't see why the paring knife has to be on the left, and the vegetable knife…" George raised an eyebrow. "Anyway, as long as it makes you happy."

"It does," George assured him. "But do you understand what I'm saying?" Josh nodded. "And do you still think being in love with someone means wanting to have sex with them?"

"No. I guess not."

"What do you think now?" Even though he'd had confirmation that the text message was for real, George was as desperate to hear those words as Josh was to say them, but to do so would be to finally admit it to himself and he was frightened; that in spite of all that George had said, the truth would send him away, only this time it would be forever. However, he was here now and maybe that was enough. Josh took a deep breath and surrendered his soul.

"I think I'm in love with you, George, but I don't know."

"Because you don't want to have sex with me?"

"No. Yes. How the hell am I supposed to answer that?" He blushed and put his head down so that his hair fell over his face.

George laughed and gently lifted Josh's chin with his finger. "You know? Whichever of those it is, I'm OK with it."

Josh didn't dare look at him, terrified it would turn out to be another lie.

"Hey," George prompted, and Josh glanced up. He saw the sincerity in those beautiful green eyes. And he knew.

CHAPTER TWENTY-TWO

From the sublime to the not so much ridiculous, but ridiculously loud, Eleanor's hen party was a very different celebration to the low key night in the jazz club two days previously. In attendance was the bride herself, of course, her sisters Charlotte and Tilly, her mother (not staying long, too much to do), Shaunna, Adele, Jess, Mrs. Brown (Rosa, please), Krissi, Karen (Krissi's current and Eleanor's previous assistant manager), Kris, Josh and George, the latter three 'honorary hens' for the evening, by reason of orientation or allegiance. Tonight's venue: a crowded live music bar with no less than three bands performing and a late licence 'til 3 a.m.

"No prizes for guessing who organised this," Shaunna shouted to Adele. Charlotte was already up and dancing, pint glass in one hand, camera in the other, so as not to miss a single photo opportunity. Mrs. Davenport and Mrs. Brown were also up on their feet, not dancing as such, but definitely swaying in time to the music.

"Does it have to be so loud?" Adele shouted back.

"Yeah. I think it does, although it's no louder than what we used to listen to." They were part way into the second band's set, which was significantly louder than the opening act and didn't bode well for their hearing surviving the headliners. Kris came over and joined them.

"They're good aren't they?" he said.

"Yeah. Very good," Shaunna agreed. "I like this folky rock music." Adele scowled and Shaunna laughed at her. "She doesn't though, do you, hun?" Adele shook her head. "I haven't seen Ellie for a while. I wonder what she's up to?"

"I think you might be about to find out," Kris said knowingly, as Eleanor and her youngest sister made their way over. They were carrying a bag, out of the top of which Shaunna spotted some brown feathers.

"Oh no! This is going to be so embarrassing."

Eleanor gave them a big, cheesy grin as she approached and held open the bag. "One head-dress, one pair of wings. And yes, Adele, you have got to wear them."

Shaunna put her hand in the bag and pulled out a pair of brown wings on a piece of elastic, attached to which was a hat with matching feathers and a red beak-shaped protrusion. She tutted and handed her drink to Kris so she could put them on. Eleanor nodded to Adele, who reluctantly followed suit, her own selection consisting of a white pair of wings and hen face.

"Don't think you're getting away with it, either," Eleanor said to Kris.

"Have you got cockerels in there too?"

"Do you want everyone calling you a cock all night?" Eleanor asked.

Kris laughed. "Nope."

"Good, because you're a hen like the rest of us."

He took out the next set—another brown one—and put them on. Eleanor tweaked his beak and then she was off in Charlotte's direction. It was Tilly's idea, but Charlotte was more than up for it: she put on her wings and hat and started strutting around the dance floor.

"Oh good God. What did I do?" Tilly asked. Eleanor was already looking around the bar in search of their next victims.

"Hmm. Jess must be in the loo. Let's do the mothers." Here she expected some resistance, but found them both to be more than willing to wear the ridiculous hen costumes. Krissi, on the other hand, was a bit more of a challenge, and only went along with it when she spotted Kris, strutting towards her from across the other side of the bar, poking his 'beak' at a table to the left and then to the right. Karen followed Krissi's lead and put on the wings she was offered. Eleanor still hadn't spotted Jess, but she had seen Josh and George standing at the end of the bar with their backs to her. George was talking, his hand cupped around Josh's ear, and Josh was nodding enthusiastically. He turned to laugh at whatever George had just said, and spotted Eleanor and her sister coming their way.

"Now, I know you'll be up for this," she said to George, handing him a pair of wings, "and you can just bloody well put up with it." She gave some to Josh.

"And where are yours?" he asked.

"Here," she said, passing the last but one 'normal' pair to Tilly, before slowly pulling her own set from the bag: a vast pair of white wings tipped with gold, followed by a hat with an enormous white and gold plume. Josh and George stared at her in amazement.

"You can blame her," Eleanor said, pointing at Tilly. "But how good is this? I'm having a brilliant time." She put on her wings and jerked her shoulders forwards so that they flapped. Josh started giggling, which made him snort, the knock-on effect being that now George was giggling, as were both women. When they finally regained some composure, Josh checked to see if Eleanor needed a drink: she already had several paid for behind the bar, so he added one more to her tab and bought a drink for her sister while he was at it. He and George were still on their first pints and had barely touched them.

"Have you seen Jess anywhere?" Eleanor asked, folding the almost empty bag over and giving it to Tilly. George shook his head.

"Not for a while, no."

"Oh well. See you later." With that, she was off on another round of socialising. Charlotte danced her way across the carpet in pursuit of her sisters.

"Those Davenports are serious party animals," George observed.

"They sure are," Josh agreed. He was getting into the party mood himself and was drumming along on the bar.

"So, how are you feeling now?"

"Confused, a bit dizzy, like I just stepped off a roundabout."

"Have you eaten today?"

"No. I was kind of busy trying to show someone how much I love them. It doesn't really lend itself to eating."

"Especially if you have to make it yourself," George smiled. "Breakfast was fantastic, by the way."

"Oh shush."

"No, it really was. And it seems so long ago."

"It was! D'you think Ellie'd mind if we popped to the chip shop?"

"She will if we don't tell her that's what we're doing."

Josh nodded in agreement and made a quick visit to the Gents', while George told Eleanor of their plan. She accepted it unquestioningly, which was what he'd anticipated: she was very compliant if you knew how to handle her—well, maybe not compliant, but she'd usually go along with most things. She still hadn't found Jess, but by now had a pretty good idea why. Josh and George were able to confirm her suspicions when they returned a short while later, having seen Jess get onto the back of a motorbike and speed off down the road. She didn't see them.

"I'll never forgive her for this," Eleanor said angrily.

"That's understandable," Josh consoled her, "but don't let her ruin your night."

"Ha! I have no intention of that happening." She went to the bar to collect one of her pre-paid drinks and glugged thirstily. "I've expressed enough milk over the last week to freeze some so I can have a drink tonight," she explained. Josh nodded in illustration of his newfound understanding. George looked puzzled.

"I can explain it to you if you like," Eleanor offered.

"I'm just fine with being ignorant, thanks," he said, looking a little worried that she might yet elaborate. She laughed at his reaction, then made her way back to the dance floor to join her sisters for the second band's last song. Meanwhile, the three members of the headliners were bringing in their equipment and Krissi was helping them.

"What're you doing?" Shaunna asked, crossing paths with her daughter on the way out, so Adele could 'get some fresh air'.

"I know the guitarist from college," she explained, "so I thought I'd give them a hand while we catch up."

Shaunna followed Adele outside, equally relieved to give her ears a break. She stepped aside to let the drummer pass by with his drums, Krissi trailing behind him, carrying a guitar case and chatting to whom she correctly assumed to be the guitarist. The vocalist was at the bar, talking to the guy who owned the place and waiting for the current band to clear the stage.

"I'd listen from out here, if I were you, Adele," Krissi said as she passed by. "They're amazing, but they're really loud."

"What?" Adele said, her ears ringing from the battering they had already taken.

"The Late Poets. They're really loud," Krissi shouted.

"Oh. Thanks for the warning," Adele smiled falsely. She wasn't sure she could take much more. "Do you think we'd get away with going home soon?" she asked Shaunna in what she thought was a quiet voice.

"No, you won't!" Eleanor had also come outside and shouted from right behind her, startling her. "I'm sorry, Adele, but Jess has already let me down."

"It's not you, sweetie. It's the music. It's really hurting my ears."

As she said this, the drummer was on his last leg of bringing in his kit.

"I've got just the thing," he said. "Stay right there." He went inside to deposit his cymbals and returned a moment later. "There you go." He handed Adele a small plastic bag containing a pair of ear plugs. "I forgot mine a couple of weeks ago," he explained, "and my mate went back home to get them, but somebody gave me these, just in case. They're not great, but they should help a bit."

"Ooh. That's very nice of you, thank you," Adele said,

fishing the small, silicone plugs out of the bag with her finger.

"No problem," the drummer smiled. "Hope you enjoy the show." He went back inside to join the other two band members, now setting up on stage. Shaunna and Adele followed.

"How lovely is he?" Shaunna remarked, watching him start to build his kit. "I could quite take a fancy to him."

"Never mind him. Have you seen the singer?" Adele said, now she was back in the mood to enjoy herself.

"See, that's just like your crush on Gary Barlow," Shaunna laughed. "Just because he's a musician. You used to be mad for him, but you hated him in *The X-Factor.*"

"I've never even watched *The X-Factor.*"

"No. Because you hate Gary Barlow. Anyway, it's your round." Adele tutted but still headed straight for the bar so that they could replenish their drinks before the band started.

Josh was visiting the toilet again, on account of the several litres of coffee he had consumed during the day, topped off with two pints of lager. Kris took the opportunity to chat to George, who had been so completely engrossed in conversation with Josh all evening that he hadn't wanted to butt in.

"Shaunna tells me you got an interesting text this morning."

"Yeah," George said, taking out his phone and loading the message up. He passed it to Kris to read.

"Wow! That's unexpected! Have you had a good day?"

"The best day of my life—so far." He couldn't stop smiling.

"Oh, I'm so happy for you, but I won't hug you, just in case there's any misinterpretation."

"Thanks. It does mean that I want to skip the wedding now and get to the holiday part, though. We need some time to work things through, you know? Somewhere away from here."

"Yeah. Well, you'll have plenty of opportunity in Wales. There's absolutely nothing to do there, other than walk hills or sit in cabins looking at hills. Or if you're Andy, jump off hills." They were both still laughing at this when Josh returned from the toilet. He eyed them suspiciously, interpreting what had taken place.

"You told him."

"Yes. I did. That's OK, isn't it?"

"I guess it'll have to be," Josh said sulkily, but his heart wasn't really in it and he had to turn away to hide his face.

"Joshua! Don't be so mean!" George poked him in the back and he turned around again.

"I'm just so totally happy for you guys that I might actually start crying in a minute," Kris said, and he really looked like he would too. He picked up his drink and set off across the bar towards Shaunna and Adele.

"He's so soppy," George remarked as they watched him wipe his eyes and make his way over to the far side of the dance floor.

"Hmm," Josh said, "not like you, huh?"

"You know I'm not!" George shot back at him, aware that the mutual declaration of their inner-most feelings had well and truly destroyed his chances of being otherwise perceived. It didn't matter; there was still a long way to go, but Josh loved him. That was all he'd ever wanted.

"By the way," he said, reaching into his inside pocket, "I think you might have lost something?" He slowly opened his hand, to reveal a blue and gold pen. Josh's mouth dropped open.

"Where…"

"Underneath the camp bed. I didn't send it back, because I'd decided you weren't bothered enough to notice, but, well, now I know different." He unfurled Josh's fingers and pressed the pen into his hand, so that it was momentarily sandwiched between their palms. "Are you cold?" he asked.

"No. Just my hands, from our little jaunt down the road. They'll soon warm up in here, I'm sure."

George found this a little strange, as his own hands were still clammy from holding a bag of chips, but any further thoughts or conversation were well and truly blasted out of existence when the band struck up their first number, after a deceptively quiet tune-up and soundcheck, which meant that Adele still jumped, in spite of the ear plugs. Charlotte cheered and immediately recommenced her madcap dancing. She really didn't care what anyone thought of her, although by now Shaunna was also ready to throw caution to the wind and joined Charlotte, Tilly, Eleanor and Kris in front of the stage. Even the mothers of the bride and groom joined in for a final dance before they bade the party farewell. Adele was left standing all alone and faced the choice of dancing right in front of the enormous speakers, or going to chat with Josh and George; she chose the latter, not that they appeared to be taking much notice of anything going on around them. All the same, she loitered nearby, tapping her feet and singing along wherever she knew the lyrics.

After the band finished their first song, the singer thanked the audience for their raucous applause, receiving even louder whoops and cheers from the women in the bridal party.

"There seems to be a bit of party going on tonight. Is that right, girls?" he asked the wing-wearing group on the dance floor. Charlotte cheered loudly. "Who's the lucky lady?" They all pointed at Eleanor and she blushed so brightly that she could see the red of her cheeks underneath her eyes. "Well, congratulations. When's the wedding? Saturday?" Eleanor still had her head down, in a kind of 'if I can't see them…' pose, but Charlotte shouted out to confirm that the singer was right. "Fantastic," he said. "Hope you're having a great night, guys. We're going to do one of our own songs now, just for our blushing bride. This is '24 Hours Alive'."

Eleanor scowled at him for the choice of song. Charlotte thought it was hilarious and gave her sister a nudge to get her back on side. As the guitarist started up the intro, the crowd (including the bride-to-be) cheered and soon they were all dancing along manically, even though they'd not heard the song before. At first, the band were waving their hands to get the audience to join in, and to begin with only a few did, but by the third chorus, the singer had them absolutely under his control, and everyone was singing along. The final chord struck and the place once again erupted with applause and whistles. The drummer went straight into the next number, and the energy level stayed right up there through four more songs. Another short bout of banter between the vocalist and members of the hen party (including a couple of double entendres aimed at Kris, who flapped his wings flirtatiously, accompanied by encouraging cheers from Charlotte) and they were off into the next song: the last of their first set. Once the noise died down a little, Adele nudged George in the side.

"Where's Jess?"

"Don't know. She left with Rob about an hour ago."

"What?"

George pointed at Adele's ears and she giggled and removed the ear plugs. George explained again.

"Ah. Right, well that explains why Ellie said she'd let her down."

"Yep, and I'm pretty certain this is the last chance she'll get to attend one of Ellie's hen parties. Her loss, really."

"You know, I really don't like Rob Simpson-Stone. There's something a bit creepy about him."

"He was always all right with me," Josh remarked, "not that I've seen any more of him than anyone else, I hasten to add. He's one of the last people I'd expect to find knocking on my door."

"Yeah," George agreed. "He was one of the nicer lads at school. What makes you think he's creepy, Adele?"

"I'm not sure. Just something about him. Then again, it's probably because I know how gutted Andy is about the whole thing."

"Does he know she's seen him since the reunion?"

"Err, yes? I told Dan and…"

"Oh, Adele, why did you do that?"

"Because what she's doing is wrong. If she wants to go off and have a fling with Rob, then fine, but she needs to finish things properly with Andy first. It's only right."

Adele folded her arms indignantly, aware that her past

history of continuing a relationship with Dan whilst being married to Tom put her on really shaky ground. However, it was for this reason that she felt the way she did. She never meant to hurt Tom and genuinely tried to end things with Dan, but that wasn't how it worked out. The way Tom supported her through the pregnancy, and to a lesser extent, during the birth, filled her with remorse for what she'd done, and it could all have been avoided if she'd been brave enough to end the relationship, instead of allowing herself to be dragged along in the undercurrent of wedding plans and other unrealistic romantic ideals. Besides, Andy deserved better. She'd always thought this, not that she wished any ill on Jess. She was one of her friends, but she wasn't right for Andy and that had always been so.

Having said her piece, Adele wandered off to the Ladies' and joined the queue behind Krissi and Karen, all three appreciating the opportunity to remove their head-dresses and wings and willing to try keeping them off for the rest of the night. The woman who happened to be standing in front of Krissi when she turned to greet Adele was far from impressed at having her drink knocked out of her hands by a pair of enlarged chicken wings; they were a bit of a liability and were also getting very uncomfortable.

"Tell you what, girls," Adele suggested, "we'll put up a united front. I'm sure Ellie will understand." She smiled hopefully.

The queue moved on slowly, and they passed the time chatting about how the evening was progressing, what they thought the wedding would be like, and the travel arrangements for the trip to Wales, the latter being a bit of a sore point with Karen, so she gladly took the first free cubicle. She had booked her holiday long before Eleanor came up with the group honeymoon idea, and Krissi really didn't want to go, but her assistant manager thought she was just trying to make her feel better about the fact that they couldn't both be away from the restaurant at the same time. Insensitive as ever, Adele chattered on enthusiastically all the while they were in the toilets and continued to do so on their way back, until they were interrupted once more by the band. If anything, their second set was even louder, and Adele quickly re-inserted the ear plugs, the drummer waving a stick at her in acknowledgement. She smiled and waved back.

"Oh aye. Looks like you've pulled there, mate," the singer grinned at the drummer. Adele giggled and joined her female friends on the dance floor, doing her best to blend in, even though she could do little more than nod whenever anyone spoke to her.

"Are you listening?" Shaunna shouted. Adele removed an ear plug. "I said, look who's back." She nodded towards the door, where Jess was standing, acting as if she'd been there the whole time. Eleanor had seen her too, and turned to face the other way. She had nothing to say, or at least, she had lots to say, but she was having too much fun and it would wait.

"Where've you been?" Josh asked Jess. She readied a lie, took one look at him and knew she'd been found out.

"With Rob. We went for a little ride on the bike."

"Why?"

"He wanted to show me something. I've only been gone about an hour."

"In the middle of Ellie's hen night?"

"It couldn't wait. Otherwise you know I wouldn't have gone at all."

"Well, it's done now," George said. "You'll just have to tell her you're sorry and hope that she forgives you."

"Ha!" Josh said. He hadn't meant to vocalise it and immediately covered his mouth with his hand.

"Thanks for the support, guys," Jess snapped and stormed off to the other end of the bar to order a drink; that's where she stayed for the rest of the evening.

The band were into a run of their own songs now, and they were really good, although the hen party posse had been dancing non-stop for most of the evening, so took the opportunity to go and buy drinks and rest their aching feet. Eleanor kept her eyes averted from Jess, who was busy with her phone, and instead watched Josh and George, still standing in the same place they'd been earlier and still deep in conversation. It was the first time she'd really paid them any attention all night.

"What's with those two?" she asked Shaunna, who happened to be right next to her.

"What d'you mean?" Shaunna mumbled, doing a very unconvincing job of hiding her only vague knowledge of what had been going on over the past few days.

"They're very close together. For them, I mean."

"Err, yeah. I suppose they are."

"Spill the beans, Hennessy!"

"It's really not my place to…" Eleanor glared at her, but she didn't crack.

"Fine. I'll just have to go and ask them myself. Look after my drink for me."

"Sure." She watched Eleanor approach Josh and pull him by the arm. He had no choice but to allow himself to be led outside.

"What's that about?" Adele asked, climbing onto a barstool alongside her friend.

"Oh God, don't you start!" Shaunna groaned. "Ellie's already given me the third degree."

"Have they fallen out?"

"As if that's gonna happen!"

"So?"

"Forget it, Adele." Shaunna turned to face the bar, hoping it would ward off any further questions.

"Is it exciting?" Adele pushed. "It is, isn't it? Ooh, tell me."

"Nope. Not telling you." Shaunna sucked hard on the straw in her glass, draining it in one go. The bar owner was immediately on the case.

"Girls, what can I get you?" he smiled.

"Bacardi and Coke, please," Shaunna replied. "Adele?"

"Martini and lemonade, ice and lemon."

The owner nodded and set about preparing their drinks.

"Please, Shaunna?" Adele tried again. "I won't tell anyone, I swear."

"Yeah, whatever, Adele."

"Three guesses?"

"No!" Shaunna glared at her, then switched her attention to watching the bar owner, who had been listening in, but pretending not to.

"Are you enjoying yourselves?" he asked.

"Yeah. It's been great fun," Shaunna said enthusiastically.

"Glad to hear it." He looked her over while he waited for the glass to fill with Coke. "Nice pair." He nodded at her wings and gave her a cheeky grin.

Shaunna raised an eyebrow. "I bet you say that to all the girls."

"Only the ones with wings. So, does heaven know they're missing an angel?"

Shaunna fluttered her eyelashes and smiled. "You're good."

"So I've been told," he smiled back. "I don't think I've seen you here before."

"No. We've not been here before." Shaunna glanced around the venue, then settled her gaze back on the bar owner, taking in his navy blue designer suit and pink, open-necked shirt. She nodded approvingly. "Got a good feel to it."

"Thank you." He placed her drink in front of her. "By the way, I'm Andy."

"Figures," she said. Adele giggled. The bar owner looked puzzled.

"She's got a thing for blokes called Andy," Adele explained.

"Adele!" Shaunna pushed her and she nearly fell off the barstool.

"Oh, really?" Andy said. He casually leaned an elbow on the bar. "I bet none of them have been as suave as me." He winked playfully at her.

"Nope, you're definitely the suavest," she laughed.

258

"Yeah?"

"Definitely. And debonair."

"Debonair, you say?"

"Oh yes."

Adele's eyes flitted from one to the other of them. She coughed lightly into her hand.

"This is Adele," Shaunna told him.

Adele passed over a ten pound note and gave him a quick smile. "And she's Shaunna," she said.

"Do you only come as a pair?" he asked.

"Why? Don't you think you can handle us?" Shaunna challenged. Adele quickly gulped her drink, making sure she got an ice cube at the same time. It was all very well for Shaunna to flirt, but she was trying to be on her best behaviour.

"So, are you here for the night, girls?" Andy asked.

"I hope so," Adele answered quickly. Shaunna gave her a look. "What?"

Shaunna stood on tiptoes and pouted. "Ooh, it's too loud, Shaunna. D'you think we can go home yet?" she said, twizzling a lock of hair around her finger and trying to sound ditzy. Adele scowled at her.

"Can you do that again?" Andy asked, his face registering appreciation as she carelessly tossed her hair back over her shoulder. The bar was getting busy and he was already serving another customer.

"If you ask me nicely," she smiled. "See you later." She gave him a little wave and turned away. Adele slid down from her stool and followed her friend across the bar to the dance floor. It felt just like the old days.

Outside, Josh was leaning against the wall, watching the smokers, all congregated under a single parasol. It wasn't even raining.

"Talk to me," Eleanor commanded.

"About?"

"You know exactly what about. Come on. Out with it."

"I don't know what you mean," he said, working so hard not to smile that he looked as if he were sucking a hard-boiled sweet.

"You and George. I can tell there's something I don't know, and I'm the bride-to-be," she said. "I have a right to know."

"Oh do you now? Well, Mrs. Brown-to-be, I have a right not to tell you."

"Joshua!"

"But I don't necessarily have to exercise that right, I suppose. George and I have spent the day together, talking things through. I told him how I feel and he…"

"Hang on. Can you backtrack for me a bit? Didn't he already know how you feel? The whole 'it can never be' thing? Me fielding phone calls and holding broken hearts together with my bare hands?" Josh burst into laughter. He couldn't help himself. It was the 'holding broken hearts' that got him for some reason.

"I'm sorry, Ellie," he stammered, finally, "but that's hilarious. Yes, you are quite right. You have been an amazing friend to us both. And I love you, for everything you are, unconditionally. Promise you won't get cross with me?"

"I can't do that, unless you tell me what it is you think might make me cross, can I?"

"Good point."

"You're stalling."

"I am."

"So stop it."

"OK."

"Josh, come on. I'm missing my party here!"

"Well, if you put it like that." He paused just once more. "I've told him I'm in love with him. I always have been." There was a further pause, in which Eleanor nodded slowly and stared at the floor, as if she had been watching his words flutter to the ground and was waiting for them to settle.

"Can you just repeat that last bit again? Only I think the music's done something to my ears."

"I'm in love with George, Ellie."

"Yep. That's what I thought you said. I'm going in now, but don't think you've heard the end of this."

"Oh, I'm quite sure I haven't," Josh said, following her back inside. She stopped by George and spoke into his ear, then returned to the dance floor with the rest of the women, and Kris. Josh took up his previous position next to George and looked him over inquisitively.

"What did she say?"

"She said—actually I don't know if I should tell you."

"No secrets, remember?"

"I'm sure it was no lies."

"Secrets lead to lies, and lies lead to more secrets and even more lies."

"Ah, man! This is so unfair." Josh stared him straight in the eyes until there was no way he could possibly keep it to himself. "All right," he sighed in exasperation. "She said 'I told you so'."

CHAPTER TWENTY-THREE

Task number one on Mrs. Davenport's Friday morning list: remind Eleanor and James about meeting with Father Maverick. His name was in actuality Terry Mallick, an ex Roman Catholic priest and authorised celebrant of marriage, which was about as far as Eleanor's mother was prepared to go in respect of a compromise. With Kevin serving a prison sentence for murder, the Church would undoubtedly have annulled Eleanor's previous marriage, but she didn't want to go through the trauma of petitioning, and as such, Terry Mallick would be officiating. He was due to arrive at the Davenport family home at ten o'clock, by which time all family members would be otherwise engaged in their allocated duties for the morning, leaving the coast clear for Eleanor and James to meet with him and discuss the ceremony.

Being an *ex* Roman Catholic did not preclude him from taking a traditional stance on the wording of vows, and he was very pleased to find that this not-so-young couple were in agreement. The meeting was over within twenty minutes, much to Mrs. Davenport's chagrin, as it didn't fill the hour slot she had allocated in her schedule (as prescribed by "Look after boys for Eleanor and James"). Now she was standing in the kitchen, looking a little panic-stricken at the prospect of having nothing to do for the next half an hour.

"Mother! Will you please sit down and have a rest?" Eleanor ticked her off.

"I can't, sweetie. You know what I'm like."

"Yes, I do, so here's what's going to happen. You're going to sit on that chair," she pointed to the seat closest to her mother, "and I'm going to put the kettle on. Then we're going to have a nice half an hour or so of quality mother-daughter time. How about that?"

Her mother ummed and ahhed for a moment, trying to come up with a valid-sounding reason for why she couldn't take up the offer.

"I shall take the boys home," James decreed. "It will give you both a little peace and quiet."

"There you go," Eleanor said, filling the kettle. "No excuse." She grinned at her mother.

"Oh, all right then," she relented and flopped wearily onto the chair. It was the first time she'd sat down all week and a very welcome break. Once James had taken the boys out to the car, Eleanor made the tea and sat opposite her mother. The peace that descended on the house was wondrous and unusual, but for one small niggle. Both women moved to get up at the same time.

"Stay," Eleanor commanded and ran upstairs to silence the dripping tap; she resumed her seat a few seconds later, suitably satisfied.

"I sometimes forget how like me you are," her mother laughed. It was a remark that naturally led into a comparison of the traits they shared, then to her sisters. Charlotte and Eleanor looked alike, and had similar personalities in many respects, although it was always Charlotte who was loudest and most outgoing. Tilly was more like her father: anything for a peaceful life was their way; her pre-marital pregnancy had obviously caused ructions, but she did 'the right thing' in marrying Ashleigh's father and they were still together, a happy family unit completed by young Benjamin, who was just turned seven, going on forty. They were currently at the chapel, as per their orders, with room for a quick lunch between checking the parking arrangements were still the same as when the booking was made, and meeting up with the rest of 'Team Bride', as Charlotte was calling them, for a final dress or shirt fitting. Ben and Luke were at the car hire company, delivering ribbons and ticking off the list of items their mother had typed out for them, which, embarrassingly, included having to check the petrol gauges themselves, rather than taking the company's word for it that the cars were fully fuelled. Teddy had suggested they might want to take a tyre pressure gauge and a spare dipstick with them too, before he was chastised and sent out to 'oversee' the catering arrangements.

Fortunately the caterer was very understanding, given that he already had extensive firsthand experience of bossy Davenport women. Eleanor and James had handed over all aspects of the arrangements to Mrs. Davenport, with just one proviso: Wotto, now proud owner of The Pizza Place Chef of the Year award, was to be their caterer. He was overwhelmed by the request, and, if the truth be told, was stressing and fussing more than the entire Davenport clan put together. James used his authority to shut the local restaurant for two days so that Wotto could use 'his' kitchen, which didn't impress the regional manager, but who was he to override the MD? Zak considered registering his gripe with head office, but then had second thoughts, seeing as he was also getting the day off for the wedding. So, poor Teddy arrived at the restaurant, thinking he would get away with a quick progress update, only to find himself elbow-deep in washing-up, whilst Wotto zipped around the kitchen with seventies disco booming from the speakers, tending to a multitude of pans, baking tins and mixers. The cake was safely stacked on the bar in the restaurant, along with anything else that wouldn't spoil before tomorrow afternoon.

"I'm gonna go and get some kip soon," Wotto explained to Teddy on his next circuit. "Gonna be working through the night." Teddy nodded and carried on scrubbing at the choux pastry stuck in the bottom of the pan, another one now sliding in underneath. Wotto grinned at him. "Thanks for helping out, mate," he said, and off he went again.

At the university, Josh was in session, enjoying the mental

break afforded by having to focus on his student clients, rather than thinking about George, or Eleanor's wedding, or any other of the myriad things going on with his friends. In between appointments, his mind lapsed back into worrying about Andy and Jess's situation, wondering how Dan was, whether Eleanor was fretting about tomorrow, if he'd done the right thing in telling George, and round again in a circle of confusion that was making him feel queasy. Meanwhile, George, who had travelled in with him, was at the library getting in some reading before he met up with Sophie for lunch. He too was struggling to stay focused, but needed to come up with ideas for what kind of placement he wanted, before he arranged anything concrete with Sean. The default was to opt for something along the lines of the generic therapy that Josh offered; after all, it was only a placement, not a long-term career choice, although his enthusiasm for either was a little deflated at present. He returned the pile of books and wandered along the shelves, looking for inspiration. When it came, it hit him with an almighty smack of 'duh!' and he immediately packed up his stuff and headed off to meet Sophie.

The walk home from her mother's took Eleanor within minor detour distance of her surgery, so she decided to stop by and see Jess. She didn't particularly want to have things out with her, but if she didn't do it now, then it would be hanging over them tomorrow, so she made her way past the empty reception desk, silently admonishing herself for being annoyed with Lois for having flu. It was only one less guest, and it wasn't her fault, bless her. Onwards, up the stairs she went, to Jess's office. The door was closed, although she could see through the glass that Jess was alone. She knocked and opened the door at the same time. Jess was sitting with pen poised in hand, her current work part-covered by piles of paper and files.

"A busy week?" Eleanor asked nonchalantly.

"Fairly. I didn't realise how hard Lois works." Jess kept her eyes fixed on the unfiled paperwork in front of her. She couldn't bring herself to look at her friend.

"Quite."

"Maybe we should consider getting another assistant to help her out."

"Maybe." Eleanor was waiting for an apology, understandably expecting it to be volunteered without prompting. However, it wasn't forthcoming, so she sat in the chair opposite Jess and folded her arms. "If I'm not getting an apology, do I at least deserve an explanation?"

"There's nothing to explain. I was only gone for an hour and to be honest I'm surprised you missed me at all. You looked like you had plenty enough company to me."

Eleanor knew precisely what she was trying to do and wasn't going to play into her hands. "Fine. Blame me for the fact that *you* ran out on *my* hen party, if it makes you feel better. For what? A last quick shag, before Andy gets back?"

"Not that it's any of your business, but that wasn't how it was. And what has Andy got to do with anything? We're not actually together, in case you've forgotten."

"No, you're quite right, you're not, because that would be far too grown-up and boring, wouldn't it? You act like a pair of irresponsible teenagers, with no thought whatsoever for the consequences of your actions. Well, I've got some news for you, Jess. They hurt people."

"You're being over-sensitive. I'd say it's pre-wedding jitters, but you're always like this. I was gone for an hour, at most. What did I miss, really? Your Charlotte making an idiot of herself on the dance floor. That's about all. Oh, and not having to wear those stupid chicken wings."

Eleanor was so angry she could readily have grabbed Jess by the hair and smashed her head into the desk, but she knew she was in the right and wasn't going to give her the satisfaction.

"If you're not careful, you're going to lose everything. I hope for your sake that Rob's worth it. You're one of my best friends, and I love you dearly. But I will never forgive you for leaving last night."

With these words Eleanor left, fighting the tears of rage just long enough to make it downstairs and out of the door. She wiped her eyes, took a deep breath and continued on her journey home. Jess watched her leave, then phoned Rob to tell him all about it.

Sophie was very cool with George, not because of the broken promise of lunch all week that had transpired into a singular date, but because he was, well, she couldn't quite put her finger on it. He kept flitting between conversation topics, one minute chattering on about the wedding, the next the outcome of his research that morning. She was having trouble keeping up, although she wasn't really paying much attention, because everything he was saying was superficial repetition of what he'd already said. She was actually finding it quite amusing to listen to him, and eventually reached a point where she couldn't stop herself.

"What are you smiling at?" he asked in puzzlement. This time he had been rambling on about Buddhist wedding vows.

"You," she said. "What's got into you?"

"Nothing. Why?"

"Because your head's all over the place."

"Oh." George picked up his sandwich and once again half the filling fell out, although this time it hit the plate. "Sorry." He grinned sheepishly and lowered his eyes.

"It's OK," Sophie comforted, patting his hand. "I think I can probably guess what's happened, and you can tell me when you're ready, or don't tell me. Whichever you decide, I totally understand." He glanced up from the mess of salmon and cucumber.

"It's a bit…"

"Complicated? It always is with you. Maybe we should talk about something that doesn't involve Josh?"

"I thought that's what we had been doing."

"That's one interpretation, I suppose, if we ignore the 'Josh and I have to be at the chapel by one-thirty', 'Josh says he needs to buy some new shoes before tomorrow', 'Josh suggested I ask Sean if he knows any animal behaviourists', 'Josh blah blah blah...'."

"Ah."

"Hmm. So, when d'you want this *Crash Team Racing* re-match." George shook his head. "Really? Err, all right then. Is your suitcase all packed for Monday?" George shook his head again. "Right, well how about—tell me how you suddenly realised you were more interested in animal psychology than human psychology." George cocked his head on one side. "Oh, for goodness' sake. I give up. You need to get a life, or at least try and fit some around the edges of Josh."

"I've got a life, thank you very much, it's just..."

"A bit complicated." she interrupted.

"I wasn't going to say that. I was going to say it's just that as you said, my head is all over the place. I'm having a bit of a problem thinking straight."

"I'd never have guessed!" Sophie laughed and George tried his best to join in.

"Sorry."

"Don't be sorry," she said. "I'm sure it'll all start to make sense once the wedding is out of the way."

"I hope so," George said doubtfully.

As a preamble to their academic meeting that afternoon, Sean had sent Josh an email, apologising for his late visit and generally drunken and disorderly behaviour. Josh was reading it on his phone as he arrived outside Sean's office. He could hear two voices coming from inside, one instantly recognisable as the rogue Irishman himself, the other, it turned out, a dissertation student who was about to leave. She gave Josh a bewildered smile as she passed him in the doorway. He smiled back and watched her shuffle away, probably feeling even more confused now than when she'd arrived for her supervision session, if his own experience was anything to go by.

Sean was sitting at his desk, surrounded by the usual stacks of books and journals, his computer screen displaying Maslow's 'hierarchy of needs' pyramid. Josh waited by the door, knowing that he would want to adjourn to the bar, although he was going to be sticking to orange juice himself. Three nights out in the past week was already three more than normal, and he still had the wedding to contend with. Sean logged out of his computer, picked up his battered briefcase and followed Josh out of the room, pausing to lock the door, before they headed for the Students' Union bar, all without a single word spoken.

It was quiet at this time on a Friday afternoon, and they settled into a corner seat, spreading their papers out across two tables. This was their last meeting before the second year of the counselling course commenced, and was really just to put the final touches to assignments and argue out a few issues regarding who would teach what. It took a little over an hour to deal with these matters, at which point they were each sat with an empty glass, willing the other to be the one to suggest another drink so they could say what needed to be said, though neither of them wanted to be the first to do the talking. Eventually Sean took the plunge, more to do with his thirst for Guinness than courage, and in the temporary absence of his colleague, Josh rehearsed his lines. It was the only way he was going to do this.

When Sean returned, he took his time putting everything back in his briefcase, then spread his hands out, palms down, on the table.

"You may have noticed I've developed a bit of a drink problem over the years," he said.

"You do drink a lot," Josh observed. Sean lifted his hands a few inches off the table's surface. "Ah," Josh said, now understanding the full extent of the problem.

"Unfortunately, I've come to the reluctant conclusion that abstinence is the only cure," Sean added sorrowfully.

"You've tried cutting back?"

"Many times. Anyway, so, I'm going to be trying some of those God-awful pills—see if I can't kick the stuff once and for all." He moved his hands away and took a long, thirsty glug of his pint. Josh mimicked with his orange juice.

"Can I ask you something?" He waited for eye contact before going any further. "Did you tell George what happened?"

"I told him some of it, like your thing for trashing the place and that I let you down."

"But you didn't tell him about—you know."

"No. That's still our secret, Joshy. I haven't told a soul."

"I do wish you wouldn't call me that."

"It suits you."

"It's very patronising. Perhaps I should start calling you Seany?"

"I wouldn't care a jot if you did."

"Hmm, I don't suppose you would."

"Well, as I say, I made a promise not to whisper a word about it, and I've stayed true to it." Sean took another gulp of beer. "Although, if you ever…"

"No. I made a promise too, remember?" Josh held the eye contact a second or so more, but then had to look away.

"You're letting me in again," Sean acknowledged. "After all this time."

"Yes, I guess I am. So have you still got them?"

"Locked away, safe and sound. Do you want them back?"

"Not yet. Soon, maybe, but not yet."

"And will you tell me now what I did that was so wrong?"

"It's hard to explain." Josh fiddled with his glass, trying to capture the words, to say what he had refused to give voice to for so long. Sean floundered in the ensuing silence.

"When I followed you to Eleanor's, she didn't understand why I'd gone to so much trouble."

"She doesn't know any of what went on and we don't talk about it. But the thing is, you see, what I couldn't tell you then, well, it seems so foolish now. I was very young."

"And you're as hard on yourself now as you were back then."

"I was so angry with you, Sean. You betrayed me. You betrayed *us*."

"By doing what Harrington wanted me to do? Did we not have this out last Christmas?"

"Last Christmas was bullshit and you were too fucking drunk to give a damn, as always."

"You're way out of line!"

"Am I?" Josh sneered. "Are we not people? What was the next bit again?"

"I was merely trying…"

"To get the low-down on me and George. You want the truth? I was in denial and you caught me on the rebound."

"You were in love with me?"

"Ha! Don't flatter yourself! True: I thought we were two of a kind, so yes, I loved you and I respected you. I hated watching you go crawling to Harrington, doing his bidding, in return for what? The promise of a first class you'd have got anyway? But you just carry on telling that fairytale, of how I left you with a year's rent to pay and a house full of broken furniture, if it appeases your guilt, when it was you who walked out on our friendship, not me; right when I needed you most."

Now he was starting to understand. "You were in love with George."

"And without him all that was left was my degree…and you."

Josh's words momentarily stunned Sean, and he rubbed his face with his hands, slowly bringing them down to his chin, where they stayed. It took him several minutes to put together what he wanted to say and his eyes remained closed as he spoke.

"He had my grades in front of him, all neatly tabulated—you know what he was like—and he says, 'Look here, Mr. Tierney? This two one average of yours? Let's turn it into something special.' There was nothing I could do; no way out."

"But you already had a clear first. We both did."

"That's what I'm trying to say, don't you see? Harrington threatened me, and if I'd known about George—I honestly had no idea."

"Well it's done now," Josh said. In his agitation, he had separated a beer mat into its constituent layers and now busied himself with re-constructing them into a neat pile.

"Have you told him?" Sean asked. Josh frowned but didn't look up. "Have you told him how you felt? Or, should I say, how you feel?"

Josh picked up another beer mat and began the process all over again.

"He's in love with you too. Do you know that?"

Josh tossed the beer mat to one side and folded his arms. "Yes, and yes. The only reason we're having this conversation now is because of him."

Sean was hurt by this and he didn't try to hide it. He'd hoped that explaining what their professor had put him through would clear the air, but there was still more, so he sat, and he waited. Josh picked up the beer mat again and peeled it in half.

"And you lied to me."

"Of course I lied to you! What choice did I have?"

"You had the choice to tell me the truth. I was going to find out you were leaving eventually."

"I took the coward's way out. Would you have done any differently in my situation?" Josh didn't reply. "I'll take that as a 'no' then."

"I don't know what I would have done, but I hope it would have been the right thing."

"That's the trouble though, isn't it? It's not always easy to know what the right thing is, but I assure you that I believed I did know back then, regardless of all those months of..." Sean trailed off and picked up his pint, swallowing half of it in one go. "But perhaps you're right. I should've told you I was planning to go to Bristol, instead of you finding out by accident, and for that I'm sorry. So very, very sorry. For you and for me. For us."

"How many have you had today?" Josh asked. The route the conversation was taking was the one it usually meandered when Sean was drunk.

"The two pints since we've been here. This isn't the drunkard speaking. This is the friend, who…" Sean's voice broke and he was unable to go any further.

"I'm sorry too," Josh said, reaching out to him. "I know you did what you thought was right." Sean's eyes lit with gratitude and Josh allowed the feeling to rest there for a moment, then raised his eyebrow. "Even if your academic choices still suck, big time."

Sean nodded. "All right, so. Up with the shields again, is it, Sandison?" He was still struggling, but managed a watery smile. Josh picked up his orange juice and held it up in front of him. Sean did likewise with the little that remained of his pint.

"Sláinte!" Josh clanged his glass against Sean's. It was back to business as usual.

CHAPTER TWENTY-FOUR

That glorious feeling of lying in bed on a Saturday morning, the curtains gently glowing with the low September sun, in that perfect position, where duvet and pillows unite to create the most comfortable, snuggly cocoon, a not-so-distant rumbling, a rapid crescendo of bangs, and a tremendous thud. Eleanor sat bolt upright and listened for more.

"Bollocks!"

Her dad's voice, just the other side of the bedroom door. Cautiously, she crept across the carpet, inhaling the scent of coffee, tea, porridge, toast: the breakfasts of the Davenports gathered en masse. She opened the door and looked down.

"What you doing down there?"

"Lost my bloody footing, didn't I," her dad explained, pointing at the ladder positioned a few feet away and poking up into the loft.

"What were you doing up there?"

"Putting your mother's mannequin away." He tried to pull himself up off the floor, but his left leg wouldn't take the weight. "Give me a hand, love," he said. Eleanor reached down and he grabbed her arm, slowly drawing up until he was standing on his right leg. He put his left foot down, then quickly lifted it again.

"What's taking you so long?" Eleanor's mother shouted up the stairs.

"Dad's fallen off the ladder," Eleanor shouted back. There was the thump-thump of feet landing, heavy and surly, on each stair, louder, closer. They looked to each other in terror.

"What the hell did you do that for?" her mother screeched as she arrived on the landing.

"You say that like I did it on purpose," her dad protested.

"I know you didn't do it on bloody purpose, you fool!" She flung her arms in exasperation. "Today, of all days. Have you broken it?"

"I don't think so," he said, trying his ankle for weight-bearing again, with the same effect.

"Come and sit in here a minute," Eleanor suggested, supporting him into the room and to the bed she had just vacated. He eased himself into a sitting position and she knelt down beside him. Trying to roll down his sock made him shrink back in pain and his ankle was swelling rapidly.

"What's the verdict, doc?" he asked.

"You need an x-ray. It's probably only tissue damage, but to be on the safe side…"

"Oh, just bloody terrific, that is," her mother cut her off. "And who's going to take you to hospital, do you think?"

"Would you stop going on like I did it on purpose?"

"I'm not!"

"I'll take you, Dad," Eleanor said. "I'll get dressed while the lads…"

"You can't do that!" her parents exclaimed in unison.

"Why not?"

"It's your wedding day."

"Mother. I'm not getting married until two o'clock and you're all 'up to your eyes'. It makes sense, you know it does." She left the room and stood at the top of the stairs. "Luke, Pete, come and carry Dad out to the car."

Her parents looked at each other. Her dad shrugged and her mum threw her hands in the air.

"I give up," she said, and stormed off back downstairs. Luke and Peter arrived a moment later, and seat-lifted their father down the stairs, then supported him as he painfully hopped his way to the car. Eleanor was ready a couple of minutes after.

"Right, here's what we're going to do," she heard her

mother begin as she closed the front door. A change of battle strategy was underway.

Eleven hundred hours, local time: the flight from Istanbul was on schedule. Dan and Andy boarded the plane and took their seats. If all went as it should, they'd be back in the UK by 14:00 and home by six.

It's amazing how much difference a few words can make, and Eleanor felt a bit guilty about it, but "I'm a GP, my dad's hurt his ankle and I'm getting married today" saw them immediately jump to the front of the queue, x-ray done within ten minutes, back to A&E to be told "tissue damage, as expected, Doctor Davenport", then back in the car and home again. The tea was barely cold in the pot. The rest of the troops had been taking a well-earned rest while they awaited news, and immediately shot up from their chairs or other positions around and about the kitchen.

"At ease, men," her dad joked, as he hobbled in on his standard issue NHS crutches, gratefully accepting the chair Tilly offered.

"Shaunna and Adele are here," she told Eleanor, nodding towards the lounge. They had to come to do hair, nails and make-up, and Eleanor went off to greet them.

"Hi," she beamed hugging first Adele, then Shaunna.

"Hi, Ellie. Are you excited?"

"I am, actually. How are you both?"

"We're excited too!" Adele clapped her hands and bounced up and down.

"Yeah," Shaunna agreed, "especially Adele!" Eleanor laughed.

"Don't suppose you've seen my mother?"

"She's having a shower, so I can make a start on her hair," Shaunna told her.

"Ah, right. Saves me having to break the news for a bit, then."

"Is your dad OK?"

"He's fine. Just a sprain. Unfortunately, he's now on crutches. Mum's going to have a fit." She was becoming aware of increasingly loud voices coming from the kitchen. "Excuse me one moment, ladies," she said, and went to investigate.

"It makes sense, Dad, you know it does," Ben was saying.

"But why you? You did it last time," Luke argued.

"Because I'm the eldest."

"So? I'm not a teenager anymore."

"But I'm still the eldest."

"I'm sure I'll manage," Eleanor's dad said.

"What's this all about?" Eleanor interrupted, having already figured it out, but she wanted to hear the full explanation before commenting.

"Clearly Dad can't walk you down the aisle," Ben reasoned.

"It's only a short one," Tilly said, having spent enough time at the chapel the day before to estimate to the nearest inch the length of the walk from the doors to the altar. Ben ignored her.

"So I was saying it makes sense to let me do it."

"Except you did it the last time," Luke repeated. Off they went again, around the same argument, with Eleanor trying to interject and failing, due to the shouting. Suddenly there was an ear-piercing whistle, and they all stopped mid-sentence with their mouths still hanging in the shape of whatever word they had paused on.

"There ya go, sis," Charlotte grinned, wiping her fingers on her t-shirt.

"Thank you! Right, now this is how it's going to be. Dad: you are still giving me away. Ben: I'm not being funny, but as Luke says, you did it the last time, and, well, let's just say it didn't have a wholly satisfactory outcome." Luke grinned smugly at his older brother. "And you can stop smirking, as well," Eleanor scolded.

"But Dad's never gonna get down that aisle," Ben started again. Eleanor held up her hand.

"No. You're quite right. He's not." She took out her phone,

pressed the screen a couple of times and started to walk away. "Josh, I've got a massive favour to ask you…"

As she disappeared back into the living room, the brothers glared at each other, as if to blame each other for losing out on the chance to give their eldest sister away.

Oliver came hurtling down the slide, straight off the end, then up the stairs again, and down and around, and around, George watching with one eye tightly shut. As if this wasn't dangerous enough, he'd already had to confiscate a tiny handful of colourful and very sharp drawing pins—God knows where he'd got those from—not to mention having re-tied Oliver's shoelaces no less than three times since they arrived at the park, the last occurring after he went flying face-first towards the floor, George's arm skilfully intercepting before contact. But it was all for a good cause: James was at the barber's and it was a perfect opportunity for burning off some of the little boy's over-abundant energy and excitement. However, Josh was now equally excited and re-organising his plans for the next couple of hours, to make sure he got to the chapel in plenty of time.

"Do you think I'd be better wearing the silver tie instead of the grey one? It's a bit more flash," he was saying.

"Wear whichever one you like the best," George suggested wearily. He'd already answered this question twice.

"I wish I'd been to get my hair trimmed. I was going to do it on Thursday, but with our discussion and everything, I completely forgot. Are you sure it isn't too long? I mean, I could probably go and get a last minute appointment…"

"Joshua! Stop fretting! Your hair looks perfectly fine. Wear the silver tie. I will clean your shoes and re-iron your shirt."

"OK. Which means all I have to do…"

"Is go home and have a bath," George finished, shaking his head and smiling.

"Yeah," Josh said absently, pushing his fringe out of his face. It promptly flopped back in front of his eyes. "I still wish…" He sighed and went for a retry, at the same time as George reached out.

"Your hair is fine," he assured him, brushing a thumb gently against his cheek. "Please stop worrying."

Josh sighed again and nodded. George was right. He needed to calm down a bit, or he'd end up having a panic attack.

"Push please, Dorge," Oliver called, having already positioned himself on the swing, his trousers all scrunched up around his knees from shoving his legs through the holes in the seat.

"All right, Ollie. Another five minutes and then we've got to go and get ready for Daddy and Eleanor's wedding." George rubbed Josh's arm. "Better now?"

"Yeah. Sorry."

"Hey, I'd be just the same! Can you manage another five minutes? If not, go, and I'll see you back at home."

"No, no. I'll wait." He watched as George went over to the swing and retrieved an object from the floor beneath the seat.

"What did I say, Ollie?" he asked sternly.

"I sorry, Dorge," Oliver replied, his lip quivering. The last thing they needed now was a tantrum.

"No more playing with drawing pins, do you understand? They're very dangerous."

Oliver nodded. George put the small box in his pocket and grabbed the chains of the swing.

"Ready, steady…"

"Go!" Oliver finished, giggling with excitement as the swing went higher and higher. Josh watched on, thinking what an incredible parent George would make, with his endless patience and kindness. He was firm, yet fair, and Oliver utterly adored him, even joining in with the countdown to the end of playtime. It was a cunning move, which meant there was no protest whatsoever when it was finally time to go. George lifted him down from the swing and held out his hand. Oliver took it and looked up at him sincerely.

"Are you coming, Dorge?"

"To Daddy's wedding?"

"Yes, silly Billy."

"Of course I am."

"Is Josh coming?"

"Yes. He's coming too." George glanced across to Josh, who appeared equally bemused by the question.

Oliver turned George's hand over and examined his bare fingers. "Where is your wedding ring?" he asked.

"I don't have one."

"Why?"

"Because I'm not married."

Oliver looked up at Josh and shook his head.

"You not propose to Dorge?"

"Err, no, Ollie."

"Why?"

Josh didn't know how to answer, and George came to the rescue once again. He picked Oliver up and swung him onto his shoulders.

"Why, why, why, Oliver Brown. Why are you all the way up there?" he said, tickling the little boy on the back of the knees. He giggled and kicked his feet. "Why are you kicking me. Ugh, huh," George pretended to cry.

"Poor Dorge," Oliver said, doing it all the more.

"Ouch!"

"Thanks," Josh muttered.

"No problem," George said, with a wink. "But don't think you've got away with it that easily."

As the jet lined up for its final approach to the runway, so too were Eleanor and Josh standing just the other side of the double doors, the aisle stretched before them, the muted tinkle of a harp coming through the speakers.

"Are you ready?" Josh asked. Eleanor was fluffing out her skirt and generally checking herself. It was nerves, and he was feeling them also, but he couldn't show it. She looked up at him, her eyes glistening with held-back tears.

"I hope so," she said, and looped her arm through his.

"You are so beautiful," he told her. She smiled and squeezed his arm, then the ushers opened the doors and she focused on the vision of James, waiting for her just a few feet away. She felt her stomach turn over, and tried to cast the thought from her mind. Josh sensed it and placed his hand on her arm.

"Thank you," she whispered.

Evidently, the congregation shared his view, for many of them gasped and murmured, and she could hear their words, but best of all was when James turned his head to watch Josh pass her to her father to give away. She held Josh's gaze for a moment, a lifetime of love cascading across the small space between them. He nodded—an almost imperceptible movement—and walked to his seat, next to George, who took his hand and squeezed it in silent congratulation. He released it, expecting Josh to move away; instead he laced their fingers together and they stayed that way for the rest of the ceremony.

It was now apparent how subtle the difference was in the bride's gown and the bridesmaids' dresses. Eleanor's gown had looked white as she walked down the aisle, but now, as Charlotte, Tilly and Ashleigh moved away, that slightest hint of blue was set off by the barely lemon hue of theirs. Later, the more observant of the guests noticed that James was wearing a blue cravat, whereas Oliver was wearing a yellow one, but for now, their backs were turned, as Father Mallick began the ceremony with the usual declaration:

"James and Eleanor, have you come here freely and without reservation to give yourselves to each other in marriage?"

"Thank you for flying with Turkish Airlines," the captain finished, as the seatbelt sign switched off and passengers began to gather their belongings together. Dan and Andy were first at the doors, out of the economy passengers at any rate, and almost ran through the terminal. They jogged back to the car— a good ten minutes across the enormous car park—and they were on their way.

"James Tobias Johnson Brown, do you take Eleanor Jane Davenport, to be your wife..."

Even if they had wanted to write their own vows, Eleanor's mother had decreed that it wasn't 'Catholic' enough, but they didn't mind, for they'd said all that needed to be said already. This was merely the formality.

"...all the days of your life?"

"I do."

"Eleanor Jane Davenport, do you take James Tobias Johnson Brown..."

The only difference was going to be the omission of any form of 'you may now kiss the bride' at the end, because public displays of affection did not fit with James's Buddhist beliefs—apparently something his mother didn't hold with.

"...all the days of your life?"

"I do."

Next came the declaration of consent, followed by the blessing of the rings, and the congregation of guests let out a unified 'Ahhhh' when little Oliver, the best man, gave the rings to Father Mallick.

"Eleanor, take this ring as a sign of my love and fidelity."

Mrs. Davenport had, however, given James permission to leave off 'in the name of the Father, and of the Son and of the Holy Spirit'.

"James, take this ring as a sign of my love and fidelity." Eleanor completed the sentence.

Prayers followed, and Eleanor's cousin took her position at her harp once more.

"That's got to be the shortest Catholic wedding ever," Josh whispered to George.

"I know!" George whispered back, both receiving a glare from the bride's mother, in the pew in front. After that they remained quiet, as the bride and groom signed the register and returned to the altar, making their way back down the aisle and out into the fresh air soon after. The congregation filed out of the tiny nineteenth century chapel, into the Victorian rose gardens that surrounded it, stopping to congratulate the newly-weds, and whichever parents they were familiar with. Charlotte, Tilly and Ashleigh stood around trying to look glamorous yet discreet, whilst Oliver went tearing around the grounds in pursuit of his new cousins.

Now it was time for the photos, and the photographer was already herding people into makeshift groups to get some 'natural shots', before the formal ones of the bride and groom, the bridal party, the couple and their parents, Eleanor and her multitude of siblings, followed by any other combinations they wanted. They were saving the big one until last, even though they were still depleted in number.

Andy was taking a turn behind the wheel, and had to admit he rather liked Dan's new 4x4. With its gas-guzzling turbo kick, it didn't perform too badly, although they were still half an hour away from the motorway turn-off, and they'd been pushing it as fast as they dared, having stopped off just long enough to grab a sandwich and a coffee. Dan's SatNav was proving to be highly accurate at picking up speed traps, so they had made very good time indeed and were optimistic they would make it for the start of the evening reception.

"Right, you move in a bit there, darlin'," the photographer said, pushing Jess's hip. "That's it. And if you come this way, just a little," he pulled Adele's shoulder. Shaunna was obviously giving off a 'touch me and you die' vibe, so he just nodded at her and Kris. "Great stuff, and you mate..." This was directed at Josh, whom he signalled to also move forward, so that he was level with Adele and now standing more or less in front of George, who ran a finger down his spine and made him shiver. He turned around and gave him something between a warning glance and permission to continue.

"Lovely," the photographer said, taking his position up in front of them and snapping several shots while they chatted, then one final 'smile' pose, although it was Shaunna who'd got them all laughing, as the photographer made his way around the group, imitating him in a gruff, dirty-old-man kind of voice, saying things like, "That's it love, just a touch more, let me see a peep of those nipples, oh yes, that's the one. Lovely!" James was trying his best to keep a straight face, but in the end he couldn't help himself.

The wedding guests were starting to make their way back to their cars now, and with the photos finally complete, James and Eleanor departed in the blue vintage Rolls Royce, with its pale blue ribbons and lemon flowers, off to a local hotel, where they were to be spending their first night as husband and wife. Mr. and Mrs. Brown senior were looking after the boys until tomorrow, which is to say that Mrs. Brown would be looking after them, with the occasional and stern advice of Mr. Brown in respect of his eldest grandson, who was to be permitted to attend the early part of the evening, providing he first had a nap. The friends were all heading home to change, then meeting at a pub near the reception venue: the old Irish club that was, these days, somewhat more tasteful and discerning in the functions it allowed within its walls, but still hadn't quite lost its 'Irishness' and was thus perfect as far as all Davenport extended family members were concerned.

Dan and Andy missed Adele by a matter of minutes, for as she took off in a taxi going one way, they turned into the other end of the street, and pulled up outside the flat.

"I've never, ever been this pleased to be home," Dan said, stretching and knocking arms with his brother, who was doing the exact same thing.

"I'm OK to get ready here, aren't I? I really don't want to see Jess yet."

"No worries, bro," Dan assured him, as they made their way inside, to where Alice was already entrenched in her knitting, and little Shaunna was happily eating a plate of jam sandwich fingers.

"Addy!" she shouted gleefully, waving one of the mini sandwiches in the air. Dan went straight over and gave her a hug.

"Hello, baby girl," he said, kissing her on the head. "I've missed you."

"Addy!" Shaunna called out again, this time directing her sandwich at Andy.

"Hiya," he said.

"Hiya," she repeated and offered him a big jammy grin. She held out the sandwich to him and he pretended to chew the end of it.

"Hi, Alice. How's things?" Dan asked, wiping the jam off his hands and onto the jeans he'd been wearing for the past two days.

"Very well, thank you, Dan," Alice said, dabbing her nose with a tissue.

"Sorry about the smell. We've been travelling for the best part of eighteen hours."

"Oh no, it's perfectly fine," she said. "Although I have dropped a stitch or two in my haste." She smiled, Dan assumed from the crinkles around her eyes. She was now trying, and failing, to re-loop the stitches onto the needle one-handed.

"Well, we're going to be out of your way again soon," he assured her, picking up his bag and heading for the bedroom. Andy followed.

"I'm gonna have to borrow some clothes."

"Yeah. In there," Dan indicated to the wardrobe furthest to the left. "Anything except the white brushed denim shirt and black pants hanging next to it. I'm taking first dibs on the shower."

Andy nodded in thanks and started searching through the array of shirts in the wardrobe, many fitting the description of the excepted item, although only one had trousers hanging next to it. He found a blue shirt and pulled it free of the rail, only to discover it was missing a button. He tried a pink one (which would look ridiculous on him), but that had a lipstick mark on the collar. The grey shirt had a torn pocket, the red one was stained with something he didn't want to guess at, and the stripy one was creased to the point that the stripes looked like the readings from the ECG he'd had after a nasty brush with a Portuguese man o' war a few years back. He huffed, selected a white shirt at random, checked it for flaws and laid it on the bed. Next for some trousers, although he could already see what was going to happen here.

Dan emerged from the bathroom, the beard he'd been sporting for the past week gone, his hair curling into slight ringlets, as it was a bit longer than he usually kept it.

"Ah, fuck. See if you can find me a shirt that isn't white, will you?" Andy asked, exchanging places with his brother. He showered as quickly as he could, and impressively managed to shave without cutting himself, then returned to the bedroom, where Dan was dressed and slipping on some shoes.

"No shirts that aren't white," he said. "What's wrong with that one, anyway?"

"You'll see in a minute."

Andy took the clothes back to the bathroom. He was still damp, so it was a bit of a struggle to get into them, although Dan was slightly broader, which helped. He returned to the bedroom, pulling the belt from his jeans.

"Yeah. See what you mean, bro," Dan chuckled. They stood in front of the mirror and looked at each other's reflections, the only real difference being Andy's ear-ring and their hair, which was far less distinct than usual.

"Let's see what Alice has to say," Andy suggested, poking his belt through the loops of the trousers and securing them, before splashing on some cologne. He followed Dan through the lounge and they stopped next to each other in front of Alice. Shaunna tilted her head on one side and frowned.

"Addy?"

"Oh my goodness!" Alice said. "How fortunate for me that you smell more different than you look."

"We're screwed," Dan said.

"Yep," Andy nodded, "although looking like you is about the only way *I* will be tonight."

Alice, luckily, didn't catch the gist and just bid them a good evening. They'd decided to walk to the club, as it wasn't far away and they were fed up with sitting in passenger transport. Neither had brought a jacket, but it was a warm evening for the time of year and it didn't take them long to reach their destination, with Dan telling Andy a dreadfully longwinded story about a girl he once dated who had worked in the Irish club, other than on Thursday nights, when she was a lap dancer who went by the name of Kayleigh Ukulele.

"I didn't know you drank in the Irish club," Andy said, as they crossed the road.

"I didn't," Dan replied, with a little cough to cover his embarrassment. "Of course, we don't need to mention Ms. Ukulele to Adele."

"No, of course we don't, bro," Andy grinned, but then his face dropped, and he slowed right down. Dan followed his brother's gaze, across to where Jess was dismounting a motorbike and removing her helmet. Andy lunged forward and Dan grabbed him with lightning-fast reflexes.

"Don't, Andy. Let it go," he said, holding on with every bit of strength he had.

"I'm going to kill him," Andy snarled, fighting to free himself. Jess leaned in and said something to the man on the bike, whom Andy had correctly assumed was Rob. She waved, as he revved and roared out of the car park, down the road and right past them.

"I swear, I'm going to fucking kill him," Andy repeated, shaking loose of his brother's grasp.

"Come on." Dan walked in the opposite direction, away from the club. "Let's go and have a pint round the corner, give you a chance to calm down."

Andy followed, still grunting and growling, animal-like. He was barely containing his anger, and Dan took him down the side of the pub, telling him to stay where he was while he went inside and bought the drinks, thinking it would be OK to leave him unsupervised for five minutes. However, when he returned, he found Andy kicking the hell out of one of the pub's wheelie bins, and all because he'd caught his sleeve on it. Dan stepped in between.

"Enough," he said. "You'll get yourself arrested if you don't watch it." Andy backed off; Dan handed him his pint and he downed it in one.

"Let's go."

"No."

"I'm ready to talk to her now."

"Ha! Do you really think that's a wise move? This is Ellie's wedding, in case that testosterone infused brain of yours has forgotten."

Andy was still spoiling for a fight, but Dan's words had filtered through the rage sufficiently for him to get it back in check. His panting slowed and he pushed his hands into his pockets.

"Better?"

"A little. Just hurry up with that fucking pint."

Dan was drinking as fast as he could, but he still wasn't back to full health and ended up passing half of it to Andy, who necked it and launched the glass across the car park. Dan grabbed him by the arm.

"Come on."

On the way back, he sent Josh a message with a brief explanation and asked him to meet them outside. He was waiting at the entrance to the car park when they arrived.

"Josh. Good to see you, mate," Dan said, clapping him on the back. "You too, George," he added, spotting him standing a few yards away.

Josh nodded an acknowledgement, but was already weighing up Andy's state of mind. He wasn't sure there was much he could do without a punchbag or some other form of physical outlet, but he was going to have to try. He stepped to Andy's side and spoke so quietly that neither of the other two men heard what he said. Andy shrugged and turned away, walking with Josh, slowly, across the road to a stretch of grass verge.

George walked over to Dan and they watched, from a distance.

"This is a quick fix, to get you through tonight," Josh explained, "but it's not dealing with why you're feeling this way, so don't expect it to last. However, it will help you to stay on top of your anger, until you can address the situation. All right?" Andy nodded his consent.

"OK," Josh continued in a quiet, yet assertive tone. "Firstly, I want to you focus on your breathing. Do you remember how we did this in the hypnotherapy session? It's exactly the same. You're going to count slowly to six, taking a deep breath in, and then the same to exhale. Good, and again. Concentrate on your abdomen, imagining that you're filling it with air, then push it out with those same muscles."

Josh stayed quiet for a moment, to allow Andy's breathing to fall into a slow, steady rhythm.

"That's great, Andy. Now, maintain that pattern for me as best you can, but I want you to think about how you're feeling, physically, not mentally.

"I can feel my pulse in my neck throbbing against my collar. And in my temples."

"Do you know why that happens?"

"Yeah. It's a stress response. Fight or flight, or something."

"Spot on. Your body's running in survival mode. What else do you feel?"

"I'm sweating like a pig in a sausage factory," he joked self-consciously. "And my shoulders are aching. I should try and relax them, presumably?"

"That's right, but try tensing them even more first, as you'll be able to feel the sensation better. And then release that tension as you breathe out. Let's do that once more with your shoulders, and then we're going to carry on down your back, and then the rest of your body."

Josh talked Andy through each stage, occasionally reminding him to breathe deeply, but as they progressed the need to do so became less and less.

"What does it feel like now?" Josh asked finally.

"Better," Andy said, "as in I'm still angry, but I've got it under control."

"It's not helping that you've had such a rough couple of weeks. You look exhausted. I'm sure Ellie would be fine with you just popping in."

"You really are very good at your job, aren't you?" Andy said, attempting a smile.

"I don't do so bad at times," Josh replied bashfully. "If you were physically able to escape from the situation you'd have naturally come down anyway. Your nervous system does that automatically."

Andy nodded in understanding. "Thanks for giving it a helping hand. I'm ready to go inside now."

They walked back across the road, to where Dan and George were still standing, their expressions both of obvious and utter amazement. Dan fell in step next to Andy and they walked in together; Josh and George hung back, until they had cleared the doorway, not wanting to steal their thunder.

"You are just incredible," George gushed.

"Ah, it was nothing," Josh dismissed.

"Whatever you say, Joshua, whatever you say."

They started to walk back towards the building.

"Will you teach me how to do that?"

"Sure. I think it's in week seven, or thereabouts, in the 'Anger Management for Amateurs' topic. See page sixty-seven of your module guide."

CHAPTER TWENTY-FIVE

Sunday morning: George awoke a little after six and scowled at his clock, as if it were entirely responsible for the earliness of the hour. He'd had just two alcoholic drinks the previous night, one of those being the Champagne for the toast, which somebody (a member of the Irish branch of the Davenports, at a guess) drank on his behalf. Charged with the task of keeping a close eye on a certain Jeffries brother meant having his wits about him, particularly as the more Andy drank, the more likely it seemed he was going to act on his suppressed rage. Thankfully, it came to nothing; Jess was, by and large, ostracised by them all, and spent the night sitting at the bar and looking woeful.

So, all in all, it had been a sober evening, and hard-going at times, but what a beautiful day! Eleanor and James seemed happy and relaxed, and even Mrs. Davenport stopped fussing once the music started. The food was unbelievable, with so many things George had never tried before. Some dishes originated in Trinidad and Tobago, he assumed, with lots of fish, fruit and vegetables, and rich, hot sauces. There were also traditional Irish wedding foods, such as soda bread and salmon, as well as the finger buffet standards of cheeseboards and things on cocktail sticks. He recognised the sausages; as for the rest: 'things on sticks' pretty much covered it for now.

Then there was the cake; Wotto really had pulled out all the stops for this. It consisted of two tiers, with small, pale lemon-yellow rose buds in various stages of opening, that started from the base layer and climbed the side, then up to the top tier, with no obvious means of the two being joined together, other than via the delicate stems of the climbing roses, and he would know; the only time Andy got close to approaching Jess was when George was trying to figure out how the top cake hadn't come crashing down onto the bottom one, although in his defence, he wasn't the only one who was supposed to be 'on watch', but at that stage Josh had gone to talk to Eleanor.

Fifteen minutes had passed in this state of reminiscing, and the bed was really very cosy, so he decided to give it a little longer before he gave up on sleep entirely. It turned out to be a good choice, as the next time he awoke it was almost eight o'clock, and he could probably have slept even longer still, but for one reason.

"Fuck, fuck, fuck," Josh cursed, as he stumbled at the top of the stairs and lifted his foot. "Ouch!" He pulled the drawing pin out of his heel and rubbed at the injured spot. "The one bloody day I don't put any shoes on. Typical." He hobbled back to his room, slid his feet into a pair of loafers, and tried again, this time succeeding in getting all the way downstairs without further injury or lewd language. He filled the coffee filter with the last of the ground coffee, made a note on the magnetic shopping list, and had a good stretch. Not a bad night's sleep, all things considered; he'd drifted off as soon as he'd got into bed, awoken with cramp at two, was asleep again by three, and then straight through until eight. Based on his previous bouts of insomnia, this was an outstanding achievement, and he mentally congratulated himself on finally cracking the best approach to falling back to sleep, which had always been his problem. The solution? To replay George's words: he knew the truth and he still loved him. It was as simple as that.

George tried once more to turn over and go back to sleep, but the aroma of fresh coffee had floated up the stairs and under his door. He wasn't a big fan of coffee; however, when freshly brewed it smelled divine, and was enough to bring his pseudo lie-in to an end. Reluctantly, he got out of bed, pulled his dressing gown from the hook on the door and left the room, all without opening his eyes.

"Jesus!" he shouted at the top of the stairs and lifted his foot. "Where the hell did that come from?" He braced himself and pulled the red-topped pin free from his big toe, then hobbled the rest of the way down.

"Morning," Josh greeted him.

"Good morning. I just stood on a drawing pin."

"You too? They must've fallen out of your pocket yesterday."

"Or we brought them home on our shoes last night?"

"That's a good point. Oh dear. I know I'm up too early when I open my mouth and terrible puns fall out of it. Coffee?"

"Yeah, thanks." George seemed a little distracted, but then he hadn't long woken up, Josh reasoned, and didn't question it further. He poured two coffees and they took them through to the lounge so they could sit and talk about the wedding and the reception, revisiting Andy's rage and Josh's 'taming of the beast', agreeing that aside from this relatively minor interruption, it was definitely the best wedding they'd ever attended. Better still, they hadn't had to choose a wedding present, because Eleanor had gone along with James's wishes that they all donate whatever they would have spent on a gift to a charity of their choosing. George had already made his donation to a local horse and donkey sanctuary, although Josh was still trying to decide on a suitably worthy cause, which wasn't anything to do with him seeing some as less deserving than others. Rather, he had yet to find one that inspired him to give his money over.

"I'd best get dressed," George said, swirling the last inch or so of coffee around in the bottom of his cup. "I need to go and see my mum today, seeing as I'm not going to be about until after next weekend. I forgot to tell her, otherwise I wouldn't bother."

"Why don't you give her a ring instead?"

"No phone."

"Not even a 'pay-as-you-go'?"

"Nope. She's the only person I know who still uses the phone

293

box when she needs to make calls."

"Wow. I'm really shocked by that."

"I did offer to buy her one," George said, fighting a smile at the memory of it. "But she said 'no thanks'."

What she actually said was more along the lines of "You can stick your fuckin' mobile phone up yer arse. What fuckin' use am I gonna get out of it? And they give you cancer." And then she lit another cigarette.

"Well I'm not doing anything today," Josh said, intending it to be a subtle hint that he was available for transport, if George wanted it. He'd have just made the offer, but he didn't feel it was right to do so; not yet. George missed the hint, and took his cup to the kitchen, then went straight upstairs. Josh finished his coffee and refilled the cup, taking this with him to his room, to wait for the bathroom to become free. His current reading material was temptingly close by, and he reached out and picked it up. It was Freud's *Three Essays on the Theory of Sexuality*: a volume that had always caused him more trouble than it was worth, for it was here that he could always find a particular passage, known off by heart, and capable of destroying everything he had read to the contrary since he first happened upon it at the age of nineteen:

> The character of hysterics shows a degree of sexual repression in excess of the normal quantity, an intensification of resistance against the sexual instinct (which we have already met with in the form of shame, disgust and morality), and what seems like an instinctive aversion on their part to any intellectual consideration of sexual problems. As a result of this, in especially marked cases, the patients remain in complete ignorance of sexual matters right into the period of sexual maturity.

What got him every time was the "instinctive aversion…to any intellectual consideration of sexual problems", because he could intellectualise them perfectly well—in everybody else. As

294

far as his own sexuality was concerned (or lack thereof), the only reason he kept returning to any attempt at its intellectual consideration was because of this damned passage of text. But then he wasn't a hysteric, usually.

The bathroom door opened and Josh glanced up in time to see George walk past on the way to his own room. He backstepped and looked in.

"You OK?" he asked.

"Sort of. I don't want to talk about it now. It'll make me miserable and I don't want to be miserable."

"OK," George said and stepped off once more, but again, backtracked. Josh's question came out a split second before his own.

"Would you like a lift to see your mum?"

"Do you want to come and meet my mum?"

The effect was a stuttered delivery of the word 'mum', followed by a silence, as they both waited for the other to answer, and then they did it again.

"Yes, please."

"I'd like that, thanks."

George shook his head. "We really must stop doing that." He continued on his way, this time making it to his room.

Josh opened one of the cupboards above his fitted wardrobes, shoved the book inside, and went for a shower, although out of sight was the easy part, for the words were etched into his brain. It was a long time before he emerged from the steamy bathroom, by which point George was dressed and waiting very impatiently in the lounge. Josh ran a brush through his hair, gave it a brief blow with the dryer and picked out a sweater and jeans at random, feeling under pressure due to the constant movement back and forth downstairs.

"What do you do in there?" George said, trying and failing to hide his irritation.

"I get lost in thought," Josh said vaguely, because he still was. "Sorry." He smiled guiltily.

"Never mind. Are you ready?"

"Err…" He patted his empty pockets and ran back upstairs for his phone, picking up his keys on the way down again. He'd snapped out of it and now noticed that George was very jumpy. The question should perhaps have been whether *he* was ready, but soon they were in the car and on their way, so there was little point to asking.

"Can we stop for breakfast somewhere?" George asked, fidgeting with his seatbelt. It always dug into his neck when he was worked up.

"Anywhere in particular?" Josh asked, calculating various routes that would take them past fast food restaurants, cafés or petrol stations.

"Somewhere that sells bacon toasties."

"Right you are." They turned left at the next junction and pulled up at a burger van; George was out of the car almost before it stopped. Josh turned off the engine and followed, arriving in time to be handed a slimy white roll with a droopy rasher of bacon stuffed slapdash in its centre.

"No bread, so no toast," George explained, passing over a five pound note. The young lad behind the counter fished some coins out of the cash box and dropped them into George's hand. "Thanks," he said, wiping the grease on his jeans in disgust.

They walked back to the car, eating the bacon rolls in silence, but for the occasional crunch of stale bread. Josh didn't like food being consumed in his car, which was always meticulously clean, a fact that was further exacerbating George's anxiety. At some point soon—preferably before they arrived at the flats—he was going to have to warn Josh what to expect, for even if he had unknowingly been followed home one day, the place was far worse now than it had been back then, when there were two other blocks, flowerbeds, and maintenance people who kept on top of the litter and vandalism. In comparison to where Josh had grown up, it was a slum. There was no other word for it.

Josh wiped his hands on the rough napkin the bacon roll had been served in and looked around for a bin.

"Here," George held out his hand, "I'll keep hold of it for now." Josh handed over the scrunched up, greasy paper, and then they were back in the car, with less than five minutes' drive to their destination.

"Just so you know," George said cagily, "the flats are due for demolition, so the council have stopped doing any work on them."

"OK," Josh acknowledged casually. He'd been waiting for something like this ever since they left, and there was still more.

"Also, my mum…" George began. How best to describe her? A rough diamond? A bit unpolished? The 'salt of the earth' type? It all sounded so twee and in any case was completely inaccurate.

"What about her?" Josh prompted.

"She's as rough as a bear's arse," he said. It was a phrase she used all the time, aptly. Josh had never heard it before and it gave him the giggles.

"Define, please," he spluttered, wiping the tears from his eyes. George didn't look too impressed.

"She's got a mouth like a docker, she chain-smokes and sleeps in her clothes. The flat hasn't been decorated for years and her staple diet is tea and biscuits, supplemented by ale. She does clean though. Sort of."

"I see. Thanks for the warning," Josh said, becoming serious once more in order to attend to the road ahead. He was now driving into the estate and the tarmac was like a moonscape, with more potholes than level bits between. As he drove on, past the two-storey, concrete maisonettes, he was overwhelmed by the poverty and ugliness of it all. Ahead loomed the solitary tower block, its front face in full shadow, a formidable blot on an otherwise beautiful skyline.

"See what I mean?" George said, shifting uncomfortably in his seat. He was suddenly regretting asking if Josh wanted to meet his mother. At this time on a Sunday morning, she'd be watching one of the TV programmes about the countryside and telling the presenters what she thought of their rustic cottages and scenic vistas. "Pull in over there," George indicated to a space next to a shell of a car, burnt-out and rusted almost beyond recognition. Josh did as he was told. "And make sure you lock up," he warned.

He'd figured that much out for himself. He wanted to stop and tell him that all of this was fine. Better than fine, because here he was, not invited round to play as such, but granted access to the secret side of George's upbringing. The respect and love he felt for him right at that moment was overwhelming. They stopped in the foyer and both sniffed, then quickly resorted to mouth-breathing.

"Stairs or lift," George asked, sounding like he had a cold.

"Lift," Josh replied in a similar fashion. George pulled his jacket sleeve over his hand and pressed the 'call' button. The lift could be heard rattling its way down from whichever floor it had last stopped. The indicator light hadn't worked since—well, ever, now he came to think about it.

They stepped inside the steel box and it started its juddering ascent to the ninth floor. Josh braved a quick breath in so he could speak.

"Thank you for doing this," he said, then added: "I know how hard it is for you, but I'm glad you invited me. It means a lot." He ran out of breath. George wasn't taking the same risk and merely nodded to confirm he had heard and understood. The lift stopped suddenly, and the doors opened part-way, George giving them a helping hand (again, with protective sleeve) so they could both step into the draughty, urine-scented corridor. He walked slightly in front, mapping out Josh's path for him. They stopped outside a door.

"It still looks the same," Josh said in awe.

"Of course it bloody does," George snapped, but then checked himself. "Sorry. That was out of order. You know I'm shitting myself about this, don't you?"

"I do. Plus, you appear to have inherited what you tell me of your mother's propensity for cussing on the way up in the lift."

"Says he, who woke me up this morning by shouting 'fuck'

no less than three times!" Josh grinned and waited while George took out his keys and unlocked the door.

"Hi, Mum," he called. She didn't reply straight away, which was entirely usual, and when she did acknowledge him, it wasn't with a standard greeting.

"Did that gobshite have bulls like this? Look at the size of the fuckers! They're fuckin' enormous. And look at the balls on 'em. That can't be normal, surely?"

George squinted at the miniscule TV screen. "Yeah, they're normal," he assured her.

"Aye fuck. They'd proper make yer eyes water." She stubbed out her cigarette end and immediately lit another.

"Where's Monty?"

"Buggered off."

"When?"

"Don't bloody start. A bit ago, when I went down Paki's. He'll come back. He always fuckin' does, unfortunately."

George opened his mouth to say something and coughed instead, as a cloud of blue smoke was exhaled in his direction.

"You makin' a brew, or what?" his mother asked, although it wasn't a question really. "Best check the milk first, mind, it came out in friggin' lumps yesterday. Oh." She stopped, having suddenly noticed George was not alone. "Who are you?"

"Mum, this is Josh. We went to school together."

"Never saw 'im before."

Josh smiled, but for the first time in his life couldn't string together an introduction. He'd always known about Mr. Morley abandoning them both when George was young, so should he call her Mrs. Morley? Or did she go by a different address these days? Whether he got it right or wrong probably wouldn't make much difference to her response.

"Hello," he opted for instead.

"You're not another one of them fuckin' woofters, are you?"

"Err, I..." Josh stammered.

"She means are you gay," George helped him out. "Mum! You can't just ask people things like that. It's personal!"

"Well you answered me question anyhow, so go and get that kettle put on. I'm spittin' feathers 'ere."

George stepped over the vacuum cleaner and made his way across the room, leaving Josh loitering next to the sofa.

"Go with 'im, if you like. I'm not proud," she told him.

Josh followed George into the kitchen and looked around. His description was very accurate, he'd give him that. In general, the place was spotlessly clean, but there was so much stuff—clocks, little china dogs, vases, pots, pans, mugs—and the entire flat was covered in a sticky yellow film. George unplugged the toaster so he could plug in the kettle, jumping back in advance of the shock he knew he'd receive.

"The wiring's a bit shot," he explained. Josh was slowly spinning on the spot, taking in his surroundings. When he came back round, George had the biggest grin on his face.

"What?"

"I think it might actually be worth all this trauma just to see you speechless for once."

Josh laughed nervously. "She's a bit scary, your mum."

"She's not really. It's her accent, makes her sound hard. All the lads around here used to be terrified of her."

"She's from Manchester?"

"Yeah. Grew up on a council estate that makes this place look like Knightsbridge." George went through his usual routine of rinsing and scrubbing the generally unused mugs. "Wonder where Monty is? I'm gonna have to go and have a look before we leave."

"Who's Monty?"

"The dog. A Westie with an identity crisis—thinks he's a pit bull."

"Ah. I understand now. He ran off when she went to the corner shop."

"Congratulations," George said, "you have completed your first lesson in Mancunian." He filled up the three cups with water, the tea bags bobbing to the surface. "A couple of other things you should know," he continued. "The 'Paki Shop' has never been run by Asian people. I think the current lot are Polish. Whatever, it's just a figure of speech—shorthand for the 'open all hours local convenience store'. Secondly, there's no coffee, because it's too expensive."

"Right. Got all that."

"And she'll no doubt tell you all about Julian in a minute. He runs the hairdresser's next to the 'Paki Shop' and is as gay as a daisy. The rest of the shops are shut now. Anyway, she thinks the sun shines out of Julian's you-know-what."

"I did wonder what she meant by 'another one of them'. Does she know about you?"

"Yeah, and she doesn't care. She says it how it is—Pakis and woofters—but it's not meant in the way you'd think. The gay community in Manchester isn't a new thing, she says. Lots of the men where she lived were gay and had their own places to meet long before the trendy bit opened in the city. In fact, the only people she really doesn't like are straight men."

"Because of your dad?"

"My dad, her dad, most of the men around here. They're all the same." He didn't get any further than this, as his mother shouted from the living room.

"Oy. Don't you be bummin' in me kitchen. I keep me food in there."

George shook his head. "She doesn't." He beckoned Josh over to the fridge and opened the door. The light didn't work, but he could see that it contained only a carton of milk and a tub of margarine. "And for the record, the only person I ever brought home was Jono, from number thirty-four, and only because his mum was a smackhead, I mean heroin addict." George took the milk out and sniffed it cautiously. She'd obviously bought more, because it smelled fresh enough. He poured some into two of the mugs of tea and looked to Josh to see whether he wanted any, as he rarely drank tea, and when he did it tended to be Earl Grey or the herbal stuff. Josh nodded.

"I wasn't going to ask about your past conquests, by the way."

"You know pretty much all there is to know. Kris, Jono, Kris again, a couple of one night stands at college, Sam—that's for another time—and Joe." George fished out the tea bags with a spoon and held up one of the mugs for Josh to take. It was the tiniest flicker, hardly noticeable at all, but he saw it. "Are you bothered about Joe?" he asked.

"What?"

"The flash of the green-eyed monster."

"Damn. I tried to hide that," Josh blushed.

"Well don't," George chastised gently. "So?"

"No. Not Joe. Sam. You've never mentioned him before."

"It's a long story, and not a good one. And yes, before you say anything, Joshua, it is complicated, which is the only reason I said it was for another time. OK?"

Josh nodded his acceptance, even though he was still fighting the jealousy within. George tutted.

"Just drink your tea and forget about it for now," he said, thrusting the mug at him. Josh took it and tried to do as he'd been told. He glanced at the tea and wrinkled his nose.

"There's nothing wrong with the milk," George restated, taking the lid off the carton again to double check. It still didn't smell sour. He went over to the fridge and took out the margarine tub. It was rock-solid and covered in ice crystals. "It's frozen," he said, checking the temperature dial. It was on the highest setting and he turned it down, making a mental note to ask his mother why. He deposited the milk and picked up the other two mugs, taking them through to the lounge, Josh trailing a step behind.

"Ta, love," his mother said, taking her tea and shoving her old empty mug across the cluttered table with her foot. Josh observed the appallingly worn old slippers, holes cut in the sides to allow her bunions to protrude, and followed them upwards: the brown pop socks, rolled down to her ankles, men's grey jogging pants, baggy, off-white t-shirt, and finally the rollers.

"Grown an extra 'ead again, have I?" she asked him with a twinkle in her eye that was pure George. Josh smiled. He was feeling a little less awkward, now he had some understanding of where he was. The people with whom he came into contact on a daily basis used words to convey how they felt, and to fill voids. Those words, as George had told him so many times, were nothing more than cleverly measured bullshit, thought up by the middle classes in an attempt to convince the listener that regardless of how it looked from the outside, they too were suffering. His surgery and the work he did there were of no relevance to this world and he felt like he had stumbled into a different reality. It was a real effort to stay grounded, because the researcher in him was desperate to step back and observe these phenomena from afar. That's how they all did it—the sociologists. It would be easy to detach himself from this experience. Easy, but wrong. This wasn't some nameless 'ethnographic insight'; it was real life, and it was George's.

The sound of scratching at the door broke Josh out of his trance, and George went to let Monty in.

"It's rude to stare y'know," George's mother remarked without taking her eyes from the TV.

"Sorry," Josh mumbled. "George looks a lot like you."

"Course he does, you daft bat. I'm his mother. D'you not look like your mother?"

"I don't remember. She died when I was little."

"Ahh. Fuckin' shame, that is."

Monty trotted into the living room, head up, ears pricked, stub of docked tail vertical and stiff. He stopped in front of Josh and started to growl, slowly backing off, the growling getting louder.

"Shut it, Mont," George's mum ordered. The little dog wandered off behind the sofa, still grumbling and very disgruntled, then suddenly appeared next to Josh's end.

"You're sitting in his spot," George explained.

"Oh." Josh shuffled along.

"Don't fuckin' move, just for the dog," George's mum said, still watching the TV. "Christ. What a soft shite." She patted her lap. "Come 'ere, Mont." Monty prowled past the sofa, glancing up sideways at Josh, and jumped onto the arm of the chair.

"I turned the fridge down," George said, trying to lighten the atmosphere. It backfired somewhat.

"What the hell did you do that for?"

"Because the milk was frozen. Why was it turned up so high?"

"It's broken, that's why. You always have to bloody interfere."

"You need a new one, I keep telling you that, but…"

"There's nowt wrong with it, if you keep the fuckin' thing on full."

"I'll get you a new one."

"You fuckin' won't."

"I'll do it when you're at work. Then what you gonna do?"

"Throw the fucker out the window, that's what I'll friggin' well do."

"Mam, come on!"

"Enough!" She turned and glared at Josh. "Brought you along for moral support, did he?"

"No, err…" He looked to George for assistance.

"Drink up," was all he said. Josh did as he was told, appreciating the coldness of the milk, as it had cooled the tea quickly, and they were done in less than ten minutes.

"Right, Mum." George leaned over her chair and kissed her cheek. "We're off. See you in two weeks."

"Why not next week?"

"Going away tomorrow."

"So you're not staying for tea?"

"No. Got to pack still."

"Right, well you best hop it then. I think I've got some of that tinned spaghetti shite in the cupboard anyhow. Have a good time and behave."

"I will," George said and kissed her again.

"Bye," Josh called.

"Ta-rah, love," she said. He followed George out to the

door, but just as he was about to step outside, she called him back. He was horrified. George shrugged to indicate he had no idea why. It looked like he had no choice in the matter: he went back to the living room and stopped just to the left of the chair, Monty growling and every so often flashing his teeth. George's mum put her hand on the little dog and glanced at Josh, then returned her gaze to the TV as she spoke.

"He thinks he's a big hard man, my Georgie, but he's a soft lad. Got a big heart, he has, and doesn't think to hide it. So you look after 'im, right? Or I'll break your fuckin' neck. Do you hear?"

"I hear."

"Good. Now fuck off." Josh didn't need telling twice. He almost ran back out to George and didn't care any more that the corridor stank of piss, nor that the lift clanged dangerously, nor that there was a strong probability his car was now resting on bricks. He was glad he had come, but he was absolutely overjoyed to be going.

When they got back to the car (still with its four wheels attached, although some young lads with skateboards were taking more than a passing interest in the petrol cap), both of them fell into their seats, and Josh put his foot down as hard as he dared without risking damage to his suspension. Only when they cleared the final row of maisonettes did either of them speak.

"What did she say?" George asked.

"She said I had to look after you."

"OK?"

"And a bit more besides, but that was the gist."

"She likes you. She didn't mention Julian, so she must do."

"Yeah. I like her. She's…"

"Don't you dare say 'down to earth'!"

"I wasn't going to." Josh drove on, processing all the new information tumbling around his mind.

"What were you going to say, then?" George asked after about five minutes.

"I was going to say she's made me appreciate just how lucky I am. I know that sounds really condescending, and it's not meant to be. Seeing the way she just gets on with it, with no complaints…"

"Ha! She's no stranger to moaning, when the mood takes her."

"But that's just it. She's got plenty to moan about, unlike those bloody awful people who pay so they can come and dump their meaningless woes on me. They don't know the half of it and neither do I."

"And Josh finally gets a social conscience."

"Hmm. Don't you worry about her not eating and stuff?"

"Yeah, but what's the point? She'll eat if I cook something, which is why she was pushing for us to stay for tea, or dinner, whichever you want to call it."

"Was she?"

"That comment about the spaghetti. She tries to make me feel guilty, and it works every time, because I've been thinking maybe we could have stayed a bit longer ever since we got in the lift."

"Why didn't you say?"

"Oh, I didn't want to stay. It's tough watching her struggle on, but she won't accept help from anybody. She's got her cleaning job in the primary school and her housing benefit. That's it. She won't take any money off me. And she still won't bloody move out of that flat. I swear one day she's going to burn the place down. It's probably why the council have stopped hassling her—it'll save them having to pay for the demolition."

They'd arrived back at the house and remained in the car for a few minutes more, while Josh surveyed his own little corner of leafy suburbia through fresh eyes, and George continued to beat himself up over his mother's spaghetti remark.

"I suppose we should go and pack," he said finally.

"Yeah, you're probably right."

CHAPTER TWENTY-SIX

Jess wasn't going on the holiday. She'd reached the decision during the wedding reception, when everyone was ignoring her, and she could totally understand why, but how could she explain? Rob wanted to keep the full extent of his heart condition to himself, and whilst he hadn't sworn her to secrecy, it was more than apparent that he didn't want her to tell the others. When Eleanor lambasted her on Friday, she was desperate to share all that Rob had told her since the reunion, because the stress of keeping it to herself was immense. Much as she was attracted to him, the time they were spending together was for his benefit more than hers, and when he was finally gone, she'd be able to tell them the whole truth. She only hoped it wouldn't be too late to save her friendship with Andy.

Unbeknownst to her, Kris was on his way round right at that moment. He would arrive to find her sitting on the sofa, stilled by indecision. Should she unpack the suitcase, or not? Kris knocked on the door and waited. This wasn't his idea; it was Dan's. They needed to get Jess out of the way, he said. Andy was still spoiling for a fight and was insistent that he was going to the house to get his things. How long Dan could contain him, he didn't know, but something needed to be done, and Kris was the only one talking to her. So, here he was, knocking for a second time, having seen her through the window when he arrived, and as reluctant to be here as she was to let him in. She relented on his third knock.

"Hi," she greeted him, her eyes ringed with last night's mascara and sleeplessness. "Come in." Kris stepped inside, noting the open suitcase in the lounge, the piles of clothes half-packed or half-unpacked; it was impossible to say.

"How are you feeling today?" he asked. A stupid question. He could see the answer right before him.

"Like shit," she said, and sat with her head in her hands. He watched her cry from across the room. He didn't want to be here. He didn't want to have any part of this. But Dan had said it was essential.

"Hey, come on," he tried, a little more sympathetically than he'd intended, which was a good thing. He sat beside her and put an arm around her. She collapsed against him, her body shuddering with each sob. It was unusual to see Jess in such a state. She was always so together. He waited, said no more, patting or rubbing her back whenever it seemed appropriate to do so. He didn't want to be here.

"If I tell you something," she gulped between rasping intakes of breath, "will you promise not to tell anyone?"

"Erm. I guess?" he agreed, quite sure as he did so that the promise was destined to be broken at the first opportunity that presented itself.

Jess sniffed and wiped her eyes, leaving black trails on her sleeves. She steadied herself, took a deep breath, and began.

"Rob's got a serious heart condition. He's on a waiting list for surgery, but it could take months, and he doesn't have that long." The sobs erupted again. Kris put his arm back around her. He still didn't want to be here, but at least he was beginning to understand why she had acted so inconsiderately over the past week.

"That must be very hard for you," he said, once again impressed by how genuine he sounded.

"It is," she gasped. "He loves me."

"And you love him, I understand," Kris said. He'd been here for ten minutes already. How on earth was he going to turn her from gibbering wreck to someone who would consider leaving the house before the next ten had also ticked by? That's all he had.

"The thing is," she continued, "I don't love him at all. I care about him and find him very attractive, but I don't love him."

"Oh." Kris stopped patting her back. "So you're doing this for him?" She nodded and sniffed. Well, he thought, that makes it quite admirable then, even if she has trampled all over her best friends along the way.

"And I can't go on the holiday, because…" The sobbing again, for goodness' sakes! And now the long sniffly silence. "Because he might…" She didn't get any further than this, and Kris finished the sentence in his head.

"But he might not," he reasoned. "Then not only will you have missed out on a holiday for no reason, you'll have probably lost Ellie's friendship for good. Listen." This was it: not the ideal moment, and if he'd been going from a script instead of improvising, he'd have hoped for a more convincing build-up, but he had just nine more minutes. "Let's go for a walk." She didn't protest. An encouraging sign. "Maybe stop off for some lunch and a drink somewhere, get you out of this place for a while." And out of Andy's way, he added silently.

"I don't know, Kris. I'm in no fit state. I haven't showered. I'm not even dressed." Cue blubbering, interspersed with snotty sniffs. Time was ticking on.

"I'm not suggesting we go to a five star restaurant, just a pub lunch. Throw on some old jeans and you'll do just fine." Eight minutes and counting.

"Oh, I just…"

Tissue: she needs a tissue. Kris searched the room frantically. No tissues left! He ran upstairs to the bathroom and grabbed a length of loo roll.

"No excuses," he said, shoving the wad of toilet paper at her. "Come on. You can cry on my shoulder, or we'll talk about something else entirely." Seven minutes.

She blew her nose and sighed. That was a good sign, surely? She was about to rally, but…no. More blubbering.

"Come on, Jess," he said gently, although behind the scenes the director was cursing her for turning it into a melodrama.

"Go put some clothes on. I'll wait here."

Finally the gasping chugged to a halt. She wiped her nose and peered at him through her hair. He pushed it from her face and nodded encouragingly. Six minutes.

"OK," she said at last. She hugged him. He felt such a fraud.

"What're you waiting for? Chop chop!" he said. This really was pushing it to the wire, and he had a feeling that even slinging on a pair of old jeans was going to take an awful lot longer than five minutes. Jess went upstairs. Kris took out his phone and typed frantically.

Give me 10 more mins if u can

Much banging about overhead. The flush of the toilet. Brushing of teeth. A slammed door. More banging and then footfall on the stairs. Thank God. They were playing in extra time now.

"Ready?"

"Yeah. I just need to..."

"Get a coat. It's a bit chilly out there today."

"I need to put on a bit of eye liner."

"You look gorgeous already." And you've still got plenty on from last night, he thought.

"OK." Jess grabbed her jacket and they were out of the door. Kris glanced furtively in both directions, picking what he hoped was the alternate route to Dan and Andy's. He quickened his pace and Jess caught him up.

"What's the big rush?"

"Just keeping warm."

"I don't think it's too bad today, as it goes."

They turned the corner just as Dan and Andy did, at opposite ends of the street. Kris checked his phone screen.

Are we all clear?

He typed to confirm they were and shoved his phone back in

his pocket, affording Jess an overly bright smile. Was she on to him? Damn.

Andy let himself into the house and went straight upstairs, armed with a suitcase and his rucksack. He was taking everything he could fit inside these two receptacles, working on the assumption that this was the last time he'd set foot in the place. Anything he didn't take now he was prepared to abandon. He'd work out where he was going to live when they got back from Wales.

Dan wandered restlessly between the downstairs rooms, collecting bits and pieces he knew belonged to his brother: a couple of DVDs; his phone charger; the keys to his written-off Audi. He picked up the photo of Andy with Jess, at her graduation ball, and slammed it face-down. Keeping his brother from retaliation was unbelievably tough, and made all the more difficult by his own barely contained rage. At least here, Adele wasn't around to further stir things up.

Kris directed Jess over into a dark, quiet corner of the pub. It was a funny little place, with a few regulars standing at the bar, chatting about football, the landlord pulling pints and joining in with the conversation. Drinks poured and food ordered, Kris took the chair opposite.

"The reason I left the hen party," Jess began to explain. Great, he thought, more excuses, although the effects of Shaunna's poison were beginning to wear off. "Was to go and see Rob's bike."

"OK." Surely she'd seen it plenty of times already, seeing as she'd spent most of the week with her legs spread either side of it?

"Not the one he rides," she added. Kris wondered if he'd accidentally asked the question out loud. "He has another one. An Indian Scout, or something, totally rebuilt and worth about twenty-five grand. He's selling it, to pay for the operation privately. Anyway, he'd been going on about this bike all week, and how he wanted to show it to me. He's so proud of all the work he's done to restore it." She stopped to drink. Kris waited.

"So," she continued, "he sent me a text on Thursday night to say this guy was coming to look at the bike on Friday morning and he was gutted I wasn't going to get to see his pride and joy. And I thought, it won't take long. I'll just go with him now. He can show me the bike and Ellie won't know a thing about it. She was busy with her sisters and everyone else. How was I supposed to know she was going to come and find us all to give us those stupid wings?"

"And the bike?"

"Meh. It's a bike. Nothing special, as far as I could see. But it's a classic, which is why it's worth so much."

"So he's sold it now, has he?"

"Yeah. The guy who came to see it is bringing the cash tomorrow, Rob says."

A young girl arrived at their table and laid plates before them. Kris's phone vibrated.

"Just popping to the loo," he said, making a quick getaway and pulling his phone from his pocket as soon as he was out of sight.

"All done," Dan said.

"Good stuff. Everything OK?"

"Yeah. Andy's waiting in the car so I've got to go. See you tomorrow. And thanks."

"No problem," Kris lied. As much as he really was feeling a little bit more sorry for Jess than when Dan roped him into this, he was as angry as the rest of them. Whether it was for Rob's benefit or not, she'd been extremely selfish. He returned to the table and glanced at the unappetising baguette. He'd not long had lunch, and he picked at it until such time as it was suitable to suggest they left. Jess hugged him and thanked him for listening. At least he had the heart to feel a little bit guilty that it was all an act.

CHAPTER TWENTY-SEVEN

Coordinating transport and re-jigging the cabin arrangements was a military operation befitting the extraordinary talents of either of the most senior Davenport women, but Eleanor was not to be worried with such trivialities, Adele had declared. And due credit to her, she'd thought of everything, right down to motorway stops and consideration of the positions of the three cabins they would be staying in. She'd even printed off the driving directions and map of the holiday village, so she could check all was unfolding as it should be.

Thus, Andy and Jess were no longer travelling together. Instead, Jess was going with George, Josh and Kris, while Shaunna and Andy were with them in the 4x4, and Casper was in the half of the boot that wasn't piled with suitcases and toddler accessories. It was this, or put Shaunna with Jess—a suggestion the former rejected in very clear and none too polite terms. Eleanor, James, Oliver and Toby accounted for the final car and the only unchanged unit in their group. Alas, the cabin arrangements were somewhat more complex, because neither Kris nor Shaunna was prepared to spend the week sharing with Jess. They wanted to stay together, which surprised Adele and she felt she had to say something to Shaunna about being a mug and giving Kris another chance, after what he'd done. Shaunna told her she was absolutely right, but asked her to let it go, for the sake of not causing further trouble, not with the situation with Jess and Andy. However, she was insistent, and in the end it was easier to give in than to try and explain.

So the cabin arrangements were essentially the same as the

travel ones. The Browns had a two-bedroomed cabin, with a double and a single room; Josh, George, Jess and Kris were sharing the first of two three-bedroomed cabins, each with a double, a twin and a single; Adele, Dan, Shaunna and Andy were, of course, sharing the second, although how that was going to pan out was yet to be seen. At the moment, they seemed perfectly content, sitting either side of little Shaunna's bumper seat, taking turns at Peek-a-boo, re-dressing dollies, or playing 'Where's Teddy?'. The toddler was giggling away happily and the radio station they were tuned in to was playing decent music, so all was well. Adele checked off the next set of directions on her printed map, even though the SatNav was doing perfectly fine without her assistance. Dan resisted the urge to tell her what she was doing was utterly pointless, and moved into the left-hand lane, as instructed.

"It says 'stay right' on here," Adele said purposefully.

"But *she* said 'keep left'." A few miles further on, Dan smoothly transitioned onto the next motorway; Adele folded her arms and turned her attention to some sheep in a distant field.

Fifteen miles behind them (a gap that continued to increase the further they travelled) Eleanor was on the phone to the husband of her dying patient, who was still holding on, incredibly. She was trying her utmost to tactfully explain that she was not going to be around for the next week, and Doctor King would be making a home visit after surgery. The husband was very understanding, and wished her a pleasant honeymoon. The words were empty, yet she was so moved by them that she remained quiet for several minutes after, scrolling back and forth through the screens on her phone and temporarily unaware of her surroundings, until James had to swerve to avoid a lorry that had pulled out without indicating just as they were passing it. He drew in breath and exhaled very slowly; Eleanor looked over her shoulder to check on the boys. Poor little Oliver was totally wiped out, having spent the first half of Sunday under the control of his paternal grandfather, and the second half burning off all the pent-up energy he'd accumulated during the morning, through a variety of tried and tested techniques, including throwing himself off the couch, racing from the kitchen to the bedroom, bouncing on the bed and screaming until he was hoarse, and finally crying he didn't want to go bed for an hour, then passing out before James made it to the door. So, with both boys fast asleep in the back of the car, Eleanor turned on the car stereo and set it at a low volume, settled back in her seat and let the sleepy jazz music float over her. James tapped along on the steering wheel, whistling sections of melody wherever it was loud enough for him to get away with it.

Running almost parallel with the Browns' car (as in close enough to witness the lorry incident and currently behind, but they'd been passing each other intermittently ever since they joined the motorway) were Josh, George, Kris and Jess—not a particularly communicative group, with Kris listening to an audio book on his headphones, and Jess listening to music through hers. George turned to the front again and flicked over to the next page of the heavy text book on his lap.

"The anger management they describe in here is exactly the same as the prison psychologist uses. The success rate is appalling." Josh heard but didn't pass comment. "What you did the other night with..." George didn't say, just in case Jess could hear him. "That works really well."

"In limited situations." Josh indicated to pull out, and passed James again, Eleanor and George wearily exchanging waves. "It was all down to trial and error, really. Having worked on *certain people* with *certain problems* for so long, I figured it would probably work on a *certain person's* you-know-what too." Josh pulled in again and settled behind a coach for a while. "But they will still have to have it out, and soon." George glanced back at Jess, who was oblivious to their conversation, lost in the maze of her music and thoughts.

"Our first stop is in sixteen miles," he said, as they passed a 'Services' sign. Josh brushed his hair out of his face and shifted his position.

"Perfect. I'm ready for a large cappuccino or two."

Dan pulled into the services, and parked up. He was eager to stretch his legs and was flagging, with the last of the flu virus clinging on for dear life. He opened his door and stepped out, suddenly coming over dizzy.

"Whoa," he said, grabbing hold of the back door as Andy opened it.

"You OK?"

"Yeah, but I think you'd best take over for a bit."

"No worries." Andy turned back and reached inside, ready to lift his niece out, once Shaunna released her from her seatbelt. She couldn't quite reach far enough across.

"Can you unclip that for me?" she asked him. Andy obliged. As he was pulling his arm away, she noticed his knuckles were bleeding. "What've you done to your hand?"

"Had a minor collision with a hard object," he said, lifting little Shaunna clear of her seat.

"Right. What kind of hard object, exactly?"

"One that wasn't quite as hard as it first thought." He smiled swiftly and closed the door. Shaunna opened the boot and waited for Casper to jump out, grabbing hold of his lead just in time to stop him tearing off across the car park. Adele beckoned her close and waited until Dan and Andy had walked on ahead.

"They went out last night, to see Rob, I'm guessing," she said.

"You're kidding!"

"No, I'm not. Andy said something about going to have a word and Dan offered to take him. They came back and didn't mention another thing about it."

"Oh crap. Kris told me last night that Rob's got some kind of heart complaint."

"How does he know?"

"Jess told him, when he took her out yesterday. Apparently he's selling his bike to a collector so he can pay to go private for the surgery. It sounds pretty serious."

"So he says," Adele said haughtily.

"You think he's lying?"

"It wouldn't surprise me. There's something very shady about Rob Simpson-Stone and he always did fancy Jess, but she knocked him back for Andy."

"So he's going for the sympathy vote, you reckon?" Shaunna asked.

"Yeah. I do. Anyway, I'm dying for the loo."

The two women followed the brothers towards the service station, taking turns to visit the Ladies' toilets, while one of them remained outside with Casper.

Fifteen minutes later, Josh pulled up next to Dan's 4x4, and shortly after James arrived, reversing into the next space along.

"Why doesn't that surprise me?" Josh said, watching him expertly manoeuvre the long estate car into the very narrow stretch between the two white lines.

"Do you have to park next to *them*?" Jess asked. She'd taken her headphones off and was glaring at the 4x4.

"Yes, Jess, I do have to park next to *them* and for the next seven days, you're also going to be living in a cabin next to *them*, so I recommend you try and reach some sort of truce."

George pulled his seat forward and waited for first Kris, then Jess, to climb out. She stormed off sulkily towards the building and Kris rolled his eyes.

"This is not going to be pretty," he said, as the three of them set off, watching her make her way to the toilets. Andy was standing by the games area, holding Casper's lead whilst Shaunna attempted to control a virtual racing car; he was making a big deal out of laughing at her futile efforts.

"Last!" she groaned.

"Never mind," Andy consoled. "They're not as easy as they look, these games." She pushed him and he flexed his chest.

"Oh. Now that's very interesting," George remarked, as they veered off towards the café. Kris had also gone in search of the toilets.

Josh frowned. "Hmm. As Kris said, or at least to paraphrase him a little, things could get ugly. You get the coffees and I'll find us a seat with a view."

"Right you are, boss," George said and wandered off towards the coffee franchise. Josh sat down at the table closest to the exit and took out his phone to use as a ruse. Andy had gone into the newsagent's by this point, so Shaunna intercepted Kris on his way back from the toilets, swapped Casper's lead for his drink order and went to queue behind George.

"Whatcha doing?" Eleanor asked, coming up next to Josh.

"Keeping a strategic position, in case anything kicks off."

"Ah." She followed the direction of Josh's gaze, observed Andy flicking through a car magazine, and scanned the vicinity. "Enemy fighter at seven o'clock," she said, spotting Jess emerge from the toilets and also enter the newsagent's. She walked straight over to Andy's location, picked up a magazine, and stood right next to him. Neither of them spoke, nor did they look directly at each other, and then Andy put his magazine back and walked off. Jess kept hers and went to pay for it.

"Well that was boring," Eleanor said, clearly disappointed. "I was hoping for some fireworks." She walked around to the other side of the table and Josh shuffled over to give her space to sit. Toby was awake and rooting for food.

"What would you like?" James asked her.

"Hot chocolate, please," Eleanor replied, lifting her t-shirt and positioning Toby inside. James nodded and left to buy drinks, sleepy Oliver plodding along beside him. Josh was trying not to watch what Eleanor was doing, but he was fascinated by the endearing, yet increasingly loud gulping sounds the baby was making.

"My God! He's a noisier eater than George!"

"Yeah, he is," Eleanor laughed. "You know that let-down reflex I was telling you about? Well this is it. And it's really, bloody uncomfortable." She put her arm under her non-feeding breast to support it.

"Is it worth the hassle, though?"

"Definitely. If you think about it, I would've had to sterilise and prepare two bottles this morning, just for a five hour drive, not to mention how much more stuff we'd have had to pack up for this holiday, but instead, I can just get my boob out."

"You can't even tell that's what you're doing," Josh observed, although his attention had shifted elsewhere, as Jess had followed Andy outside and they were once again standing very close together, but didn't appear to be saying anything. George placed Josh's cappuccino in his hand and sat on one of the chairs opposite.

"Where are Dan and Adele? Anyone seen them?" Eleanor asked.

"No, come to think of it," George replied.

Shaunna stopped to say hi on her way back to Kris, who had taken Casper out to the dog exercise area. "D'you know where Dan and Adele have got to?" he asked.

"Yeah. They're on the massage chairs. Over by the toilets. They've been pumping money into the things ever since we got here."

"I've got to see this." George took a quick swig of his coffee, and went off towards the toilets.

"A-a-a-gh," Adele groaned, her voice fractured by the vibrations.

"This is the business," Dan said to George, as the chair came to a stop again. "You want a go?"

"No, thank you," George laughed. "You carry on."

"I think five in a row is probably more than enough already," Dan admitted and slowly eased himself out of the plush, black leather. Little Shaunna put her arms up and he lifted her from Adele's lap, where she'd been sitting throughout their extended electronic massage. Adele's chair stopped, and she stayed where she was.

"Ooh. I don't want to get up now," she said, reluctantly doing so anyway.

They walked back to the café with George, and he filled them in on the current state of play in the Jess and Andy situation, or at least, how it was when he last saw them. However, things had progressed considerably since then, and whilst the glass building was sufficiently soundproof for them not to be heard, it was more than apparent that they were yelling at each other. George kept his eyes on them all the way back to his seat, only looking away to pick up his drink, so that their whole group was now staring at their two friends warring right outside the main entrance of a very busy motorway service station.

"Excuse me."

The voice was small and apologetic and directed at Eleanor. She looked up at the not so small or apologetic-looking owner.

"Err, sorry to ask this," he continued, "but could you do that somewhere else?"

"Like where?"

"Somewhere a little more private. There is a changing facility in the disabled toilets."

"And do you eat your dinner in the toilet?"

"Obviously not," the man said with a false laugh. Josh leaned in and read his badge.

"John Docherty, Assistant Manager." He looked him straight in the eyes and smiled sweetly. "You realise that you are discriminating against my friend, Mr. Docherty?"

"Not at all," he laughed again. Nonchalance with a touch of nervousness. He evidently hadn't expected a fight. "It's just that it distresses some of our customers."

"Then surely you should be tackling their bad attitude, instead of proliferating it?"

"In an ideal world, sir. Unfortunately, we have to cater for a diverse range of customers, and..."

"Including breastfeeding mothers," Eleanor interrupted. "Can you actually see anything?"

"No, but..."

"And has anyone actually complained? On this occasion, I mean."

"Well, no, but as I said..."

"Then go away and harass someone else."

He backed off, but had to get the last word in.

"I'll have to pass this on to my manager."

"You do that," Eleanor shouted after him. He'd wound her

up and she was just in the mood for taking on his manager, as well. Their attention had now switched from Andy and Jess, to John Docherty, in muted discussion with a woman they presumed to be the aforementioned manager. He kept pointing over to their group, then turning his head away to talk.

"If he points at me once more, I'm going to go right over there and break his sodding finger," Eleanor growled.

The manager was shaking her head now, and her assistant walked off, collected a couple of trays of dirty crockery from the trolley and stomped into the kitchen. She watched Eleanor for a moment, then she also walked away.

"Unbelievable!" Josh said. "No apology, or anything! Bloody unbelievable!"

"Ah. I'm used to it." Eleanor freed herself from Toby's grip and straightened her top. "Some places are great, but some, like this one, have yet to catch up. Still," she looked down at Toby's satisfied, sleepy face, "he's happy, and that's all that matters. I'm ready whenever you are, James."

It was another two hours before they stopped again, but this time it was in the nearest large town to where they would be staying, to stock up on provisions, with Shaunna and Kris taking turns to hold Casper, while the others traipsed the aisles of the tiny supermarket. And once again, they were privy to Jess and Andy's argument, although were far enough away to avoid hearing most of it. It didn't look like they were making much progress.

Back to the cars, then, for the final ascent into the mountains, a picturesque ride, as described by Dan and Andy, who weren't even remotely perturbed by the narrowness of the road, nor the steep drop to their right. Adele clung to the dashboard with her eyes shut.

"Take it easy, Andy," she squealed for the third time.

"Oh please shut up," Dan snapped from the back. "You're in safe hands."

"I'd much rather you were driving."

"Andy knows what he's doing."

"Ooh-ooh," Adele wailed. Andy chuckled.

"Don't worry, we'll be there soon," he tried to console her. He wasn't even concentrating, as his mind kept returning to Jess's attempts to explain herself. He didn't want to know and told her as much, but she wouldn't let it rest and it was starting to make him angry again. He flexed his fingers and balled them into a fist, to remind himself that at least he'd already dealt with half of the problem.

In the Browns' car, it was James who was feeling the tension the most. Eleanor trusted his driving completely, and the boys were too young to appreciate the potential danger. He switched off the music to help his concentration, and kept a good distance behind Josh.

"We're not coming here again until you pass your test," he was saying to George.

"Then we're not coming here again," George said ruefully. He'd failed his driving test a couple of months back and had been having enough problems finding the motivation to book another one, without the prospect of this kind of driving to look forward to.

A few cabins, tucked away between the trees, were now coming into view.

"They're more hills than mountains," Dan remarked, as they took a hairpin bend upwards; Adele let out a little squeak.

"The cabins look lovely," Shaunna said. Adele couldn't see them, because she still had her eyes shut, but Shaunna was right: they really were very impressive. Some were two storeys high, with balconies running around the top floor. Others were on one level, and in all cases they were sturdy, well-kept and very much like what they'd all expected George's house on the ranch to be, prior to their visit.

"You're going to have to look soon, Adele," Dan told her. "You've got the directions for where we need to turn off." She felt around for the sheets of paper and passed them over her shoulder. Dan snatched them from her.

"You're looking for a right turn, signposted 'Treetop View'."

"That's imaginative," Andy said dryly.

"How can we turn right?" Adele asked. "We'd fall off the mountain."

"I really can't be bothered to explain," Dan said, rubbing his temples with his thumb and forefinger.

The same conversation was taking place in the car behind, although George was patiently telling Josh the answer.

"I see," Josh said when George was done. He felt a bit silly for not thinking it through and could feel himself becoming all hot and bothered. George patted his thigh.

"Never mind. It wouldn't do to know everything about everything." Josh gave him a sideways glance and he grinned.

"I've never claimed to know everything," he retorted.

"I'm sorry to have to ask this," Kris said, leaning forward, "but are we nearly there yet? I've got a dreadfully numb bum."

"Yep," George said, pointing to the sign up ahead.

They followed Dan's 4x4 round to the right, then into a steep decline, which levelled out, before turning uphill again, through a copse of trees and to the three cabins. There were others not too far away, but theirs were close enough to be 'next door' to each other. Josh waited for Dan to park up outside the furthest of the two larger cabins, then pulled into the space at the side of the other. James rolled past a moment later and reversed into the driveway of the smaller cabin, set on a slightly higher level and at a forty-five degree angle to its neighbour.

"Here we are, then," James said, unbuckling his seatbelt. Eleanor left the car to talk to the owner of the cabins, the cheque for the key deposit in her hand. The others waited in their respective vehicles, until she had the keys in her possession.

"Shall I go?" George asked, although he was out of the car before anyone had a chance to answer. Adele, representing the 'Jeffries Contingent', had already beaten him to it.

"Right," Eleanor said authoritatively. She passed them each a set of keys. "The little brown one is for the windows. The other two are for the external doors—you'll have to work out which is which. And this," she took the keys back from Adele and lifted the one in question free from the rest of the bunch, "is for the lid of the hot tub."

"Yay!" Adele squealed and jumped up and down.

"And don't think you're keeping it all to yourself," Eleanor added, before she got any ideas.

The rest of the friends were now out of the cars, with Casper liberated and tearing around after Oliver, who was all of a sudden wide awake again and ready to go off exploring. James called him back and told him to stand still.

"We will go and find the playground tomorrow," he said. Oliver was crestfallen, as he'd already spotted the primary colours of the swings peeking enticingly through the trees.

They all made their way to their homes for the next week, opening cupboards, checking out the bathrooms and trying the beds. Each cabin was the same on the outside, with slight variations in the way the interior was arranged. The two-bedroomed cabin consisted of a lounge at one end, and the largest of the two bedrooms at the other, with the kitchen area separated from the living area by a breakfast bar, the smaller bedroom and bathroom at the juxtaposition of the two larger rooms. The cabin with the hot tub had the same set-up of lounge and kitchen area, with French doors opening out onto the veranda, opposite which was one of what turned out to be two doubles and one twin. The furthest bedroom was the one set out with two single beds, and was where the two Shaunnas were sleeping. Adult Shaunna helped Dan to set up the cotside on the bed nearest the window, before changing out of the clothes she had been travelling in and rejoining the others in the lounge.

The other three-bedroomed cabin was proving to be something more of a challenge. Again, the lounge and kitchen area took up the whole of one end, but this time the single room and bathroom ran along one side, with one of the double/twins opposite and the other across the end of the cabin. However, the problem was that both large bedrooms contained double beds. Even if it hadn't been necessary to separate Jess and Andy, they would still have been stuck, and the only solution they'd come up with so far was for Josh and George to share a bed. Kris didn't care where they put him, and offered to share with George, or take the single room—whichever suited them best. Jess, on the other hand, had already taken herself off to the double room at the far end and shut the door, leaving the three men standing in the lounge and scratching their heads.

"I'll go and get my bags out of the car," Kris suggested, to give the other two a chance to discuss what they wanted to do. Josh tossed the keys to him and leaned against the breakfast bar.

"I suppose I could always sleep in here," George said, trying out the sofa for comfort.

"For the whole week?"

"That's not so long. My mum slept on the sofa for eight years." Josh raised an eyebrow in query. "It's only a one-bedroomed flat and I got too big to share with."

"I really don't want you sleeping on there. It's not fair. And it'll drive Kris insane. You know what he's like about people sleeping on sofas."

"I think that only applies to his own," George said. He assumed a horizontal position and rolled onto his side. "It's perfectly acceptable, unless you have any better suggestions?"

Josh blew his hair out of his eyes and chewed the inside of his cheek. The pressure was of his own making.

"We can share," he said in a quiet voice, but not so quiet as to go unheard. George sat up again.

"You don't want to though."

"To be honest, I've not had long enough to think about it to tell you whether I do or I don't."

"But your first instinct was to say no."

"My first instinct is always to say no. And I don't really care if you share with Kris, either."

George sighed. He needed to use the loo, and could hear Kris struggling with his bags at the door. He got up and let him in on his way, leaving Josh to inform him of 'their' decision.

"I'm in the single room then, yeah?" Kris called from just outside the bathroom. There was a pause, in which presumably Josh replied, but George didn't hear what he said. A bedroom door opened, then the outside door opened and closed. George flushed the toilet and washed his hands, impressed to find clean towels and toiletries were included. He opened the miniscule bottle of shower gel and sniffed; it didn't really smell of anything, but he'd brought a bottle with him anyway. The soap was the generic standard found in hotel rooms, and the shampoo had the same vague floral quality as the shower gel. He put the bottles back where he found them and opened the bathroom door at the same time as Josh opened the bedroom door opposite.

"We're in here," he said, dropping the two suitcases next to the bed and sitting down, "and I'm having this side."

George held back the smile that was trying to fight its way out, but the twinkle in his eyes gave him away. "We can make a wall out of a blanket or something, if you like," he suggested, for the second time in as many weeks, although the last time it was to Shaunna.

Josh shook his head. "I don't think that will be necessary, do you?"

CHAPTER TWENTY-EIGHT

It was much too early in the morning to be crying with laughter, but Dan's comeback was so quick and captured the moment so perfectly. Andy had woken to find that Casper had crept onto the empty side of the double bed at some point during the night, and had made himself very comfortable, with his head on the pillow, a paw positioned under his cheek, just like a human. It was quite a surprise and Andy got a very slobbery lick for his troubles. When he told Dan, he patted his brother on the back and said:

"Well, let's face it, bro, it's not the first time you've woken up next to a dog, and I don't imagine it'll be the last."

Still giggling in the aftermath, Andy didn't care that what Dan had said was a cruel insult, because he hated Jess with a passion right now. He didn't want to have to see her, listen to her, indeed have anything whatsoever to do with her, but was determined that if their falling out did anything to ruin this holiday, then it wouldn't be of his doing. Thus, when he went outside to hang his towel over the balcony rail and she was doing the same thing, he said good morning and even went as far as asking if she'd slept well. She grunted a response, of sorts, and went back inside.

"And fuck you too," he said through gritted teeth, and returned to the kitchen, where Dan was trying to make a mat out of a plastic bag to go under his daughter's highchair so that the inevitable spilt breakfast didn't land on the carpet. Adele was in the shower and Shaunna was eating toast in the lounge. Andy sat at the breakfast bar and watched little Shaunna bang her spoon into the bowl of cornflakes. Dan froze and put his hand to the back of his neck, scooping away a clump of soggy cereal, which made Andy and grown-up Shaunna hide their faces so that he couldn't see them laughing. Twice already and it wasn't yet eight o'clock, Andy mused. He was either having a really great time, or investing heavily in the theory that if he didn't laugh then there was only one other alternative.

"So," he said, clearing his throat, "what's the plan for today. Anything?"

"Nope. Probably go and have an explore of the woods, but I'm up for sitting around and drinking beer for the next seven days. You?"

"There's a sports centre in the next clearing up, apparently. If I can be bothered, I'll take a walk up and see what they've got on offer. Otherwise, I'm happy to keep you company while you drink beer, make sure you don't get lonely."

"Sounds good on both counts. Let me know when you're going. I might come with you."

"Well, I'm off to take Casper for a walk," Shaunna said, rinsing her plate and loosening her still-damp curls with her fingertips. She went to her room to grab her shoes and Casper's lead. "See you later." Dan watched her give one last swish of her auburn locks on the way out.

"Her hair is damn hot," he said. Andy had been thinking the same thing. "Don't tell Adele I said that."

"Goes without saying, bro."

Shaunna knocked at Kris's cabin and waited. It was Jess who opened the door.

"Hi," Shaunna said brightly. "Is Kris up yet?"

"Come in," he called. Jess turned and walked back inside. Kris was tying his shoelaces and now had to contend with the big stupid Labrador's nose, as he acted like they'd been separated for weeks, not hours.

"Casper, shift!" He pushed the dog to one side and pulled the lace tight. This only reinforced Casper's belief that it was a game, and he went tearing up and down the cabin at speed, poking his nose at Kris's hand each time he completed a circuit.

"Come on then, mutt," Shaunna called.

Casper pushed past as they descended the steps, and the three of them headed off into the trees behind the cabins. Jess flopped onto the sofa and looked at her phone despondently. There was very little signal here, although some places were better than others. She went out to the balcony and checked the screen again, just as a text message arrived. She read it and smiled, sending a reply back straight away.

Inside, George was wide awake, but didn't want to move. As he'd come to, he'd felt the presence of someone else behind him, and it had taken a moment or so for him to remember. Since then, Josh had stirred and put an arm over him in his sleep. It was the best feeling and hence he wanted to stay right where he was. He lay there for some time, taking in the sensation of having him so close and the prolonged body contact. He could feel himself becoming aroused. It would pass. Hopefully. Josh stirred again and his fingers brushed against George's bare side, where his t-shirt had risen up during the night. Even though the hand was cold, the touch was like fire and it made him buck. Josh pulled the fabric straight and laid his arm over the previously exposed place.

"Josh?"

"Mmm?"

"Are you awake?"

"Mmm."

"How long for?"

"A while."

"Oh." George smiled to himself.

"Why?"

"No reason." He was concentrating all of his energy on pushing away the erotic thoughts charging into his mind without permission. "I need a pee." He slid across the mattress, and sat on the edge of the bed for a moment. That was easier, without the physical contact. Slowly, with his back to the bed, he sidestepped through the small gap between the footboard and the wall, then made a dash for the bathroom. When he opened his eyes, it was upon his reflection in the mirror above the toilet and he looked away, suddenly bashful. The coldness of the water on his face soothed away the guilt and gave him back some rationality. He turned off the tap, rubbed his hands with the towel and went to make coffee.

So that was the first big challenge fought and won, and in the aftermath, he was starting to comprehend what it was going to take to really 'be OK' with what was required of him if and when their relationship took off properly, for at present it still felt more like a prelude; a series of courting rituals halted before they could reach their natural and much more gradual conclusion, simply by the geography of this cabin. As he waited for the kettle to boil, he examined his surroundings in a new morning's light, feeling a sense of both gratitude and loathing for what the building had brought into being. He and Josh had spent their first night together; it matched no prior fantasy he had encountered, apart from the waking up beside each other, the warmth of their bodies welling and mingling beneath soft, perfumed linen, an arm wrapped around him. It was stirring in him again and he found a welcome distraction in watching Jess, just outside the French doors, smiling and talking into her phone, idly pushing at a knot in the banister rail with her thumbnail. She sensed that he was watching her and turned away. The kettle came to the boil.

Back in the bedroom, Josh was sitting cross-legged, the duvet cast to one side and pillows positioned in an ad lib fashion against the wooden headboard. He saw the coffee and smiled.

"Thanks," he said, taking the cup from George and shuffling over to make space. Instead, George sat on the other end of Josh's side, mirroring his pose.

"You know when you stay in a hotel?" Josh asked. "That first night, in a strange bed, when it's almost impossible to sleep and you're glad when the alarm releases you from the scratchy covers and pillows that aren't yours? Well, that's what I was expecting last night and I wasn't looking forward to it at all."

"But?"

"But I slept right through. Eight whole hours of glorious, undisturbed sleep. I feel unbelievably good this morning."

George thought on this statement; having shared a house with Josh for the past nine months, not to mention the short time after he first returned from the States, he was aware of the bouts of acute insomnia, and at the best of times, it was rare for a whole night to pass without hearing him get up at least once. Being the sort of person who could fall asleep anywhere and had no trouble getting back to sleep if woken, George wasn't bothered by being disturbed every night and didn't mention it. He worried for Josh though, especially when he detected an increase in the frequency of his awakenings, for it came and went in a relatively predictable pattern. The last few weeks had seen an escalation from one or two nightly visits to the toilet, to hearing him go downstairs and turn on the TV, where he would sometimes stay for as long as three hours before he felt it was worth returning to bed.

The gentle touch of Josh's fingers on his cheek. "What's on your mind?"

"Lots."

"Tell me."

"Just then? I was thinking about your insomnia. It must be difficult to cope with."

"It used to be. When it first started, I regularly went for three or four nights at a time without sleeping at all, although I was working on my dissertation, so it was probably self-perpetuating. Other than that, the only time it really got to me was 'the dream', but it's normal for me, so I try not to worry about it."

"Can I ask you something?" George asked hesitantly. He hadn't considered how he was going to word the question, and didn't want to put any pressure on him, but their knees were touching and he needed to address it.

"Go on."

"It's about the sex thing."

Josh sipped his coffee, hoping for a 'couldn't care less' effect, even though his heart had quickened and he was dreading what came next.

"It's only a little bit about the sex thing," George reassured him. "You see, other than that one hug when I came back from the States, you've avoided bodily contact with me since we left school, and I understand it was because you didn't want to mislead me. But what I don't get is why that suddenly changed, not that I'm complaining, although it's hard, err, what I mean is…"

"It turns you on."

"Yes," George blushed, "that's where I was going. Like when we were getting ready to leave for the reunion, and you fixed my tie. It was almost more than I could stand, because you'd never done anything like that before. And then in the limo, you held my hand. Your hand was so cool and smooth and I wanted to—I'm really confused. To wake up with you this morning, with your arm around me and your fingers on my skin; I'm fighting with everything I've got, I really am, but I just don't know how to respond."

"How would you normally respond?"

"Normal doesn't apply."

"Why not?"

"Because normally it might lead to sex."

"Ah. I see." Josh closed his eyes and inhaled deeply. He wasn't ready to compromise yet, to seek out some middle ground that would satisfy them both. "How do you want to respond?" he asked.

"Well, ignoring the really dangerous situations, like when I woke up this morning with…" George swallowed and reworded. "Feeling very aroused. Forget that bit for now."

Josh laughed. "OK. It's forgotten."

"I don't believe you, but anyway, when you touched my face just before, what I wanted to do was take your hand in mine and kiss your fingertips."

"So why didn't you?"

"Boundaries, or lack thereof. If we go for a walk today, for instance, and you go to hold my hand again, do I leave my hand dangling at my side all unresponsive?"

"Like you have been doing."

"Quite. Or do I hold your hand back? Am I allowed to put my arms around you in bed?"

Josh hummed thoughtfully.

"I said I'm OK with it," George continued, "and that's still the truth, although I need to know where the line is and even then I'm pretty sure I'll step over it plenty of times, especially in the heat of the moment."

"When does a touch become a caress?" Josh mused.

"That's what I mean. How will I know if I've gone too far?"

"Which is why you resist when I do touch you."

George nodded. "That and the whole getting hot under the collar thing," he confessed.

Josh watched him blush again and turn away. "Can we try something?" he asked. He put his coffee cup to one side and shuffled down the bed, opening his legs so that they were now either side of George.

"Oh, this is dangerous," he said shakily.

"I know. That's why I'm doing it, although the only way I'm actually doing it is by pretending this is a consultation, not that I've ever done anything like this with a client, you understand, and I'm really nervous, but if we're going to draw the line we need to find out where it is, because I really want to be able to touch you without you freaking out about it." He kept moving forward, until his legs were bent up and he couldn't get any closer. "Uncross your legs," he instructed. George looked at him dubiously, but did so anyway. Josh gently removed George's coffee cup and put it on the floor, then took his hands and positioned them on his own hips. "How are we doing so far?"

"Not so good." George breathed out slowly and focused on the smoke detector above them.

"Did you want to go and—sort yourself out?"

"It's not going to come to that just yet," he said and they

both started laughing at the innuendo. "Doesn't this turn you on?"

"Yes, but only because it turns you on. I can't...I don't want..."

"It's OK. I was only asking because I want to understand."

"So do I." Josh allowed him to move his hands away, wrongly anticipating that he would try and take it further. Instead, he lifted them clear of their thighs and took hold of Josh's hands, lifting them to his face and kissing them in relief. Josh smiled encouragingly. "We'll find a way, I know we will." George kept his lips against Josh's skin and closed his eyes. He was teetering on the edge of the most exquisite precipice and found he was enjoying the sensory overload, but it was no longer purely sexual. He opened his eyes again and leaned forward to kiss his cheek.

"I think I'm beginning to."

Oliver hadn't forgotten his father's promise the day before, and was pestering him to go to the play area. James was about to tick him off for being impatient, but didn't. He had eaten all of his breakfast, as requested, and had taken his bowl and cup over to the sink without being asked, which was where he was standing now, holding them up to Eleanor. It was difficult to say no when he was trying so hard.

"Come on then," James said, strapping the papoose to his front.

"Leave Toby here, if you like," Eleanor suggested.

"I thought you might prefer some time to yourself."

"I would, but it's a hassle having to carry the baby and push a swing at the same time."

"We will cope, won't we Oliver?" James smiled.

"OK then. See you all later." She wiped her hands on a tea towel and gave each of them a kiss as they made their way outside, glancing up at the sky as they variously strode and trotted away. The weather was a bit on the dull side today, but it was dry and still quite warm. She finished tidying away from breakfast, then dug a book out of her bag and settled in the armchair for a quiet read with a cup of tea. It was so peaceful up here, and the signal on her phone was non-existent, for which she was very grateful.

In the absence of a Frisbee (on the kitchen table back home so they didn't forget it), Casper was quite happy collecting pine cones, and the most muddy, smelly, half-decomposed ones at that. He was like a little truffle hunter, sniffling in amongst the fallen needles, scratching them back with his paw, before proudly carrying his prize back to whichever of his humans looked most likely to appreciate it. It was Shaunna's turn and she praised him briefly, before he lollopped off in search of his next find; she surreptitiously disposed of the pine cone and wiped her hands on the closest tree trunk.

They'd been walking uphill for half an hour or so, and stopped to look back down the footworn path through the trees, the cabins long since out of sight, with nothing but greenery and the sounds of birds and other creatures around them. It was perfect. Kris picked up a fresh pine cone and sniffed it.

"I could live here," he said.

"You so could not," Shaunna retorted.

"I so could!" he protested. "It's beautiful, and peaceful, and…"

"Missing all the little comforts of modern life. How long d'you think you could stand not being able to just hop on a train, or pop to the supermarket when we run out of milk?"

"Or to the petrol station to buy you chocolate?"

"That too," she grinned. She eyed a large, flattish stone sticking up through the composted forest floor, brushed away the pine needles and sat down. Kris sat next to her.

"Jess was in a foul mood this morning," he said.

"I noticed. Has she said anything else?"

"Not since we got here."

Shaunna watched, as Kris took another pine cone from Casper, then off he went again.

"Neither has Andy," she said.

"It's depressing, isn't it?"

"Yep."

"So," Kris rubbed his hands together, mostly to remove the mud transferred from the pine cone, "here's the plan."

Shaunna leaned in conspiratorially.

"I'm going to get Jess talking again," he said, "get the low-down on the Rob situation."

"OK."

"And your mission, should you choose to accept it, is to find out how Andy's feeling."

"That should be easy enough. A couple of beers and he'll be at it for hours."

"Challenge accepted?" Kris held out his hand and Shaunna shook it.

"Accepted."

CHAPTER TWENTY-NINE

After the third attempt at trying to unlock the lid of the hot tub, Adele relented and passed the key to Dan, who spent several minutes struggling on, whilst she repeatedly reminded him that she'd told him the lock was jammed, before he passed the key to Andy. He tried turning it upside down, rattling the lid to see if it was misaligned, indeed, all the tricks his brother had just tried, but it wouldn't budge.

"Looks like you'll have to do without," he informed Adele.

"I'll get it open," Shaunna said, heading back inside the cabin. Dan and Andy looked at each other smugly, then stood with their arms folded, watching as Shaunna came back out, squirted some oil into the lock and lifted the lid clear of the hot tub.

"There you go, hun." She smiled at Adele, flipped the oil can, caught it and blew the nozzle as if it were a pistol, then sauntered back past Dan and Andy, who both swooned and coughed nervously. Adele was too engrossed in trying to make sense of the controls to even notice. She pressed one button and nothing happened. She pressed another button and the number on the LED increased. She pressed it again, figured out it was the temperature setting, and that two of the buttons were marked with arrows, reset the temperature to what it was originally and pressed the final button. Success! A motor whirred to life and the water erupted in a bubbly mass.

"Yay!" she said excitedly. Josh and George had just arrived, and were helping Dan to set out chairs, while Andy was loading beer into the fridge.

"Hope you've got your trunks on," Adele said to George. He pulled a flap of red fabric from the top of his jeans to show he had. She was already out of her clothes and about to step into the hot tub. "And you too, Josh."

"Err, no, thanks. I'll sit this one out, if it's all the same to you," he smiled. The lights around the edge of the veranda suddenly illuminated and Shaunna appeared a moment later, armed with a bottle of red wine and two glasses.

"That's better," she said, inspecting the golden glow she had instigated. She poured the wine and placed the glasses on the ledge alongside the hot tub, then stepped out of her bathrobe and climbed in, scooping her hair into a large clip as she sat down next to Adele. This time, Dan had his back turned, but Andy didn't and he busied himself with passing bottles around. George and Josh took their beers and settled into their seats.

"Is it me," George whispered, "or is Shaunna being a dreadful flirt?"

"The second one," Josh whispered back. It was as if she'd reverted back to her old ways, and she was clearly enjoying every second of it, as were the Jeffries brothers, it would seem. Luckily, Adele remained oblivious to all of this, sipping her wine and letting her legs float up on the air bubbles rising through the wonderfully warm water.

Eleanor and James arrived and left Toby in his carrycot just inside the door. Oliver had been permitted to stay up late, and immediately went off to play with little Shaunna, who had napped for a short while earlier, but was wide awake now and no doubt would stay that way for most of the evening. James positioned his chair so he could keep an eye on his sons at the same time as enjoying the evening. Jess and Kris arrived soon after, and everyone stopped talking, anticipating trouble.

"Andy," Jess acknowledged with a nod.

"Hi," he said airily. "Want a beer?"

"Thanks."

He took the lids off two bottles and handed them to her. She passed one to Kris and followed him outside, where things were gradually returning to normal. Dan brought out his speakers and set his MP3 player to a low volume, the music providing an inconspicuous backdrop to the interactions between the friends as they flitted in and out of each other's conversations. The last time they had properly been together like this was when they went en masse to visit George on his ranch, a fact that had not been lost on Josh, but he waited for someone else to point it out first.

"At least there was plenty of space to spread out," George was justifying, having taken yet another round of jibes about the warm beer he'd served them. Looking back on it now, he wondered how he'd coped for so long without a fridge, or any form of heating (he never did master lighting the wood burner). It was easy to forget that he had gone from living at home in a draughty tower block, to sharing a house at uni with three others who all came from farming backgrounds and tended to prioritise food and alcohol over heat and light, with the end result often being that the meter would be out of money for days at a time. Only since he'd come back to the UK had he really enjoyed the luxury of reliable refrigeration, central heating and constant, running hot water.

"Look at us," Josh said, sensing George's discomfort. "We're sitting on a balcony, drinking beer and watching the sun set over the mountains."

"We are too," George grinned, "although I always imagined we'd be doing it on our own."

"There's plenty of time for that," Josh assured him. "We've got the rest of our lives."

George was momentarily stunned by the realisation. He and Josh were *together*.

"Come on, George, get your kit off!" Shaunna shouted through the cloud of steam hanging over the hot tub. Adele whooped.

"Oh, all right then," he said, only partially affecting a reluctant tone. "If you insist." He unbuttoned his shirt and pulled it open, receiving a wolf whistle from one of the girls (he couldn't see which one because of the steam, but had a pretty good idea), and unzipped his trousers, stamping his way out of them and his socks at the same time. He turned to put his clothes on the chair and winked at Josh.

"Are you sure you won't join us?"

"You're making me cold just watching!" Josh said, pulling his sleeves down over his hands. George shrugged and climbed in between Shaunna and Adele. Eleanor didn't skip a beat and made a beeline for Josh, lifting George's clothes onto the table and sitting down.

"So, as you were saying," she said. Josh kept his eyes fixed straight ahead.

"What was I saying?"

"About telling George how you feel."

"Oh that."

"Yes that."

Josh swigged at his beer and said nothing. Conversations were trailing off all around them, as the others started to pay attention.

"Come on, Joshua, spill it. Are you together, or not?"

"Perhaps we could do this some other time?" he said, raising his voice slightly, "when there aren't seven other people trying to listen in!"

All eyes were on him, except George's, and he was too far away to be of any help in getting him off the hook.

"What's this?" Dan asked.

"Did I hear right?" Andy looked to Eleanor for confirmation.

Shaunna and Adele both turned to George and he raised his arms in surrender.

"Don't look at me!"

"I hate you, Eleanor Brown," Josh said, screwing up his eyes and glaring at her, pretending to be angry. She'd put him on the spot, and now he had no choice in the matter, but he actually felt really good about that.

"So?" she prompted.

"Agh. All right then. George and I are officially together, in a relationship," he announced.

"About bloody time," Andy said.

"Agreed," Dan seconded.

"You waited long enough, hey George," Eleanor called across.

"Yes," Josh replied for him. He found his face through the dense steam and looked deep into his eyes. "And I'm so very, very glad he did."

If it hadn't been for Shaunna and Adele ambushing him, George would probably have started blubbering there and then, but instead he was being squashed by two scantily clad, very slippery women, who were rubbing his hair and kissing his cheeks.

"That's where we've been going wrong all these years, bro," Dan said.

"Ha, yeah." Andy had finished his beer and took orders from anyone else who needed another drink before he went back inside, and found Jess, standing on her own, watching the rest of them from a distance.

"You heard Josh's announcement?" he asked her. She nodded. "I'm really happy for them, aren't you?"

"Of course I am," she snapped.

"I didn't mean it like that."

"No. I know. I'm sorry." She wanted to look at him, but couldn't.

"We can't go on like this, Jess. It's not fair on everybody else."

"That's what I was trying to say at the service station, but you wouldn't listen."

"You were trying to justify what you'd done, and I don't want to hear it. I'm too angry to even try, but we have to put this aside and make a good show of getting on, for their sake." He looked out to the others, all laughing and drinking and sharing stories. Jess watched them too. She was missing her friends so much.

"They're all on your side," she said.

"Yeah. And much as I'm enjoying their support and hate you for what you've done, I don't like to see you being left out like this."

"I deserve it."

"Maybe you do. It's not my place to say. But we're going back out there, together, and we're going to act like everything's OK between us." He wasn't asking for her permission. He was telling her how it was going to be. He picked up as many drinks as he could carry and left her to bring the rest.

"Jess! Go put your bikini on!" Kris shouted. He had joined the others in the hot tub. She looked at Andy and raised an eyebrow.

"Best do as the man says."

"OK. I'll be right back," she shouted to Kris and returned to their cabin. Andy circulated, handing out the drinks.

"What did you say to her?" Dan asked, taking a beer from him.

"Basically to stop being selfish, but not in those words, obviously."

"Seems to have done the trick."

Andy shrugged. "We'll see." He didn't want to talk about her anymore and made his way over to sit with Josh and Eleanor. Dan stood next to James, looking in on their children, both curled up on the sofa and watching cartoons on Dan's tablet, which was propped against a cushion on the armchair. Their eyelids were drooping and little Shaunna had her thumb in her mouth.

"Sorry about missing your wedding, by the way," Dan said.

"Don't worry. It's perfectly understandable. Are you recovered now?"

"Almost. As soon as we get back we'll have to rearrange the meeting with Jason."

"Yes. I spoke to him briefly on Saturday. He is keen to get things in motion."

"A bit too keen for my liking. Don't get me wrong, I've been known to jump in without looking myself a few times. Well, most of the time. But this is a bit different."

"I think he understands that, which is why he's asked for our support. I still miss Alistair terribly, but if I can help Jason to do this, then at least his death won't have been a total waste."

"Absolutely. I miss him too, although I wasn't as close to him as you were, of course. Has Jason said anything about Alice?"

"Nothing."

"Hmm. I ask only because she's mentioned him a couple of times. I think she's considering getting in touch," Dan explained. "We'll just have to play it by ear on that one." James nodded his agreement.

"What're you two scheming?" Eleanor asked, coming up behind James and putting her arms around him.

"Boring business matters," James said. Dan excused himself and went to talk to Kris, who was sitting on the rim of the hot tub. It was a bit too warm for him and was making him feel sick.

"I need to have a chat with you, in private, at some point," Dan told him. "It's not urgent."

Kris stepped out and wrapped a towel around his waist. He followed Dan inside.

"We've been in here too long," George said, holding up his wrinkled fingers. Adele and Shaunna followed his lead and giggled. "Seriously, you're not supposed to stay in these things this long. Let's get out for a while. We can always come back later." He tried to stand up and they kept pulling him back down, but eventually he managed to fight his way over the edge, and back to Josh, leaving a trail of wet footprints across the decking.

"Having fun?" Josh asked, handing him a towel.

"Definitely. You?"

"Ah. You know." Josh shrugged. George play-slapped his arm and he mouthed an 'ouch'.

"Don't be such a baby."

"Don't be such a baby," Josh mocked. George put his finger on Josh's lips to shush him, and he tried to bite it, then grabbed his hand and pulled him closer, water dripping from George's nose onto his chin. Their lips were mere millimetres apart.

"I'm wearing Speedos," George implored, holding the towel in front of his groin.

"Yes. I can see why that might be a problem." Josh smiled teasingly. He tilted his face upwards, until their lips were just touching, and gazed into George's eyes, lingering a moment longer before he released him.

"I, err...I'm just going to sit here for a while," George said, shivering as he fell into the cold chair, unable to use the towel.

"Good idea," Josh agreed, then leaned in and whispered: "Thank God I'm wearing clothes."

Dan took Kris through to the bedroom and checked they could not be overheard; he closed the door.

"Is it true? What Adele said?"

Kris frowned. "Depends what she said."

"That you had an affair?"

"Ah. Yeah," Kris nodded sadly. He'd forgotten that Dan hadn't heard directly from him about the marriage break-up. "Yes, it's true."

"Why? I thought you were happy."

"So did I, but...when I had my breakdown I started to realise that I needed more."

"More than Shaunna?"

"More of me. I love Shaunna, and I didn't mean to hurt her, but it turned out for the best in the end, because now we're having so much fun together, and Krissi's fine with it too, which was..."

"Hang on," Dan interrupted him. "Adele said Shaunna was devastated and that you were still trying to work things out."

"Err..." Kris screwed up his nose. "The thing is, we kind of made that up, for Adele's benefit."

Dan scratched his head. "Now I'm really bloody confused. Are you separated or not?"

"Yes, we are separated. No, we are not trying to work things out. That's just what we told Adele."

"Right. Gotcha. So…" Dan was still trying to decide if he should tell Kris or not, and in his hesitation had planted the seed of curiosity.

"So?"

"Before you confirmed the facts, I was going to tell you to have words with your wife, because she's been flirting big time with Andy since we got here."

"She's a free agent now." The words were dismissive; Dan watched him for a moment and decided it was safe to continue.

"And how would you feel if she and Andy ended up together?"

Kris laughed haughtily. "Even if he and Jess are finished for good, that's not very likely, is it? Not with…" He spotted Dan's raised eyebrow. "You think they might?"

Dan shrugged. "Whatever, I thought I'd mention it." He wasn't going any further with this. "Seeing as I thought you were trying to work things out." There was no point.

"Well, as I say, she's a free agent, although, with all due respect, I'd be bloody amazed if she went after Andy." Dan faked a laugh and opened the door. The conversation was over.

Jess had returned in her bikini and bathrobe, to find the hot tub empty. It hadn't been intentional, and George felt really bad about it, but there wasn't a thing he could do right at that moment.

"I'm coming back in a minute," he called over. "I'm just having a drink." He held up his beer as evidence, and tipped the bottle to his mouth, half the contents running down his face. Josh caught a drip with his finger as it raced towards George's belly button.

"Don't!" he spluttered on a mouthful of unswallowed beer. "I'm having enough of a problem as it is." Josh grinned and sucked the beer off his finger; the sexual overtone was probably unintentional, but even so, George had to concentrate to block it out. "I'll get you back, you know that," he said, twisting as he got up from the chair, so that his back was to everyone else. He pulled the towel over his trunks, a bulge still evident through the thick fabric.

"Ahem," Josh said, averting his eyes. George struggled off towards the hot tub and stepped in as far as he could without taking the towel away, then whipped it off and threw it on the floor, submerging his lower body before anyone noticed. Jess joined him, and a minute later, Kris also climbed back in. The water was slightly cooler now, and the three of them sat chatting, enjoying the view and each other's company. Adele and Shaunna were taking a breather, sitting in their bathrobes on the edge of the tub, and listening to the conversation. This was how things stayed for the rest of the evening, until people started making their way back to their own cabins or rooms; first Eleanor and James, then Dan and Adele, closely followed by Josh and George. Shaunna waited until Kris and Jess left, and locked up behind them, while Andy collected the empty bottles. He stopped at the kitchen sink for a glass of water. Shaunna waited until he became aware of her watching him.

Kris slowed to a stroll before they reached the steps to their cabin; Jess matched his pace. It was too dark to see her clearly.

"Did you get things sorted?"

"Not really."

"Oh. It looked like you were getting on OK."

"We're on speaking terms, if that's what you mean."

Andy sipped at the water and grimaced. It was warm. He emptied the glass into the sink and tried again.

"I don't wish to pry, and I know it's difficult for the pair of you, but it's pretty hard on the rest of us too."

Jess sniffed. Kris reached into the darkness and gently rubbed her arm.

"It's over between us."

A silence followed. Their plans to intervene had not extended to this eventuality.

"Have you talked it through? Explained how you feel?"

"Why bother? Friends don't lie. They don't cheat. They don't hurt each other. There's really nothing left to talk about.

It's over."

No more to be said, each wished the other a good night at the junction of their bedrooms and went to bed.

The next day saw everyone heading out on different excursions. Dan and Andy went back up to the sports centre, which was, in essence, a large log cabin with a shop full of equipment and a bored-looking student type sitting behind a desk. The previous day they'd booked a hang gliding session, and were given insurance forms to fill in while they waited for the equipment to be brought out and checked over. Meanwhile, Josh and George were going to explore the nearest village, which they'd passed through on their way here: a forty minute drive back down the mountains. Shaunna, Kris and Casper were hitching along for the ride to do the same thing, but independently. This left Adele, Jess, Eleanor, James and the children at the cabins, and the Browns offered to take little Shaunna out with them for a short ramble around the local area, culminating in a stop-off at the playground, which was distant enough from the other cabins to be almost a private facility. Hence, they were quite surprised to find three boys of around eight or nine years of age, playing on the roundabout when they arrived. Their bikes were dumped across the path, and they immediately apologised and came over to move them out of the way.

"Thank you, boys," James smiled, setting Shaunna down. She immediately toddled off after Oliver, but he was too fast for her. Eleanor was carrying Toby in the papoose, and sat down on the tiny yellow park bench to rest her back.

"I don't know how you cope with this," she puffed, lifting Toby out and sitting him against her arm.

"I imagine it to be a lot like pregnancy," James contended. She knew better, although it would most certainly have afforded him an insight, as the aches and pains she'd had in her lower back throughout the last three months of carrying Toby had returned in full force. James set off after Shaunna, who had made it as far as the slide, and was now pointing up to Oliver at the top of the steps.

"I-do-it," she said. Oliver came flying down at speed, straight off the end, then back up again.

"I-do-it," Shaunna repeated. James examined the slide. It was too narrow for him to fit, and Oliver was too small to hold on to Shaunna. All the while, one of the boys had been watching and now approached.

"Excuse me," he said politely. "Would you like me to take her?"

"It's very kind of you to offer," James said, trying to think of a plausible reason why this boy—a stranger—shouldn't take his friend's daughter down the slide, other than the truth of it being exactly that.

"I've got a baby sister," the boy added helpfully. "She loves the playground and I do it all the time." James looked to Eleanor for guidance. She shrugged.

"I don't suppose Adele will mind," she said. It wasn't as if they were leaving Shaunna with this boy and he sounded genuine enough.

"All right then. Thank you," James said. The boy smiled and held out his hand to Shaunna.

"Come on," he encouraged. She took his hand and he lifted her up, carried her to the top of the steps and sat her on his knee, dragging the soles of his training shoes along the sides of the slide to slow their descent, while she giggled with excitement.

"I-do-it," she said again, once they'd stepped off the bottom. Dutifully, he carried her back to the top and down they came a second time, then a third, and so on until everyone had lost count. James was splitting his attention between this activity and Oliver's swinging, in between the other two boys, who were showing him how to kick his legs so he could do it for himself without being pushed. So far, he'd set the swing wobbling from side to side, but was having some trouble with backwards and forwards. He was becoming quite frustrated by this, and one of the others came over to set him off with the right motion, before returning to their own swing. James was quite overcome by the kindness these boys were showing to the younger children, and made his feelings very clear several times over. He had learned from Alistair Campion the value of praise in encouraging the right kinds of behaviour, and it really couldn't be given too often. He took over the pushing of Oliver's swing to allow his new friends to enjoy their playtime; not long after this, one of them pulled an old and battered mobile phone from his pocket and signalled to the other two. Little Shaunna was just coming to the bottom of the slide, and James took her from the boy, placing a one pound coin in his hand, as he had for the others.

"If your mother wishes to know where this came from, tell her she is welcome to find us. We are staying in the cabins over there."

The boy nodded and darted off after his friends, all three of them tearing back down the track, wheels leaving the ground as they cleared bumps and stones.

"Come on," James said, taking Oliver's hand. "It's time for lunch."

"Can I have a bike, please?"

"You already have a bike, at your mother's."

"I bring it here?"

"I don't think so."

"Why?"

"Oliver. Please don't ask silly questions."

"Because it is too far away," Eleanor explained patiently. "Maybe your dad might think about buying you a bike to keep at our house." She looked at James as she made the suggestion. So far, her 'interfering' had been allowed to pass without comment, but she could see that he wasn't happy.

"I will think about it," he said sternly. Eleanor and Oliver both knew to say no more. They started making their way back to the cabins, with Eleanor giving little Shaunna a piggyback and James carrying Toby in the papoose. As they walked, they hit a pocket where there was phone reception and a beep sounded from Eleanor's pocket. She took out her phone: missed call and voicemail, from her dying patient's husband, which could mean only one thing. James took Shaunna from her and walked on ahead so that she could listen alone. Her patient had died the previous evening, with her family around her; it had been very peaceful and she was in no pain. The widower ended the call by saying how much he appreciated her compassion and care for his wife, both so grateful for all she had done. One of the last things she'd asked was that he personally thank Eleanor and tell her she wasn't to feel guilty about not being there, but that she would honour her memory best by enjoying her new husband and family and making the most of every precious moment they had together. The line went quiet, and then the voicemail options sounded. Eleanor saved the message, intending to delay a while longer to allow the tears to subside, but her patient had been right. Every moment was precious. So what if she didn't agree with some of James's decisions? So what if she was crying like a baby and Oliver would have a hundred questions why? She cleared her throat and made her way back to the cabin, where James immediately put his arms around her.

"Why are you sad, Enna?" Oliver asked. And so it began.

While they were alone, Jess and Adele had taken the opportunity to enjoy a soak in the hot tub, and clear the air, albeit in a very superficial way. Adele was feeling very important indeed, with Jess telling her that she felt she ought to explain why she had been spending so much time with Rob, although it was only a means to an end, inasmuch as she knew that Adele would tell Dan, and therefore Andy would get to find out. Rob had got the money for his surgery now, his last text message confirmed, and he promised to call as soon as he had an admission date. Adele made all the right sympathetic noises and even gave Jess a hug and an apology. None of it was heartfelt, but both believed they had gained sufficiently from the experience to at least act like they were friends for the rest of their time in Wales.

Things weren't much less tense a few miles down the mountain, where George had led his reluctant companion up a winding cobbled road that opened out onto the village green, across from which was a pub called 'The Ferret's Hat'. It was old and tatty, with missing roof tiles and flaking window frames. Outside there were three weather-bleached picnic tables and a sandwich board penned by an illiterate:

Fine Cask Ale's
Fresh food served dayly

"We've been walking around this place for almost an hour," George pre-empted, expecting Josh to dismiss the pub, like he had the three others before it.

"All right," he sighed, stopping to wipe off the apostrophe with a dampened fingertip.

"Joshua!" George admonished, grabbing his sleeve to pull him inside. Josh jolted his arm away and made a big deal out of straightening his shirt. "Would you please stop moaning? It's this or the chip shop."

Josh followed him sullenly to the bar and glanced around the place listlessly, shrugging at the suggestions being made, leaving George to decide that they were having steak and ale pie and a glass of Coke.

"What's the matter?" George asked, as they took their drinks and sat at a table outside.

"Nothing. I'm not that hungry."

"You're very fidgety today."

"Am I? I feel fine," Josh dismissed, whilst at the same time becoming very aware that he was jigging his leg up and down. He stopped immediately.

"You would tell me, wouldn't you, if there was something wrong?"

"Stop worrying!" Josh smiled quickly and broke eye contact.

George didn't ask any more questions. Clearly there was something bothering him, and he knew not to probe if there was to be any chance of receiving an explanation. It was just so infuriating to see him revert to his previous mood when things had been going so well and they'd been so open with each other for the past few days. The chill in the air wasn't just because they were sitting in the shade, with the silence only temporarily suspended to thank the person who brought out their food. It was very well presented and tasted just fine to George, but Josh hardly touched his, so clearly desperate to leave. George ate as quickly as he could, giving himself indigestion in the process, and they were back on the cobbled road again thirty minutes later.

"So what do you want to do now? We've got another hour before Shaunna and Kris are due back."

"Can we just go and find somewhere quiet, away from people?" Josh suggested. George looked around the deserted village. It was half-day closing and they had hardly seen anyone at all. To his left there was a signpost for the marina, which had already been dismissed as being too full of tourists; to his right was a footpath arrow pointing to a gap in a dry-stone wall.

"This way," George said, heading off in the direction of the footpath. Josh held back, then ran and caught up.

"Sorry. I don't feel very well today."

"Too much beer last night?"

"Err, a bit more than that."

They stepped through the gap, emerging into a field of cows. George stopped dead. "Ah," he said.

Josh walked on, up the footpath which ran along a wall separating this from another field, fully expecting George to be right behind him and only realising that he wasn't when he was thirty feet or so away.

"George!"

"Could you come back here, please?"

"No. They're not even paying any attention to us."

"Not yet, they're not, but it's only a matter of time. Please?"

Josh refused to move, so George slowly, carefully, walked up the field towards him, trying to ignore the cows. One of them turned and stared at him, steadily chewing her way through the mouthful of long grass that was hanging down from either side of her enormous nose. George drew level with Josh and stopped again.

"Don't make me do this."

"I'm not going to make you go any further. Just stay here, with me, for a few minutes, and we'll watch them."

"No way. I know what you're up to and I'm quite happy to keep this phobia, thank you very much."

"Are you sure? Only it seems a shame to miss this perfect opportunity to do something about it." By now the herd had started moving towards them, and George was already backing off. The wall was too high to climb over, which meant the only other escape was right up the top of the field, in which case they would have to come back this way again later, or the hole through which they had come, beyond the expanse that was now filling with cows.

"I hate you for this," George muttered through tightly clenched teeth, and although he didn't mean it, the words were tinged with the venom of someone whose every instinct was telling them to flee.

"I'm beginning to hate me for this too," Josh said. He didn't share George's fear, but they were getting a little too close and even he was starting to feel nervy. The path back to the gap in the wall was still clear, and he took George's hand.

"We're going back," he instructed. "Close your eyes if you need to. I'll guide you."

George kept his eyes wide open and followed, stumbling a couple of times, watching the nearest of the enormous beasts plodding slowly in their direction. If he'd been on his own he'd have made a run for it, which was the worst thing to do, but as it was, his pace was being controlled by Josh, and they were now almost at the exit. Without warning, a guinea fowl, disturbed from its hiding place in the long grass, flew out in front of the cow; it startled and ran, and so did George, dragging Josh out of the field and back onto the road. He stopped and leaned against the wall, panting and trying to catch his breath. Josh shook his head in amazement.

"How in God's name did you cope on the ranch?"

"I didn't," George replied breathlessly. That was part of the reason he'd so readily given it up, although only a very small part.

"You know this animal psychology idea of yours?"

George knew where this was going and Josh was right. If he had any intention of taking things further, he was going to have to deal with his ridiculous phobia. However, his whole interest in anything to do with psychology, counselling and therapy was at an all time low, as a result of his bad experience at the prison, so now was not the right time to be making quick career decisions. Josh sensed he wanted to let it go and respected his wishes.

"On the plus side, you've distracted me from my moping. Let's go take a look at this marina," he suggested. George frowned grumpily. "Come on. I'll even throw in an ice-cream."

CHAPTER THIRTY

Only their third evening at the cabins, and they were already settled into a routine, which began in earnest once the children were fed, the dog was walked and those intending to make the most of the hot tub had surpassed the disappointment of their bathing attire still being wet from the day before. Andy wasn't the first to suggest skinny-dipping as a viable alternative, but all those concerned decided that a few moments' discomfort was preferable to spending an entire evening exposed to the elements and to each other. Dan and Andy had bought some disposable barbecues from the shop up by the sports centre, where there was also a launderette, should the people in the hot tub feel the need to avoid the wet swimming costume problem in future, although by the time it came up in conversation they were all so warm and tipsy from yet again spending too long sitting in the hot water that no-one really cared.

This time, rather than leaving the occupants of the centre cabin to clear up (and after several not-so-subtle hints from Shaunna), each took their empties away with them when they left at the end of the evening: a much more respectable eleven o'clock, although Josh and Kris—the only ones from their cabin not to go in the tub—were still wide awake, and stayed up playing pontoon for chocolate buttons. Jess had put on a convincing façade of enjoying herself, but her dark mood returned as soon as they were away from the celebratory atmosphere, so when she came for a glass of water at two in the morning, having been woken by the pair of them laughing at how many chocolate buttons Kris had piled in front of him, she didn't say a word, although her silent glare told them exactly what she thought of their little card game. George had also gone to bed, assuming he wouldn't be alone for long, and had fallen asleep quickly, emotionally and physically drained from their excursion to the village, and from trying to cope with Josh's mood swings. It was to be expected, he supposed, given that it was only last week that they had both finally owned up to how they really felt, and now they were sharing a bed, which would have been a bit of a shock in any relationship, even more so in one requiring so much negotiation and compromise. It was almost three o'clock when Josh finally came to bed, and he curled up close, once again sending George into an immediate state of arousal. He concentrated on his breathing and was asleep again within minutes.

The next morning they were both sitting in bed, reading books and sipping coffee. It was all very conventional and made them feel a bit like an old married couple, although the main reason they were still in bed was to avoid Jess, who had been up since seven, flooding the lounge with her misery. When they did eventually make it out of their room, it was only en route to the car, from there driving to a pub on the way to the village they had visited yesterday, to eat lunch and be somewhere inside where Jess, or indeed, any of their friends, was not. They were having something of a minor disagreement, because George really wasn't being obstreperous in asking so many questions; he just couldn't get how an 'intimate' relationship was possible without even the most occasional sex, which was not what he said in so many words, but Josh knew what he meant and kept switching between patiently explaining—again—the difference between romantic and erotic love, and dissolving into sulky silence, where all George could do was say sorry, knowing that any time now he would receive an apology back; and on it would go.

They stayed in the pub for as long as they could without loitering, which was difficult, seeing as Josh was driving and the only non-alcoholic drinks available were mixers. After a half an

356

hour of further chatting, with no drinks on their table and lots of funny looks from the barman, they left and returned to the cabin to find they were alone.

"See now," George began cautiously, trying to make his observation sound carefree and not a bit important to him, "this would usually be a perfect opportunity for a bit of afternoon nookie. Is there a romantic equivalent to that?"

Josh folded his arms and leaned on the breakfast bar, a bemused smile settling on his face.

"Why is that funny?"

"Because you really have no imagination, do you? You want afternoon nookie? Come on then."

George frowned. He couldn't see how this was going to work, but Josh was already in their room, so he had no choice but to follow.

"So, what are we doing?" he asked.

"Thought we could make it up as we go along."

George flexed his aching back. The firmness of the mattress wasn't doing him much good, but it was more tension than anything.

"Perfect," Josh said, flipping off his shoes and getting into a kneeling position on the bed. He patted a spot in front of him. "I'll give you a massage."

Now it was George's turn to look bemused. He sat where indicated and tried to relax, as Josh's fingers gently came into contact with his skin. He ignored the stirring of interest inside his jeans and focused on the sensation of the light pressure on his tense neck muscles.

"Take off your t-shirt."

George turned his head and gave him a 'Do you think that's wise?' kind of look.

"I can't very well rub your shoulders through it, can I?"

George complied, aware of the rumblings of lust starting up within. Josh continued to knead and stroke, round his neck, into his shoulders, working his way down each arm, before moving on to his back, at which point he told him to lie on his front.

With Josh now straddled across his buttocks, it was all he could do to stay where he was, convinced that, for the first time since he was a teenager, he was going to make a terrible mess in his boxers. The whole 'purpose' of these exercises, aside from intimacy, was to try and establish the point at which the sensual became the sexual, and he really ought to admit that he was so far beyond it that there was probably no going back. He was on his way to the crest of the wave when Josh moved away, and he heaved a sigh of relief. Alas, it was optimistic and short-lived, as the next thing he knew he was lying on his back, with Josh sat astride his waist, his hands coming down on his chest and it was all too late. He wanted to cry with embarrassment.

When he returned from cleaning himself up, Josh put his arms around him.

"I'd have stopped if you'd said something."

"It's not as easy as that." He couldn't get his head around it, and the more he tried, the worse it got. How could Josh not be aroused by what they were doing? His self esteem was plummeting through the floor.

Josh waited for George to put his shirt back on and indicated that he should sit down. He looked so dejected.

"Please don't be embarrassed."

"I'm trying! But when I find you so…it's this whole sexual attraction thing. I'm struggling with it being all one-sided. It's making me feel so inadequate."

"Honestly, you're such a goon sometimes. First off, there's more to good looks than sex appeal. I mean, look at Shaunna, who, let's face it, neither of us have any sexual or romantic interest in, but does that mean we don't find her attractive?"

"No, I guess not."

"And for the record, I am attracted to you, as I told you before, but it doesn't work the same way for me. That doesn't make you, or me, inadequate."

George wasn't convinced, but he gave him the benefit of the doubt.

"We made it to here, didn't we? After all that time apart."

He nudged George and he nodded dolefully. "And perhaps that's the way we're going to have to do it, because I really don't mind if you…do what you did before."

"It feels like I'm being selfish." Josh was about to protest, but George continued: "I know what you're saying, but it's a whole new concept to me."

For all that they had shared so far, Josh didn't want to say that this was new to him too, which was why he'd accidentally tipped George over the edge. Even now he was struggling to comprehend how a massage was erotic, just as much as George was struggling to see how it wasn't. To think: all the time they'd known each other, and yet they barely knew each other at all.

The awkwardness of their 'afternoon nookie' was soon forgotten once they were in the company of others again. Tonight's activities: Shaunna and Kris had cooked a colourful array of Indian dishes, which were going down very well with a bottle or two of their chosen beverage. And Shaunna was on fine form once again, regaling them with stories of Adele's first visit to an Indian restaurant, where she'd thought the hot cloth delivered at the end of the starter was another course and politely informed the waiter that she hadn't ordered it. Even Adele laughed when Shaunna mimed the actions of someone trying to bite into a piece of wet flannel and saying "Mmm…chewy!".

Overnight it rained so heavily that there was a virtual stream running along the stretch of tarmac in front of the cabins, before it coalesced with the river that was the road down the mountain. By midday it started easing off, and Dan was back on Andy's case about the bungee jump he'd been threatening to undertake. However, the previous afternoon, after they'd checked in their hang gliding equipment, they'd got talking to a couple of skysurfers who were about to go up, and being the adrenaline junkie that he was, Andy challenged Dan to a rematch. Before they knew it, they were both freefalling towards the mountains (this time with the benefit of expert advice and the right equipment), each catching occasional glimpses of the other attempting basic manoeuvres. It was an exhilarating and successful dive, until they came in to land, when Andy jettisoned his board so late that it bounced back and hit him on the side of the head.

Thus, as soon as anybody mentioned bungee jumping (which they were all doing at a far greater frequency than usual—amazing how it could be worked into a conversation on almost any topic), Andy would put his hand to his head and complain that he felt sick and dizzy, although not so sick or dizzy as to stop him drinking beer, and with the weather so bad, they'd started early. Poor Oliver was tearing around the place, so desperate to play outside that in the end George took him for a short spell at the playground. The boys on bikes were there, making the most of skidding in the muddy terrain, but they stopped to come over and play for a while with Oliver. When it started raining again, George got to experience the tantrums firsthand, and stood in heavy downpour for a full five minutes, while Oliver stamped his feet and screamed. He didn't mention any of this to James later.

Friday morning was a little brighter, and everyone headed off to the village, to hire boats on the marina, which sounded a lot more glamorous than it was in reality, as what they ended up with were brightly-coloured, numbered pedalos, in which they spent more time going round in circles and almost colliding with each other, than racing to the island in the middle of the lake, which was what they were trying to do. The entire adult contingent blamed their fuzzy heads, from the previous day's extended drinking session, and refused to surrender their hopes for victory, even though the weather looked set to turn again soon. Inevitably, it was Dan and Adele who made it to the island first, closely followed by Andy and Shaunna. Jess and Kris were in third place, although it had taken them a further twenty minutes to get there, with the Browns giving up when they crashed into a moored yacht. Josh and George didn't even look as if they were trying to compete (although they were), and took a strategic early retirement, following Eleanor and James back to the jetty, where they ate ice-creams and watched as the others made their higgledy-piggledy voyage back to shore. Their communal failure to steer their vessels didn't detract from the enjoyment of the experience though, and by the time they disembarked, their sides were aching from laughing, a situation made profoundly worse when Shaunna remarked that it gave a whole new meaning to their once overly utilised nickname of 'The Circle'. Needless to say, they were stiff-legged and still feeling too toxic to do much in the way of drinking that evening, so all retired early in order to make the most of their last two full days in Wales.

Andy was sweating, and his hands were shaking so much that he could barely keep a grip on the smooth steel karabiner, let alone clip it to the harness. And he could afford to surrender. After all, he reasoned, he'd stacked up a few achievements this week: hang gliding and skysurfing on Wednesday, a day off to recover from concussion on Thursday, another day off to recover from a hangover and paddle around a lake on Friday, and even though Dan came first, it was still the best holiday ever, because he was getting over Jess. Yes, he was enjoying every minute, whereas she appeared, by and large, to be having the exact opposite experience, and he was kind of pleased about that, but was too nice a guy to gloat that her misery was of her own making.

So, today was the day. He was going bungee jumping, over whitewater, and this one was on his own. Dan had been up for everything else, and was only too happy to drive him here, but there was no way on earth they were attaching that harness to him and dangling him from a bridge. Adele had also complained, entirely reasonably, that he had left her to look after little Shaunna for most of the week, although the truth was that James and Eleanor had done more than their fair share of babysitting. Nevertheless, he'd strapped his daughter into the car, to accompany him in delivering her crazy and much idolised uncle to his madcap adventure for the day, leaving

Adele free to head off with grown-up Shaunna on the weekly bus to the nearest town. It was a two hour ride each way, with almost six hours to see the sights in between, the bus picking them up at a quarter to nine in the morning, and set to return them at seven that evening. So far they'd visited a tea room and a traditional sweet shop and spent a small fortune in each, their bags now laden with pear drops, cola cubes and all kinds of other sugar-based delicacies they hadn't much liked in their youth, but were deliciously loaded with nostalgia. They stopped off at a couple of fashion boutiques, mostly so Adele could criticise the dreadfully outdated lines on display, and then crunched their way along the rest of the high street, towards the tiny shopping precinct and hopefully lunch.

Kris returned from walking the dog and scrubbed his hands vigorously in order to remove the sticky sap from the various sticks and cones Casper had retrieved for him, not that he'd thrown them in the first place. Contrary to what Shaunna had said, he was still enjoying being out in the wilderness, so to speak, and was also loving the fact that they had a little longer left before they went home. The same, alas, could not be said for some of his cabinmates, or one of them in particular, for Jess had spent the past couple of days making, at best, half-hearted attempts to join in with barbecues and nights in the hot tub, her mind elsewhere. Even now, she was once again standing on their balcony, her phone at her ear and a worried expression on her face. She moved her phone away, checked the screen and returned it to her ear. Kris was curious to know what it was all about, and armed himself with a magazine, under the guise of sitting outside to read. Jess flashed a brief smile at him and turned away. He put his feet up on the chair opposite and opened a page at random, paying very little attention to what he was reading. Jess put her phone in her pocket and sighed. She ambled over to where Kris was sitting and perched on the edge of a chair. Evidently, she wanted him to ask, so what else could he do?

"Everything all right?"

"Ha ha. No," she said tearfully. "I think I might have done a really stupid thing."

"OK. What's that then?" He asked the question almost sarcastically, because what he was expecting to hear was some almighty confession of how she'd made a dreadful mistake in spending all her time and energy on Rob, at the expense of Eleanor's wedding celebrations, and even most of this holiday.

"You know I told you about Rob's heart condition, and that he was selling his bike to pay for the surgery?"

"Yes?" He glanced up from the magazine he wasn't reading.

"Well, he did sell the bike, apparently."

"Oh, that's good. So now he can have the operation?"

"Err, the thing is, I received a phone call from his boss yesterday. Or should I say, ex-boss? He was having a problem getting hold of Rob—Lord knows how he got my number, but anyway, the bike wasn't his. It belonged to his boss. And now he's reported it stolen, and says he thinks Rob stole it."

"What?" Kris looked at her in disbelief. It was the same expression she imagined she'd had when the owner of the motorcycle garage called yesterday to tell her.

"I've been trying to get hold of him ever since, but he's not answering his phone."

"Are you sure you've got all the facts? Maybe it's just a coincidence, and the bike was stolen by someone else."

"I don't know. I checked what make the bike was, and it's definitely the one Rob showed me. But he said it was his."

"Right." Kris thought for a moment. "Do you think he stole it to pay for the surgery?"

Jess didn't answer. Her lip was trembling and she was ready to burst into tears. Kris put the magazine down and moved his chair closer.

"Jess? What's happened?"

She let out a couple of sobs and got up, putting her hand out to distance herself from him.

"Rob told me the sale fell through on the bike. The guy who was supposed to come on Monday never showed."

Kris frowned. "Hang on a second. You just said he sold the bike."

"His boss said he sold the bike, which wasn't his to sell. He told me he didn't. And he sounded so upset..." At this point she trailed off and started to cry again, so completely inconsolable that if the sounds she was making were real words, he had no chance of deciphering them. He went inside to get her a glass of water, waiting for Josh to finish filling the kettle.

"Bugger!" Josh said, shaking the excess water from his hands. In his haste to get out of Kris's way, he'd turned the tap full on, forgetting the water pressure here was stronger than at home. Now his t-shirt was totally drenched and it was his last clean one. He went to the bedroom, grabbed a jumper and turned towards the wall to change.

"Had an accident?" George asked.

"Yeah. Bloody tap. I'm going to have to do some laundry. That's my last clean top."

"It'll dry."

"And in the mean time?"

"I've got a couple spare, if you want to borrow one."

"Thanks, but I prefer long sleeves."

"But you only wear them in bed. Does it matter?"

Josh glowered at him. "It matters to me! Is that not enough?" George looked a little hurt by his reaction, and Josh immediately softened. "We don't all have perfect biceps, you know."

"Like anyone's going to be looking when you're in bed!"

"You might."

"I might, but then I think you're perfect anyway." Like Josh, he was trying to gloss over this latest outburst and they each appreciated the other's effort enough to sustain the pretence.

"Excuse me while I go and throw up," Josh teased, leaving the room again in order to make the coffee. George threw a pillow at him and it hit the edge of the door. Josh peered back through the gap.

"Missed," he grinned and dodged out of the way of another

well-aimed shot. The kettle hadn't quite boiled yet, and as he waited he heard Kris and Jess talking outside. He moved closer to the partly open French doors to listen, catching the very end of what Jess was saying.

"...no surgery without the money, and without selling the bike, he wouldn't have the money, so I lent it to him."

"You didn't."

"Yeah. And that was the last I heard from him."

"Oh, Jess," Kris said. She started to cry and the kettle clicked. Josh crept away from the doors and made the coffee, stirring the cups as quietly as he could, in case there was more to follow, but other than the sound of Jess sobbing her heart out, there was nothing. He took the coffee back to the bedroom and explained what he had heard.

"Hmm. I'm intrigued now," George said. "I think it's time we found out what's going on."

"How?"

"If we can get Kris on his own—I bet he knows *everything*."

"Good idea. As soon as I've drunk my coffee."

George tutted. Josh was well and truly back on the full caffeine diet this week: he didn't seem to be suffering so much for it at night, but during the daytimes he was restless and agitated, stressing out over silly things, like getting his shirt wet.

"I'm also thinking," George said, crawling across the bed and putting his head in Josh's lap, "maybe we should go and commandeer the hot tub." Josh looked down at him, tracing his finger across that mischievous smile.

"You know that line we talked about?"

"Yes. And have I done anything to breach it all week?"

"No, you haven't. That's true."

"In fact, I quite like the whole tightrope-walk aspect of it. Not that I'm suggesting we get up to anything. It's just that everyone next-door's out, and I get the feeling that you've wanted to go in it all week, but felt a bit shy about stripping off in front of people." He felt Josh's leg muscles tense under his head. "Hey. It was only a suggestion."

"I know," Josh said, "and you're so right. I really do want to go in the hot tub, but I just can't."

"Does it have anything to do with 'the dream'?"

"No! That's fear of heights, if it's anything at all."

"Your scrawny biceps then?"

"I didn't say they were scrawny!"

"True. But you do keep yourself covered up," George argued gently. He could feel Josh mentally pulling away from him.

"I know what you're thinking," he said, "and you're wrong." He eased his legs out and sat on the edge of the bed with his back turned.

"I'm not thinking anything." George put his hand on Josh's shoulder and he shrugged it away. "Don't shut me out."

"This isn't me shutting you out. This is me getting angry at having to justify who I am."

"No, you're misinterpreting what I said."

"Am I? Don't you think I've been through this a hundred times before?" Josh was up on his feet and pacing the short expanse of floor between the door and the bed. "Maybe he was abused as a child. Maybe it was because his mother died when he was so young. Maybe it was the lack of a father figure. Maybe this, maybe fucking that. There is no reason for it. It's just the way I am, so stop trying to fix me!" He left the room, slamming the door behind him, and locked himself in the bathroom, leaving George sitting on the bed, alone and confused.

Andy was strapped into the bungee harness, balanced on the rail along the side of the bridge, the uneven banks of the river giving him vertigo and a touch of cold feet. The instructor was splitting his attention between watching him and repeating his explanation of the process to the next jumper. Dan was standing a short distance away, with little Shaunna perched on his shoulders.

"Addeeeee!" she shouted, bouncing up and down and grabbing her dad's ears.

"Hurry up, bro. I'm suffering here," Dan complained. He could see Andy was scared, but he'd also seen him bottle it before and knew that if he didn't do it now, then they'd be back tomorrow, and the day after if necessary, until he finally found the nerve. "You've jumped out of planes and off mountain tops without a safety harness. This is nothing!"

Andy glanced down again and felt himself go dizzy. Dan was right. He had done all those things, and technically they were of far greater peril than this, yet somehow the prospect of plunging a hundred feet down into the rock-strewn rapids below, should his bungee cord snap, was infinitely more terrifying. However, failure was definitely not on his agenda for this holiday, and with this thought firmly planted in his mind, he fell forward and tucked in his toes, keeping his arms in a swan dive and falling, falling, the fast-flowing river rising up to meet him at an ever-quickening speed. For a split-second he felt icy water slicing at his fingers, and then he was lurching back up, up, his stomach barely arriving before he fell again, then up, and finally down once more, until he was bobbing like a badly wound yo-yo. He didn't know what all the fuss was about.

Driving back to the cabins, little Shaunna couldn't get enough of her Uncle Andy, shouting his name over and again, pulling at an elasticated toggle on his sleeve and releasing it, as if she understood that the principle was the same. He was still buzzing with adrenaline, because the other things he'd done this week were fun, but he'd done them before. He remembered now: it was never about the quest itself, but the journey to get there, which was why he'd hated being stuck in Kathmandu so much. All of the preparation and planning for the trip: that was the part he loved, just like standing on that rail, waiting to dive off the edge of the bridge.

Dan observed his brother through the rear view mirror, so completely enthralled by his niece and the attention she was lavishing on him. It was the first time he'd seen him look happy since they left for Nepal, and a sign that his heart was on the road to recovery.

Back at base camp, Kris had given Jess a large vodka to steady her nerves, not that he thought alcohol was a particularly effective medicine, but at least she'd stopped crying and had permitted him to explain the full story to George, as she had conveyed it to him. Josh had waited until their room was vacant before he unlocked the bathroom door, and was now sitting on the bed, rehearsing an apology for his earlier irrationality. A short while later, he made his way outside, and sat down next to George, listening intently as Kris explained what Jess had done, while she sat staring into the depths of her vodka. George glanced sideways and he met the glance briefly, hoping it would be enough to convey how dreadfully sorry he was. George hooked his fingers through Josh's and continued to listen.

As Kris reached the end of his narration, Dan and Andy pulled up outside their cabin. Jess knocked back the rest of the vodka and went to get a top-up.

"So," George said, by means of clarifying what he'd heard, "Rob told her he needed the money to pay for an operation, she lent it to him and now she can't get hold of him."

"That's the long and short of it."

"He's done a runner."

"I don't know. A reunion is one hell of a length to go to just to prime your victim. Maybe he does have a heart condition and something's happened to him, which is how she's interpreting it."

"Well, there's one way to find out," Josh said, as Eleanor came up the steps to their cabin, with James. He was all set to fill her in and get her professional opinion, but he didn't get that far. There was something very wrong; he could see it in her face.

"Ellie? What's happened?"

"Oliver's gone missing. He was playing outside on the balcony, and I called him in for dinner, but he didn't answer. I just thought he was having one of his sulks."

"We don't know how long he's been gone," James said. He was operating on automatic, his face drawn, yet expressionless.

"Could he have gone off to play somewhere? He really likes the playground," George suggested. Eleanor shook her head.

"We've already checked and he's not there. Some older boys who were playing with him the other day said they haven't seen him either." Eleanor's voice was rising in panic. Josh put his arm around her and led her over to the sofa.

"Don't worry. He can't have gone too far. When did you last see him?"

"About two hours ago," James told him.

"Presumably you've called the police?"

"They're on their way, but the nearest station is in the town. It will be dark before they get here."

"Right," George said decisively. "We need to organise ourselves into search parties. Jess, go and tell Dan and Andy what's going on, and ask Dan to bring the map Adele printed."

Jess left without hesitation, the priority now to get out looking for little Oliver Brown as quickly as possible. Kris grabbed his coat and George went to put on his shoes; Josh followed him into the bedroom and unhooked his jacket from the back of the door.

"I'm sorry about before," he said. "I over-reacted. There's something I need to tell you, but it will have to wait."

"It's OK. I'm sorry too, for pushing you. I shouldn't have."

There was much more to be said, but for now it was put on hold, as they joined the others gathered in the lounge of their cabin, the printout of the site spread out on the table. It wasn't a particularly detailed map to work from, but it at least gave them some idea of the main forested areas and footpaths. Andy marked off the map with a grid of squares, pencilling in darker lines to indicate which area each of them would search. They all took pictures of it with their phones and headed out to their respective zones, keeping an eye on the time so that they could make check-ins every half an hour. As James and Eleanor made their way back towards the playground, the three boys on bikes came up to meet them, and for a moment, James dared to hope that they'd seen Oliver, but they hadn't. They did, however, offer to search downhill, and alert their parents to what had happened so they too could join the search if necessary.

Half an hour passed and still no sightings; each of the group checked in with Andy, and moved on to their next area. It was starting to get dark, and Shaunna and Adele had arrived back to find all three cabins deserted. After several attempts, Shaunna got through to Kris's phone and he explained about Oliver's disappearance.

"What can we do?" she asked.

"Wait at the cabins, just in case he comes back."

She hung up and went outside to sit with Adele. Casper was locked inside the other cabin, barking and scratching to be let out, but they didn't have a key. He started howling, the eerie sound piercing the petrified silence.

"Surely he can't have gone that far," Adele reasoned. "He's only four. How far can someone so small go in a couple of hours?"

They, like all of the other adults, didn't want to consider the possibility that he hadn't simply wandered off, but that someone had taken him, although they hadn't seen anyone other than the three boys at the playground in the entire time they'd been staying here, so it was, thankfully, the least likely of the two possibilities.

"Kris said they're all heading back now. The police should be here soon."

"Oh God. This is awful," Adele cried.

Kris was the first to return, closely followed by Andy, then Dan. They'd found nothing. Kris let Casper loose and he went tearing around the place in circles and greeting everyone—a trait they usually found endearing, but not today. Shaunna called him over and told him to stay, whereby he sat next to her for a couple of seconds, but then he was back on his feet, pushing his nose into her hand, wagging frantically and wriggling to break free. He was picking up on the anxiety and she only just caught him by the collar as he got set to start all over again.

Eleanor and James walked up to the cabins and stopped in front, so worried by now that neither of them could even speak. Toby was hungry and Eleanor sat on the wooden steps to feed him. They too had found nothing; nor had they heard from the boys on bikes.

In the dulling twilight, the sudden illumination of the police car headlamps was blinding. James took the two officers inside and explained the situation, as best he could. Torchlight shone through the trees up ahead, and George and Josh came into view a minute or two later. George shook his head. Eleanor started to cry and Josh sat next to her on the step, pulling her close and stroking her hair; all the while Toby suckled noisily and contentedly. Adele was putting little Shaunna to bed, and Dan and Andy were sitting in the 4x4 with the lights on full beam, shining them along the path and through the trees towards the playground, for this was the most likely route Oliver would have taken. Shaunna's feet were aching from traipsing around the shops, and she'd popped inside to put on a pair of flip-flops, which sounded so ridiculous in the awful, black silence of the situation. She flip-flopped her way over to the 4x4 and stopped.

"Ouch!" She leaned down to remove one of the thin rubber shoes and plucked out the sharp object with her finger and thumb nail, passing it to Andy.

"Ooh. Nasty! I got one in my hand before," he said sympathetically. "I went flying on the wet grass. It didn't half hurt."

"I bet it did."

The others were paying little attention to their conversation, for it only existed as a fleeting distraction.

"Yeah," Andy continued. "I found a few more on the steps." Carefully, he groped around in his pocket, and deposited the evidence in Shaunna's hand. She frowned.

"Hmm. I wonder how they got there?"

Josh and George had gradually tuned into this dialogue and now looked at each other in disbelief.

"Drawing pins!" they said in unison.

"Pardon?" Eleanor asked.

"When we looked after Ollie before the wedding, he was playing with drawing pins," George explained.

"Ah, so that's where they got to! My mum was going mad looking for them."

"Well, obviously we confiscated them, but then we found a couple on the floor, went to put them back in the pot, and Ollie had taken it again. Maybe if he's still got them, he might've..."

"You do realise how crazy that sounds?" Kris interrupted. "You think there's going to be some gingerbread style trail of drawing pins leading the way to Oliver? Even if there is, how the hell would we see them? Casper's got more chance of finding him than..." He stopped, as his brain did a double-take, then sped off in overdrive. But it was absurd, or was it?

"You don't think..." Shaunna said, running the possibility through her mind.

"What are you two on about?" George asked.

"Casper was bred to be a search dog, but he failed the training."

"That's not a lot of good, is it?"

"Is it more or less stupid than your drawing pins idea?"

"That's cool," Andy said, trying to keep things as positive as possible. "One time I went snow-boarding they had to call out the dogs for some skiers buried under an avalanche. It works by tracking human scent, doesn't it?"

"Yeah, pretty much. Basically we present him with a piece of clothing and then we command him to seek out the owner. The thing is, although there's not much wrong with his nose, he doesn't quite get what he's supposed to do."

"I bet George could get him to do it," Josh said. George turned to him, aghast.

"Are you mental?"

"Think about it. What did that horse whisperer say? You could sense their fear?"

"I don't see how that's going to help."

"And then there's Sphinx. Do you have any idea how much of a psycho that cat is? But you! You just walk in there and he sits right on your knee!"

"Come on, George. It's worth a try," Kris egged him on.

"Ellie?" George was hoping for a bit of sense, even if she was out of her mind with worry. She shrugged.

"What've you got to lose?"

George looked around him at all the hopeful faces, and opened his mouth, about to refuse, when the two police officers came outside and got back in their car. James reappeared a moment later.

"They're going to call out the helicopter," he explained. "It should be up here within the hour."

"Within the hour?" Ellie repeated. "Oh, James." She pulled herself upright and they held each other, enveloping Toby between them. Josh looked away, struggling to cope with seeing her in so much pain.

"Right then," George said, "I guess I've got no choice. Let's do this thing."

Kris nodded and asked James to go and get Oliver's pyjamas: the ones he'd been sleeping in this week. James wasn't sure why he needed them, but went and got them anyway. Meanwhile, Shaunna brought out Casper's running lead and attached it to his collar. George took the lead and knelt on the floor next to the dog, stroking his head and taking deep breaths, trying to tune in to that sense of connection he'd felt with the horses. It was so hard, with everyone watching him, and he closed his eyes to concentrate. Casper had been panting and wagging, but now he stopped and sat quietly and calmly.

"Wow!" Shaunna whispered, not to anyone in particular. "How did he do that?"

"I know! It's amazing, isn't it?" Josh whispered back.

George took the pyjamas and held them in front of Casper, turning them over so that he could sniff all aspects of them (this part he'd got straight off the TV).

"What command do you use when you want him to fetch his

F-R-I-S-B-E-E?" George spelled out so as not to break Casper's calm state of mind.

"We don't usually have to," Kris said. "He just does it. But if he doesn't, 'go find it' should do the trick."

George nodded and held the pyjamas to the dog's nose again, then swiftly moved them out of the way and hid them in his jacket. "Go find it," he commanded and Casper shot off, almost ripping George's shoulder out of its socket as he reached the end of the running lead. Down the path towards the playground they went, with everyone in pursuit, other than Adele, Eleanor and James, the latter of whom was under strict instructions to wait at the cabin for confirmation from the mountain rescue team.

"Go on," George goaded, panting for breath. "Go find it." Casper pulled onwards. He was a tremendously strong dog and it was a real struggle to keep up. They were now entering the playground area, and Casper toured each and every piece of equipment, correctly identifying the swing Oliver had been on most often, sniffing the slide and climbing halfway up the steps. It was apparent that Oliver wasn't here, and his residual scent was causing confusion. George took the pyjamas from his jacket and held them to the dog's nose again.

"Go, Casper. Go find it."

On they went, down the dirt track where the boys on bikes had ridden, back towards home. They were going at such a speed that George kept losing his footing, and he tripped, but saved himself, as Casper suddenly veered off to the left. Here, the footpath was less well trodden, low branches and brambles snagging on George's clothes as he careered along behind the determined Labrador, the canopy so dense now and the path so winding that he kept losing sight of Casper as he rounded corner after corner, the running lead alternately becoming slack and almost being pulled from his hand as he momentarily caught up, then fell behind again. George's arms were aching from the effort of keeping a grip on his flashlight and the lead, and once again he tripped, but this time it was over Casper, as he came to an abrupt stop, barking, yelping and wagging his tail. And there, on a ledge six feet below where they were standing, was Oliver, curled up and shivering, his leg glistening in the harsh beam of the torch.

"I falled down, Dorge," he said, looking up at the light. "Carry me please." He held his arms up in the air and George swallowed back the tears.

"He's here," he shouted, assuming the others were somewhere nearby, although it was now too dark to know for sure. "He's here and he's OK," he said, crouching down and rubbing Casper's ears. The dog nuzzled into his hand and George felt tears roll down his cheeks.

"Good boy, Casper. Good boy." The dog licked at his face and it made him cry all the more, but he pulled himself together again, for Oliver's sake.

"OK, Ollie. I can't carry you, because your leg is hurt. I'm going to come and sit with you, though. And soon, you're going for a ride in a helicopter."

"Why?"

George climbed down onto the ledge and sat next to him. "So they can take you to a hospital and fix your leg." The way it was bent under him, it had to be broken, but otherwise he seemed fine.

"I don't want to go hospal," Oliver said, blinking up at him with anxious, round eyes. "I want to go home with Enna."

"You can, soon," George promised.

Immediately on hearing the shout that Oliver was OK, Dan and Andy had doubled back to tell Eleanor and James. Adele took Toby from Eleanor and she ran, with James, all the way down the hill. They were both standing above the ridge now, tears flowing freely in relief. George was shivering, from the shock and the cold, having wrapped Oliver in his jacket, and when the helicopter arrived, it took some persuading to get the terrified little boy to let go of his hand, but he did so as soon as they winched him up and his dad gave him a huge cuddle.

"I sorry, Daddy. I wanted to play bikes. I be a good boy."

George turned away and collapsed into Josh's waiting arms. Together they made their way through the trees and up to the playground, from where they watched the helicopter until it was nothing more than a distant dot of light blending into the stars. The others had already started walking back to the cabins, but they stayed a moment longer so that George could get his legs working again.

"You ready?' Josh asked. George buried his head in Josh's jacket. "Hey." He gently lifted George's face so he could look him in the eyes. "You were awesome."

George tried to laugh it off. Josh wiped the tears away with his thumb.

"Can you show me how to do that?"

"Yeah," George said, stepping unsteadily. "See page sixty-eight of your module guide: 'Animal Psychology for Amateurs'."

CHAPTER THIRTY-ONE

Cuts, bruises and a broken foot: little Oliver Brown had got off fairly lightly, and was so enthralled with his blue plaster-cast and crutches 'like Granpad', as he called Eleanor's dad, that he'd forgotten all about swings and slides and bikes. This temporary amnesia was being helped along by a visit from the older boys, who brought him sweets, followed up with a hefty dose of paediatric pain relief once his visitors had left, with the other welcome side effect being that he was drowsy and somewhat more compliant than usual, which was a good thing, for a sleepless night at the hospital had made James ill-tempered. He began the phone call to Oliver's mother with a gentle and, Eleanor thought, very convincing reassurance that everything was well; he remained silent during her scathing indictment of his capabilities as a father, interspersed with frequent reference to the likelihood that Oliver's schooling, due to commence on his fourth birthday two weeks from now, would undoubtedly have to be delayed, with disastrous and somewhat overstated consequences; he even managed to utter a polite farewell at the end of the conversation, such as it could be called that. However, the terms in which he referred to her after he hung up were far from polite and so unlike James that they left Eleanor agape. When she recovered, she ushered him off to bed, promising (with fingers crossed) to wake him if he were needed.

Fairing just as poorly, in the cabin next-door-but-one, was Jess, who had woken with nausea and a banging headache and at first assumed it was due to the vodka, thus refused to give voice to what she believed was yet more self-inflicted suffering. An hour later and Kris was sent for the 'doctor in residence', even though the sum total interactions Eleanor and Jess had engaged in since the wedding came to less than one. Kris stayed with Oliver and Toby (both fast asleep) whilst Eleanor tended to the patient, whose high temperature, muscle stiffness and general state of lethargy could mean only one thing.

"Flu," Eleanor announced, stripping the cover from her thermometer.

"Terrific," Jess groaned. "And there was I, thinking it couldn't possibly get any worse."

"At least it waited until almost the end of the holiday."

Jess didn't say what she wanted to say to this. It had been a truly awful week, with no contact from Rob for three days and the whole thing of pussy-footing around Andy. She was staving off telling him, in the hope that, in spite of the evidence, she was wrong; that she hadn't been ripped off.

"So, how is Rob?" Eleanor asked without a trace of sympathy or interest. "I'm assuming he's still alive?"

"How would I know?" Jess responded, trying to sound equally uninterested and failing miserably.

"He's not been in touch?"

She shook her head, the dizziness combining with the irrepressible tears and making it impossible to hold back any longer.

"Oh, Ellie. I don't know what's going on anymore. I wanted to do the right thing and I messed up and I'm so sorry for everything." Each sob was making her wheeze, and each wheeze was hurting her chest so much that she didn't know what to do with herself. For all that she had done, Eleanor couldn't stand by and watch her suffer like this.

"Oh dear. What's happened?" She sat down and Jess collapsed against her.

"I think Rob's conned me," she gasped, struggling to catch her breath. "I gave him everything in my bank account and now he's disappeared."

"Why did you give him money?"

"To pay for his operation. How could I have been so stupid?" Jess was breathless and doubled up in pain, but there was little more Eleanor could do than rub her back and wait for her to stop putting herself through this.

"OK, honey. Here's what's going to happen. I'm going to help you get into bed and make you comfy with some painkillers and a cool flannel. Then I'm going to ring Lois and ask her to get him to call you. How does that sound?"

Jess nodded listlessly. Eleanor helped her to her feet and escorted her to bed, making sure she had plenty of cold water nearby and forcing her to take paracetomol. She located Jess's phone and made the call.

"Hi, Lois, it's Eleanor. How are you?"

"Oh, hello, Doctor Davenport, oh. I mean, Doctor Brown. I'm much better, thank you for asking. I'm so sorry to have missed your wedding. Did you have a lovely day?"

"It was wonderful, Lois, thank you. Please don't apologise. As long as you're on the mend now."

"Very much so. I felt so awful, leaving Miss Lambert without any assistance."

"Ah, yes. It's safe to say she's realised how indispensable you are. We're thinking of hiring another assistant, actually, to help you out a little, but I'll talk to you about that later in the week. What I phoned for was to ask a small favour."

"Of course."

"I wondered if you could pass a message on to your Uncle Rob?" The line was silent. "Are you still there, Lois?"

"Err…yes." Her voice was suddenly much quieter. "That might be a bit of a problem."

"Why's that?"

"I can't say too much, but we haven't seen him since before your wedding and my mum is furious with him. He borrowed some money—quite a lot of money, in fact—from the trust fund set up for my sister and me."

"For his operation?"

"I'm sorry?"

"He's waiting for surgery for a heart condition, isn't he?"

"I don't know anything about that, I'm afraid. No, this was for his business. He held a big investors' meeting at a hotel, and invited Mum along. She said she wasn't interested. Then he came to the house with a fancy bike he was supposed to be selling to meet the shortfall, but the sale fell through. She offered to help him out in the short term, and he hasn't been back since, on top of which, his phone's going straight to voicemail and emails are bouncing."

"Oh, that doesn't sound too good," Eleanor said. "Has he ever gone off like this before?"

"I, err…"

"It's OK, Lois. You must all be very worried."

"Not really," she said lightly. "Has he taken money from you too?"

"Not from me, no, but I can't really say any more than that. Look, we'll have a good chat when I get back, see what we can sort out."

"All right, Doctor Dav…Brown. Enjoy the rest of your honeymoon. Bye now."

"Bye, Lois."

Eleanor hung up and spent a few minutes weighing up her options. It was risky, and if she got caught she could get into trouble. Of course, it was possible that Rob was trying to protect his family from worrying about his health, but she was far from convinced, for the implication was that he had done something like this before. And then there was the investors' meeting, which, coupled with the reunion, pointed to a rather more elaborate scheme to defraud not only Jess, but quite a few other people. In light of all of this, she didn't see there was much choice: she went out to the car and retrieved her laptop from the boot (where it had remained all week), and logged in to the patient database. The connection was frustratingly slow, but even so, it didn't take long to establish the truth: Simpson-Stone wasn't exactly a common surname, and there was only one patient registered with the first name of Robert. Apart from an overnight stay and follow-up for gall stones a couple of years ago, the only other entry was from the minor injuries clinic the previous Sunday, for a cheek wound requiring a couple of steristrips and a preventative course of antibiotics. Rob had been lying all along. She wasn't sure how she was going to break the news to Jess, but for now it could wait, because she was resting and Kris was still looking after the other invalid. She left Jess's phone within arm's reach and returned to her cabin.

"Time to swap patients."

"So soon?" Toby had woken up not long after Eleanor had left and was now sporting a clean nappy and a full tummy. Kris looked very disappointed that she'd come back.

"You're a superstar. Thanks."

"Well, he smiled at me so beautifully, I just couldn't resist," he said, rubbing the gurgling little chap's back until he let out the most enormous belch and sicked up all down his front. "Although…" Kris grimaced and handed him back to his mum.

"Yeah. He does that when he's fed from the bottle, don't you Toby?" She rubbed her nose against his and he smiled again. "And one for Mummy too? What a clever boy!"

"So how is she?" Kris asked.

"Jess? She's got flu. She's in a dreadful state over this thing with Rob. I haven't told her yet, but I've just spoken to his niece and he's gone AWOL. He's a conman."

"Oh no! Did Jess tell you she gave him everything from their joint account?"

"Yeah, although she didn't mention the joint part. That's really going to see the you-know-what hit the fan."

"Think I might go AWOL myself," Kris joked. "Right, well I guess I'd best go and keep an eye on her. Thanks, Ellie."

"No problem. Thank you for saving me from the joys of nappy-changing."

"Oh, the pleasure was all mine!" he said dolefully and returned to his own cabin for an afternoon of reading and care-giving.

Their final night: James chose to stay 'home' and look after his sons, leaving Eleanor free to join the rest of her friends for an evening of eating, drinking and general merriment. There was a real party feel in the air, with just one dark cloud looming: Jess was now aware of the full extent of Rob's trickery and had sent for Andy. Some thirty minutes later, the door of the cabin was slammed so hard that it bounced, and the seven of them watched as Andy marched off up the footpath and into the woods without so much as a backwards glance. Dan moved to follow and Kris stopped him.

"Leave him. He'll come back when he's got it out of his system, if his little brother's anything to go by." Dan accepted these words of wisdom and opened another beer. Casper, on the other paw, did not, and tore off after Andy, with Shaunna and Kris shouting themselves hoarse, but to no avail.

"All the praise has gone to his head," Shaunna said, watching as Casper's tail disappeared from view.

"He'll come back when Andy does," Kris consoled her. "Once he's happy they've collected their full quota of pine cones."

"Who? Andy or the dog?" she asked wryly.

As it was their last night, Adele contended, they had to make the most of the hot tub, and it had been burbling away for the best part of two hours before Andy (and Casper) strolled back into their midst, acting as if nothing had happened.

"Come and join us," Shaunna called from in amongst the steam and bubbles."

"D'you know what? I think I will!" he said, pulling off his jacket. Adele started up a raucous rendition of 'The Stripper' and Andy slowed down, making a big show of lifting his t-shirt inch by inch, before spinning it in the air and launching it in Eleanor's direction. By this point, everyone was singing along and producing the most atrocious, tuneless noise that it was as well no-one else could hear them. One button at a time, his jeans were next, landing at Josh's feet, then his socks, until all that was left were his boxer shorts, and he started to push them down at the back, with much whooping and encouragement from the women, whilst Dan's smile melted into a look of pure terror.

"Nah," Andy grinned and jumped in the water. "Just kiddin'!" Dan had never been so relieved, although he was also feeling a little unsettled at seeing his girlfriend and her best friend flirting with his brother, all of them semi-naked in a hot tub.

"You know the simple solution?" Kris said, noticing his friend's jealousy. "Get your kit off and join them."

"Ooh, I don't know about that." He flexed his shoulders and started acting all macho.

"Go on, Dan!" George said. "It's great fun!"

"So why aren't you in there tonight?"

"I thought I'd give everyone else a chance."

"Well, if you put it like that." Dan kicked his shoes off, and removed the rest of his clothes on the way. "Shift over, bro," he said, climbing in between Andy and Adele. Shaunna leaned across to get the wine bottle and emptied the rest of it into their glasses.

"A toast," she said, "to the absent Mr. James Brown, esquire, and his lovely lady wife, El-e-a-nor." Eleanor laughed and hid her face.

"To El-e-a-nor," they all repeated, over-emphasising James's pronunciation of her name.

"Thank you for an amazing honeymoon," Shaunna continued, "and for letting us share it with you." A chorus of thank-yous followed, and Eleanor cleared her throat. They all fell silent, and Adele turned off the water jets, delighted with herself for getting the right button first time.

"Can I just say how honoured I am to have friends like you. Who would have thought it, that twenty-two years on…"

"Twenty-three," George corrected.

Twenty-three years on from..."

"Nearly twenty-four, actually," Adele interrupted again.

"Good grief! However many years it's been since that first

party..."

"Don't remind me," Shaunna said, shoving her elbow into Andy's ribs. Eleanor rolled her eyes and continued.

"...that we'd still all be together, enjoying a night in the mountains and sharing a drink or two."

"Or three," Adele said.

"Or five!" Shaunna laughed, examining her glass in mock horror.

"I don't want to keep going on, so I'll finish by saying thank you." She turned and looked at Josh as she said this. "For always being there for me." He smiled and nodded tearily. "And here's to the next twenty-something years. I love you all." She stopped speaking and turned away, overcome with emotion.

"Aww, Ellie, that was beautiful," Adele said, and everyone applauded.

"OK, OK, enough already!" Eleanor chastised. "Now why the hell's my glass empty?" She took it over to Shaunna, who had set up all of the wine bottles within easy reach of the hot tub, and sat on the steps, chatting to Kris, who was getting ready to join the others.

"I don't mind, you know," Josh said to George. "Go in, if you want to. I'm quite happy spectating."

"And I'm quite happy sitting here, spectating with you," George said, taking Josh's hand and giving it a reassuring squeeze. Josh looked down at their hands, entwined in his lap, and moved closer.

"Kiss me," he said.

"Really?"

"Really."

"Umm. OK." George leaned forward and planted the quickest, lightest kiss on his lips.

"No. Kiss me properly."

Josh was staring deep into his eyes and even if he'd wanted to resist, which he didn't, there was absolutely nothing he could do now to stop himself. He felt his lips part of their own volition, compelling him forwards, to meet with Josh's, the soft perfume of his hot breath filling his nose and his mouth, the gentle pressure of those wonderful lips against his, opening them further, until he could resist no longer and pushed back. For those few seconds everything else in the world melted away and they were all that there was.

"Josh-u-a and George on a bal-con-y. K-I-S-S-I-N-G," Adele chanted, breaking the spell. George opened his eyes to find that Josh was laughing, but he wasn't backing off.

"Yeah, yeah," he said, waving a hand in Adele's general direction without breaking eye contact with George. "As you were." Shaunna and Adele started giggling and Andy splashed them.

"That was the best kiss I've ever had," George said, still unable to move away.

"That was the only kiss I've ever had," Josh told him.

"Well, you're obviously a natural."

"Hmm. I don't know about that. I think I might need to practise a bit more."

"I see. So you liked it then?"

"Yes, George. I liked it."

"That's good to know."

"Yes," Josh said, trying to be serious, "I do need to ask you to do something for me, though."

"What's that then?"

"Please don't say 'I see' like that."

"Like you say it, you mean?"

"Exactly."

Andy lay there for a while, listening to his niece in the room next door, shouting 'Addy'. She probably wanted her breakfast, so it wasn't him she was after at all. With that thought, he rolled over and pulled the duvet, giving it a good tug to free it from where it had hooked over the edge of the bed, and covered his head. He felt a bit rough, not surprisingly, as they'd all carried on drinking late into the night, which perhaps wasn't the best idea with a five hour journey ahead of them. These thoughts were just drifting from him when the duvet was suddenly snatched away, and his eyes flung themselves open. He rolled onto his back and turned his head.

"Shit."

Shaunna sat up and pulled the covers around her, leaving him completely exposed. He grabbed the bottom corner of the duvet and quickly covered his lower half.

"Please tell me we didn't…"

"Erm, well. Let's see. You're naked. And I'm naked, so…"

"Did we use any protection?"

Shaunna leaned forward and glanced around the floor, taking the duvet with her. "Erm…"

Andy pulled a pillow from behind his head and put it over his groin. She gave him a quick smile.

"Oh God. Not again!"

CHAPTER THIRTY-TWO

The journey home was a subdued one in most quarters: Jess was sleeping fitfully, lying across the back seat of Josh's car with her head on Kris's lap, whilst he tried to ignore how hot his legs were and read a script. George was reliving that kiss, the memory of the sensation bringing with it both fulfilment and a hunger for more. Josh was flitting between a similar mind state and much more complex thoughts about what the immediate future held. James and Eleanor had turned off the motorway to head across country in order to drop Oliver back at his mother's, which left just the two cars in convoy, with Dan, unusually, trailing far behind. Andy and Shaunna were acting very strangely, and Adele was restless, clearly preparing to say something that she didn't think Dan was going to like. If she was going to start an argument, he hoped she'd wait until they got home, although a quick glance in the back was enough to tell him that if Adele suddenly turned into a giant cup of coffee, the other two wouldn't even bat an eyelid. This ridiculous vision brought with it an awareness that he was getting very sleepy, and he wound down the window an inch or two.

"Can you ring George and see if they're stopping off anytime soon?" he asked. Adele did so and five minutes later they pulled in at the next service station, where the others had been for around ten minutes. Josh was standing outside, drinking from a vast takeaway cup and evidently having the same problem with fatigue. It wouldn't have been half as bad if they'd been able to leave earlier, but they'd waited until they were sure they were no longer intoxicated from the night before, and now it was getting dark. Dan gave his back a good stretch and headed inside to get his own dose of caffeine. Another couple of hours and they'd be home.

Back in the cars, with Andy taking the final leg again; Adele decided to sit in the back, behind Shaunna, who was watching the tiniest bead of water make its way along the rubber sill of the window. As they left the services and picked up speed, the droplet was squashed flat and ceased to exist. Now she had nothing to distract her.

"Want some music?" she asked.

Andy shrugged. "If you like."

Shaunna switched on the stereo and turned it up to a volume where it could be heard over the road noise. Andy checked his rear view mirror and signalled to pull out, catching a glimpse of Adele's pensive expression. He couldn't decide whether it was because of his driving, or something else, but it was obvious that she was about to start one of her mini rants. Less than five minutes down the motorway, and predictably as ever, he saw her turn to Dan and smile ever so sweetly. Not wanting to be party to another of their arguments, he focused his attention on the road ahead and tried to tune her out. However, it soon became apparent that the people in the back were unaware that everything they were saying could be heard, loud and clear, in the front. Andy chanced a peek at Shaunna and saw that she too was pretending not to listen. The conversation went something like this.

Adele had been so worried when the plane crashed in Kathmandu; they all had, and for a while it looked like she was going to be bringing up little Shaunna all alone, to which Dan pointed out that she had lots of very good friends and as such would never be alone. She told him to stop interrupting and he did accomplish this for a short time, while she continued to relive the horror of being at home, so helpless and 'sick to the stomach' each time the phone rang, dreading the terrible news she was convinced would arrive every minute of every day. Dan remarked that he only had flu; she let out a shrill squeal and he backed off again. Her relief at finding out he was alive and on the mend was immeasurable, and she'd been having a good long think over the last week (Andy knew what Dan wanted to say at this juncture, but he refrained from doing so), and, the thing was, she still wasn't ready to say yes to getting married, but, if he'd like to propose again, she would happily agree to a long-term engagement.

Now, at this point, if Andy had been Dan, he thought, he'd have just said yes and got on with secretly congratulating himself for finally snagging the girl of his dreams. Instead, he asked her if she was 'out of her mind', because, and he thought it a reasonable consideration, they weren't teenagers anymore. They were an almost middle-aged couple with a child, not to mention the fact that his brother was going to be forty next year (thanks for the reminder, bro). Adele listened and said no more. The music played on. Andy kept his eyes on the road; Shaunna traced circles on her knee with her finger, the silence stretching on through the miles ahead. Dan started fidgeting and shifted his position. Shaunna took her lip balm out of her bag and pulled down the sun visor to use the mirror. Andy grinned, impressed with her cunning.

"Adele," Dan said finally, turning in his seat as far as he could and shuffling over so he could reach across the sleeping toddler between them. Shaunna lifted herself in an attempt to see what Dan had in his hand.

"Where did that come from?" Adele asked.

"My pocket, where d'you think?"

"And do you normally keep it in your pocket?"

"Always."

"Oh."

Ever the optimist, Andy thought. He briefly made eye contact with his brother in the mirror and gave him an encouraging wink. A few seconds passed before Dan addressed Adele again.

"I can't very well ask you if you'll marry me, when you just said you won't, can I?"

"So be creative."

"I'm trying!" he snapped in exasperation.

Shaunna's neck was beginning to ache from holding it in such an unnatural position. It was futile anyway, because she couldn't see a thing, as they were now on a section of motorway with no lighting. Andy pulled out and overtook the car in front. Come on, he urged silently. What is he waiting for?

"Adele," Dan began for what he hoped would be the very last time. "When we were in juniors, I asked you to come to my birthday party, and you said you didn't want to be the only girl there. When we started high school, you refused to come and watch the football team, and gave me the same excuse. And again when I asked you to come visit me at uni."

"What has that got to do with anything?"

"The thing is, Adele, after thirty years I still ask the question, hoping that one day you'll give me the answer I want to hear. You always were and will always be the only girl. So please, will you just say yes?"

The pause that followed wasn't very long really; Andy knew this because he was counting down the signs to their turning, and even then he almost missed it.

"Yes."

"Yes?"

"To getting engaged," Adele clarified. "As for getting married? One day, maybe."

She held out her hand and Dan lifted the ring from its box, a ring that had been transferred from pocket to pocket, forever waiting for the singular word that would set it free. He slid it onto her finger and held it there. Andy and Shaunna breathed a united sigh of relief and bumped fists.

At Jess's request, Kris had phoned her mother when they stopped at the motorway services, to tell her that Jess had flu and also that she and Andy had broken up. Thus, her mother was at the door the second they arrived and came out to the car to greet her very sick daughter. Kris carried Jess's bags inside, then Josh dropped him off too; Shaunna was just returning from taking Casper for a quick circuit of the block, having got back a good twenty minutes ago, thanks to Andy's inability to stick to the speed limit. Casper went crazy when he saw Kris, and was obviously still feeling very proud of himself, strutting with his head held high. Josh waved wearily as he pulled away, glad to be almost home.

Alas, the relief was short-lived, for it was only when he pushed the front door open against the pile of mail and the rubberised underlay folded back on itself, concertina-style, that he remembered the state in which he had left the house; in an instant all of the pain of the weeks preceding their holiday came rushing back. George stepped past him, picked up the post and straightened the underlay with his foot, watching patiently as Josh found the courage to once again face the demons he had yet to exorcise.

"Come to me," George beckoned. "Forget about the carpets and everything else. They're just things. Come on. Come to me." Josh took a deep breath and held it. "I'm going to make coffee," George offered hopefully. Josh tried his best to smile. George moved away, towards the kitchen, listening out for the sound of the door closing.

"How can a house make me feel like this?" He'd made it as far as the hallway and couldn't bring himself to face the devastation all around him.

"How does it make you feel?"

"Out of control." He edged closer.

"In what way?"

"Like everything's wrong. It all needs to go. Look at the kettle, for instance."

George examined it and shrugged. "It's a kettle. It serves a purpose."

"But it's old and noisy and takes too long to boil."

"You bought it two months ago. I was with you, remember?"

"I should've bought the other one, with the blue LED."

"And if you'd bought that one, we'd be having the same

discussion about how you should have chosen this one instead. Wouldn't we?"

Josh sighed and turned away from the kettle, the urge to pull it from the wall socket and throw it across the room almost too hard to resist.

"You know I'm right. This isn't about kettles, or carpets, or wallpaper. You can keep on replacing them forever more and they'll always be wrong." George put his arms around him and kissed him gently on the forehead. "We're both tired and it's late, but if you want to do this now, then that's what we'll do."

"No," Josh withdrew and patted George's arm. "I'm shattered. Let's just make the coffee and go to bed." George nodded and filled their mugs, following him to the top of the stairs, where they both stopped.

"So," Josh said cautiously, "do we just go back to our own rooms, or——"

"If you're asking me what I want to do, then you already know the answer. It's up to you."

He didn't know the answer. It would be so easy to bring an end to the incessant battle he had been fighting for the past week, so desperate to be close to George, yet always anticipating that moment when things would go too far, knowing he didn't have the strength to see it through, nor to tell him that this was how he felt. The doors to their rooms felt like they were falling towards him, closing in, crushing him into submission.

"Help me," he urged. "Don't let me hide. I need you to make the choice for me, because if you don't I will push you away and I don't want to push you away, but I can't help it."

George reached forward and opened his door.

"Then tonight we stay in here, where there are carpets and curtains and things you can't change, because they are my things. Tomorrow, who knows? Maybe we'll try your bed instead."

The next morning, Josh was up and dressed, ready for a full day of work, with back-to-back appointments from nine onwards. George watched him going through the motions of his daily routine: coffee brewed; bread in the toaster; laptop next to the coffee machine, ready to check through his client list, emails arriving in the background. The toast popped up and Josh buttered it, dangling a piece from his mouth as he opened his diary on screen. George leaned forward and took the toast from him, bit off a corner and handed it back, examining the full page of appointments.

"Last one at seven," Josh said, scrolling down the list. "There's nothing like ten hours of lamenting housewives to keep your mind occupied. What's your day got in store?"

"Not much. I'm meeting Sophie at the farm, if that's OK with you."

"Why wouldn't it be?"

"The whole *Crash Team Racing* thing?"

"Ah. I see what you mean. I honestly don't mind you spending time with Sophie, but…"

"Just don't play *Crash Team Racing* with her?"

"Yes. It's irrational, I know."

"It's actually not that irrational, knowing what I know now, but anyway. Could I take on some of those appointments? Share the burden a little?"

"You've done your time with me already."

"But your clients don't know that, do they?"

"That doesn't make it acceptable. No. Thank you for offering, but I'll be fine." Josh gulped down his coffee, closed his laptop, picked it up and was halfway to the front door, when he backtracked and kissed George.

"See you later," he said and then he was gone, leaving George standing trancelike. He shook himself out of it, went for a shower and unpacked his suitcase.

It was very strange to have so much to say and not be able to find the right words in the right order to even begin to explain what had occurred since he last met Sophie for lunch. Much of it was too private to share, and so he stayed quiet, encouraging her to tell him about her antics at the farm over the previous week or so, hoping she would understand his lack of communication was not due to unwillingness. He needn't have worried on that score, and she regaled him with tales of her latest victory with a five year old girl with ornithophobia, supposedly, whom she'd been working with for several weeks and finally had a breakthrough with some newborn chicks, getting her to hold them without her realising they were birds, soon moving on to ducklings, then ducks, chickens and finally geese—from a safe distance—all producing no reaction, until the geese took off in flight, at which point the girl started screaming. It turned out that she had partial hearing loss and it was the air vibration caused by the flapping wings that was upsetting her. She was now undergoing further hearing tests and looking forward to showing off her 'ear-ring aids' to Sophie.

This and other stories took them through lunch and they made their way back to the farm, with George pondering over whether it was worth having a chat with the farmer himself. Perhaps it was something for another day, because at the moment the future felt very much beyond his control. Sophie gave him a hug and a knowing smile, and he turned to walk back down the lane to the main road. He got no further than about five yards from her before she shouted him back.

"I forgot to ask. Is there anything you and Josh don't like? Only I'm going shopping for tomorrow night on my way home."

"Tomorrow night?"

"Sean's birthday? You're coming round for dinner."

"I am?"

"Well, Sean got a reply from Josh this morning to say you were."

"He didn't mention it. Maybe it was after he'd gone to work." He checked his phone for missed calls, of which there were none. "Oh well. No. We'll both eat pretty much anything."

"Good stuff. About seven?"

"Sounds good. See you." George headed off and caught the bus ten minutes later, puzzling all the way home over why Josh hadn't told him (or better still, asked him) and also why suddenly they were being invited to Sean's as a couple, as it wouldn't be enough for Sophie to have mentioned it. The dynamic between Josh and Sean was too complex for anyone else to make decisions as to where and when they should socialise together. The one thing he did know for sure was that he was going to have it out with Josh when he got home from work, because wasn't that what he'd requested? And much as he'd rather not have to take the lead, it looked like he had no choice.

Back at the house, he did his best to tidy up and undo the damage Josh had caused before they went away, but short of laying new carpets, there was little he could do to improve things. He turned on the vacuum cleaner and lightly ran the vented brush nozzle over the underlay, with the predictable outcome of sucking half of it into the hose on more than one occasion, and in so doing, discovered that underneath was a perfectly serviceable solid wood floor. It would be a bit drastic, but surely it had to be better than dusty, tattered underlay? He quickly folded it up and shoved it into a black bag, which he hid under the stairs, before resuming his vacuuming and giving the whole place a thorough going-over with a mop. Next, he rubbed the remaining scraps of lining paper off the lounge wall and temporarily re-hung the painting that had been there before. He was done and had dinner ready just as Josh's key turned in the lock.

"Hi..." He stopped in the doorway, taken aback by the expanse of beautiful, dark oak.

"What do you think? I wasn't sure if it would be OK, but I didn't want you to come home and feel like you did last night, and when I was vacuuming I saw this underneath. Is that OK? Oh, and I put the painting back on the wall, just until you decide on some new..."

"Yes!" Josh said, putting his hand over George's mouth. He

stopped talking and Josh released him.

"If you want, I can go and get the wallpaper for you, but I might pick something you don't like, so maybe it would be better to…"

Josh silenced him with a kiss this time. It was no more than a peck on the lips, but it had the intended effect.

"Please shut up, George. And thank you, for doing this, for me. I couldn't even face making a start on it yet and it was really getting me down. So, how was Sophie? Did you have a good chin-wag?"

The change of subject was obvious and deliberate. They were to talk of his destruction no more.

"Yeah, it was nice, although she did all the chin-wagging and I did the listening. She also asked if there was anything we didn't like. You know, for Sean's dinner party tomorrow?" George was watching closely as he said this, trying to read the reaction as it was in the making, but there wasn't even a flicker. Like a daisy at dusk, Josh had shut him out, concealing his fragility, the secret he could not stand to share, that had the potential to lay to waste the honesty and closeness they had begun to explore, and their relationship.

"I assume we are going to Sean's tomorrow?" George asked, instead of making any further attempts to address why he hadn't been informed or consulted.

"I suppose we have to really, seeing as he invited us especially. I wouldn't want to let him down."

"Right. I'll go and buy some drinks in the morning then, to take with us. What does he drink, apart from Guinness? Whisky, I seem to recall from that night in the SU last Christmas."

"Err, yeah," Josh confirmed hesitantly. Sean's confession of alcoholism was not his to pass on, but he had also pushed it from his mind almost as soon as it had been made. "What I'd rather do is buy some speciality coffee. Sean's got one of those snazzy bean-to-cup machines, so he keeps telling me. That's something we can all share, as I'm going to be driving, and I guess Sophie will be too."

"A great idea," George agreed. This superficial start to their evening was filling him with a pernicious sense of dread. Even though to have Josh in his prior state of mind would have seemed far worse to outsiders, he knew where this was leading. Josh was forcing his hand, for sharing the poem had been the first bold step in breaking down the walls they had constructed around themselves. For now, though, just for this one last night, before he took a demolition ball to that final and mighty bastion, he was content to play along with the domestic bliss routine, pretending that all was well and that he was as happy to leave things the way they were as he was making out.

And so they sat and ate the meal George had prepared, in the lounge he had tidied, no longer distracted by the underlay that had served as a reminder of what still had to be entirely undone before it could be rebuilt. Then they went to bed, where George draped his arm over Josh as he slept and later lay in silence on his own, listening to the sounds of insomnia echoing around the emptiness of his heart.

The next morning, when the pretence of sleep was done, the shower took George's tears to the sewer, but the aching still remained. He returned to his room alone, and waited. He heard the bedroom door, the sound of running water, footsteps back and forth. He crept stealthily from his room, pulse racing, hands clammy.

"Hey." He stood in the doorway to Josh's room, watching as he pulled the duvet straight.

"Hey. I'm sorry. I couldn't sleep."

"I know." He advanced into the room. Josh turned briefly and smiled.

"If you're going out to buy coffee this morning, can you pick me up some shower gel? I think I left mine at the cabin."

"Sure." George sat on the bed. Still Josh kept his back to him, making clear that the putting of distance between them was intentional.

"I really must catch up with Ellie later," he was saying, and much more beyond this, but George couldn't hear the words.

He kept watching and waiting. Slowly he stood up and stepped carefully, ensuring at all times that he was between Josh and the door.

"I've got to go," he protested.

George pressed into him with his body and kissed him, open-mouthed, searching. "This is more important," he breathed shakily, moving from his lips, to his chin and down to his neck, sensing the urgency, the desperation to flee.

"I'm not ready for this," Josh said, his eyes becoming wide as he searched for the right words to say to stop it from happening. George's hands continued downwards, peeling open each button of Josh's shirt.

"Please." His voice was almost childlike. "Please stop."

"Forgive me," George pleaded, "but I can no longer wait for you to be ready. You asked me to help you. Forgive me." There were just two more buttons left fastened, and he was staring right into Josh's face, his weeping wrenching him apart, until he almost couldn't take it. Josh was frozen, in fear and horror, paralysed, and he felt like a murderer, or worse. His hands shook as he pushed the shirt back over Josh's shoulders, slowing it as it descended, his own sobbing indistinguishable as he let it fall to the floor.

"Please, George, please," Josh cried out, but it was too late now. There was no going back.

Slowly George retraced his path of kisses, the taste of their tears mingling bitterly in his mouth, down, down, he was drowning in his own wretchedness, his sobs almost screams, raking at his throat and stealing his breath. He caressed each shoulder blade, his lips now his only sense of touch to seek out and to heal; each seared round pit a bleak biographical moment, the chaotic criss-cross of years deprived of light and life, those final paths cutting deep into the darkness, searching in solitude, desperate for release.

Josh collapsed, his soul so empty yet so heavy that his legs buckled under its weight, his bare back slamming into the wall with each new wave of hysteria that engulfed him.

George fell to his knees and begged for mercy, unheard and unseen. "I didn't want to do this to you. I knew it would be like this. Please forgive me." He kept repeating over and again, his own loss long since buried in a place he had fought to forget, now reawakened and clawing, tearing, eating him alive. He pulled his hair, his head colliding with his knees, but still it wasn't enough. "I'm so sorry. So sorry." A voice echoing and dying away into the nothingness that surrounded him.

"George?"

Someone was speaking. Were they calling his name? They seemed so far away. Was he dreaming?

"All right now, George, everything's going to be just fine. Take your time."

Yes, it had to be a dream. Or a terrifying nightmare. Oh, why? Why couldn't it be a nightmare? For now he recalled how he came to be lying on this cruel, cold floor. Terrible betrayal. Most horrendous violation. How could he have done such a thing?

"OK now, I'll give you a little hand there."

The hand was strong, and warm, and pulled at his arm. He felt it rise and fall down dead. Two of them now, one on each shoulder, righting his wrongs.

"Open your eyes, George. That's it. Open them for me. There you go."
His breath was sweet, familiar, like his voice.

"Sean? Why…"
"He called me. He was in such a dreadful state, so worried for you. We came straight away."
"He was pleading. How could I…he was pleading, Sean, and I…"
"He needed your help and you gave it. Whatever you believe at this moment, you did the right thing. You love him, so how could it be wrong?" Sean held out his hand and George took it.
"Where is he? Is he all right?"
"No. He's not. Not yet, although I must say you're probably a little bit the worse for wear than he is. But he's safe now. He's downstairs. My Soph is looking after him for us."

"Sophie." George smiled at the memory of her face and her stories. They always did make him feel like nothing else mattered.

"We came straight away," Sean repeated, but it still made no sense.

"Can I go to him?"

"Of course you can. He'll be pleased to see you back with the living."

"What happened? Did I black out?"

"You shut down. Nothing to worry about, it's only natural. How do you feel now?"

"Confused. In pain. Not physical, you understand." George crumpled again and Sean caught him.

"More than you know," he said, holding him tightly and rocking him from side to side. "But it gets no worse than this, I promise you."

Some time later, George couldn't tell how long, Sean helped him down the stairs, supporting under his arms as he led him into the lounge. There was Sophie, her face lit up in the most beautiful smile. And there next to her was Josh. As soon as he saw that George had come, he ran to him and they fell into each other, apologies and confessions of love and sorrow, joy and loss, tumbling in a torrent of tears. Sean left the room, and Sophie quickly followed.

"I'll make some more drinks. They'll be needing them," he said to her, but she just took the kettle from his hands and held him. She wasn't fully aware of what was happening, but she had to keep it together, for Sean, for all of them.

"I'll make the drinks," she said. "You do whatever you need to." He wiped his eyes and nodded.

Somehow they had made it to the sofa and were sitting, still and silent, giving each other the chance to recover, to build some courage in the hope that it would be enough to make it through the next round. Sean stopped in the doorway and watched them, huddled together, each with their arm entwined around the other. Josh felt his presence.

"Can you give us a little time?"

"Sure, Joshy. I'll just be in the kitchen." Josh watched him leave, then slowly drew away from George. He resisted and clung to him.

"No. Don't go."

"I'm not going anywhere. Not ever."

George released his grip and watched, as Josh rolled up first one sleeve, then the other. He laid out his arms, palms up, hands resting on his knees. George blinked away the tears and one dropped onto the bared wrist, snaking its way downwards, along the lifeline; Josh cocooned it in his palm.

"How long have you known?" he asked.

"Always."

The word hung in the air on a hiss of breath and he delayed so it could dissipate.

"I always knew what, I just didn't know how, or else I wouldn't have pressured you to go in the hot tub. That's when I figured out the 'how'. You were drifting away and I kept reaching out. I wanted to tell you, and the words escaped me. You escaped me. I needed for you to see that I loved you, because…" George traced his fingertips over the long, maroon scars. "I thought I could stop you if only you knew, that you'd never try to leave me again, and it just pushed you further away."

"And you've kept it to yourself all this time?"

"What else could I do? It was your secret."

"But it is such a burden to bear. That's why I did it. It was not yours, nor Ellie's, nor anyone else's to carry, but mine."

Within these words was the key to what George wanted to understand, but should not. How could he tell him that it was because of him, that he still wished he had died, because of the love of him?

"You wanted to know why I hated Sean. I hated him so much once, but not anymore. He did what he had to do, what he thought was right."

402

"He saved your life."

"Yes, you could say that. I didn't want him to." Josh laughed, but it was empty. "After the first time, when I took the overdose, I fooled him and everyone else into believing that it was an accident, a cry for help rather than a real attempt. The next time, as you can see, I went for the dead certainty, but he came home, and found me, pulled me out." He pushed his sleeves even further up to reveal two very faint, banded impressions, but these were not the scars of once-open wounds. George frowned, unable to comprehend their significance.

"Tourniquets," Josh said. "The rest were my own doing." He pointed to the dark circles, too numerous to count. "Cigarette burns." And then to the diagonal slashes. "Pen knife, razor blade, letter opener, I wasn't fussed. I even got hold of a scalpel for a while." And finally the two-inch long scar on each wrist. "It was the only way I could ensure I did the job properly, alone for the weekend, or so I thought. And as soon as I woke up in hospital, do you know what I did? I told him I was going to do it again. Make sure he wasn't there to save me the next time, to think he knew better than I did, because I wanted to die."

"Did you try again?"

"No. And I won't. Sean could've walked away. God knows most would have, but he stayed, got me through the first few months, used every trick he'd learned to try and help me to get better. I promised him I'd never put him through that again."

Josh was fighting his guilt, the constant reminder that he had hidden so well now in plain sight. George pulled down the sleeves and took hold of his hands.

"What made you do it?"

Such a simple question that could be asked of any and every activity. Why did you choose one tie over the other, to stay for that one drink too many, to die instead of live?

"Lots of things. The bullying, as I perceived it, was a big part of it, because I didn't know how to answer their questions. Have you got a girlfriend? A boyfriend? Everyone else was doing it, all the time. At school you all talked of losing your virginity, your little trophy for your triumph over adolescence. In university it was even worse, the prerequisite for every relationship, meaningful or otherwise, but what did I know? To feel the way I did about you and that it couldn't go any further—I wasn't in love, because being in love means giving yourself, entirely, over to another, and the world said I was incomplete. So I started to read up and found out it was true. I was abnormal. Every book told me so, thrusting its empirical arrogance into my life, making me dredge through my past, turning it into a pack of lies. There was no abuse, and whilst I would have liked to have known my mother better, I was hardly starved of affection. Of course it was devastating when Dad died, but my grieving followed a normal pattern. And yet, they all wrote, there must be some reason. My obsession with Freud was a form of self-flagellation, I think, in retrospect. For his verdict was the most damning. Because I loved you, and I wanted to be in love with you, but I was flawed, broken, worthless."

"I wish you'd trusted me to make that judgement."

"It would have been selfish, and not just because of the sacrifices we each would have needed to make. I convinced myself that whatever I felt for you, however much I thought I loved you, I wasn't in love with you. I kept waiting for that feeling to come, to feel like everyone else told me I should feel, to want to be with someone, with anyone. I was so lonely. I didn't even think what it would do to you, or to Ellie. It took me months to realise what it had done to Sean. In fact, I didn't truly appreciate the way it affected him until he told me—"

Even in the state he was in, Josh was aware that his defence of keeping a confidence would be an outright lie.

"Sean's an alcoholic, because of what I did. Because he's had to live through seeing what I did every day, over and over again. That's how I knew he wouldn't have deliberately overdosed last Christmas. That's why I hated him, because every time I saw him I remembered what I'd done, and how I ruined his life. He had a brilliant mind. They wanted him at Cambridge and he wouldn't leave me, but in the end he had to, for his own survival. When I came out of it, and started to realise how things would've been if I'd succeeded, I knew I had to find a way to stop the loneliness. So I kept on caring for you all the only way I knew how. I had to, so that I could keep going, so that I'd never break my promise to Sean. I convinced myself I didn't love you, and I truly believed it. But you never gave up. No matter how hard I pushed, you never really went away. You never left me. Even when you were in America, you were always there, waiting, and loving me. I called out to you and you came back. For everything you saw of how I lived, and everything you've seen since, you stayed, and you still love me."

"Yeah, I'm a stubborn bastard."

"I never wanted you to feel that you were the reason why I did what I did. Those were dark days. It was out of my control."

"You didn't even say goodbye."

"Oh, I did. It was the hardest part of all."

"I need to…" George began, but Josh squeezed his hand to silence him.

"I know, but I'm not sure you're strong enough."

"Nor am I, but what are the options? We pretend it didn't happen and hope we can keep on ignoring it forever, or we face it down now and go forward knowing that we are free of the past."

George was seeking to liberate them both, to fully comprehend how it could be that Josh attempted to take his own life, less than a year after graduating with top marks.

"Tell me about Sam," Josh said. George frowned at him in puzzlement. "Please? I need you to tell me, because—I just need you to. I don't know why."

He was trying to delay. That much was obvious. George took a deep breath.

"He was a veterinary science lecturer. I used to see him in the bar on a Wednesday, when all the athletic teams were in after a hard afternoon's sport. I thought he was a bit of a perv at first, but then one Wednesday he came over when I was waiting at the bar and asked me if I wanted a drink. So I said yeah, why not? We went and sat down, and he told me all about his partner, launched straight into it, like he needed me to know before things went any further. He came home one day, he said, and all of his partner's things were gone, and I felt sorry for him. He looked so sad.

"So anyway, we had a few more drinks, left and got a takeaway, and he was after an invite back to mine. I didn't really want to, but, well, it was sex and he was a nice-looking guy. Next morning he was gone before I woke up, so there's me thinking that's that then. I went off to uni, didn't see him around on the Thursday or Friday, which was normal, and pretty much forgot about it.

"Saturday nights, me and my housemates, because we were skint, would club together and buy this bloody awful cheap lager from the supermarket. Honestly, there's more alcohol in piss after a night on real lager than there is in that stuff, and it'd probably taste better, but it was a laugh. This Saturday, after the Wednesday I took him home, he turned up. It was late and I was in bed, but I let him in, and—you can work out the rest. Next morning, he's gone again.

"It went on like this for weeks. Wednesday night: bar, takeaway, back to mine. Saturday night, or sometimes in the afternoon when no-one was about, he'd come round, usually stay over and go early in the morning. And I know what you're thinking, but I didn't cotton on for a while. Stupid, I know. So, I figured it out and—remember I was only twenty at the time—I thought what the hell? So he's got a partner. Not my problem. If their relationship was OK, then he wouldn't be having an affair with a student. We carried on, same thing, Wednesday, Saturday, for the rest of the term, I came home for Christmas, and…"

George stopped and covered his face with his hands, not because what he was saying was bothering him particularly, even though he'd had much time to think about what happened and realised that he had been at great risk. All the while he'd been narrating the story, the full truth of why Josh tried to kill himself had been sinking in and he was suddenly overwhelmed by such grief that he almost couldn't bear it.

"Keep going," Josh urged gently. George sniffed and continued, his voice quivering with the effort.

"And I thought what's the point? Yeah, he's attractive, and intelligent, but I could be doing this with anyone, and probably people I like more. It's just sex."

The words were a revelation.

"Ha. It's just sex. That's all it is. Anyway, the next Wednesday after New Year, we were on our way back to the house, and I told him how I felt. He seemed a bit disappointed, but not upset as such, said he'd walk me back and call a taxi. But as soon as we got inside, he pinned me to the wall by my neck. I couldn't believe it and it took a minute to get my head around it. I kneed him really hard and he doubled up. I pushed him out the door and locked it. I can look after myself, so I wasn't that worried, but I should've known, I guess. He was always so intense, so serious, although he didn't try coming back and didn't turn up on the Saturday, so I thought it was finished. Back to normal.

"The following week, I'm in the bar again, and I was a bit nervous, wondering how things would be after what had happened. He came in as usual, and ignored me at first, but then he walked over and sat next to me. And he's smiling and laughing, so it looks to everyone else like we're having a nice friendly chat, but he's saying, 'I'm going to get you when you're sleeping, no-one makes a fool out of me,' and stuff like that. As far as everyone else is concerned, there's nothing going on, so I slipped out, telling him I was going to the toilet, which is where I went. Next thing he's in there too, smashing my head into the cubicle door. See that scar? That's from the lock. When I finally got free, I punched him in the stomach and he fell backwards, hit his shoulder on the sink. I left him there, told my housemates not to let him in if he came round.

"Needless to say, it wasn't over. He came round on the

Sunday morning, when everyone was still in bed, and kicked the front door in. This time he punched me in the face, and one of my housemates rang the police, who turned up about two hours later, said they didn't like to get involved in domestic disputes, and fucked off again. It just went from bad to worse. Apparently, if he was telling the truth, his partner had found out he was seeing someone else and left him. So that was my fault, obviously. Not that I thought that. To be honest, it was pissing me off more than anything, and it had got to be almost every day. He'd come to the house, or follow me around the campus. I lost count of how many times he hit me, but I wasn't going to be his victim.

"Eventually, after about three weeks of this and he still wasn't giving in, I phoned Kris and told him what was happening. Right after I put the phone down, Dan rings back and says he's coming to 'sort it out'. Well, I don't even want to know how they got from London to Aberdeen in under five hours. And predictably as ever, Sam turns up, thinking I'm going to be on my own, because it's Saturday afternoon, and he hammered on the door for ages. I shouted to him to go away— we'd put loads of bolts up by this point. So he's outside, kicking the shit out of the door, and Dan's inside, getting all worked up and me and Kris are looking at him, thinking he's gonna kill him.

"The banging died down and I thought maybe he'd given up, but the next thing, the back window goes through and he's in the house and he looks wild, like he's on drugs. I'm not sure what happened next, because Dan was on him and the noise was unbelievable. I'll never forget the sound of Sam's head smashing into the floor. He didn't stand a chance. Of course, I know now why Dan was so angry. He was like an animal and it took both me and Kris, plus one of my housemates who'd just got back from football, to pull him off.

"And that was the last trouble I got from Sam. I saw him once or twice around uni after that, but he wouldn't even look at me, and Dan's never mentioned it since."

As soon as he stopped talking, George wished he'd thought ahead and fabricated a more pleasant version of his relationship with Sam. Even so, it was a necessary distraction, and far less horrific than what they were about to face. Josh gently cupped George's cheek in his palm and stared deep into his eyes, seeking confirmation that he still wanted to go through with this. The answer gazed back at him; resolute, unwavering.

"I love you," he whispered.

George nodded. "I know."

Josh smiled and released him. "I'll tell Sean it's time."

CHAPTER THIRTY-THREE

Part I

Sean had forgotten his notes, which was a sure sign he was either working too hard, or losing it, seeing as he could essentially have taken them and nothing else and have been entirely equipped to speak at his first conference. So that was a wasted journey: two and a half hours' drive to the host university, only to get right back in the car and drive two and a half hours home again. If only Josh had been about, he could have faxed them, but he must have gone home for the weekend. The house was silent and horribly empty without his frantic typing and reading and pacing to and fro, as he tried to get theories straightened out in his mind. Sean chuckled at the thought, grabbed his notes from the desk and threw them on the passenger seat. Except that these were not his notes. They'd come from his printer, sure enough, for that dratted black line ran through each and every one of the meticulously typed sheets. But these were not his notes.

He began to read, each page bringing him closer and closer to the realisation of why the house was so still. Driven by some macabre desire to reach the end, or perhaps he simply didn't want to believe what he was reading, he continued until he had read every last word. The truth sank in and he sprinted back inside, ripping his belt from his jeans as he ran up the stairs, two at a time, and shouldered the bathroom door with such force that he'd have been surprised and impressed at any other time but this. Josh was cold, no breath, no colour but the deep, deep red of the water he lay in. How long had he been there? Was it already too late? He couldn't lift him, had to wait for the water to drain away, but there was no time. He strapped the belt around Josh's left forearm and pulled as tight as he could, then did the same to the other arm, with Josh's own belt, wrenched from the jeans lying lifeless on the floor.

The ambulance was quick, much quicker than he could ever have hoped for, and they said he'd done everything— *everything*—that he could. A blood transfusion; so many stitches; so much blood loss, but they had to make it to the hospital first. The iron filled his lungs and made him vomit. And then they drove away, blue flashes filling the sky, paddles searching out and somehow sustaining that precious wisp of life within.

The letters: he took them inside and prayed to a god he didn't believe in to save him from ever having to deliver those letters.

Part II

Dear Kris,

It's only right that I let you all know why I have done this, even though you and I have never really been very close. I wanted to tell you how much I admire you for what you have done for Shaunna and her baby. She is so lucky to have you. I'm sure you will be happy together forever, and I'm sorry I won't be around to see you get married, and maybe give Krissi a little brother or sister, but I'm really sick.

Please try not to think badly of me. I worry that you will most of all, because you have such courage. You were an inspiration to me in school, being who you are and staying true to yourself in spite of the trouble it caused you. I know what a sacrifice you have made for Shaunna. If nothing else comes from this, make a promise to yourself that you will never let the life you are living drown you the way mine has drowned me.

What's most important is that you have each other, and whatever the future holds, I know that this will always be true. Look after each other and have a wonderful life.

See you in the next one,

Josh.

Dear Shaunna,

I used to watch you and Adele sitting cross-legged at the back of
the playground, taking turns with the skipping rope. I bet you
didn't know that. You used to play some stupid game, where you'd
tie one end of the rope to a drainpipe and then the person on the
other end would shake it until it made waves - something about
seashells, cockle shells...Ironic really, considering you ended up
with someone who is allergic to shellfish.

I remember wishing I had a best friend like that, and I got one
eventually - two, in fact. Ellie and George are the most wonderful
friends I could have asked for, and it's going to be hard for them to
understand why I have left them. I tell you this even though I know
it is unfair of me to do so, but you are the strongest of us all.
Nobody could be a better mum than you are, and I know you will
be the one to look after Ellie and George now. I've also told Kris
he's got to look after you, and you must let him, because he has
given up everything for you. He loves you so much, Shaunna, I
hope you know that.

I'm truly sorry that I won't get to see Krissi grow into a beautiful
woman, but when she is old enough to understand, please tell her I
loved her. Tell her that I'm sorry I couldn't be there to see her
graduation, for her twenty-first birthday, her wedding. Unless I'm
wrong and there is an afterlife after all.

You will always be beautiful. You will always be strong.

Josh.

Dear Andy,

We weren't friends for very long, but I wanted to say thank you, for showing me - for showing us all - how to live life to the full. I only wish I had the energy to take up the challenge the way you do. You're totally insane, in a good way, and you must never change.

I've been diagnosed with acute depression, not that I needed a doctor to tell me. It's been so hard to keep going, to keep living, and even though we're not very close, I wanted to explain why I have done what I've done. I'm sorry I can't be more like you.

I know that when people leave the way I am leaving, it plays on the minds of those who loved them, so many questions that can never be answered. But next time you're up there, flying through the clouds, I want you to remember that what I have done means that now I am as free as you and that is something to be glad for.

Keep on enjoying your life and make sure that little brother of yours does too. I'm sure one day he'll tell you why he's so angry, but you must be patient. Never give up on him, because he needs you and you need him.

Take care of each other,

Josh.

Dear Adele,

I haven't seen you for such a long time, but Ellie tells me you've had your boobs done. She also said they've all been giving you stick because of it. Well, sod them, I say. It's your body. You do what you like with it. I bet they look awesome, although you have always been very pretty anyway, whether you had big boobs or not.

This letter is to say goodbye, because I'm sick and have made the choice to go before the illness takes me. You have a wonderful group of friends, especially Shaunna, and I really think you should give Dan another chance, but that's up to you.

I wrote the same thing to Shaunna, but I wanted to share my memory with you, of you both playing together at primary school, with that stupid skipping rope. She always had you holding the end while she did all the skipping, and I know she was a terrible cheat, so you can tell her that from me! You are a wonderful woman and one day I hope you feel confident enough to be who you really are, instead of hiding inside your pretty shell, because the real you is much more beautiful than you think.

Be happy Adele, and don't let them boss you about.

Josh.

Dear Dan,

You called me queer once. I don't suppose you remember that, but I do. I didn't understand what it meant at the time, and although I do now, I still don't get why you thought I was. In case you do remember, I want you to know that there's no hard feelings. I also want to tell you to stop being so cruel to Andy. You're so lucky to have a brother, and he needs you to keep him out of trouble. I think you need him too.

In case you haven't realised, this letter is to say goodbye, because I am terminally ill. That's not strictly true, but it's the best way to think of it. They insist I'll pull out of this, eventually, although I think they're wrong, as usual. Whatever, I know that this will be with me for the rest of my life, which is why I have to end it now, before it takes its toll on all of you.

Whatever happens with you and Adele (I'm certain you will be together forever), be happy and be good to each other. Above all else, stop being angry. It will eat away at you and everyone around you.

You're worth more than that. Don't you ever forget it.

Josh.

Dear Jess,

Thank you. You have been such a support to me over the past few months and I am grateful to you for not telling Ellie what I was going through. I didn't want any of you to have to see me like this, and even you haven't seen how bad it can get, which is why I have made the decision to end it now.

There is nothing any of you could have said or done to make it better, because they tell me it's more than just a bout of depression. The psychiatrist said I'm probably going to go through this every so often, but that it will get easier if I face up to why I feel like this. I can't take the pain again.

Even though I'm not worth it, you'll probably still all grieve for me. Ellie and George must find peace. My one last request is that you come together to find it.

Good luck Jess. You are going to be the best lawyer ever and you are a truly wonderful friend. Thank you with all my heart.

Josh.

My dearest Ellie,

It's tearing my soul apart writing this letter to you, after all we've been through together. I know that I am not important in your life anymore, that you've moved on. It's been wishful thinking on my part to believe that you cared as much for me as I care for you. And I've missed you so much since we each went our separate ways to uni. I want to thank you for being my friend, even though sometimes I know it was hard for you to deal with anything but what was going on with you. I hope that it will help you to understand why I have done this.

But most of all I want you to know that it is not your fault. I'm so deeply unhappy and it's not anyone's fault. The worst part of all of this is knowing what my future holds. You see, I've been diagnosed with depression - they even mentioned the word 'manic'. The jury's still out on that one, although it explains a lot, about how I got through the last year on so little sleep. Well now it's sucked me into its black heart and I can't find a way out.

The psychiatrist I saw yesterday didn't help at all, telling me I had a long way to go before I'd feel any better. I haven't got the strength to make that journey. More than that, I can not burden you, or George, or any of the others with this terrible thing, and that is why I have to go. I hope you can forgive me. In time you will forget me too and get on with your life. I want you to be happy, Ellie.

Be happy.

Josh.

To my best and oldest friend, George,

You are the love of my life.

There are so many things I want to say to you, and I wish I'd had the strength, for telling you now will make it even harder for you to let go.

From the moment you walked into Mrs. Kinkade's class you were my best friend, and I still miss our bike rides to this day. But I'm afraid it's all too late. This depression seems to have two sides to it and it's probably what got me through my degree - maybe I should be grateful for that. Now I get to see the other side and it feels like I'm being buried alive.

I've never hurt so much as this, George. It makes me want to tear out my hair to stop the pain that's growing inside me, like a massive tumour. I'm broken and they tell me they can fix me, if I let them. I can't do that.

I know you're a tough guy and you'd probably beat this thing, but it has me beaten and I can't take it. It's no-one's fault I feel like this and no-one can save me from it. So I have to leave you all.

What I need to tell you before I say goodbye is that I love you. You must go on - find some rich, handsome man who will look after you. You deserve the best and I am not it. I never deserved to be your best friend. For that I am sorry.

Goodbye George.

Josh.

Part III

The convulsions had stopped. The recovery position had slowly morphed, and now he was tightly furled, like a foetus, the breath leaving his body in shuddering jerks, his eyes staring, unseeing. She stayed, her hand gently resting on his hand, her mind tuned to his mind, watching, waiting.

"It's your birthday. I'm sorry."

Josh was on the floor, his back to the sofa, so he didn't have to witness again what he had done. Sean was perched on the end of the coffee table, hands clasped together, tight and tighter still, to alleviate the shaking, numb the pain.

"I know. It's all right."

It was a day no different from those that had passed before it, filled with the visions, the replays of then. Josh watched them flash before Sean's eyes.

"I wish I could take them away," he said.

Sean swallowed hard and took Josh's hand. It was cold, as always, the consequence of the nerve and tissue damage. Josh tightened his grip around Sean's fingers. Cold, but still alive.

"These things make us who we are. If we could go back and change them, would we? Should we? We are Gestalt."

George stirred.

"He knew," Josh said. Sean didn't seem surprised. "He always knew and he kept it locked safely away, my secret that made a liar of him."

"That's what people do when they love you." Sean retracted his hand. "We carry those pieces around with us, waiting and hoping for the time to come when we can give them back, when we can complete the jigsaw." His gaze drifted of its own accord, settling on the eight pristine sheets of A4 paper. "I've often wondered if it would help *them* to know how this feels. To share those letters, to surrender my shield and tell them: what you are thinking of doing? It will destroy the people you love, the people who love you. Their lives will *not* go on with or without you. They will never be the same again."

420

Josh shook his head.

"It's a place far beyond reason, beyond words. If you had shown me those letters, I'd have believed them to be a fiction created by do-gooders like us, with our theories and statistics and our pretence of understanding. And if you'd somehow convinced me they were real, they'd have still made no difference. All they offer is more guilt, and more pain."

"So how, then?" Sean asked.

It was not a simple question to answer, for it was in itself a multitude of questions. How to stop someone from attempting to take their own life; to help them if they fail; to find a way to live.

"First, you have got to stop blaming yourself," Josh replied, understanding at once. "You did everything right."

"How can you possibly say that? I ignored it, hoped it would go away, even though I knew that those first sixth months…"

"Trickery and misdirection," Josh stated, cutting him off. Sean put a hand to his forehead, the pain now registering physically, his other hand hanging, limp and trembling, between his knees. Josh took a hold of it and gently tugged. "In the general scheme of things, you don't do so bad at it yourself."

Sean raised an eyebrow in acknowledgement. "Thanks. I'll take that as a compliment," he said; empty words. "I had to work so hard not to blame you, that was the thing. I should've seen it coming, been able to prevent it. All that knowledge cluttering up my big, conceited head, thinking a piece of paper could save a friend. I missed the signs. I missed them all. Every single one of them. The talk of dropping out, giving away your books, your sudden obsession with my research. *My* research. I was arrogant—I should've seen it coming when you took the pills and the fact that I didn't? I told myself it was your fault."

"Yes, Sean!" Josh was barely able to keep the frustration out of his voice. "It *was* my fault. It wasn't up to you to stop me. You couldn't have stopped me. All those signs? Of course they're there, but we talk about them as if they're carefully measured and deliberately emitted, but they're nothing of the sort. I didn't think to myself 'tomorrow I'm going to take an overdose' or 'as soon as Sean's away I'm going to slash my wrists'. Those letters—I wrote them in my head for years, but they weren't part of some cleverly thought-through plan. When I overdosed I wasn't even thinking I wanted to die, because I didn't care one way or the other. All I knew was that if I took those pills, whatever happened it couldn't possibly be any worse than how I was feeling at that moment. So I took them and went to sleep. Then I woke up and carried on. It was no better, no worse. It was just the same as before, other than interfering fools too fond of their labels, who think they understand because they can 'see the signs'.

"That day, when you went to the conference—it was exactly the same. The opportunity was there, so I typed the letters and ran the bath while they were printing. If you'd have come home then, I wouldn't have done it then, but I would have done it at some point and not because I'd planned it. You don't decide you want to die. You realise you don't want to live and if the chance arises to do something about it, that's when you decide. And once you make that decision—once *I* made the decision—there's no going back. What keeps me here is my promise to you that I will never do it again."

"Present tense?" Sean asked the question almost before Josh had finished speaking.

"A slip." The realisation cut deep into him, reopening the wounds in his mind. Sean watched quietly, giving Josh time to reconcile this newly uncovered 'truth', before he spoke again.

"It doesn't always have to be a slip, but since you brought it up, do you still want to die?"

Josh didn't respond straight away, in part because Sean was forcing him to admit that wanting to die and not wanting to live were one and the same. But more than that, he needed to be sure that the answer he gave was the truth, and searched his mind, digging into every deep, dark corner, no thought or memory left unturned.

"No," he said, finally. "I want to live. Do I wish I'd died in that bath? Yes. You can't even begin to imagine what it's like to wake up alive, and then keep waking up and remembering—I say 'alive', but I wasn't really, not for a long, long time.

"And you did help me, simply by asking how you could. You listened when I talked—I should've told you everything and I chose not to, but knowing I could if I wanted to? That was enough. As for your survival kit idea—I'll admit I was wrong. It wasn't idiotic. Those photos, letters, silly little keepsakes—it's so easy to ignore how much you are loved when you're in that place. But I've ignored it long enough. I'm sick of dragging myself through every day, hanging on to a guilty promise."

He felt George's leg twitch against his back and reached behind him, seeking out his hand.

"The past two years have been torture, watching him tiptoe around me, trying so hard to say and do the right thing, believing as he did that one wrong move could be fatal."

George was fully conscious again and was listening to Josh, but looking at Sophie. She was stroking his head, stopping occasionally to wipe away a tear from the corner of his eye, or her own.

"I want to live," Josh repeated, "for him, and for me. He makes me feel alive and I owe this much to you, Sean. You gave me the chance to stay and fight, and believe me when I tell you that it has been a fight. Your methods got me through the darkest time of my life, until I was ready to take down the wall, to let myself feel again, the good and the bad. Looking back—maybe they weren't so far off with the bipolar diagnosis, but it's symptomatic. I'm ready to live, and to love, even if it means going without sleep for days on end, even if there are times when the black dog is constantly snapping at my heel, even if it means…"

"Ripping up carpets."

He turned to George and smiled.

"Even if it means ripping up carpets," he said. "I love you, George Morley. I want to make you happy, prove that I am worthy to be your best friend."

"You already have." Slowly George pulled himself into a sitting position. "But that's it. No more lies, or secrets, because these—what are they called again?"

"Dissociative seizures," Sean told him.

"Yeah, those. Man, they suck."

Part IV

Josh parked up outside Sean's house and turned the ignition key to the 'off' position. It had been just a few hours since Sean and Sophie went home, but it felt like days ago. In the aftermath, he and George had cuddled up on the sofa, using the silence to reorientate themselves in this brave, new world. Then they played *Crash Team Racing* and George was defeated again, but only on-screen. Afterwards they went to nap in Josh's room, setting the alarm for 6 p.m., and snuggling together under the duvet, Josh finally able to let go, no longer caring if his sleeves rode up in his sleep, which they did; George awoke just before the alarm, with Josh's arms wrapped around him, the scars a reminder of how far they had come and where they had yet to venture. He covered them with his palms and closed his eyes again. The future, whatever it held, was before them and he was ready for it. The alarm sounded and Josh rolled away. George turned over.

"Hey."

Josh opened one eye and looked at him, using his trapped arm to pull him close.

"Hey," he smiled. "How are you feeling?"

"OK. You?"

"Like I want to stay here, like this, forever."

"Well, Sean and Soph aren't expecting us for another hour, so you've probably got…" George looked at the clock, "…thirty seconds or so, if you want to have a shower before we go." Josh pretended to be offended.

"Even *I* can be ready in an hour," he protested.

"We'll see."

"Actually," he turned onto his side and propped himself on his elbow, tracing the outline of George's lips with his finger, "why don't you come with me? Hurry me along." George stared at him in disbelief.

"I'm not sure that's a good idea."

"I am. I'll even wash your back."

"No. Definitely not a good idea." The mere thought of it was proving too much.

"And your front, if you like."

"Would you please stop?"

Josh laughed and kissed him.

"Come on," he said, "it'll be fun." With that, he was out of the bed, pulling George behind him.

What happened next was a bit of a blur, and a dreamy, blissful one at that. To begin with George kept his eyes tightly shut, focusing his energy on staying in control, which worked for all of sixty seconds. After, when he opened his eyes and saw that Josh didn't care, he let the sensation of his hands, his lips, the cascade of water over their naked bodies, wash over him and set him adrift.

"Yes," he said finally, "I'm OK with it."

Part V

Sean heard the car pull up outside, and wiped his hands dry on a tea towel.

"I'll go," Sophie offered, but he dismissed it and was already on his way.

In the few hours that had lapsed since they returned, Sean had confessed and they had rid the house of alcohol: a practical strategy to keep his mind from wandering back down the years. At times, as they prepared the meal together, if she noticed the regression, she would wait to see if he pulled himself out, only going to the rescue if he was struggling. After all, he'd said this was what he wanted: to face down the ghosts and set them to rest.

"Always bang on time, aren't yer, Sandison?" Sean grinned, flinging the door wide open.

"I try my best."

Josh and Sean embraced on the threshold. George edged around them and walked through to the kitchen, where Sophie was trying to stir two pans at once.

"Hi," he said, setting the coffee beans down and taking over one of the wooden spoons.

"Everything OK?" she asked.

"Better than OK, sort of," he smiled.

"Same here." They were distracted by the raised voices now coming from the lounge. Sean and Josh were still winding each other up, taunting each other with insults, arguing over trivialities (the merits of red versus green wallpaper) but this time it was different. They were laughing.

"It's gonna totally throw the rest of them when we start back at uni next week," Sophie remarked.

"Yeah," George agreed absently. He and Josh had been talking when they were sitting outside in the car, and he'd reached a decision about the counselling course. He was dreading telling her, but he had to do what was best for him. She stopped stirring her pan and watched him.

"You're dropping out."

"Err…Yes. I am."

"Why? Because of what happened to Josh?"

"Partly. I don't ever want to go through that again, and I know it won't be the same when it's someone else who's facing all that pain. It's just not for me. My head needs a break."

She examined him for a moment, to decide if it was worth trying to talk him out of it, but she could see that his mind was made up.

"Plus," he continued, "I need to find a job. We're going to get a house together."

This was where their conversation in the car had started: the house next door but one to Sean's was for sale, and whilst they weren't necessarily thinking of buying that one in particular, Josh had suggested that getting somewhere together would help him to control his destructive tendencies, should they ever return, although he was hopeful they wouldn't. Even so, George pointed out that they would be best finding somewhere with wooden floors instead of carpets. It was said with 'tongue-in-cheek', of course; he'd lived with Josh long enough to fully comprehend what he was letting himself in for. He was sure he could cope, but not if he also had to listen to everyone else's problems all day, every day. So tomorrow he was going to see if he could pick up some work at the farm, and maybe, at some point in the future, look into training as an animal psychologist. For now, though, he just wanted a nice, easy job that he didn't have to think about, so he could heal; so he could love.

"You're making the right decision." Sophie's voice interrupted his thoughts. "I can see it in your eyes. But you have to promise to stay in touch."

George listened to the banter continuing to come from the lounge and raised an eyebrow.

"Somehow I doubt that's going to be a problem."

CHAPTER THIRTY-FOUR

The final scaffolding poles were secured in the back of the van.

"There you go, mate," he said, smiling expectantly.

Cheeky bastard, Andy thought. They'd been paid before it was erected, as per their terms. He pulled a ten pound note from his jeans pocket and shoved it in the man's grubby hand, eager to see the back of him so he could get on with the rest of the jobs.

"Nice one. See you again."

And off he went, the van and its contents rattling loudly as the tyres sank and left grooves in the deep gravel drive. Andy followed at a distance and watched as it trundled out onto the road, then disappeared into the Saturday afternoon traffic. He shut the gates and paused for a moment: it had been a close call, but he'd made the deadline. He started making his way back towards the house, so busy congratulating himself that he didn't hear another van pull up to the gates. The sounding of the horn made him jump.

"Oy! Knobhead! Wanna open these for me?"

Andy closed his eyes, took a deep breath and turned back.

"Not really, but seeing as you asked so nicely." Once again, he dragged the heavy gates across the gravel, and stepped out of the way to let Michael pass. They nodded a frosty acknowledgement at each other and his older brother put his foot down, skidding to a halt between the house and the statue outside.

"You can't leave it parked like that," Andy stated, once he'd completed the fairly lengthy walk back. "You're blocking the way for everyone else."

"So?" Michael had the rear doors open, an untidy pile of paint trays, rollers, brushes and dust sheets accumulating at his feet. One of the trays had tipped and a blue puddle was forming beneath it.

"So shift it, if you wouldn't mind very much, thank you," Andy told him curtly. Since when was he a painter and decorator? It was rhetorical and he wasn't about to ask, because he didn't care.

Michael grabbed a suit bag from inside the van, shoved it at his brother, threw his equipment back in and slammed the doors.

"You do know I'm staying here?" he half-asked, half-told him.

"Yeah. Mum said."

"It'll be just like old times, hey, *bro*," he grinned falsely. Andy returned the sentiment.

"With you leaving your shit everywhere, you mean?" He glared at the patch of blue gravel and Michael scuffed it with his boot.

"Nothing a good hose down won't sort," he said. "So, what's with you? That posh lawyer bird finally saw some sense, did she?"

"Don't fucking start."

"I was only asking."

"Oh, right, and how's Anne these days, then?"

That shut him up. This was the third time Michael's wife had kicked him out, and no doubt she would have him back again, but he didn't want to discuss it any more than Andy wanted to talk about Jess, or indeed engage in a conversation about anything else with him. Andy handed the suit bag back and went inside, Michael following not so far behind. He stopped in the entrance hall.

"Fuck me!" he said, looking around the expanse of polished black and white marble.

"This is the first time you've been to see her? She's lived here for almost a bloody year, Mike!"

He didn't respond, overwhelmed by the size of the place and its lavish décor. It was one of those nineteenth century vast country homes, with twin staircases curving up either side of the 'atrium' and what was effectively a balcony running around the top perimeter of the upstairs storey, a good twenty feet or so above which was a stained-glass dome, fans of multi-coloured light extending and fading to nothing as they transcended the stark white marble walls, to the black and white chequered floor, currently covered in cables and debris.

"She could've cleaned up the place," Michael joked.

"Yeah," Andy agreed, adopting the same change in tone, because there was still much to organise and he really could do with a hand. "They've only just taken down the scaffolding," he explained carefully, "so I've not been able to get things straight yet. We're gonna have to get those lights up before we do anything else, though."

"We?"

Andy ignored his protest, knowing that when it came to the crunch, Michael would do whatever he told him to, so long as it pleased their mother, which, of course, it would, because it was for 'her baby'.

"The sound system's coming at five, and they're setting up the bar in there at six." Andy indicated to a door to their right and Michael wandered over to take a look.

"You could fit a bloody pub in there, never mind a bar," he said. "Dad The Fourth's minted then, yeah?" The title derived from their mother's insistence that her three sons always refer to their current stepfather as 'dad', and the present incumbent was a definite material step up.

"Yeah, like lottery win minted, as opposed to posh," Andy told him. Len, his name was, and he didn't like to talk about how he'd 'earned' his millions, but it was safe to say it wasn't by legitimate means.

"I take it she's buggered off for the afternoon?"

"Nope. She's in the pool."

"A pool as well? Bloody hell! She's well and truly hit the jackpot this time. Just goes to show really, if at first you don't succeed…Well I best go and say hello, I s'pose."

He waited for some indication of the general direction in which he might find the aforementioned pool, and Andy pointed to the passageway ahead of them. Michael wandered off with his suit bag still slung over his shoulder, and Andy set to work on clearing the brick dust and marble off-cuts. It wasn't as bad as it looked, and a few loaded shovels later, all that remained was a pile of cables and lights. He wiped the sweat from his forehead and looked up, scanning the banisters and mentally plotting out his lighting. It was going to be tricky running the cables back without them being seen, and he was a bit concerned about overloading the circuits. He was in the middle of calculating maximum loads in his head, when the sound of someone behind him sucking air through their teeth made him lose his train of thought. He turned around.

"It's gonna cost ya," Dan said, shaking his head, "but I think I can do it."

Andy grinned, but not at Dan.

"Addy!" Little Shaunna squealed, wriggling to break free of her dad's arm. Andy grabbed her and tipped her upside down, which made her squeal even more.

"You all right, bro?" Andy asked.

"Pretty much. Other than having to walk half a mile up the drive with Madame here. She's a lot heavier than she looks."

"Oh, poor girl. Daddy's saying you're a fatty. Are you a fatty?" Andy blew raspberries on her belly. She giggled loudly and grabbed him by the nose with both hands. He pretended to fight her off. "Why didn't you bring the car up to the house?"

"Couldn't be arsed opening the gates. Aside from which, some idiot's blocked the driveway with their van. Ah," he said, as someone emerged from the passageway in front of them, "that'd explain it. Alright, Mike?"

"Dan," his brother acknowledged. Little Shaunna turned to

see who the voice belonged to and suddenly became quiet, a very serious frown crumpling the dainty bridge of her little nose. Michael clapped his youngest brother on the back, with no more than a passing glance at his niece. He'd only seen her once before, when she was first allowed home from hospital and Dan and Adele were doing the rounds.

"Glad you could make it," Dan said, suppressing the urge to say something about Michael's ignorance towards Shaunna. It was much easier that way; both he and Andy had long since stopped fighting or arguing with him, because he really wasn't worth the effort. "I want to ask you a favour," Dan continued, and put his arm loosely around Michael's shoulders, guiding him towards the room opposite the one that would later become a bar. This was where the food would be. Andy watched them go inside and close the door.

"Shall we go see Nana?" he asked little Shaunna.

"Nana!" she repeated enthusiastically and they set off in the direction of the pool, Andy twirling her upside down and around and around until she was shrieking and squealing with excitement again.

The pool was located in an elongated conservatory that extended from the back wall of the house and was where they probably once grew all sorts of herbs and vegetables for the kitchens. Unlike modern conservatories, this was a good, solid structure, with large, arched, leaded windows. Years of condensation gave it an overall green hue, and it smelled like a hothouse that had been flushed with bleach. Andy wondered what Alice would make of it later, and made a mental note to show her around, just to see if it looked as green to her as it did to him.

His mother had seen them coming, and was already out of the pool and wrapped in a thick, fluffy bathrobe.

"Hiya," she called to little Shaunna. Her granddaughter gave her a toothy grin (she was very proud of her new teeth) and planted a soggy, open-mouthed kiss on the puckered lips presented to her. "Dan and Adele are here then?"

433

"Dan is. Adele's probably at the hairdresser's, or something."

"Hmm," his mother said, tending to little Shaunna, but with a thoughtful look in her eye. "Surely she won't let him down again?"

"She won't," Andy asserted. She still didn't seem convinced. "Not now they've got this little lady to contend with." He gave his niece another flip upside down with the usual result.

"I hope you're right, for my sake as well as his. I was banking on having at least a couple of grandchildren before I hit seventy."

"That's another five years away, Mother. Plenty of time." It was an automatic defence, because she still didn't know and now seemed the perfect time to tell her. She had her back turned and was bent over, drying her hair with a towel; relatively defenceless.

"And anyway," he ventured on, trying to sound as if what he was about to say was as trivial as thanking someone for holding a door open, "you already have two granddaughters."

His mother carried on rubbing her hair for a few seconds before what he'd said registered. She lifted her head slowly and carefully pushed the curls out of her face, turning towards him; a gradual, drawn-out motion intended to intimidate. It did the trick.

"Care to explain?"

"Shall I make us a drink first? Coffee? Tea?"

"Andrew. Sit down." She pointed at the loungers and he sat, uncomfortably balanced on the edge, not wanting to lean back and leave himself any more vulnerable than he already was. "Right, lad," she said, folding her arms. "You'd best get talking."

"Erm, well…" Little Shaunna turned and looked at him with big wide, enquiring eyes, as if she too was waiting to hear what he had to say. "In all honesty, Mum, I didn't know until quite recently."

"When?"

"A couple of years ago."

"So you've got a two year old daughter that you haven't even bothered to mention?"

"Err, no. She's a bit older than that."

She glared at him and he shrank back behind his niece, who bent over so she could keep her eyes fixed on him.

"She's, erm..." There was no way he could just come straight out and say it. He went for the roundabout route. "You remember Adele's mate, Shaunna?"

"Not really."

"You will do. She used to come round and sit in the lounge looking miserable, while Adele went upstairs to see Dan." Still not a flicker of recognition. "Red hair down to her waist, cropped jeans, high heels?" Finally.

"Oh yes. The Giggler."

"The who?"

"Me and your dad (by whom she meant 'Dad the Second') called her The Giggler, because that's all she did when you or Dan were anywhere nearby." Andy nodded his understanding. "They're still friends, I take it? Adele and Shaunna?" She looked at the wriggling toddler as she said this, by way of confirming the origin of her name. Andy nodded again. "Yes, so what about her?"

"Well it's her daughter. I mean she's our daughter." His mother raised a solitary eyebrow. He took a deep breath and tried again. "Shaunna's daughter, Krissi, is mine."

"And how old is this Krissi?"

"She'd be about, err..." He pretended to think, but he knew exactly how old she was. He even knew when her birthday was, as well as the day of the week and time she was born. "She's just turned twenty-three," he said quickly and ducked. Little Shaunna gave him a terrible look; the same expression as her grandmother.

"I think I'm going deaf in my old age," his mother said, shaking her ear for effect, "but I swear I heard you say she's twenty-three."

He smiled sheepishly.

"So what you're telling me is you got a girl pregnant when you were still at school? What in hell's name were you thinking?"

"There wasn't a whole lot of thinking went into it, Mum."

"And is Krissi coming here tonight?"

"Erm…" The answer was yes. His mother shook her head in disdain and picked up the towel again.

"Honest to God. Kids!" she said and walked off, muttering about not being surprised she had so many wrinkles and her hair was so grey. Little Shaunna reached out and grabbed Andy's nose. It hurt.

"Ouch," he said and she started to giggle. "I think Nana might be a bit cross, eh?" She grabbed his nose again and he pretended to do the same thing back, then went inside to find Dan and Michael.

On reflection, telling his mother hadn't been anywhere near as bad as he'd anticipated, but that was only the start of it. She'd expect a full introduction later, and he had no idea how Krissi was going to react. They didn't have a father-daughter relationship, because she still saw Kris as being her dad, and treated Andy as if he were little more than a sperm donor, which, he supposed, wasn't that far off the truth.

Now he was out of the conservatory, he put his niece down so she could toddle ahead, catching a whiff of her nappy in the process. Dan and Michael were walking towards him, with Michael narrating some story involving lamp-posts.

"What's that about lamp-posts?" Andy asked.

"Oh, nothing," Dan said dismissively and gave him a sly wink.

"Well, you'll be pleased to hear that your daughter has filled her nappy."

"Again? I've already changed it once today," Dan sighed. "Come here stinker." Shaunna grabbed his legs, coming over all coy again with Michael nearby. Dan picked her up and sniffed. "Pooey!" He retrieved the bags he'd left by the entrance and headed off upstairs.

"I never thought I'd see the day," Michael remarked, and whilst it was true that neither he nor Andy had ever envisaged their younger brother so expertly fulfilling the role of doting father, it was merely a means to maintain some form of communication.

"No, me neither. Shall we get on?" Andy suggested, grabbing a reel of cable.

"Yeah, I suppose I'm gonna have to pull my weight, really." Andy didn't look to see his brother's expression, but knew it would be all smug and sneering, before he continued with the rest of what he wanted to say. "Seeing as he's asked me to be his best man."

"Oh right," Andy said, keeping his back turned until he'd mastered his sincere face. "Congratulations."

"Thanks. I hope you don't feel too put out, but I think he saw it as only right, me being the eldest and everything."

"Absolutely," Andy agreed, handing over the coils of cable and turning away again.

"Plus, he was my best man, so, yeah. What're we doing with this, by the way?"

Andy picked up the speakers and walked towards the stairs, indicating to Michael to follow. He wanted to laugh so much that he didn't trust himself to speak, instead pointing to where he should leave the cable and trying to explain his lighting plan through a combination of hand gestures and strangled grunts. Michael didn't notice a thing, and obediently went downstairs to retrieve another load of cable. Dan emerged from the large bathroom (there were four in total) and started walking over.

"Don't say anything," Andy warned him, as Michael came back up the stairs. Dan grinned mischievously. "Seriously, or I'll knock that grin right off your face."

Michael put the cable on the floor and brushed his hands.

"Andy informs me you've told him the good news," Dan said. Andy muttered something through gritted teeth. "What was that, bro?"

"Nothing," Andy snarled, picking up a light and carrying it

to the far end of the landing.

"As I was saying before," Michael stated pompously, "I feel honoured that you've asked me, and I think it's fair to say that although Andy's obviously disappointed you didn't ask him, he understands why."

"You don't feel put out then?" Dan called across.

"No, I'm just fucking dandy."

Dan put his hand over his mouth and gasped loudly, his daughter imitating the action perfectly.

"Uncle Andy! Go wash your mouth out, right now!"

Michael backed away. "I'll err…just go and check that's all the cables," he said and beat a hasty retreat.

Andy sidled up to Dan, trying to maintain a furious expression, but he couldn't do it. He started laughing and put his hands over his niece's ears.

"You complete and utter bastard," he said. Little Shaunna was shaking her head and making a sound that didn't translate into words, but went something like 'yai-yai-yai-yai-yai-yai'. Andy took his hands away and she grinned up at him. Dan patted his brother on the arm.

"Just so you know, if I thought there was a cat's chance of us ever getting married I wouldn't have asked him." Andy tutted and was about to pass comment, but the sound of Adele's heels on the marble downstairs distracted him.

"You'd best go and brief her, before she drops you in it," he advised.

"Yeah. Good thinking." Dan went off to intercept, leaving his favourite brother to his lighting.

CHAPTER THIRTY-FIVE

Given the size of the place, it was surprisingly crowded. Adele had invited all of her colleagues, customers and acquaintances from the gym, which accounted for upwards of forty guests; then there were her ex-colleagues from the department store, including Tom, who had been Dan's friend long before his ill-fated marriage to Adele. He was trying not to feel bitter, but it was going to take a lot more than two glasses of Champagne, he justified, collecting another one from the bar. Kris saw him, excused himself from the conversation he'd been having and went over to say hi and generally offer a bit of distraction from Adele's antics: she was currently on a circuit of the room, laughing outrageously and shoving her engagement ring in everyone's face. Tom smiled quickly as she traipsed past him and out into the atrium to further tantalise people with her disgustingly large diamond set in platinum. It had cost Dan a fortune, but then he'd had a very, very long time to save up, and it was worth it to see her enjoying herself so much. Better still, she hadn't sniped at him once all day, and was leaving him to catch up with Aitch and his other mates in the police, numbering around twenty, with wives and girlfriends; his other business associates, past and present, left the total number of guests just shy of the one hundred mark.

Adele spotted Shaunna and tottered over to give her best friend an enormous, heartfelt hug.

"You look beautiful," Shaunna gushed, as Adele stepped back and gave her a twirl. She was wearing an ankle length, pale yellow dress, with the back of the bodice almost entirely cut away and a skirt that flowed out to a broad, swooshing hemline.

"Thank you," Adele beamed. "So do you, it goes without saying. And your hair smells gorgeous." She lifted a handful of the shining copper curls to emphasise her point. Shaunna raised her eyes, pretending, as always, to be sick of hearing this, for she knew her hair was her best feature.

"See you later," Adele said, giving her a little wave and heading off into the crowd for more mingling. Shaunna waved back and put her foot up against the wall she was leaning on. Her feet were killing her. Across the room, George and Josh watched on, having previously discussed whether she was a) flirting, and b) aware that the man she had been having a much-touching conversation with for the past twenty minutes was not her type, in the same way that Kris was 'not her type'. Now, with her knee pressing against the guy's leg, George was absolutely convinced she was in full pick-up mode.

"I think you're wrong," Josh said smugly. "I've seen that look on Ellie and it's the shoes that are doing it."

"We'll see, won't we?" George said, moving away, his intention to get a formal introduction and clear up the matter once and for all. Josh grabbed his hand and pulled him back, spinning him so that he came to a stop with their lips less than an inch apart.

"You do realise there's a lot of people here who don't know us?" George said nervously.

Josh shrugged and let him go, watching as he made his way over to Shaunna, who immediately introduced him to the man she was standing with. George exchanged greetings and turned back to stick his tongue out at Josh. He just smiled.

"Are you OK for a drink?" Dan asked him on his way to the bar.

"I'll come with you," Josh said, and they walked together, sidestepping as Michael came past carrying a tray loaded with glasses of Champagne.

"Does your Mike always look so miserable?"

"He's actually in a good mood today."

"Really? I'd hate to see him in a bad one."

"You probably will before the end of tonight. Maybe you could work a bit of your magic on him."

"Yeah, I think I might give it a miss. Two Jeffries brothers is already two more than I can handle."

"And we appreciate it. I've given you some shit over the years, Josh, and I'm really sorry."

"No need to apologise. I've given plenty back."

They both laughed, then Dan became serious.

"Thanks, mate. For everything. I don't know what I'd have done if you hadn't been around."

They held eye contact a moment longer, then Dan broke away, instantly reverting to his usual self.

"Andy!" he shouted across the bar. "Want a drink?" Andy gave the thumbs up and started making his way over. Josh stayed a little longer—just enough to bow out politely—and went back to find George.

"I was right then?"

"Yep."

"So who is he?"

"Not telling you."

"Fine."

George wasn't falling for it. "Jess is here, by the way."

"On her own?"

"No. She's with Lois, over there." He pointed across the atrium, to where the two women were dancing away and seemingly enjoying themselves. "Rob's disappeared off the face of the earth," George continued. "Apparently he organised three different events, all for the sole purpose of ripping people off. Last estimate: he got away with about half a million."

"Jesus!"

"Yep. He conned us all."

"I'm kind of glad he did, though. It was a good night out."

"Hmm," George frowned dubiously, "if you say so."

"Well, I enjoyed it, anyway," Josh said. He put his arms around George and tried to pull him close, but he resisted.

"So, what've you been up to while I was gone?" he asked, avoiding eye contact. Josh backed off.

"Not much. Dan was telling me how indispensable I am. I think he's had too much to drink."

"Or maybe he's right?"

"Maybe." The shortness of his answer was less about dismissing George's reassurance and more to do with having spotted Andy and Shaunna, now standing upstairs, leaning on the banister and looking out over the room below. George followed the direction of his gaze.

"I wish I could lip-read."

"I can a bit, and they're not saying anything interesting."

Had they continued to watch a moment longer, it would have been a very different matter, because they had both gone up there at the same time, with the sole intent of speaking to each other away from everyone else, but neither had yet mustered the courage to do so. It was Shaunna who found her voice first.

"We're off the hook this time, you'll be pleased to hear." She kept her eyes steady on the movement of the lights as they flashed across the floor, up the wall and disappeared into the darkness of the glass dome above.

"Right," Andy replied quietly, or as quietly as was possible given the volume of the music and the fact that they were standing between two large speakers. "Thanks for letting me know."

Her gaze settled on Kris and the guy she'd been standing with a short while ago.

"Who's that?" Andy asked.

"Ade-wee-an."

"Who?"

"Adrian, his name is, but he's got a pwoblem saying his 'r's."

Andy laughed.

"He met him at work," Shaunna explained. "He's really very nice and seems to care a lot about Kris."

"That's good. How do you feel about it?"

442

"I don't know. A bit weird, but it's OK. I think I'm only bothered at all because I feel I ought to be."

"And Krissi? How does she feel?"

"She thinks it's the best thing ever, like having two dads, well three, including you."

"I don't really count." He wasn't looking for sympathy.

Shaunna glanced sideways at him and smiled. "Maybe not as Krissi's dad, but you do in lots of other ways."

He turned and studied her profile as she continued to follow the trail of light chasing around the atrium walls. Every so often it passed across them, illuminating her full, glossy lips and transforming her hair into a vibrant veil of cherry-red. She briefly met his gaze and he turned away.

"What I told you before," she said, "you sounded disappointed."

"I suppose I am, a bit."

She gave him an enquiring look. He shrugged.

"What can I say? I'm nearly forty. I want to settle down, maybe start a family."

"You? Settle down? Where did that come from?"

"Kathmandu."

"Blimey! Must be some amazing place, that Kathmandu!"

"Yeah, it is."

Neither of them spoke for a while, comfortable with each other's company, but with things still to say, and again, it was Shaunna who took the lead.

"I'm not ready for another relationship yet, Andy."

"I understand that," he smiled ruefully. "But I'm not getting into the whole friends with benefits situation again. It's all or nothing for me, I'm afraid."

"Well, as I say, I'm not ready—yet—but who knows? Never say never." She brushed her hand across his back as she passed him and then she walked away, back down the stairs and into the crowd. He spent a moment on his own, thinking over what she'd said, before he too returned to the party, hoping his mother had forgotten about her estranged granddaughter,

443

however unlikely that was. He had seen Krissi arrive with Jason, so he knew she was here somewhere. For now, though, he was going to keep a low profile and see if he could get away with not having to formally introduce them.

Jason was also having a hard time finding Krissi. She'd told him she was going to the bathroom, but that had been quite some time ago, and now he was standing alone, next to the buffet table, picking at celery sticks and poking them in the hummus, and he didn't even like the stuff. A few other people wandered in and out, grabbing at bits of food and staying just long enough to eat, then leaving him with his own company. He was glad to be out of the lights, which weren't likely to trigger his epilepsy, but he'd rather not take any chances. He was so deep in thought, wondering whether he should just give up waiting and go and find Krissi, that he didn't see the woman come into the room, until she was standing right next to him, with a look of horror on her face. He smiled nervously and moved away.

"You were there!" she gasped. Jason raised a worried eyebrow but otherwise kept his usual cool. "You were there," she repeated. "The day Mr. Campion was murdered."

He gulped and felt a cold sweat descend over him.

"In the boardroom. I know you were there. I saw you."

He shook his head, panic now starting to rise within.

"No. You've got it all wrong," he said. "I only went to talk to him about a job."

"Did you see him? Did you see the murderer?"

"No. I didn't see anything, I swear, but the police—I wanted to tell them. I was scared."

He had turned white with fear. Not one single witness had reported seeing him at Campion's that day, and if they had, he would have come clean, because he had done nothing wrong.

"Please believe me," he beseeched. The duress of his arrest and interrogation was flooding back to him. He couldn't go through that again.

The woman stepped towards him, her prior expression now

transforming into a kindly smile.

"You look just like him. His eyes. And you're a good boy, I can tell." She was looking at him, but she wasn't at the same time, like she was studying his outline. It was making him feel even worse.

"I don't want to get in trouble for not coming forward, but I promise, I didn't do it."

"I know, dear," she said, reaching into the side pocket of her handbag. She opened his hand and placed something inside it. "A mother knows these things." She smoothed his hair, and then she turned away and left the room. Jason opened his hand, unsure what he was going to find inside, and did a double-take.

"Cool," Krissi said, glancing at the small, silver ring in his ear and then at the identical one glinting on his palm. "You found it. Come on. Let's go dance." She grabbed him by the arm and bounced out into the atrium, pulling him along. There was no point in resisting, so he didn't even bother to try. As they danced, he kept looking for the woman who had given him the ear-ring, but he couldn't see her anywhere and eventually gave up on that too.

In spite of the loud music and jovial atmosphere, Little Shaunna was curled up, thumb in mouth, fast asleep and looking tinier than ever, snuggled in amongst the plush pillows and duvet of her grandmother's super-kingsize bed. Dan watched as her long, dark lashes flickered against her rosy cheeks, wondering about the dreams of innocent two year olds. Momentarily, her little nose wrinkled and her brow creased in worry, then all was tranquil once more. For a second or so, the music became louder; Dan turned and smiled at his mother.

"Sound asleep?" she asked.

"Yeah. It's been a long day for her," he yawned, for he too was exhausted, having been up with his daughter since six that morning. His mother rubbed his arm sympathetically. When her own boys were small, she was still married to their father, a man who would readily engage in all the fun stuff—the birthday parties, football matches, and so on—but didn't trouble himself with the day-to-day tribulations of bringing up three boisterous young sons. By the time Dan was four, she'd had enough and sent their father on his way, and it was hard-going, being a single parent. She wouldn't wish it on anyone.

"So you and Adele are finally settled?" The question was the natural progression of her thoughts.

"Looks that way. She doesn't want to get married, though, but that means nothing these days." She frowned. "Stop stressing, Mum. I know it's not been the easiest of relationships, but I'm pretty sure all of that's behind us."

She took off her jewellery and walked past him to her dressing table, then turned and took his face in her hands, looking up into his eyes.

"I'm so proud of you," she said earnestly. He tutted self-consciously. "Don't be like that, Daniel. It needs to be said. You've got a successful career, a beautiful daughter..." She ruffled his hair with her fingers and he rolled his eyes. "You'll always be my baby boy, and I'm so very proud of you," she finished tearily.

"Andy's not doing so badly for himself either," Dan defended.

"Hmm." She stepped away from him and turned her back. "He told me about Krissi earlier."

Dan nodded, but didn't say anything, readying himself to take yet another bullet for his brother. And he'd do it again, and again, if he had to.

"Did you know he had a daughter?" she asked.

"Yeah."

"Since when?"

"Since he's known," he lied. No point telling her the truth, if he could get away without.

"And what about Shaunna? How did she cope, bringing up a child on her own?"

"She wasn't on her own. She's been with Kris since she was sixteen."

"Your friend Kris? I thought he was gay."

446

"He is. He and Shaunna have just separated."

"Well, he's obviously more of a man than your brother, raising someone else's child."

Dan pinched the bridge of his nose and smoothed the bags under his eyes with his finger and thumb. So, the truth it was then. She was sitting in front of her dressing table, removing her make-up and watching him in the mirror. He sat on the end of the bed and waited until she swivelled round to face him, and then he told her everything, beginning with the party, where Shaunna and Andy had got so drunk that neither of them could remember what they'd done, the part-confirmation of his suspicions when they met baby Krissi for the first time, the years of keeping this to himself, Krissi's quest to find her biological father, how his brother had tried to do the right thing by Shaunna, Krissi and Jess, finishing up with the non-dramatised version of their trip to Kathmandu and Andy and Jess's break-up.

His mother had continued to remove her eye make-up and listen intently throughout. Now she was watching him carefully, reminded of the little boy who was always so relieved when he finally owned up to whatever minor misdemeanour he had committed.

"And?"

Dan shrugged. "And what?"

"There's something else."

He frowned and examined his shoes, but she kept her beady eye on him. It was never a good thing to get caught alone with her. She could wrestle a confession from an innocent man. "Andy's in love with Shaunna," he confirmed. "Has been for a long time. Maybe even since school."

His mother nodded and turned back to her mirror. "Well, I suppose that's something," she said. She was about to send him on his way, so she could change and go to bed, when the door opened again. Adele edged through the gap and closed it quietly behind her, unaware that there was anyone else in the room. She jumped when she saw them.

"I just came to check on the baby," she whispered. Dan nodded over his shoulder at their sleeping child.

"Have you had a nice evening, Adele?" his mother asked.

"Oh, yes, thank you, Barbara. It's been lovely. Thanks ever so much for letting us have the party here."

"That's quite all right, although it's your future brother-in-law you have to thank. He did everything, including getting the cracked marble replaced. Don't know how he managed that. Leonard's been trying since we moved here."

"He got it off this man he and Dan..." Adele began, but Dan coughed to shut her up. He might have told his mother the truth about the rest of it, but there really was no need for her to know the ins and outs of their business 'negotiations'.

"I'm going to get a drink before the bar closes," he said as their cue to leave. "What d'you want, Adele?"

"Just a lime and soda." She busied herself with giving little Shaunna one last check.

"Really? Too many Martinis?"

"No! I've only had one glass of Champagne!"

"So what's up then?"

"Nothing."

"Who's upset you this time?"

"No-one. There's nothing up." She folded her arms.

"You fallen out with Jess again?"

"No."

"Shaunna?"

Adele gave out a little shriek. "I wasn't going to say anything, until I got past three months."

It took a moment for her words to sink in, at which point Dan's confused expression spread into a wide grin. He put his arms around her and kissed her.

"We're going to have another baby. I'm going to be a daddy again."

His mother raised an eyebrow, then she smiled too.

"Congratulations," she said. "Now, bugger off, so I can go to bed!" She shooed them from the room and soon after climbed under the duvet, beside her tiny, unstirring granddaughter. Dan and Adele returned, arm in arm, to their party downstairs.

The night was almost over and the music began to slow in tempo, with some people taking to the 'dance floor' in couples, while others stood around and chatted.

"Do you want to dance?" Josh asked George.

"Slow dance, you mean?"

"Yes."

"I don't know if that's such a good idea. As I said before, we don't know most of the people here and they don't know us."

"So?"

"So sometimes you have to be a bit less—"

"Out?"

"Yeah."

Josh kissed him.

"That's, erm, not quite what…"

Josh kissed him again, and this time it was a full, long, lingering kiss that left George both speechless and breathless. He backed away, feeling ashamed, but for the first time in his life it wasn't because of who he was.

"I, err, I think I need another drink," he stammered.

"Hurry back," Josh smiled, but George wasn't going anywhere. He felt like his feet were glued to the ground. All this time he'd been worrying about what people would think of him—his social class, his sexuality—yet no-one had ever tried to fix him, or told him he was abnormal. When at last he found he could move again, he didn't run away to the bar. He put his arms around Josh's neck and pressed himself hard against him, so hard that he had him pinned to the wall. Now he kissed him properly, his tongue pushing and probing, their lips crushed together, wet, penetrating, his whole body flooding with desire, overwhelmed by the taste and the scent, oblivious and not giving a damn about who might or might not be watching. When he finally, reluctantly pulled away, he saw that Josh's cheeks were flushed red, and could feel his own burning too, but not with shame or embarrassment.

"Wow!" Josh said, breathing out slowly and shakily. Their eyes met again and George didn't even try to hide that twinkle. He moved forward, their cheeks brushing and remaining in contact as he breathed into Josh's ear.

"I'm sorry. That was way over the line."

"Yes, it was." Josh gasped, as George ran his tongue down to his neck and bit him gently. He still wasn't letting up. Josh slid his hands into George's back pockets. "Maybe we need to have that chat about compromise soon?"

"Are you sure?"

"I'm sure."

"It's not just sex."

"Isn't it?"

"I want to make love to you."

"I can tell!" Josh pushed back against him. "But isn't that what we've been doing? Making love."

George thought on this for a moment.

"I want to make love to you my way."

"I see. And did you still want me to propose?"

"When did I say that?"

"In the park. Before Ellie's wedding."

"Ah yeah. You can propose if you like, but I don't need your ring to know that you love me."

"George!"

"Sorry." He smiled impishly. "But I mean it. You don't want to do *it*, so we won't."

Josh smiled back. The reassurance was unnecessary; he had already given himself completely. "Can I ask you something?"

"Sure."

"What the hell is 'TTWDTA'?"

"You still haven't figured it out?"

"Would I be asking if I had?"

"It's a defunct acronym."

"But an acronym for what?"

"That Thing We Don't Talk About."

"What thing?"

"This thing." George kissed him again, but this time it was a gentle, soft-lipped kiss, conveying the tenderness, the love, and the promise they had made to be honest and true to each other.

"Got it?" he asked.

"Got it," Josh replied.

"Good. I'm going now. To get that drink."

"OK. Go then."

"I love you."

"I love you too. Shoo!"

As George made his way to the bar, Kris intercepted, dragging him over to meet 'Ade-wee-an', even though Shaunna had already introduced them earlier. He looked back helplessly to Josh, but he just shrugged. Eleanor was now standing next to him, and he was pretending he hadn't seen her, knowing that the time for the real inquisition had finally arrived.

"Come with me," she said, and stepped off. Josh huffed like an uncooperative teenager, but still followed her, through the dancers, across the atrium and down the passageway, until they were standing in the dark space by the doors to the conservatory. She was looking away from him, not that it mattered, as he couldn't really see her; he didn't need to. They remained, in the dark, listening to the slow thud-thump of the bass escaping through the thick old walls, the occasional high-pitched chink of glasses and the fuzzy murmur of many distant voices.

They had no need for words; they communicated the way they always had, through a sensing of each other's presence and how it felt. He knew she wanted to ask why he'd kept his feelings hidden from her. She knew that he would not answer if she did. There were some things that even she could not know; he was protecting her. It had always been like this and she accepted it as part of their friendship, for Josh was like a treasured, ancient book, a keepsake from childhood that has lost some of its pages, consigning them to fleeting memories; glimpsed recollections of a once complete story. And she had seen that George was now the guardian of those pages. He completed Josh.

He reached into the darkness and took her hand, pulling her close and encircling her with his arms, and they danced, to the echo of the bass and the whispers of conversation, their cheeks pressed together, hearts beating as one. When finally the dance was done, they stepped apart, their hands outstretched until only the very tips of their fingers were touching.

"You love him absolutely."

"I would die for him."

They moved on and the dance began again.

Sometimes I wish I'd known you the way I know your brother, although the fact that I didn't kind of makes me glad - for myself, at least - for I only have to watch the consequences of what you did from afar.

Many would say that you were a coward; still others would say it was an act of sheer stupidity; your mum says it took courage. I don't know if it's any of these things, but I did know once.

If only I could say this to you, in person, now. Would what I say make any difference? To be standing there with you, as you gather the strength to see it through. I'd have to try. I'd have to tell you this:

What you are thinking of doing? It will destroy the people you love, the people who love you. Their lives will NOT go on with or without you. They will NEVER be the same again.

I'm not saying don't do it. I'm just begging you not to do it right now, even though I understand that the only thing you believe right at this moment is that this will make the pain stop, make it go away. But you haven't really thought it through. I bet you only reached the conclusion that this is what you needed to do a few hours ago, yet now you believe you've felt like this forever, that there is no way out, but this. It's not true.

You might feel like this tomorrow, and the next day, and the one after. It might feel like this for the next ten years. But it won't feel like this forever, I promise.

So please don't do it. Don't take you life, because it isn't just yours, don't you see? Part of you lives on, in your mum and your brother, and in all the other people who love you. If you do this - if you 'succeed' - those pieces of you will stay with them.

And you will take part of them with you. Sounds comforting, you might think. Not so. Now you are gone, your mum is torn between this world and yours, between the past and the present; between her two sons.

So please, just stay. Just for now.

Lightning Source UK Ltd.
Milton Keynes UK
UKOW041804310513

211588UK00001B/6/P